What the Heart Sees

OTHER NOVELS BY KATHLEEN FULLER:

THE HEARTS OF MIDDLEFIELD SERIES

A Man of His Word
An Honest Love
A Hand to Hold

THE MYSTERIES OF MIDDLEFIELD SERIES
FOR YOUNG READERS

A Summer Secret
The Secrets Beneath

What the Heart Sees

A COLLECTION OF AMISH ROMANCES

KATHLEEN FULLER

THOMAS NELSON
Since 1798

NASHVILLE DALLAS MEXICO CITY RIO DE JANEIRO

Published in Nashville, Tennessee, by Thomas Nelson. Thomas Nelson is a registered trademark of Thomas Nelson, Inc.

Thomas Nelson, Inc., titles may be purchased in bulk for educational, business, fund-raising, or sales promotional use. For information, please e-mail SpecialMarkets@ThomasNelson.com.

Scripture quotations taken from the King James Version.

Publisher's Note: This novel is a work of fiction. Names, characters, places, and incidents are either products of the author's imagination or used fictitiously. All characters are fictional, and any similarity to people living or dead is purely coincidental.

ISBN 978-1-59554-919-8

Printed in the United States of America

11 12 13 14 15 RRD 5 4 3 2

Glossary

ab im kopp: off in the head, crazy
aenti: aunt
aldi: girlfriend
appeditlich: delicious
bauchduch: napkin
boppli: baby or babies
boyfriend: boyfriend
brechdich: magnificent
bruder: brother
bu, buwe: boy, boys
budder: butter
daag: day
daed: dad
danki: thanks
demut: humility
dochder: daughter
du bischt wilkumm: you're welcome
dumm: dumb
dummkopf: dummy
Englisch or Englischer: a non-Amish person
familye: family
frau: wife, Mrs.
Frehlicher Grischtdaag: Merry Christmas
freind: friend
geh: go
grosskinner: grandchildren
grossmammi: grandmother
guder mariye: good morning
gut: good

gutguckich: good-looking
guten nacht: good night
gut-n-owed: good evening
halt: stop
haus: house
herr: mister
hochmut: pride
hungerich: hungry
kaffi: coffee
kapp: prayer covering or cap
kinn, kinner: child, children
liebschen: dearest
maed, maedel: girls, girl
mami, mamm: mom
mammi: grandmother
mann: man
mei: my
meiding: shunning
mudder: mother
narrisch: crazy
nau: now
nee: no
nix: nothing
onkel: uncle
Ordnung: the written and unwritten rules of the Amish; the understood behavior by which the Amish are expected to live, passed down from generation to generation. Most Amish know the rules by heart.
Pennsylvania Deitsch: Pennsylvania German, the language most commonly used by the Amish
recht: right

rumschpringe: running-around period when a teenager turns
  sixteen years old
schpass: fun
schwester: sister
sehr: very
sehr gut: very good
seltsam: weird
sohn: son
vatter: father
wunderbaar: wonderful
ya: yes

CONTENTS

A MIRACLE
FOR MIRIAM

To my family: my husband James,
my son Matthew,
and my daughters Sydney and Zoie.
I love you all very much.

Prologue

Miriam Fisher

Mrs. Miriam Fisher

Miriam and Seth Fisher

Mrs. Seth Fi—

"What's this?" Caleb snatched the spiral notebook out of Miriam's hands.

She grappled for the book, but Caleb, who was three inches taller, held it out of her reach. "Give it back," she pleaded.

Caleb gave her a malicious grin. "Or what? You'll tell the teacher? Go ahead, she won't do nothing. Not when there's only a month left of school."

Panic flowed through her. "Caleb, please. Don't read it—"

"Miriam Fisher?" He glanced up from the page, looked at Miriam, then guffawed, his laugh bordering on a donkey bray. "Miriam *Fisher?*" He looked back down and kept reading, then turned another page and started laughing again.

Miriam wanted to die. Right there in the middle of the school yard, she prayed the earth would swallow her whole. It did not. Instead, she watched with horror as Caleb ran across the playground to the object of her affections, Seth Fisher, and interrupted the game of bare-handed baseball he was playing with his friends. Caleb thrust the notebook in front of him.

Miriam had harbored a secret crush on Seth since sixth grade but never dared tell anyone, not even her best friend,

Hannah. Now they were both fourteen and near the end of their eighth-grade year. Soon she wouldn't get to see him every day, to watch him from across the classroom, pretending to be engrossed in her schoolwork when all she could think about was how good-looking he was. For two years she'd hoped he would notice her. For two years she had spent her recesses, not with her friends but sitting in the corner of the school yard, journaling her dreams in her notebook.

She couldn't breathe as she watched Seth take the notebook and thumb through it. His expression never changed while he glanced over page after page filled with crudely drawn hearts and their names written in various combinations. Her palms grew slick as he looked up from the notebook and caught her gaze. He tossed the baseball to one of his buddies and made his way toward her.

Her legs threatened to buckle. She had expected him to laugh like Caleb, but instead he strode across the playground, his dazzling blue-eyed gaze never leaving hers. Was it possible that he secretly liked her too? That he, like her, had been afraid to admit it? The thought of it brought a whole new wave of emotions flowing over her.

Could she really be Mrs. Seth Fisher someday?

Seth stopped in front of her, his friends straggling behind him. He was their leader and had been since they'd started school together. Tall, lean, he had filled out before most of the boys, and his voice had deepened last year. He wore his pale yellow straw hat tipped back on his head, giving her a full view of his handsome face. He looked much older than fourteen. More confident, without a trace of insecurity. Unlike Miriam, who was filled with it.

He held out the notebook. "This yours?"

Pushing up her glasses, she nodded, her tongue suddenly too thick to formulate a verbal answer.

"Here. Take it."

But when she reached for it, he jerked it out of her grasp, then dropped it on the ground. Stepping square in the middle of it, he said, "Four-eyed beanpole." Then he kicked the notebook at her and laughed.

Any flicker of hope she held inside died at that moment. Seth and his group walked away, some pointing and laughing, leaving her to pick up her journal. She lifted it from the ground, staring at the large heart filling the page, *Miriam + Seth* written in the middle. The dirty outline of a boot print was stamped on top.

Across the playground she could still hear the boys laughing. Seth looked at her and circled his fingers around his eyes.

Four-eyed beanpole . . .

Chapter One

Five years later

SETH LIVED WITH PAIN EVERY DAY. AT ONE TIME HE'D TRIED to blame God for what had happened, but he knew that wasn't honest. He had no one to blame but himself.

He winced as he pulled on his trousers, his movements awkward. Still, just as he did each day, he silently gave thanks to Father God. If people had said to him even six months ago that he would be grateful to feel pain, that he would praise the Lord for each twinge and ache, he would have laughed in their faces. But today, the ever-present soreness reminded him that he was lucky to be alive.

He reached for his walking stick—plain, unadorned, but stained and lacquered to a smooth, shiny finish. His older brother, Noah, had made it for him shortly after the accident. The top of the stick was straight, so he couldn't call it a cane. Neither was it overly long, like a traditional walking stick. The knob at the top reached him at hip level, giving him the perfect amount of support without being unwieldy.

When he first saw the stick, he'd wanted to throw it at his brother. Now the gift had become indispensable.

Seth turned at a loud knock at his door. "What?"

"Caleb Esh is here." His father's gruff voice penetrated the wooden door. "You ready?"

Hearing his *daed*'s voice gave Seth pause. Considering their strained relationship, he was surprised his father had come upstairs to fetch him.

"*Ya*," Seth replied, reaching for his black felt hat, the one he usually wore in cold weather. He'd pick up his coat on the way out. "Tell Caleb I'll be right down." He heard the thudding of his father's work boots against the wood floorboards as Melvin Fisher left to deliver Seth's message.

Seth placed his hand on the knob of the door and started to turn it, then stopped. Before the accident he'd never been nervous about going out. But tonight was different. The Christmas sing at the Lapps' home was his first social outing in six months, a time span unheard-of for him. For the last three years, since he'd turned sixteen, going out had been a big part of his life. Not that he had wasted his time on the Amish social circuit. Frolics and singings and other gatherings had been too tame and too lame. Seth was too cool for that, choosing instead to hang with *Englisch* friends. When he was with them he drank. He smoked.

He learned to drive a car.

He ran his fingers over the thin ridge of scar tissue that started from his left temple and cut a straight line to the top of his jaw. The facial cut had healed faster than his leg, and far more quickly than his pride.

Shaking off the raw memories, he twisted the brass knob and opened the door. He'd learned some hard lessons that night six months ago, and they had shaped him into a new man. But he couldn't hide here forever, surrounded by his family. Not only had they accepted what had happened; they'd forgiven him too.

Perhaps not everyone would show him such mercy.

He ignored the sudden stab of low confidence and headed down the stairs, determined to renew the old acquaintances he had abandoned in favor of the outside world.

❦

"I don't understand why you're helping me with this boring task when you could be at the Lapps', having a good time."

Miriam finished putting the plastic binding on a cookbook and looked into her older sister's weary face. The exhaustion she saw there explained why she chose to spend Sunday night helping her sister Lydia. But she would never say so aloud. Since the death of Lydia's husband two years ago, she'd had enough to fret over without worrying about how tired she looked.

"I like helping you," Miriam said, a little too brightly. "I can't think of a better way to spend my evening than with my sister and my niece and nephews."

"I'd believe you, except the *kinder* aren't even here right now." Lydia smirked. "The boys are spending the night with the Yoders, and Anna Marie is at the Christmas sing, where you should be."

Busted.

She had heard her niece use the term on occasion, and Miriam thought it fit her current situation. Pushing up her glasses, she glanced down at the cookbook, pretending to be engrossed in the artwork on the shiny cover.

"You can ignore me all you want, Miriam, but I know the real reason you're here." Lydia picked up her mug of lukewarm coffee, took a sip, then frowned. Rising from the table in the middle of her kitchen, she walked over to the stove, opened up the percolator, and started a fresh pot.

Lydia's bait was too tempting to ignore. Miriam's gaze shot up, and she watched her sister remove the lid from the metal coffeepot.

"I already told you why I'm here," she said.

"You told me what you wanted me to hear, not the real reason." Lydia added fragrant coffee grounds to the basket, then poured water over them and put the pot on the stove. Within minutes the kitchen filled with the coffee's comforting aroma.

"There's no other reason, Lydia." Miriam reached for an unbound cookbook. "Besides, if I weren't here, how would you get all this done?"

"I'd manage, God willing." She sat back down at the table. "Not that I don't appreciate all the help you've given me. But you're spending too much time either here or at the quilt shop. You're nineteen years old, Miriam. You should be enjoying life."

"I enjoy life. I like my job, and I have my quilting." She started inserting the binder into the square holes on the left margin of the loose pages.

"But what about your friends?"

"I have plenty of friends. A lot of them are just as busy as I am."

"What about a *boyfriend*?" Lydia leaned forward, her gaze steady and serious.

"What about Daniel?" Miriam said, eager to switch their conversation to something else. She suspected that Daniel Smucker was the main reason for Lydia's singular focus tonight.

Since her late husband's brother had returned to Paradise, her normally steadfast sister had been out of sorts.

Lydia averted her gaze, but only for a moment. "I'm not talking about me and Daniel."

"You and Daniel?" Miriam lifted a brow. "What about you and Daniel?"

"There is no 'me and Daniel'."

"But you just said—"

"Stop changing the subject." Lydia sat up straight in her chair and folded her hands on the table. "Miriam, it's time you started thinking about your future. There are several available young men in the community. Isn't there at least one you're interested in?"

At her sister's last question, Miriam's thumb slipped and slid against the sharp edge of the binder, hard enough to draw blood. She put her thumb to her mouth.

Concern suddenly etched Lydia's features. "Do you need a bandage?"

Miriam looked at her hand. The cut was tiny, negligible actually. She shook her head and rose from her chair. "I'm fine. I'll just give it a quick wash."

As she stood over the sink and lathered her hands with Lydia's homemade lavender soap, Miriam stared out of the window into the darkness of the night. A chill suddenly flowed through her, as if the cold outside air had somehow seeped through the clear glass pane and entered her body. Lydia didn't want to talk about Daniel, and Miriam certainly didn't want to talk about men, so she wished her sister would drop the topic altogether.

At nineteen Miriam was old enough to marry. Several of her schoolmates had already married or had steady beaus. But she remained single. She'd learned her lesson a long time ago. She wasn't about to open herself to ridicule again. Although she was expected to get married and raise a family, she wasn't in any hurry to do so. At least she tried to tell herself that.

Trouble was, her heart refused to cooperate. At times she had to admit she was lonely, especially when she saw other young couples together, enjoying each other's company. So she made sure not to put herself in situations where she would be reminded of what she didn't have.

"Miriam? Are you all right?"

Lydia's voice broke into her thoughts. Quickly Miriam rinsed and dried her hands, then went back to the table and delved into her work.

A few moments later Lydia placed her hand on Miriam's forearm. "That's enough. I can get the rest. You go on and have a good time."

"Lydia, I already said I'm not going."

"And I said you are. This is the last singing before Christmas, and you don't want to miss that. Go home and put on a fresh dress. I'm sure Pop won't mind dropping you off at the Lapps', and Anna Marie can bring you back home." As if to make sure Miriam would follow orders, Lydia gathered the cookbooks and binders and carried them into the next room.

Miriam frowned. The last thing she wanted to see were boys and girls flirting with each other as they played the awkward and thrilling game of courtship. Or worse, she'd be subjected to all the young people who had already found someone to love, or at least to like well enough to date.

She planted herself in the chair. She was nineteen years old, not a little girl. Her sister couldn't force her. Could she?

Lydia came back into the room, glanced at Miriam, and grimaced. "I can see this is going to be harder than I thought." She left abruptly, and returned a moment later with her black winter cloak slung over one arm. She adjusted the black bonnet on her head with the opposite hand.

"Where are you going?" Miriam asked.

"Drastic times call for drastic measures." She stood in front of Miriam, hands firmly planted on her hips. "I'll take you to the singing tonight."

"You can't. Your *kind* has your buggy, remember?"

"*Ya*, but that doesn't mean I can't drive yours. I'll drop you off, then pick you up in a couple of hours. Then you can go home to *Daed* and *Mamm*, or you can spend the night here. You know we always love having you."

A scowl tugged at Miriam's mouth. She was being coerced. "You say you love having me, but you want me to leave."

Lydia nodded, her expression resolute. "*Ya*, I do. Just know that I'm doing this for your own good. Now, are you coming, or do I have to physically force you?"

Miriam didn't doubt her for a minute. Although Lydia was a couple inches shorter than Miriam, when she set her mind on a goal, nothing would keep her from achieving it. Even if it meant making her younger sister do something she didn't want to do.

Trapped, Miriam slowly stood. "You said I needed a fresh dress."

"You look fine."

Miriam doubted that. "Let me at least freshen up in the bathroom before we go."

"*Ya*, but don't dally. The singing has already started. You're missing all the fun!"

Miriam headed for the bathroom, more than a little irritated. Why couldn't Lydia mind her own business? Entering the small room, she closed the door and turned on the battery-operated lamp on the vanity. As with all the rooms in Lydia's house, this one had also been adorned with Christmas decorations. An evergreen-scented candle burned next to the lamp, filling the small space with its fresh fragrance. A pine bough sporting a bright red bow perched above the small mirror over the sink. Nothing fancy, but a festive touch.

The light was a bit on the dim side, but she could see her reflection clearly enough. Plain, plain, plain. A stab of insecurity hit her. While she lived among a people who valued simplicity and plainness, there was such a thing as being too nondescript. She knew that firsthand.

There was nothing pretty, nothing extraordinary, nothing striking about her appearance. Her hair and eyes were the shade of brown mud while her complexion was fair, even stark. Small, wire-framed glasses with round lenses did little to enhance her features, while her chin angled to a point. Unlike her sisters, Miriam had no curves, and her dress hung loosely on her boyish frame. A sharp chin, lean hips, and a tiny bosom. No wonder men weren't falling at her feet.

She knew that inner beauty was more important than a pretty face or appealing figure. She also knew that the Lord valued the heart, not the shell that protected it. Still, that didn't keep her from secretly longing for at least one attractive physical quality. Seth Fisher's words were still true: she was a four-eyed beanpole.

Closing her eyes against the insult ricocheting in her brain, she fought the humiliation and resentment pooling in her stomach, unabated by time. Her path hadn't crossed Seth's since they left school, and that had helped—at least she hadn't been constantly reminded of how ugly he thought she was. He had turned into a wild boy and run around with a bunch of *Englisch* people, constantly getting into trouble. A few months ago he fell into more trouble than anyone would have thought, and that was the last she'd heard of him. While she had never wished him any harm, it would suit her just fine if she never saw him again.

Opening her eyes, she leaned over the sink and splashed some cold water on her cheeks. She mentally pushed the past away as she stood up, adjusting the hairpins affixed to her *kapp*. Staring into the mirror, she forced a smile. She could do this. She could do anything for a couple of hours.

Opening the door, she thought of the one good thing about attending the singing, and that put a genuine smile on her face. At least *he* wouldn't be there. She wouldn't have to worry about Seth Fisher ruining her night.

Chapter Two

"*ACH, WHAT'S WITH THAT BUGGY MOVING SO SLOW?*" CALEB tapped his foot in a rapid staccato rhythm against the floor of his buggy as he pulled on the reins. His horse slowed almost to a standstill as they pulled up to the modest white house at the end of the street.

"You sound like an *Englisch* driver," Seth remarked, shifting in his seat. Sitting in one position for very long still made his leg ache. The physical therapist who had helped him regain his motion said that the pain would subside, but it would take time.

Patience—another hard lesson learned.

"*Ya*, and they got a right to complain if they get behind someone like this," Caleb said. "We're running late as it is."

"Sorry."

"*Nee*, it's not your fault. Well, it is, but I don't blame you. I blame this!" Caleb pointed as the buggy made a left turn into a driveway. "Great. He's also going to the Lapps'. It'll probably take him forever to find a place to park."

But instead of parking, the buggy pulled to a stop just as Caleb's horse drew up behind it. In addition to their large circular driveway, the Lapps had another driveway that split off from the main one, which led to the barn in the back. There was ample parking there, so Seth wasn't sure why Caleb was concerned.

The passenger door opened, and a woman stepped out wearing a black cloak, her face obscured by a bonnet. She walked around the back of the buggy and headed toward the Lapp house.

"Finally." Caleb tapped the reins on the flanks of his horse as the buggy in front of them moved, then turned around in the driveway.

In the dim light of dusk Seth could see the driver was another woman.

"Would have been easier if she had dropped her off at the road." Caleb maneuvered his buggy into an empty space by the barn. "And faster."

Seth regarded his friend. "Why are you in such a hurry?" As soon as he asked the question, he knew the answer. "That's right. Mary Lapp."

Caleb shrugged. "Maybe."

Seth knew that was all he would get out of his friend, and he was fine with that. He was glad his first outing would be here. The Lapps were a good family, Mary included. She had always been a nice girl, friendly to all and a stranger to none. If anyone would help him not feel out of place, it would be Mary. Besides Caleb, of course. He was the one Amish friend Seth had kept in touch with during his wild years, and one of the few to visit him when he came home from the hospital.

Caleb jumped out of the buggy, and envy stabbed at Seth. He swiveled in the seat as he opened the door, then slid to the edge and grabbed his walking stick. By the time Caleb had teth-ered his horse, Seth had just gotten out of the buggy.

"Need some help?" Caleb asked.

"*Nee*. I've got it." Leaning on his stick, Seth shut the door behind him and turned around. "Go ahead and go inside. Don't want to slow you down."

"I'll wait."

Seth shook his head. "I know how eager you are to see Mary—"

"I never said that."

"You didn't have to. Now, go."

Caleb hesitated again, then nodded and walked to the house, taking long strides. Again jealousy came to the fore, but Seth ignored it. He was determined to walk one day unassisted, no matter how long it took. He would accomplish that by continuing the exercises his therapist had given him, even though they were painful.

Seth hobbled along until he reached the front door. He knocked out of politeness, though he had been to the Lapps' many times as a child.

Mary's mother, Katherine, opened the door. She stood still for a moment as she looked at Seth's face, then at his walking stick, then back up until her gaze focused on his scar.

"*Gut-n-Owed*," Seth said, breaking the silence.

She blinked a couple times, then grinned. "Seth Fisher! I'm so glad to see you."

His earlier nervousness dimmed a little at the warm welcome. "*Danki, Frau* Lapp."

"Come in, come in. Everyone's downstairs. I'm sure they'll be happy you came." She stepped aside, and Seth entered through the doorway, then turned and faced her, inhaling the sweet scent of cinnamon that wafted through the room.

He knew the brighter light in the Lapps' front room made his scar more pronounced, and that was evident by the way *Frau* Lapp was looking at him. A mixture of pity and curiosity filled her eyes, but for only a moment.

"Do you need some help getting down the stairs?"

"*Nee*. I can manage on my own. But *danki* just the same."

Katherine glanced at his walking stick. "All right, but if you need anything, just let me know. Jeb and I will be right upstairs."

Seth nodded and headed for the basement. The murmur of conversation, peppered with a few laughs, drifted up the stairwell. He couldn't help but smile. He sorely missed the company of people his age, especially after spending weeks in the hospital, then months at home trying to heal. He hadn't realized how isolated he'd been until now. But his eagerness to join the others was tempered by a hike in his anxiousness. How would they react? Would they ask a million questions? If they did, he wouldn't hold back. He'd tell them everything they wanted to know.

Realizing he was wasting time, he made his way down the stairs, using both the handrail and his stick for support. When he reached the bottom he turned left, which led to a large, open room that held about twenty-five young people. The scent of pine wafted from the boughs decorating the walls, reminding him that Christmas was only a couple weeks away.

At first no one noticed his arrival, as they were all involved in their own conversations. Then Mary Lapp, with Caleb at her side, spotted him. "Seth?"

The conversation died down to nearly nothing. It seemed that everyone in the room had turned their focus completely on him.

"Goodness, it's *gut* to see you, Seth." Mary gave him a huge smile, the dimple in her right cheek deepening. She wore a white *kapp*, and her dark hair was neatly parted and pulled back, exposing her pretty brown eyes.

He hadn't seen Mary in a couple of years, and while she had

been sort of a cute girl when they were younger, she had grown into a pretty woman. No wonder Caleb was smitten.

As if to remind Seth that Mary was his, Caleb stepped closer to her. Seth didn't miss the slight spark of warning reflected in his friend's blue eyes. He didn't blame Caleb for being concerned. In the past when Seth Fisher saw what he wanted, he took it, without any regrets.

Seth would have to earn his friend's trust. And not only Caleb's, but everyone else's as well.

"Don't just stand there; come on in." Mary, the consummate hostess, led Seth into the room. "Look who's here, everyone. Seth Fisher!"

Reactions varied, from outright gaping at the scar on his cheek to polite smiles and nods. The ages of the group ranged from sixteen to twenty-four, so it was no surprise that the younger kids were the ones staring. He didn't mind; he'd expected both surprise and curiosity.

"Are you hungry? There's plenty of food. *Mudder* prepared a feast." Mary gestured to a long table situated against the wall on the other side of the room.

Seth took in the bowls of chips, potato salad, ham slices, three different kinds of cheeses, an abundance of bread, Christmas shortbread cookies frosted in red and green, and several varieties of soda. Everything looked delicious, and normally he would have dived right in. But tonight he wasn't interested in eating, not when everyone was still scrutinizing him. "Maybe later," he said.

"That's fine. Just fill up a plate whenever you want." Mary smiled again, reassuring him that he had made the right decision in coming.

The three of them chatted. While Mary described her job waitressing at a local restaurant, Seth surveyed the room. Instantly something caught his eye. Not something. *Someone.* A young woman. Angling to get a better look, he turned his head as far as he could while still appearing to listen.

The *maedel* had caught his attention because she was standing apart from the group, leaning with her entire body pressed against the wall, as if it would fall down around her if she walked away. Her black bonnet obscured part of her face, and she took small sips from the plastic cup in her hand. He guessed she was the woman he'd seen being dropped off earlier.

"Seth?" Caleb tapped him on the arm.

"What? Oh, sorry." He tore his gaze away from her and looked at his friend. "What were you saying?"

"Mary and I are going to get a drink. Do you need anything?"

"*Nee.*" He lowered his voice. "Don't worry about me. I'm fine. Enjoy your time with Mary."

"*Danki.* I intend to." Caleb tilted his head to the side.

"What?"

"You wishing me a good time. You really have changed, haven't you?"

"I hope so, Caleb. I really hope so."

❦

Miriam wanted to throw up.

Lydia had given her a few last words of encouragement before dropping her off, and Miriam had held on to those words and entered the party with feigned confidence. While her niece

Anna Marie and some of her friends had greeted her, a quick scan of the room told her that not very many of her own friends were in attendance. Before long, several young men and women started pairing off, while others huddled into small groups of three or four, forming small cliques that Miriam had no desire to try to penetrate. How she wished her best friend, Hannah Beiler, was there. Then at least Miriam would have someone to talk to. But Hannah and her family were visiting her mother's cousin in Lititz and wouldn't be back until after Christmas.

She watched with a little bit of envy as Mary Lapp confidently greeted her guests, making everyone feel equally welcome in her home. Miriam wished she had the self-assurance to walk right up to anyone and just start a conversation. But the thought of doing that made her stomach spin, so she stayed on the sidelines.

Knowing she had to endure only an hour or so of the singing, she filled a cup with lemon-lime soda pop and leaned against the cold basement wall, a true wallflower. But being invisible to everyone else had one advantage: it allowed her to people-watch, something she did enjoy. She noticed right off that Caleb Esh and Mary Lapp were sweet on each other. They made a striking couple, with her dark hair and his lighter features. Anna Marie had captured the attention of Amos Zook, but Miriam would keep that tidbit to herself, not wanting to insinuate herself in her niece's business. She observed several others, making mental notes as she did. She was almost enjoying herself.

Then Seth Fisher walked in.

Even before Mary spoke, Miriam had seen him.

Which made her stomach turn inside out.

What was he doing here? He'd made pretty clear his disdain for Amish social activities when he was fifteen. Why show up to one tonight?

Maybe he wanted to be the center of attention, as usual. She noticed he walked with a limp and used a wooden walking stick. The stick was quite beautiful, actually, probably one of his father's or brother's designs. Both had sterling reputations as carpenters. Already she could see several people crowding around Seth, more than likely entranced as he regaled them with tales of his accident. She didn't know the exact details, but she'd heard it had been pretty severe.

Well, she really didn't care. It was callous of her, but why should she? While she would never have wished for anything bad to happen to him, she didn't have much pity for him either.

Well . . . maybe a little. *Very* little.

"Hi."

She jumped, splashing some of her drink onto her dress. Annoyed not only with the speaker but with herself for being on edge, she grimaced and tried to dry the soda off the bodice of her dress with little success.

"Sorry, didn't mean to startle you. I can get you a *bauchduch*—"

"*Nee*, I don't need it. I'm fine," she said, unable to hide her irritation. "It'll—" At that moment she made the mistake of looking up—directly into the eyes of Seth Fisher.

Chapter Three

HOW HAD SHE NOT HEARD HIM APPROACH? SHE SHOULD have at least heard the thump of his walking stick. Now there was no chance for escape. She was trapped between Seth and the wall, forced to be polite to the one and only man she'd ever dared to have romantic feelings for, the one and only man who had crushed them to dust.

"Are you sure you don't want me to get something to wipe that up?" Seth bent down slightly to look at the darkened splotches on the upper part of her dress. Then, realizing what he was doing, he jerked up and looked her in the eye. "You're right," he said, clearing his throat slightly. "It's not too bad."

"*Ya*. The stain will come out." What was she doing even talking to him? She should just stride right past him and head to the refreshment table. It wouldn't take much for her to pretend to be interested in the plentiful food the Lapps had provided. But it would only be pretense. If she thought her stomach was in a knot when Seth had walked into the room, it was a pretzel right now.

Tall for an Amishman, he had broad shoulders, slim hips, and long legs. All in perfect proportion, of course. But that wasn't his most arresting feature. Seth Fisher had the most incredible eyes she had ever seen. They were an odd shade of transparent blue, aquamarine almost, and the irises were rimmed with gray. Long, black lashes surrounded those amazing eyes, and she remembered in school how she would sit and stare at him in class, hoping he would turn around and look at her, maybe even give her a smile. . . .

She bit the inside of her cheek, hard. She should leave. Maybe she could convince Anna Marie to take her home. Searching the room, she found her niece talking to Amos. Miriam recognized that moony look on Anna Marie's face and couldn't bring herself to interrupt.

If she couldn't leave, she should at least walk away. She could go hold up the wall on the other side of the room, even. Why weren't her feet *moving*?

She knew why. Even after all this time, even after she tried to forget him and prayed for God to take him out of her mind and heart, Seth still had an effect on her. She could still be mesmerized by his unreal eyes, the perfect shape of his lips, his—

Scar?

For a moment she couldn't take her eyes off the raised ridge that traveled the length of his cheek. Crooked in some places, with a faint outline where stitches had been. Though noticeable, it did very little to detract from his attractiveness. It figured— Seth Fisher could even make a scar look good.

"I see you noticed my souvenir." Seth reached up and touched the scar with the tip of his index finger.

Embarrassed at being caught staring, Miriam looked away.

"It's not as if I can hide it. People are going to stare anyway, so why worry about it?"

She looked at him, surprised to see his lopsided grin. How could he be so nonchalant about such a disfigurement? If her face had been marred even slightly, she would have been devastated.

Not that she liked her face, but she didn't want it to look worse than it already did. Yet here he was, speaking about his scar as if he had picked it up from a store and was trying it on for size.

He looked at her for a moment, his head tilted slightly, a small frown tugging at his mouth.

She shifted from one foot to the other, wishing he would just leave. Why was he looking at her like that?

"Miriam," he finally said, then smiled again. "Your name is Miriam Herschberger."

Well, he remembered her name, at least. That was something. "*Ya.*"

"I thought I recognized you, but I just couldn't figure out where I'd seen you before. We went to school together, right?"

"*Ya.*" Wow. She was a witty conversationalist tonight.

"It's all coming back to me now. In eighth grade you sat in the same row, but on the other side of the room."

Heat started to creep up her neck. She was not enjoying this walk down memory lane.

Seth grinned, oblivious to her discomfort. "I'm telling you, I couldn't wait to get out of school. Those last two months seemed to last forever."

"I know," she said quietly.

"*Ya,* I . . ." Seth looked at her for a moment, not saying anything. Then he shut his eyes. "Miriam," he said, almost to himself. When his eyes opened, his expression changed. "Now I remember you."

Miriam squeezed her plastic cup. The only thing that kept her from crushing it in her hand was the possibility of staining her dress again.

"I wasn't very nice to you," he admitted.

That was putting it mildly. She thought about just brushing it off, acting as if being insulted to her very core hadn't bothered her a bit. But she couldn't bring herself to do that. She couldn't lie, not about this. "*Nee*. You weren't."

He scrubbed a hand over his face. "I was a big *dummkopf* back then."

Seth Fisher, admitting he had a flaw? That didn't jibe with the boy she went to school with, or the young man who had sowed some extremely wild oats these past few years. Then again, the fact that she was having this conversation with him showed he was different. The fact that they were having this conversation at all was some sort of miracle.

"I'm so sorry for what I said to you. I was an idiot."

"And a *dummkopf*." The words were out before she could stop them.

"Thought I said that already." The corner of his mouth lifted. "I've done a lot of things I regret. I hope someday you can forgive me for the way I treated you."

Miriam honestly didn't know what to say. Over the years, when she thought about Seth Fisher, it was never in the context of his apologizing or asking forgiveness.

He limped over to stand next to her against the wall. "Hope you don't mind." Uncertainty crept into his eyes. "Unless you wanted to be alone?"

It was on the tip of her tongue to say that was exactly what she wanted, but for some irritating reason she couldn't form the words.

"I can see why you picked this spot," he said, apparently

taking her silence as affirmation that she wanted company. "You can see everyone in the room."

She nodded slowly, still trying to take in the knowledge that not only had he apologized to her, but he was now standing next to her. Without much space between them. If she moved her hand over a few inches, she could touch his index finger; they were that close. Not that she would ever do something like that.

"So fill me in on what's going on," Seth said.

"What?"

"I've been gone awhile, so I've missed out on a lot." He looked down at her and grinned.

Her insides turned to mush.

This wasn't right. It wasn't fair, either. She'd spent so much time chasing him out of her mind and heart, and now with an apology and a grin he had snuck his way back in again. Would she never learn?

No, she wasn't going through this again. Steeling herself, she decided to tell him what he wanted to know, then leave. Simple as that.

"You probably know about Mary and Caleb. Eli Bontrager— he's over there by the food; he never strays far from anything he can eat—is still working for his father's cabinetry company. My niece Anna Marie is helping with her *mamm*'s business, and Marlene's sister Sarah Anne just had a baby. Now, if you'll excuse me, I need to be going."

He looked surprised. "You're leaving already? You just got here."

Prickles stood out on her arms. How did he know that?

As if he sensed her discomfort, he quickly added, "Caleb and I pulled up behind you when you were dropped off."

Miriam relaxed. A little. "He must have been irritated, then, because Lydia drove so slow. Our horse has a sore foot, so she tries not to hurry him along too much. Tomorrow the shoer is coming out to take a look at it."

Seth grinned again, then turned and faced her, leaning on his stick. "That's the most you've said to me all night."

"You find it funny that my horse has a sore foot?"

"*Nee, nee.* Of course not. I'm just glad you're talking to me, that's all."

She thought about asking why, but she stayed silent. Maybe if she didn't speak at all he would take the hint and leave.

But he must have been slow on the uptake because he leaned in closer and said in a low voice, "So what have you been up to all these years?"

Seriously? He wanted to know about her? If she didn't know it was December 10, she would have thought it was April Fool's Day, because this had to be a joke.

When she didn't respond right away, he said, "Okay, I'll go first. After I finished school I moved away from Paradise to live with my *Englisch* friends. I bought a car, and six months ago I wrapped it around a tree. Nearly killed myself. I'm lucky I only have the scar and a limp."

His initial good humor faded as he relayed his story, and melancholy seeped into his tone. By the angst shadowing his expression, Miriam could see how deeply the consequences of leaving the Amish and the accident affected him. Beyond the outward injuries, she suspected there were wounds inside that hadn't healed yet. She knew from experience that those were the toughest to mend.

"So," he said. "Your turn. Tell me something about yourself."

She still didn't understand why he was so interested. And it didn't matter, because she wasn't going to tell him anything. In a few minutes he would walk away and forget about her, so why bother?

"There you are, Seth." Mary walked up to them and smiled. "Hi, Miriam. How are you?"

"I'm well, *danki.*"

"Have you heard from Hannah since she left?"

Miriam shook her head. The three young women had gone to school together, but Miriam wasn't as close to Mary as she was to Hannah. "*Nee.* I only know she'll be back before January 1."

"I hope she has a *wunderbaar* Christmas." Mary smiled and glanced over her shoulder. "Oh, look. John Hostetler just came in. Late as always." She turned to Seth. "I'm sure he'll want to catch up with you. You guys were good friends at one time." She looked at Miriam. "You don't mind, do you?"

"*Nee,*" Miriam said, a little relieved that Seth was finally leaving. And, to her great dismay, a little disappointed.

"*Danki,*" Mary said. "Make sure you try the oatmeal cookies, Miriam. They're delicious."

Seth looked at Miriam. "Talk to you later?"

Tingles traveled through her body as his striking eyes locked with hers. Seth Fisher was looking at her. *Really* looking at her. For the briefest of moments, her young teenage fantasy had come true. She opened her mouth to speak.

Nothing came out. Not a single word.

Her cheeks flaming, she turned and fled the room.

◠◡◠

"Well, that wasn't very nice of her. She could have at least answered you."

Seth glanced at Mary, who seemed genuinely upset by the way Miriam departed. Not wanting her to be mad at Miriam, he said, "She's fine. Probably needs some air. Don't worry about it."

"Is there something wrong?"

Yes, there was something wrong, but it wasn't Miriam. It was him. "*Nee*," he said, swallowing the lie. It tasted like the bitter pill it was. He didn't blame her for not wanting to talk to him again. Not after what he'd done to her when they were young.

For the rest of the night, Seth visited with old friends, who accepted him back into the fold as if he'd never left. He was thankful to them, and thankful to God for softening their hearts. After the way he'd behaved, as if he had been too good for them, too high and mighty to be Amish, they had every right not to want to talk to him.

Like Miriam Herschberger.

He hadn't even realized the identity of the young woman standing against the wall until after he'd started talking to her. When he did, he wanted to kick himself. When he remembered what he'd said to her, and how he and his friends had laughed in her face, his spirit withered.

She could have thrown that back at him, but to her credit she didn't, and he found that a bit intriguing. Her voice was unique, soft but with a slight hoarseness to it. He didn't remember her sounding like that in school. Then again, until that day when he found out she liked him, he hadn't paid much attention to her at all.

"Seth?"

He turned and looked at Caleb.

"This is the second time you've blanked out on me. What's going on?"

Seth shook his head, giving his shoulders a slight shrug. Again, another lie. "I guess I'm just tired."

"You ready to go home?"

"I don't want to cut your night short," Seth said.

"I'm ready to go. Gotta get up early, ya know." Caleb did odd construction jobs that often took him many miles beyond Paradise.

"All right, then, let's go."

By the time Seth had made it up the stairs, thanked *Frau* Lapp, and walked out the door, Caleb had already brought the buggy around to pick him up. His leg ached from standing on it so long, even though he'd sat when he could throughout the night. The cold temperatures also added to his discomfort. No doubt the pain had slowed his pace to turtle speed.

When they were on their way, Seth stifled a yawn. He was glad he could sleep in a bit tomorrow morning. He wouldn't start officially working at his father's woodshop until after Christmas. His *daed* and brother, Noah, specialized in beautifully crafted items—carved hope chests, shelves, and smaller decorative pieces that sold well to the *Englisch* tourists visiting Paradise. Every once in a while his father would take on a larger project, like a porch swing or a pergola, but he preferred to work on smaller objects that allowed him to use his skills as an artist. Noah had also inherited his father's artistic bent and had been his apprentice since he was a young boy.

Seth didn't have that gift. He had worked in the shop for a year after he finished school, but fights with his father drove him to find work elsewhere, and soon after that he left Paradise altogether. He was determined not to let that happen again. He may not have the talent his brother and father had, but he would show them that he was a hard worker. After everything they had done for him since the accident, he owed them that much. And although his relationship with his *daed* was still strained, he was determined to mend the fences his own foolishness had destroyed.

"Ho, Seth." Caleb broke into his thoughts. "Do you see that?"

Seth squinted at the barely visible shadow on the side of the road. As the buggy neared the dark shape, he could see that it was a woman walking. Even though she wore a cloak, her arms were folded together in an effort to ward off the cold. As they pulled closer, he recognized her and grabbed Caleb's arm. "*Halt!*"

Caleb yanked up on the reins. "What are you doing?" he asked, his tone bewildered.

"That's Miriam."

"Who?"

"Miriam Herschberger. She was at the singing; didn't you see her?"

"*Ya.* What does it matter?"

"We need to pick her up."

Caleb groaned. "Have you looked in the backseat of my buggy? It's filled with junk."

"Maybe you should clean it out once in a while."

"Where is she gonna sit?"

Seth looked at the bench seat. There wasn't much room between him and Caleb, but Miriam was on the small side. It would be a tight squeeze, but better than letting her get chilled to the bone. "She'll sit between us."

"*Not* a good idea."

"Caleb, it's freezing out here." Although there was no snow on the ground, the temperatures were frigid. He didn't know where Miriam lived, but he didn't like the idea of her walking two feet out here in the cold, much less a couple miles.

"She's probably almost home anyway," Caleb said.

"What if she isn't?"

Caleb paused for a moment. "*Ach*," he said as he set the buggy in motion again. Miriam, with her quick stride, had passed them moments earlier, barely giving them a glance. "I knew you'd changed since the accident, but I didn't realize you had such a bleedin' heart."

"You should try a little compassion sometime." Seth moved his walking stick and put it on top of the pile of stuff in the back of the buggy. In the dim light he couldn't tell what was back there, and he really didn't care. All he wanted was for Miriam to be warm and safe. *Bear ye one another's burdens* . . . The verse popped into his head. Although he hadn't officially joined the church yet, he'd attended every service once he'd healed enough from his accident to leave the house. This past Sunday's sermon had been on compassion, and the bishop had singled out that particular passage from 2 Corinthians. He couldn't think of a better situation to apply it.

"*Halt,*" he said as they pulled up alongside her.

"Again with the *halt,*" Caleb mumbled. "Next time you're driving."

Seth ignored him, seeing Miriam glance over her shoulder, then rush her steps until she was almost jogging. Why was she running away from them? He opened the door and called out her name. "Miriam!"

She slowed, but didn't stop.

He hollered at her again, this time hanging halfway out of the buggy. "Miriam!"

"Obviously she doesn't want to be picked up," Caleb said. "Get back in here and let's go."

But he couldn't let it go. He couldn't let *her* go. Despite his weariness and the intensifying ache in his leg, Seth hurtled out of the buggy and landed on both feet, ignoring the pain. Surprised and grateful that he was still in a standing position, he started to yell again when his leg suddenly buckled, and he crashed shoulder first into the sharp gravel on the side of the road.

"Yeesh!"

This utterance came from inside the buggy. Now Seth was going to hear it from Caleb, probably all the way home. Maybe he deserved it. He shouldn't have bothered, since Miriam clearly wanted nothing to do with—

"Seth! Are you all right?"

He pushed up on one elbow and lifted his head. She had not only come back; she was crouched down in front of him, concern filling her husky voice. He was all right, despite the stinging in both his shoulder and leg. But the pain was worth it when she reached out and touched his arm.

Caleb had reached them by this time, hot with anger. "Are you *ab im kopp*?"

"I'm fine," Seth muttered, moving himself to an upright position. "You're overreacting."

"You're fine? Then get up and walk."

Seth looked up at him, his jaw tightening. "You know I can't." He paused, ashamed to admit in front of Miriam what Caleb already knew. "Not without help."

"Then let's help you." Miriam put her hands under his arm, prepared to either push or pull, he wasn't sure which. The idea of her slender arms lifting him off the ground would have been amusing, if he weren't so embarrassed.

"For crying out loud. I should have never stopped." Caleb, on the opposite side, did the same as Miriam, and together they lifted Seth to a standing position. A lopsided position, but Seth wasn't about to complain. Caleb was doing enough griping for the both of them.

When they led him to the buggy and started to help him in, Seth resisted. "Miriam, you get in first."

There was very little light outside to guide them, only the exterior lamps on the buggy. He couldn't see her face, but by the way her hands tensed on his arm, he could tell she was surprised. Okay, more than surprised, probably stunned, with a little bit of shock thrown in there.

"T-that's okay," she said, her eyes cast slightly downward. "I can walk home."

"*Nee*. It's freezing out here." His breath hung in the air, punctuating his statement.

"I only have a couple more miles to go. I'll be fine."

Walking a couple of miles was easy, if it was daylight and the weather was decent. But that wasn't the case tonight, and he wasn't going to let it drop. "Miriam, we can stand out here and argue about this, which will make Caleb even more ticked off than he already is—"

"You got that right," Caleb grumbled.

Seth shot him an annoyed look. "Or you can get in the buggy and let us take you home."

She hesitated again, and he thought she would pull away from him and flee down the road. He didn't think he could convince Caleb to stop again. Just as he was about to prod her one more time, she let go of his arm and climbed in.

"Finally," Caleb said.

"What's your problem?" Seth hissed.

"My problem?" Caleb countered, thankfully keeping his voice down. "I told you, I gotta get home. And since when did you care about Miriam Herschberger, anyway?"

"When did you become such a jerk?" *Like I used to be.*

Caleb grimaced but went ahead and assisted Seth into the buggy before shutting the door and dashing around to the other side. In a few seconds he hopped in, and they were on their way.

The three of them were crammed next to each other like little fish in a can. Caleb needed the use of his arms to steer the horse, so Miriam scooted over a bit until she was sitting as close to Seth as she possibly could without climbing into his lap.

For some bizarre reason, he didn't think he'd mind very much if she did.

Tossing the illicit and surprising thought out of his head, he glanced at her. Her head was cast down, her hands clasped together so tightly he thought she might snap her fingers in two.

Due to the cramped conditions, his arms were pressed tight against his sides. Way too tight to be comfortable. The position increased the pain in his shoulder, and as they rolled along the road, he knew he wouldn't be able to sit like this for very long. He needed more room. She needed more room. Caleb would definitely like more room. Maybe his friend had been right.

Maybe this was a bad idea.

Chapter Four

WHAT HAD SHE DONE WRONG?

She had to have done *something* for God to punish her like this. Okay, maybe sitting so close to Seth Fisher that she could inhale the clean scent of his clothes and skin wasn't exactly punishment.

More like torture. Sheer torture.

She should have never stopped and turned around when Seth fell out of the buggy. Better yet, she should have waited for Anna Marie to take her home instead of leaving the Lapps' early on her own. Above all, she should have never left Lydia's in the first place. If she hadn't, then she wouldn't be wedged in between one man who was sizzling mad and another who was just plain . . . sizzling.

The thought popped into her head, unbidden and unwanted. Her cheeks heated, and she dipped her head lower, despite knowing that it was impossible to see much in the almost non-existent light in the buggy. Yet she wouldn't risk Seth seeing her blush.

"Where do you live?" Caleb ground out, after a long, uncomfortable stretch of silence.

Ach, he was mad. In a way she didn't blame him. They had never been very good friends, ever since the incident with Seth years ago. In fact, for a long time she had resented Caleb almost as much as she had Seth, but she had found a way to forgive him.

While his teasing had hurt her feelings, it hadn't come close to Seth's outright meanness.

"I'm going to my sister's," she said. "Lydia Smucker." She gave him the address.

Caleb nodded curtly and sped up the horses.

"That's not a couple miles away."

She turned toward Seth slightly—very slightly because they were so close to each other—and looked at him.

"More like five," he added.

She pushed up her glasses, which were always slipping. "I'm quite capable of walking five miles."

"In the dark? In the cold?"

"*Ya.*" And she could too. But she wouldn't like it, and her hands and feet would have been near-frozen by the time she got to Lydia's. Not warm and cozy like she was right now.

They sat in silence for a few moments, the *clip-clopping* of the horse's hooves the only sound she could hear through the black curtain that covered the front and sides of the buggy, protecting them from the winter cold and wind. Tonight wasn't windy, but it was cold. Downright cold.

She felt Seth move farther away from her. Or at least he tried. There really wasn't any room to move at all. She tried to dismiss the prickle of hurt that he didn't want to sit so close to her. All she wanted was for the ride to be over.

Then suddenly Seth pried his left arm loose from in between them and swung it over the back of the seat.

A gasp of surprise nearly escaped her lips. This was the closest she'd ever been to having a man's arm around her.

"Hope you don't mind," he said. "'It's a little tight in here."

Unable to say anything, barely able to breathe, she simply shook her head.

"*Gut.*"

"I could use a little more room." Caleb's elbow lightly touched her arm. Then he glanced at her. "If you can scoot over a bit, I'd appreciate it."

His tone wasn't as harsh before, and for that she was glad. She looked to see if there was any way she could move to the right and not be up against Seth, but she didn't see how.

"Here." Seth made the decision for her as he pressed his hand on her shoulder and guided her to close the miniscule gap between them. He leaned down and whispered, "Don't worry about Caleb. His bark is worse than his bite."

But she wasn't worried about Caleb. Not at all. In fact, she forgot Caleb altogether. She kept reminding herself that Seth was only being polite, which was nothing short of amazing. She had never known Seth Fisher to be nice. Confident, yes. Cocky, even. But never nice.

He moved his hand from her shoulder and laid his arm against the backseat again. "So you're staying with your sister?" he asked in a low, smooth voice that reminded her of molasses pouring out of a jar.

"*Ya,*" she said, irked by her disappointment that he'd moved his hand. "She was widowed a couple years ago, and I help her out when I can."

"What does she do?"

"Lots of things, but her most recent project is her new cookbook. It's a collection of recipes handed down through our family."

"How original," Caleb remarked.

Miriam winced. Sure, there were a lot of Amish cookbooks filled with family recipes for sale in Lancaster County, but Caleb didn't have to be so sarcastic.

"Lydia's is special," she said, feeling the need to defend her sister. "Not because it's from our family. There are recipes, *ya*, but there are also photographs of the quilts my grandmother and I have made. The cover shows a very special quilt."

The photograph was of her grandmother Emma's favorite quilt, a beautiful masterpiece Miriam cherished beyond description.

"I'm sure it's a great cookbook," Seth said.

His kind comment set off a tiny spark of warmth, and again she marveled at the change in him. She found it hard to reconcile the kind man sitting next to her with the cruel boy from her childhood. "*Ya*. It is. I know she's going to sell a lot of copies. I'm taking a box with me to sell at work tomorrow."

"Oh? Where do you work?"

"Stitches and More," she said, stating the name of the fabric and sewing supply store in Paradise.

Seth didn't say anything, and the conversation came to a discomfiting conclusion. The silence filling the buggy grew awkward, as none of them seemed to have anything else to say. Caleb had set his horse on a brisk pace, and they soon came upon Lydia's house, causing Miriam to let out an inward sigh of relief. He turned in the drive and brought the buggy to a halt.

Before she could say anything, Caleb slipped out the door and motioned for her to follow him out the driver's side. "I don't want him taking another spill," he explained.

She understood that and agreed. But before moving away,

she needed one more look at Seth. She'd never be this close to him again, which was a good thing. She didn't like the tumult of conflicting emotions churning inside her. Against her will, her body started to shake.

"You better get inside and warm up," Seth said.

One thing she didn't need to do was warm up. She was already warm. Warmer than she had a right to be.

She nodded, pulling herself away from his magical gaze before Caleb started grousing again. "*Danki,*" she said over her shoulder to Seth, then quickly exited the buggy. "*Danki,* Caleb."

"No problem. Sorry for being a grouch. Patience is a virtue I'm still trying to master."

His apology surprised her. He'd seemed so put out with her before, and now he was saying he was sorry. First Seth, and now Caleb. She had spent years distrusting and thinking the worst of most men, save her *daed* and her brothers. Now two men were being kind to her in one night. That had to be some kind of record.

❧

"So what was that all about?" Caleb asked as he climbed back into the buggy.

Seth looked at his friend. Now they had plenty of room and he could stretch out his leg a bit. He welcomed the movement, while at the same time he kind of missed having Miriam next to him. Why, he had no idea.

"You know. You and Miriam. First you're hanging out together at the party; then you practically kill yourself making sure she'd let us take her home. What's going on?"

"Nothing." Which was the truth. Nothing was going on, and he doubted anything would. Not when he'd been such a jerk to her back in school. Some girls might have put that behind them, but he could tell Miriam hadn't. Distrust radiated from her like heat off a woodstove. And for some reason he couldn't fathom, that really, *really* bothered him.

"I'm just surprised, you know. You and a girl like Miriam. Doesn't add up exactly."

Obviously Caleb had forgotten about the playground incident, and Seth wasn't about to remind him. "First of all, there is no 'me and Miriam.' I haven't seen her since we left grade school. Second, I talked to everyone at the Lapps' tonight, not just her. Third, I would have wanted to stop for anyone walking on the road on a night like tonight. It's the right thing to do."

But Caleb wasn't buying his protests any more than was Seth himself. "Uh-huh. Well, that all may be true, but I think there's more than that."

"There isn't."

"I should hope not. I can't see you with a snob like her."

Seth turned and looked at Caleb, surprised. "You think she's a snob?"

Caleb nodded. "You've been gone a long time, Seth, and you don't know her like we do. The way she was at the singing tonight, separate from everyone? She always does that, like she's too *gut* to be with us. I'm surprised she was even there. Usually she doesn't show up at all."

"Maybe she's just shy."

"Maybe." Caleb cast Seth a sideways glance. "You gotta admit, she's kinda hard to look at."

"No, I don't."

"Oh, c'mon, Seth. Wait, don't tell me . . . you actually think she's pretty?"

He didn't respond right away. He couldn't, because in all honesty, he didn't find Miriam physically attractive. "She's not . . . that bad."

"Wow, you *really* have changed. Sure that accident didn't affect your eyesight?"

"It didn't. Just drop it, all right?"

Caleb moved on to another topic of conversation before Seth could say anything in Miriam's defense. A short while later they arrived at Seth's house.

"Need a hand?"

"I'm *gut*," he said, waving off Caleb's help. "*Danki* for the ride."

"*Du bischt wilkumm*," Caleb said in response. "But I mean it next time, Seth."

"Mean what?"

"You're gonna be the one driving."

Seth chuckled. "Fair enough."

As Caleb left, Seth made his way to the house. He entered the front room, surprised to see his parents still up.

"Did you have a *gut* time?" Rachel, his mother, gazed up at him, and he could see the worry sneaking into her light-gray eyes.

"*Ya*. I had a great time."

She let out a breath and set down the knitting she was working on. "Any problems?"

He knew she meant with his leg. Since the accident, she had been hovering, only stepping back these past couple weeks when it became obvious that he would eventually heal and be all right. If he even hinted at the fact that he'd hit the ground, bruising his arm and his dignity, she'd never let him out of the house again. "*Nee*. Everything was fine."

"*Wunderbaar*. We're glad you had a chance to go out and have some fun. It's not *gut* for you to be stuck in the *haus* all the time." She stood and cleared her throat as she looked down at his father, who was sitting in his well-worn chair.

Daed set aside his paper on the end table and followed her lead. "Bedtime," he said in his usual gruff manner, not looking at Seth. He rose from his chair. "See you in the morning."

"*Guten nacht*."

His parents made their way to their room on the main floor, while Seth climbed the stairs to his bedroom. He passed by his brothers' old room, then his sisters', which was also empty. At the end of the hall was the smallest bedroom. As the youngest of the family, he had his own room, but it was tiny. Still, he didn't mind and appreciated the privacy. Limping into his room, he went to the bed and plopped down on the soft mattress with gratitude. The fatigue he'd kept at bay during the latter part of the evening had caught up to him.

But sleep wasn't all that easy to find. And as he lay there in bed, hands clasped behind his head while he tried to ignore the throb in his leg and the ache in his shoulder, he thought about Miriam. Guilt seeped into him once again over how he had hurt her. But as her image remained in his mind, his conscience tempered a bit.

She had certainly changed since the last time he had seen her in school five years ago. He thought about Caleb calling her a snob and saying she was hard to look at. Seth thought his friend was wrong on both counts. She wasn't pretty by most men's standards—his standards too. Yet there was something unique about her, not only physically, but beneath the surface. He had enjoyed their brief conversation at the Lapps', along with their ride to her sister's. She hadn't tried to get his attention or flirted with him the way most girls usually did. That in itself was different and fascinating.

As his eyes drooped, he also realized something else about her. Behind the wire frames of her glasses, her eyes held a glint of sadness. He couldn't help but wonder what that was about. Maybe someday he would find out.

✑

"This is a lovely pattern, Miriam," Sarah Fisher said the morning after the singing. "One of your own designs?"

Miriam smoothed out the wrinkles on the quilt square with her palm. When business was slow in the fabric shop, she worked on her own quilting. Tammy, the *Englisch* owner of Stitches and More, didn't mind, as long as Miriam's work was done. That included not only handling the sales but also putting out new stock, rotating old, and making sure the myriad of fabrics, patterns, and notions were neatly arranged on the shelves and displays.

"*Ya*, this is my work, but it's not really a formal design," Miriam said, pleased by Sarah's compliment. Sarah was an excellent quilter, and she didn't give out praise lightly. "More like an experiment."

"The colors are striking." With delicate fingers, Sarah touched the intersecting rectangles. "So many different hues of red and green, and so many different textile patterns. I would have never thought to put some of these fabrics together." She glanced up and smiled. "I've seen your grandmother's quilts at Lydia's. You have your *grossmammi*'s gift, you do."

Miriam blushed. She had to be careful not to let the compliments bloat her ego—to maintain *demut* at all times. Humility was an important part of Amish life. The Scriptures said that pride goeth before destruction, and they were words to live by.

"*Danki*, Sarah. I cherish the quilts *grossmammi* gave me."

"She knew you would appreciate them like no one else." Sarah stepped to the side and looked at the quilt block from another angle, her gray eyes filled with curiosity. "I think you should continue with this experiment. It will make a wonderful Christmas quilt. Will you bring it when you come to visit David and me on First Christmas?"

Sarah and Lydia had been friends for years, and Sarah and her husband had invited all the Herschbergers to their house for First Christmas. Miriam knew it would be a bittersweet occasion for the young couple, who had lost their baby the previous Christmas.

"I'd be happy to." Miriam smiled as she folded up the quilt block and tucked it into her bag, which she had made from scraps and bits of discarded fabric.

Like the block Sarah admired so much, the bag was made with vibrant colors and vivid patterns, no one fabric the same as the other. Somehow it worked, and more than one *Englisch* tourist had spotted the bag and asked where she purchased it. A couple of them even offered to buy it from her, when they found out it was one of a kind. Miriam had thanked them, but turned down the offer. She had used some of her grandmother's old fabric, and she could never part with the bag for that reason.

"I'm surprised to see you here today," Miriam said. "Is school out of session?"

Sarah nodded. "Vacation started a couple days ago. I have to admit, even though I love my job, I'm glad for the break." She looked around the store. "Is Tammy here today?"

"*Ya*. She stepped out for a moment, but she should be back soon. Maybe I can help?"

Sarah frowned slightly. "When I was here last week, she was out of green thread. She was ordering more, and she said it should be in by today, but I don't see any."

"I haven't seen any spools up front here, either," Miriam said, "but I can check in the back."

"*Danki*. I'll just keep looking around while I wait."

Leaving Sarah to browse through the wide variety of colorful fabrics in the store, Miriam went to the back. The space was small, with Tammy's desk in the corner, a diminutive round table in the middle where they could sit and eat their lunches, and a tiny bathroom off to the side. Tammy's desk, as usual, was a mess, covered with papers, order forms, and catalogs.

As Miriam searched for the thread, she said a silent prayer of thanks for her job. She only worked three days a week, but spending the day in the fabric shop helped keep her mind off what happened last night. It had been hard enough for her to fall asleep, thinking about Seth and the buggy ride home. She didn't need to spend the entire day focusing on him. Instead she would set her attention on her work, like finding the thread for Sarah.

Amid the disarray on Tammy's desk, Miriam spotted a brown box. She opened it, finding standard spools of green thread inside, and smiled, knowing Sarah would be pleased.

Miriam took a couple of the spools back up front.

"Here they are, Sarah. What are you making with—"

The rest of the words disappeared in her mouth when she saw who was standing in front of the counter.

Chapter Five

"WHAT ARE YOU DOING HERE?"

Seth lifted a brow, not at Miriam's question, but at her tone of voice. While he certainly hadn't expected her to welcome him with open arms, he hadn't thought she would react with horror. Well, not exactly horror, but close to it.

"I came to pick up *mei mudder*'s order." When he'd found out this morning that she needed to pick up some things from Stitches and More, he didn't hesitate to offer to run the errand for her. Maybe it hadn't been such a good idea.

"Why here?" Miriam said.

"This is where she placed her order."

Miriam's cheeks flushed, and she cast her gaze downward. "Oh. *Ya*. That makes sense."

He liked her white *kapp* better. The black bonnet she'd worn last night hid too much of her face. Now he could get a good look at her, and he liked what he saw. Maybe Caleb was the one who needed an eye exam. Her skin was so smooth, not marred by a single blemish except for a small, light-brown freckle above her lip on the right side. Her eyes were a deep brown color, rimmed with long, black lashes.

She had high cheekbones, lips that were a bit on the thin side but still appealing, and a prominent chin. Why had he thought she was ugly back in eighth grade?

Because he was an idiot, that's why.

"You found the thread, Miriam?"

He turned around at the sound of a woman's voice, making sure he didn't knock anything over with his walking stick, then stepped to the side. He recognized his cousin David's wife and smiled. "Hello, Sarah."

A grin crossed her face. "Seth!" She came toward him and put her hand on his forearm. "You're looking well."

"*Danki*, Sarah. How is David?"

"Just fine. Busy this time of year."

"Sarah? Your thread?"

Both he and Sarah looked at Miriam, who held out the spools in front of her. She kept her gaze on Sarah as she asked, "Did you prepay for these?"

"I did," Sarah said. "If you could just put them in a bag for me, I'll be on my way."

Miriam reached underneath the counter and retrieved a small plastic bag. Seth watched as she carefully placed two spools of dark-green thread inside. She had such small hands. But her fingers weren't short and stubby; they were slender and proportionate. Delicate. He glanced at his free hand. Large, rough. Her hand would probably get lost in his.

He groaned inwardly at the erratic and unexpected thought. What possessed him to think about holding Miriam's hand? Like that would ever happen.

Pulling his gaze away from her hands, he glanced around the shop as Miriam finished up the transaction. He'd never been in here before—he doubted many men had. The store was crammed to the brim with fabric and sewing supplies. On the walls hung colorful handmade quilts—his mother was a quilter, and he recognized the high quality and intricate, yet artistically simple patterns that were typical Amish. There were also various gift-type items scattered around the small space. Taking a deep breath, he inhaled the mingling aromas of scented candles and potpourri, stuff women seemed to love.

"*Danki*, Miriam. Say hello to your *mamm* for me." Sarah moved toward the front door, then turned around. "I just thought of something. I remember Lydia had one of your *gross-mammi*'s quilts displayed in her living room. It was absolutely stunning. But I didn't see it the last time I visited."

"Was it a star pattern?"

"*Ya*, cream and navy blue."

"*Mei mamm* and I are repairing some of the stitching. We're doing that for all twenty of her quilts."

"Do you display them on a rack?"

"*Nee*. I have one at the end of my bed, and the others are packed away in the closet. I'd like to buy a hope chest to put them in, so they can be stored correctly. Right now that's out of my reach."

Seth saw a flush of color bloom on her cheeks as she finished the sentence. She shouldn't feel bad about not being able to afford the chest. He had very little money himself, and almost all of his future earnings would be applied to his doctor and hospital bills. Since he and the rest of the community didn't have insurance, they often pooled their resources when one of their brethren had a medical crisis. Seth's bills had been paid off, but he was determined to pay the community back.

"I'm sure you're taking very good care of them," Sarah said. "And someday after you're married, hopefully you can buy one."

Seth didn't think Miriam's cheeks could get any redder.

"Regards to Tammy." Sarah turned to Seth. "Tell your *mamm* I'll stop and see her before Christmas. 'Bye!"

Sarah went out the door, leaving Miriam and Seth in the store. Alone, as far as he could tell. Just them and the awkward silence that filled the shop.

"You needed to pick up an order?" Miriam finally asked.

Seth nodded and reached into the pocket of his trousers. He retrieved the slip of paper his mother had written her order on and handed it to Miriam.

She glanced over it. "I think I saw her fabric behind the counter this morning." Miriam ducked down and disappeared for a moment, then popped up with two different, short bolts of fabric, one a dark green with tiny, white flowers, another a plain Christmas red. Consulting the note again, Miriam tucked the bolts under her arm. "I'll just take these to the cutting table," she said, leaving him standing at the counter.

She crossed the short distance to the other side of the shop. Her steps were too quick and the store too packed with stuff for him to follow.

Spinning around, she frowned when she didn't see him. "Seth?"

"Still at the counter." He clenched his jaw.

"Oh." He heard her hesitation. "I'll just be a minute, then."

As he waited, he tried to stem his frustration at not being able to do something as easy as crossing a room. Before his accident he had been nimble and a pretty decent athlete. Now he couldn't go five feet without worrying about knocking something over or taking twice as much time as an able-bodied person. But as he always did when he came perilously close to self-pity, he reminded himself that he was lucky to be alive. God, for some reason, had spared him, and he was sure it wasn't so he could spend the rest of his life feeling sorry for himself.

Miriam appeared behind the counter again, holding two neatly folded piles of fabric. "Four yards of green and two yards of red, correct?"

Seth shrugged. "That's what she had on her list. I think she's finishing up a quilt."

"Your *mudder* quilts?"

"*Ya.* I take it you do too."

She nodded. "*Mei grossmammi* taught me."

He watched as she put the fabric in a bright-yellow plastic bag, the name Stitches and More emblazoned on the side in black letters. As she rang up his purchase, he made a last-minute decision. "Candles," he said, mostly to himself, as he spied a small, snow-white candle next to the register. "What kind of candles do you sell?"

"All kinds," Miriam replied. "We usually keep more in stock over the holidays. Why?"

"I'd like to purchase some. Christmas presents," he added. Since he'd left Paradise, he hadn't really paid much attention to Christmas and hadn't purchased any gifts in the past five years. Today he could rectify that and buy something for his mother and his sisters. He would also get something for Sarah. This Christmas marked the anniversary of her miscarriage, which had devastated her and his cousin David. In the past Seth probably wouldn't have thought twice about their loss, but this year was different. Like Caleb said, he was different, and he wanted to show everyone just how much.

"What kind of candles were you looking for?" Miriam looked up at him with her chocolate-brown eyes.

"Um . . . not sure. Something that smells good."

A smile quirked on her lips, and he realized he'd never seen her smile. It softened her features, making her seem almost . . . pretty.

The hint of a smile instantly disappeared, and her expression became all business. "First of all, who are the candles for?"

"My *mudder*, two sisters, and a cousin."

"All right. Do you know their favorite scents?"

Now it was his turn to go red. "Ah, not really. I never paid much attention."

She tapped her finger against her chin, obviously deep in thought. She seemed to be more relaxed than when he first entered the store. "I have just the thing."

Walking around the counter, she met him on the other side and led him to a tiered display of candles only a few steps away. She picked up a small, round candle that had been dyed a light purple. "This is a lavender tea light. It looks tiny, but the scent is strong. Lavender is soothing and calming. We sell a lot of these, not just at Christmas. We try to keep them in stock year-round."

Seth looked at the candle. It covered almost her entire palm. He plucked it from her, again noting the contrast in size of their hands.

"You can smell it if you want."

He brought it closer to his nose and took a big sniff. Too big. He turned away and sneezed.

"I told you it was strong."

There was that hint of a grin again. He really liked her smile. "Smells pretty good." He handed to candle back to her. "How much?"

"We sell them individually or by the box. The boxes are in the back."

"All right, how much is a box?"

When she told him the amount, he inwardly breathed a sigh of relief. He could afford that and still have a bit left over, thankfully. He would have felt stupid buying only four tiny tea lights.

"I'll get the box for you."

He watched her as she turned around and walked away. She had an air of confidence about her, one that she didn't have when he first came into the shop, and it was definitely missing last night at the Lapps'. Clearly she was in her element here.

Moments later she brought the box and laid it on the counter. "Now, what do you think your *mamm* would like?"

Uh-oh. "Actually . . . I think I'll give her the lavender tea lights too."

"Okay. I'll go get three more boxes." She started to go when he reached out and touched her arm.

"I'll just take the one."

Their gazes met for a moment, and he knew she understood his meaning.

"No problem. I'll ring this up for you."

"Make sure the fabric is separate."

"I will."

"*Danki*." He leaned his hip against the counter, relieving some of the pressure off his leg. He appreciated her not making him feel like a fool over not having enough money to buy more than one box of candles. As she punched a few buttons on the cash register, a chiming sound echoed through the store. He glanced over his shoulder to see a petite woman with dark-red hair walk through the door. A blast of cold air followed her in.

Miriam told him the amount, and he fished in his pocket for his wallet.

"Good morning," the woman said, giving him a big smile as she strode toward him. "I hope you found everything you needed."

"I did, thanks to Miriam." He glanced at her, but she had her head down, counting his change. He could only see the top of her *kapp*.

"It was my lucky day when Miriam walked into my shop," the woman said. "She could run the whole thing herself if she had to."

"I'm sure she could."

Miriam handed Seth a few coins without making eye contact. She retrieved a plastic bag from underneath the counter and started to pack up his box as if he and the woman were comparing the price of horse feed instead of singing her praises.

Demut. Miriam understood it and exemplified it.

It was a lesson he still had to learn.

Most of his life he'd been filled with *hochmut*. He'd had an ego the size of Pennsylvania and didn't care who knew it. He'd been told so many times he was handsome that he believed it. He'd been popular, not only with girls but with the guys as well. Athletic, strong, he'd done well in school without even trying. By the time he was sixteen, he knew he was the golden boy. Untouchable. Unbreakable.

He'd been broken all right. Not only his body, but his pride as well.

The shop owner stood at the opposite end of the counter. "I'm back for the rest of the day, Miriam. Why don't you go ahead and take your lunch break?"

"It's not quite noon yet. I can wait twenty more minutes."

"Don't worry about it. Go."

"All right." She handed Seth his bag of candles. "*Danki,*" she said in her usual soft, slightly raspy voice. "Have a *gut* day." Without waiting for him to respond, she picked up a multicolored quilted bag, then turned away and headed for the back of the store.

Seth limped out of the store and searched for his father. They had ridden into town together. He didn't see him right away, and even though his leg was sore, he decided to take a short walk down Lincoln Avenue. Next door to the sewing store was a bakery, and he stopped in front of the window, staring at the mouthwatering treats on display. Then he glanced back at Stitches and More . . . and had an idea.

⤜⤏

Miriam's stomach growled. Relief had washed through her when Tammy gave her the go-ahead for lunch. She'd overslept this morning, which made her late for work and caused her to skip breakfast. The reason for her bad morning had fortunately just left the fabric store.

She'd stayed up half the night thinking about Seth—and fighting with herself. But it wasn't just that she thought of him. Hope jabbed at her defenses, weakening them with each punch. He had apologized to her, talked to her, even made sure she had a ride home on a freezing cold night. That was more attention than anyone had ever given to her before. How was she supposed to resist that?

To make things worse, he had to show up here. Today. When she hadn't yet fortified the buttress around her heart. At first when she was helping him with his *mamm*'s order, she tried not to stare at the scar, remembering how rude she'd been at the Lapps' last night. Yet after a few moments she didn't even notice it. All she could see was the beauty of his eyes, which never seemed to stray from her face. Why had he looked at her so intently?

His reasons didn't matter, and she didn't need to ponder them. He completed his purchase and went on his way. Now things could go back to normal. Like her heart rate, for example. And her life.

Tammy breezed into the back room and leaned against the doorjamb, crossing her arms over her chest. "Pardon me for saying this, but that guy you were talking to a minute ago? He is way *cuh-ute.*"

Miriam looked at her, shocked. Her boss had never referred to any male, Amish or *Englisch*, as *cuh-ute.*

Then again, she'd never seen Seth Fisher before.

"I know we don't get that many men in here, at least not by

themselves. But still, he's the best looking young man I've seen in a long time. He seems nice too. Like he'd be a sweetheart once you got to know him."

Miriam clamped her teeth down on her lower lip. *Oh, if only Tammy knew . . .*

"So what's with the scar? And the limp?"

Miriam hesitated. Although she considered Tammy a friend—easy to do since she was only ten years older than Miriam—she rarely spoke with her about life in her community. Tammy, who transplanted herself to Paradise from Philadelphia three years ago after her divorce, had asked Miriam the usual questions—did she use electricity (no), did she have a phone (no, but some of her friends' families did, for business use only), did she use an outhouse (she didn't), did she wish she could drive a car (not at all), and several others. Miriam didn't mind answering those, but she made sure not to reveal too much about her family or things that happened in the community. Not that there was anything to hide; she just didn't feel it was Tammy's, or anyone else's, business.

"He was in an accident," she finally said, but offered no further explanation.

"That must have been some accident."

"It was." From what she'd heard and Seth confirmed last night, he was lucky to have survived it.

"Okay, enough chitchat. Go ahead and have lunch." Tammy hooked a lock of her chin-length, auburn hair behind an ear that held five piercings. "Take a full hour, Miriam. You deserve it." Rising from her chair, she turned around and went back out to the front of the store.

Miriam picked up her quilted bag. Besides the experimental quilting square and a few quilting supplies, it also held her lunch and her wallet. She spread her meal on the table in front of her—a ham sandwich and a banana. Bowing her head, she whispered a prayer of grace.

"Dear Father God, bless this food I am about to partake of. And please have mercy on me, Lord. Help me not to think of Seth Fisher anymore."

She ended her prayer and slipped her sandwich out of its small plastic bag. She was just about to take a bite when Tammy barged in.

"Your friend's back." Tammy's plum-tinted lips formed a wide grin.

"Friend?"

"The one that was just here? The cute one? What's his name?"

"Seth." Miriam's mouth had suddenly gone dry, and she set her sandwich down. Her appetite instantly disappeared.

Tammy nodded. "I heard him say he would see you soon, but I didn't think it would be this soon."

"Neither did I."

"Don't keep him waiting." Tammy walked toward her, making shooing gestures with both hands.

Miriam slowly rose from her chair, wiping her hands on the paper towel she'd taken from the roll in the bathroom. In her haste at home, she had forgotten a napkin. Maybe Seth had forgotten something too, and that's why he was here. Or he'd discovered she'd given him incorrect change. That was possible, especially when his mere presence made her brain go haywire. Unable to resist touching her *kapp* to make sure she didn't have a hair out of place, she left the room and walked behind the counter, the long stretch of pale-green formica-topped wood making a good barrier between them. Be professional. Professional. Professional . . .

He's so cuh-ute.

So much for professional.

"Did you forget something?" she asked, pleased that her voice sounded businesslike even though most of her mind was thinking about anything *but* business.

"*Nee.*" He leaned against the counter, and she thought she saw him flinch. Was he in pain?

"Are you all right?"

He nodded. "As fine as I can be with a bum leg. Here." He plopped a small white bag on the counter. The top was folded down and stapled together.

"What is this?"

"A little something to go with your lunch. To thank you for helping me."

She eyed it skeptically.

"Open it up. I promise nothing's going to jump out at you."

Tentatively she unfastened the bag, less suspicious of the contents than she was of his motives. Peeking inside, her eyes grew wide as she saw what the bag contained.

A nice big chunk of raspberry fudge. Her favorite.

"The lady at the bakery said you come in every so often, and you always get the raspberry fudge."

"*Ya.* She's right, I do." Miriam looked up from the bag, still inhaling the sweet aroma of sugar and raspberry. "Why?"

"Why what?"

"Why did you give me this?"

"Because I wanted to." Without saying another word, he straightened; then he limped to the door and left.

Tammy instantly appeared, as if she'd been watching them from the back room, which she probably was. "I saw him holding that bag, and I just knew it was for you." She grinned, as if she were the one getting an unexpected gift from a man. "What's inside?"

Miriam tilted the bag in her direction and showed her.

With a sly grin Tammy said, "That's your favorite."

"I know."

"You get that every time you go to Weaver's."

"I *know*."

"But he's not your boyfriend."

She looked at Tammy and hid her irritation. "*Nee*, he's not."

"Are you sure? Because a guy doesn't just surprise a girl with her favorite dessert and not have some intentions."

Miriam looked at the exit, where Seth had just been. "I know," she whispered, taking a deep breath and steadying her nerves. Part of her wanted to know what kind of game he was playing with her. The other part was scared to find out.

Chapter Six

"I APPRECIATE YOU LETTING ME COME WITH YOU TO TOWN," Seth said to his father as they headed home from Paradise.

Melvin Fisher gave his son a curt nod.

Not that Seth expected anything more. Even when the man felt like talking, his father had a staccato form of communication that used to grind on Seth's nerves. But now he appreciated the older man's measured phrases. Melvin usually spoke only when spoken to and made his points quick and concise. He did his work, took care of his family, worshipped his Lord. As far as Seth knew, his *daed* had always lived a solid Amish life. The kind of life Seth tried to run away from, with disastrous results.

When he was a kid, he never thought much about being Amish. He'd grown up in a tightknit community and never had a complaint about it. And even though his relationship with his father had become rocky early on, Seth hadn't considered leaving. It wasn't until his *daed* fired him from the shop and he got a job working in a warehouse in Lancaster that the *Englisch* world grabbed hold of him. Before long he'd moved to the city and shared an apartment with another *Englisch* friend and fully left his Amish life behind. He cut his hair to a length much shorter than the Amish wear, wore *Englisch* clothes, dated *Englisch* women.

Yet during those four years away from his family and his community, there was an empty space in his soul, one that kept growing larger with each passing day. He truly believed that

God had used his accident to bring him back to Paradise and to the Amish. Despite having his work cut out for him where his relationship with his father was concerned, Seth felt a measure of peace, something he'd never experienced living in Lancaster. As soon as he was able and had convinced his family and the church leaders of his sincerity, he wanted to be baptized into the Amish faith.

Melvin steered his horse, Gravy, onto the road. The horse's full name was Biscuits 'n' Gravy, as christened by Seth's niece, Ruth, when she was four years old. Biscuits 'n' Gravy had been too much of a mouthful even for the adults, and especially for his father, who wanted to please his granddaughter but couldn't bring himself to call the horse by its full name. Gravy was a good compromise.

"Got your *mamm*'s order?" he asked Seth.

"*Ya.*" Forgetting about the fabric he'd purchased, he thought about Miriam's reaction when he had given her the fudge. A combination of surprise and wariness. He had to admit he had surprised himself with his impulsiveness. He hadn't planned on buying her anything, but when he saw the bakery next door, the idea just came to him. That fancy treat had been quite dear and cost him the last of his money, but he didn't mind.

He frowned. He'd never had such a confusing reaction to any *maedel* before. He'd had lots of girlfriends, especially when he had been out whooping it up with his *Englisch* friends. They'd all been pretty. Actually, *hot* was a better word, one he'd learned from those same buddies. According to them there was *cute*. Then there was *pretty*. And finally, what every man wanted and what Seth had all the time, there was *hot*.

And then there was Miriam. Plain Miriam, who had liked him at one time—he vaguely remembered the notebook with his name surrounded by crooked hearts—but now seemed to barely tolerate his presence. He'd never met a girl he couldn't charm within five minutes. Yet she seemed anything but charmed.

"You're thinking deep thoughts," his father remarked as they continued down the road toward home.

Seth waited for his *daed* to ask what those thoughts were, but he didn't. They'd never shared much in the past, unless he counted the numerous heated arguments they'd had when Seth was a teenager.

But that didn't mean his father didn't love him. That had been made clear the night of the accident, when his parents showed up in the emergency room. Seth had been in and out of consciousness, partly because of the pain medication they'd given him and partly because the pain medication didn't help too much, so passing out at least gave him some relief. But before he'd gone to surgery, he remembered his father's voice as they wheeled him down the hallway. *Heal my boy. Whatever it takes, whatever it costs—heal my boy.*

No, he didn't doubt his father's love. Not anymore.

What he did doubt was that his father would ever trust him again. He had betrayed that trust, first when he had slacked off and caused trouble in his *daed*'s shop, then when he had left for Lancaster without saying good-bye. His mother had forgiven him completely, but his father, in his customary way, had said little. Seth knew it would take time for him to earn back his *daed*'s confidence. He just had to figure out a way to do it.

"Gotta make a stop at Matthew Herschberger's," Melvin said, breaking into Seth's musings.

Seth lifted his brow at the sound of Miriam's last name. He wondered if she and Matthew were related. There were several Herschberger families in Lancaster, but it was a possibility.

Twenty minutes later they turned onto a dirt drive, which led to a huge spread about half a mile from the main road. As they neared the large, pristine white house, Seth saw a white rectangular sign that read "Herschberger Lumber." When they pulled onto the asphalted driveway, he could hear the whirring of a gas-powered bandsaw.

"You don't have to get out," Melvin said, yanking on the horse's reins.

"I'd like to." Seth grabbed his walking stick.

Matthew must have seen them approaching, because he met them at their buggy. After exchanging greetings, Melvin got to the point.

"I'll need that delivery tomorrow instead of Friday. Just got a big order from Philadelphia for some fancy bookshelves."

Matthew tilted his hat back and scratched his head. He didn't look much older than Seth, but Seth didn't recognize him.

"I promised to pick up *mei* cousin Miriam tomorrow and take her to work in the morning." Matthew paused for a moment. "I think she has to be there at eight. She works in Paradise. Once I drop her off and come back, I can probably deliver the wood. I can get it to your house by ten."

"No earlier?" Melvin stroked his salt-and-pepper beard.

"*Nee. Daed* and *mei bruders* are leaving first thing in the morning for Lancaster. They have a big delivery to make. We hadn't planned on getting you your wood until Friday."

"Guess that'll have to do. *Danki*, Matthew. I'll see you tomorrow."

On their way home, Seth stared out the window. The winter sky cast a pall over the barren landscape. The fields, normally lush with grass and towering cornstalks in the spring and summer, were now empty and brown.

So Matthew was related to Miriam. An idea suddenly occurred to Seth. Maybe there was a way to get in his dad's good graces.

"*Daed?*"

Melvin nodded.

"I'm ready to start driving again."

His father didn't answer for a long time. Seth could tell he was stewing it over. Big decision or small, it didn't matter. Melvin Fisher always thought everything through. Finally he spoke. "We talking car or buggy?"

"Buggy. I'm done with cars, *Daed*. Done with all those worldly things."

Melvin paused and gave him a hard look.

"I'd like to prove it to you," Seth said. "I know I've let you down in the past, but I promise, not this time."

Gravy's hooves clip-clopped against the asphalt road as cars whooshed by them.

"How's the leg?" Melvin asked.

"Feeling better." While it still ached constantly, at least he wasn't in massive pain anymore.

Tugging on his beard, Melvin said, "Church is at the Yoders' this Sunday. You can drive there."

Sunday? He didn't want to wait that long. "I was kinda thinking I could drive tomorrow."

His *daed* looked at him. "You got somewhere you gotta be?"

"I thought I might help you out. I could pick up Miriam so Matthew could deliver the wood to you before ten."

"Sure this ain't more about seeing that girl than about helping me?"

Seth frowned. He should have known better than to offer to help. "Never mind."

"Wait." Melvin paused. "Is Miriam the *maedel* at the fabric store?"

"How did you know?"

"I was across the street. Saw you go to the bakery. Then you went back to her shop. Put two and two together." He switched the reins from his right hand to his left. "Been in the shop with your *mudder* before. Seen the *maedel* who works there. She got glasses?"

"*Ya.*"

Glancing at Seth, he said, "She's nice."

"*Ya.* She is. We went to school together, and I hadn't seen her in a long time. I'd kind of like to renew our . . . friendship."

"So that's what you're calling it."

"I'm not calling it anything right now." He leaned back against the seat and tilted down his hat slightly. He doubted he could make his father understand, and based on his past behavior, his *daed* had every right to be suspicious of his motives. But he was willing to try. "There's something about her, *Daed*. She's not like the other girls."

"Not like the *Englisch maed*?"

"She's not like *any* other girl."

Their modest house appeared in view, and Seth spied the line of plain Amish dresses, blue shirts, and gray trousers stretched across the front porch, drying. They would take longer to dry in the cold temperature, but the slight breeze in the air that lifted up the clothing would help.

After Seth's confession, his father remained silent for a long time. So long, that Seth began to regret revealing so much. By the time they turned into the driveway, he wondered if Melvin would acknowledge his words at all.

Melvin pulled on Gravy's reins and stopped the buggy. Seth turned to climb out, but his father stopped him, laying his big, beefy hand on his son's arm.

"Pick her up in the morning." He dropped his hand, opened the door, and got out.

Seth sighed with relief and said a small prayer of thanks. He knew that was the closest to approval he would get from his *daed*, at least right now. He gladly took it.

∼◦∽

The next morning a knock sounded on the front door, surprising Miriam. She glanced at the clock on the fireplace mantel. Seven o'clock. Who would be calling at this time in the morning?

"Miriam? Can you get that?" her mother called from the kitchen. "Breakfast is almost ready."

"All right." Miriam shoved a bobby pin in her *kapp*, her bare feet padding against the hardwood floor. When she opened the door, she let out a gasp, and not just from the gust of cold air that greeted her.

KATHLEEN FULLER

"I'm sorry," Seth said, looking contrite. "I didn't mean to startle you."

She opened her mouth to say something, but couldn't. Once again he had rendered her speechless. Then again, who could blame her? As usual, he looked gorgeous with his black felt hat tipped back from his forehead, giving her full view of his stunning eyes. His black coat fit his broad shoulders perfectly. She knew that with an *Englisch* haircut and clothes, he could pass for a model, like those she saw in some of those magazines at the library.

He glanced down at her bare legs and feet. "Sorry. Guess I came too early." He winked.

Something inside her crumbled. Just a bit, but that's all it would take, a small fissure in her defenses, and he would be back in her heart. She couldn't let that happen. She *wouldn't* let it happen.

"Who's at the door?" Mary Herschberger appeared behind her. "Hello. Can we help you?"

Seth extended his hand to Mary. "Seth Fisher," he said, giving her a brilliant smile. "Melvin Fisher's *sohn*."

Recognition dawned on Mary's face as she shook his hand. "*Ya*, I remember now. Nice to see you. How are your parents?"

"Doing well, *danki* for asking."

"Well, don't just stand there." She looked at Miriam. "Why didn't you invite him in?"

Miriam stepped back, allowing Seth room to walk inside. The worn end of his walking stick made a thumping sound against the floor as he entered the living room.

"I just finished cooking breakfast," Mary said. "Eggs and sausage. Would you like some?"

"*Mamm*, maybe we should find out why he's here first." Miriam glanced at her mother and nearly groaned. Even her *mamm* wasn't immune to Seth's charms.

"Oh, *ya*. Of course." Mary smiled. "What brings you by, Seth?"

"I came to give Miriam a ride to work, if that's all right with you."

Miriam sucked in a breath. "My cousin is picking me up."

He shook his head. "Matthew had to make a delivery for my *daed* this morning. So I thought I'd help them both out by offering you a ride to work."

"What a nice thing to do." Mary grinned. "We appreciate the offer, don't we, Miriam?"

"*Ya*," Miriam said slowly with little enthusiasm.

"Seth, why don't you come in the kitchen and have a bite to eat while Miriam finishes getting ready." Mary's gaze landed on Miriam's bare legs, her brow raised in disapproval.

"*Danki*," Seth said. "It smells *gut*."

As Mary led Seth to the kitchen in the back of the house, Miriam ran upstairs to her bedroom to get her socks and shoes on. As she slid her feet into the black woolen socks, she tried to stem the panic rising within her at the thought of Seth driving her to work. The trip would take at least thirty minutes. Alone with him. In close quarters.

She didn't think her heart could take it.

But she also knew she couldn't refuse him. Her *daed* had already left to help a friend across town repair the fence around his pasture, and he had driven their one and only buggy. Now, with Matthew otherwise occupied, she had no choice but to accept Seth's offer. But only this time. She would make that clear to him as soon as possible.

Slipping her feet into her black shoes, she quickly laced them and dashed downstairs. As she walked into the kitchen, she saw Seth at the table, already diving into a plate piled high with fluffy yellow eggs and perfectly browned sausage patties. Her stomach coiled into a knot. She didn't think she could eat a single bite.

Mary set another plate on the table, in front of the chair next to Seth. "Here, Miriam. Have a seat."

"*Danki*. You go ahead, *Mamm*," she said, fighting to keep a normal tone to her voice. So what if Seth Fisher was sitting in her kitchen, eating breakfast with gusto? That was no reason to have an attack of nerves. She glanced at her hands, which shook slightly. Unfortunately her body refused to be reasoned with.

"I already ate. I need to get started on the laundry. It always takes so long to dry in the winter." Mary glanced at Seth. "*Danki* again, for taking Miriam."

"You're welcome."

When Mary left, Miriam stood for a moment, watching Seth as he scooped a forkful of eggs. As if he sensed her gaze on him, he looked up. "Aren't you going to eat?"

"I'm not hungry."

Seth held up the bite of eggs. "I don't know how you can resist this." He paused for a moment. "At least sit down. I feel *seltsam* eating your *mamm*'s cooking while you're just standing there."

Pressing her lips together, Miriam slowly lowered herself into the seat next to Seth. "You don't have to do this."

"Eat breakfast?" Seth grinned. "I think I do. I'm starving, and your *mamm* is a great cook."

"I mean take me to work."

"I have to do that too. Matthew is probably already loading his wagon to take the wood over to *daed*'s. Unless you have someone else to take you?"

"*Nee.*"

He flashed her one of his trademark smiles, the kind that could melt ice in winter. "Then it's settled." Pushing his empty plate a few inches away from him, he added, "Are you ready to go?"

"*Ya.*" Apparently only capable of one-syllable answers, she stood from the table and crossed the kitchen to get her coat, which was hanging on a hook near the back door. Moments later they were outside and walking toward the buggy.

Seth took a few quick but awkward steps as he passed her and went to the passenger side. His movement confused her until she realized he wanted to open the door for her.

"You didn't have to do that." She meant it, and not because he'd done it for her, but because he had to limp the extra steps. Now she could add guilt to the mixing pot of emotions simmering inside her.

"I know." He untethered the horse, then climbed in the driver's side of the buggy. Soon they were off.

She crossed her arms over her chest and kept her gaze directed straight ahead. Miriam felt more awkward than she had the other night when he and Caleb had brought her home from the Lapps'. He didn't even try to draw her into conversation, and she thought his father must have desperately needed Seth's help for him to agree to take her to work. Finally the excruciating ride was over as he pulled into a parking lot behind the store.

"*Danki*," she said, throwing open the door, eager to get out. She had one foot on the ground when she heard him say her name.

"What time do you get off work?"

Her eyes widened. "Why?"

"So I can take you home."

She searched his face, but didn't see a trace of humor in his expression. "You don't have to do that. Matthew usually picks me up. "

"Not anymore."

She gaped. "Why?"

"Because I told him you already had a ride home. With me."

He was flashing that grin again, obviously trying to pour on the charm. And it was working. Her heart kept jolting out of rhythm. But despite her body's traitorous response, she had to keep her distance. Physical distance would be a start. She stepped completely out of the buggy and held the door partway between them.

"Miriam, did you hear me?"

"I heard you." She was just trying to process the words. "Won't Matthew be finished with his delivery to your *daed* by then?"

"*Ya.*"

"Then why would you tell Matthew you're taking me home?"

He leaned toward her, lowering his voice. "Because I want to."

This wasn't going to work at all. How was she supposed to remain unaffected if everything about him dazzled her? The husky way he answered her question made her mouth go dry. She knew the way he said those words was calculated, but for one tiny moment she didn't care.

Then she snapped to her senses. "That was presumptuous of you."

His facade faded a bit, as if her statement caught him off guard. Then instantly he was back in full form, grinning, gazing at her with those heavenly eyes in a way that threatened to buckle her knees. "Maybe it was," he said. "But it doesn't matter, because I still want to take you home. Just tell me what time you're done, and I'll be here."

She weighed her options. Should she tell him no and risk the chance of not having a ride home at all? Tammy would be glad to take her home, but Miriam didn't want to count on it. Or should she just take him up on his offer so he would leave her alone?

With a sigh she said, "I get off at five."

"Then I'll be here at five." Leaning back, he gripped the reins and gave her another mesmerizing smile.

Over the past five years he had obviously honed his skills. She had a feeling that whatever Seth wanted, especially from a woman, Seth got. Every time.

Her hands went cold. Suddenly she wished she hadn't said yes.

Chapter Seven

TRUE TO HIS WORD, SETH SHOWED UP AT FIVE O'CLOCK. Technically 4:55 . . . not that she was watching the clock.

"I'll see you tomorrow," Tammy said, walking Miriam to the door. Then she saw Seth standing outside, far enough to the right of the entrance so as not to block customers who might want to dash in at the last minute.

Miriam briefly wondered why he chose not to come inside.

"Hold on there." Tammy grabbed Miriam's arm. "Is that who I think it is? The cutie?"

"His name is Seth."

"Oh. Nice name." She smiled wryly at Miriam. "Seems like there are a lot of nice things about him. Is he here to pick you up?"

"*Ya.*" Unfortunately.

"Then I'd say you were a lucky girl. So go on." Tammy opened the door and practically shoved Miriam outside. "Hi, Seth," she said in greeting.

"Hello." He turned to her and extended his hand. "And your name is?"

"Tammy. Just call me Tammy." She winked at Miriam in such a blatant way that Seth couldn't have possibly missed it, and told them good-bye.

Miriam groaned. Why had she agreed to this?

They walked to the end of the block, where Seth had tethered the horse and parked the buggy. *Awkward* didn't even begin to describe how she felt as the silence grew between them. He hobbled over to the passenger side of the buggy and opened it for her.

She didn't know if she was up for another silent drive, but she would have to endure it. At the very least she could close her eyes and feign sleep.

They drove along in silence for a few moments, and Miriam stared straight ahead, listening to the horse's hooves click on the asphalt road. Darkness had descended, and she watched as the taillights of the cars whizzing past them disappeared into the distance. The clear winter curtain protected them against most of the cold, but she couldn't help crossing her arms over her chest anyway. She was just about to close her eyes when Seth spoke.

"So, Miriam. Tell me about your day."

His interest surprised her. Everything about him pretty much shocked her lately.

"Fine," she said, not eager to go into details, especially when she doubted his interest was sincere. It was more like a desperate attempt to break the deepening silence.

"C'mon, now. I'm sure there's more to it than that. Were you busy? Are sales good?" He took his eyes off the road for just a moment and gave her a sly look. "Did anyone buy any more green and red fabric?"

She turned away from him. He was funning her, and she didn't appreciate it one bit. But she wasn't without recourse. If he wanted to know how her day went, she would tell him. In minute detail. She'd bore him to death the rest of the ride home, and then she'd be done with him for good. And that was all she wanted.

Wasn't it?

"Well, first Tammy came in the door. She was supposed to be there at 8:30, but she was late and came in at 8:31. She had on a red sweater and blue jeans—"

"*Ya,*" he said, his brows furrowing a bit. "I saw her, remember?"

"Oh, that's right. Anyway, she had brought some new fabric catalog of summer fabrics, and we looked at those. On page 1 were the pastels, on page 17 the jewel tones . . ."

She continued talking until her mouth started to ache. She hadn't said so many words in a very long time, if ever. And she could see her banal conversation was having an effect. First he stopped grinning at her. Then he wouldn't even look at her. She took great pleasure in seeing him trying to stifle a yawn not once, but twice. By the time they turned in her driveway, she was confident Seth Fisher wouldn't be taking her anywhere again.

He pulled his buggy to a stop in front of her house. "What time do you have to be at work in the morning?"

"What?" It was the only word that would come out of her mouth. She'd used all the other ones up.

"I asked you what time you needed to be at work." He was looking at her, and despite the dimness of the interior of the buggy, she could see the expectation on his face. Instead of his charm-filled grin, his lips twitched in a half smile, making his mouth lopsided.

And adorable.

She pushed up her glasses. "Let me guess. You want to take me to work tomorrow."

"You got it."

Without warning, her bravado disappeared, and she suddenly couldn't fight him—and her feelings—anymore. Every emotion she'd been suppressing since that night at the Lapps' simmered inside her. All the anxiety, resentment, and confusion came to a boil, and she fought the tears that came to her eyes. "Why are you doing this to me?"

༄෴

Having Miriam get teary eyed wasn't the reaction he was expecting. Or looking for. Alarm dashed through him. "Miriam?"

"Wasn't it enough for you?" Her voice was thick, like something was clogging her throat.

"What?" he asked, bewildered.

"Didn't you have your fun at my expense years ago? Or do you have some unfinished business?"

"Miriam, I don't know what you're talking about."

"I'm talking about me, Seth. Plain, ugly Miriam. I have feelings, you know."

He moved a little closer to her, his chest aching from the pain he saw in her eyes. "*Ya*, I—"

"Don't *do* that!"

"Do *what*?" His voice raised in volume to match hers.

"Don't get close to me." She leaned back against the door of the buggy.

He froze for a moment, then understood what she meant. Gentling his voice, he said, "Miriam, I just want to get to know you, that's all."

"Why? Why would anyone, especially someone like you, want to have anything to do with me?"

"Someone like me?" he scoffed. "The question should be this—why would you want to be around me?"

"I-I don't."

All of his charm, energy, and confidence dwindled away. He stared straight ahead. "I don't blame you."

"What did you say?"

Realizing he'd been whispering, he raised his voice slightly. "I said I don't blame you. I haven't been a good person to be around for a long time. I'm trying to change that . . . but maybe it's not working."

He waited for her to open up the buggy door and rush out, as if she had flames licking at her heels. He waited . . . and waited.

But she didn't move. Instead, she sat there and stared at her hands for a long time. Finally she took a deep breath and said, "Eight o'clock."

"What?"

"I have to be at work at eight, but I'm off tomorrow. Pick me up at seven thirty on Thursday . . . if you still want to." With that she exited the buggy and ran inside, her cloak billowing around her thin body.

Seth remained still. Her words confused him. He had been sure she was going to refuse him, but then at the last minute she changed her mind. But why?

Even more important, why did he offer? He had only intended to take her to work and pick her up today, but then he found himself offering to pick her up again. But he knew the answer to that question. When he'd told Miriam he wanted to get to know her better, he meant it. He'd spent the entire afternoon thinking about her. She had been so quiet on the ride to work, deepening that mysterious quality he found so fascinating. Most girls he'd known gabbed nonstop or tried to impress him. Instead, he found himself wanting to impress her. However, that seemed to be the last thing she was interested in.

He turned Gravy around, then headed for the road. During the ride home he tried to sort things out, but it was useless. All he knew for sure was that she didn't hate him so much that she wouldn't let him take her to work. At this point, that was all that mattered.

‹⁄›

Lately, it seemed, Miriam collected regrets. She added one more to her growing cache by wishing she'd just told Seth to leave her alone Tuesday night when he dropped her off from work. If she had, she wouldn't be standing on her front porch this morning, waiting for him to pick her up.

Maybe he wouldn't show. The thought filled her with relief. And, of course, disappointment. She wondered how long she could handle her contradictory emotions.

She looked out into the near-barren fields surrounding her house. Across the road she could see her neighbor's herd of beef cattle nibbling at the short, frosty grass in the shadow of the huge white barn.

The days were shorter now, and dawn had just broken a little while ago, swathing the heavens in transparent washes of pale yellow and dark gold. There were only a few clouds in the sky, and she predicted it would be a sunny day, but cold. Folding her arms across her chest underneath her cloak and seeing her breath take the form of wispy puffs in the air, she wished she could feel some of the sun's warmth now.

Miriam checked the small clock fob pinned to the inside of her coat. Seven fifteen. She'd left the house early to escape her mother's probing questions about Seth picking her up. Explaining the situation would be pointless, since she didn't understand what was going on herself. She wondered if Seth even knew.

What did he mean about wanting to get to know her? She'd pondered that the last two nights, but didn't come up with any answers. She still couldn't get past the thought that his attentions were one big joke. Or maybe he was involved in some kind of community service program as part of his reparations for the accident, where he had to be nice to a lonely girl for a couple of days.

She rolled her eyes. Even her thoughts didn't make sense.

The *clip-clop* of the horse's hooves alerted her to Seth's approach. Just like Tuesday, he was a little early. She walked to the end of her driveway so he wouldn't have to pull in. When she saw he was going to scramble out to open the door for her, she held up her hand and opened it herself.

"Got it," she said. Warmth enveloped her as she sat down.

"Cold morning." He blew on his hands and rubbed them together. "Should have worn my gloves." Picking up the reins, he glanced at her. "Ready to go?"

"*Ya.*" She was still focused on his hands. They were huge. Strong looking, but not weathered like most Amishmen's hands were.

She pulled away her gaze. What was she doing, staring at his hands? They were just hands, for goodness' sake. And she had no business wondering what they would feel like, clasping her own.

"Did you sleep well last night?" Seth tapped the reins on the horse's flanks, and the buggy lurched forward.

As with every question he asked, she wondered why he cared. "Well enough." Then, before she could stop herself, she asked, "You?"

"Pretty good."

Silence engulfed the buggy once again. Not the comfortable kind. The self-conscious kind, where she wished she could just disappear and escape the awkwardness of it all.

Seth lifted the brim of his hat with two of those long fingers of his, pushing it a little farther back on his head. "Nice bag you have there."

"My quilt bag?"

"*Ya. Mei mudder* and sisters make quilts." He grinned. "But I decided it wasn't for me."

A chuckle escaped her lips before she could prevent it. "I can't picture you holding a needle and thread."

"You'd be surprised what I learned at my *mudder*'s knee."

"Then you know how to sew?"

He shook his head. "Hardly. But when I was a kid, she let me help her in the kitchen sometimes. I learned to cook a few meals. Nothing complicated."

"Like what?" Despite her vow to be uninterested, she found herself intrigued.

"Meat loaf, lasagna, tuna salad, and of course, whoopee pies."

"Whoopee pies aren't that easy to make."

"Sure they are. They're just a little time-consuming. I haven't made any in a long time, not since I was a little kid." He looked at her. "Do you like them?"

"They're okay."

"But not as *gut* as raspberry fudge?"

"Nothing is as *gut* as raspberry fudge."

They both laughed, and Seth gave her a grin. But it was a different smile this time, more genuine, not so calculated and forced. She put her hand on her stomach to calm the swirl of butterflies.

Resist!

"So what kind of quilts do you make?" he asked, nudging the horse to turn right onto the main street.

"Just your average quilt. Nothing special."

"I think Sarah would disagree. She was pretty complimentary about your work."

"It's nothing compared to my grandmother's. She made the most beautiful quilts. Every stitch was perfect, and her eye for color was amazing." Her gaze dropped back to her hands. "Sorry. I'm sure hearing about quilts is *really* exciting."

He shrugged. "Maybe not exciting, but interesting. I never understood how a woman could sit in a chair for hours making tiny stitches on small squares of fabric. That would drive me crazy."

"I could say the same for what your father does. It must take a lot of patience to cut and carve all those intricate designs he makes."

"It does. But he loves to do it."

"Just like I love quilting."

He smiled again. "Exactly."

By the time they reached the fabric shop, all the tension that had been building in Miriam was nearly gone. Their conversation hadn't been of much import, but it had been nice. Friendly. Comfortable. She'd never thought she could be comfortable around Seth Fisher.

He pulled the buggy into the small parking lot at the end of the block.

She turned and looked at him. "*Danki*. For the ride. I appreciate it."

"You're welcome. So I'll see you at five, then."

"What?"

His brows furrowed. "Do you get off at a different time on Thursdays?"

"*Nee*, but . . . Seth, you don't have to do this. There are lots of people who can give me a ride."

"I'm sure there are."

"And I'm also sure you have other things more important to do than pick me up and take me home."

He turned in his seat and looked at her straight on. "Now, that's where you're wrong, Miriam."

Her guard shot up again, but not as quickly this time. Warmth enveloped her as he held her gaze.

"You'll be late for work," he said softly. "We'll finish the conversation when I pick you up."

"But—"

He held up his hand. "No buts. See you at five." He reached for the reins and dipped his head toward the buggy door.

She complied, because he was right—she would be late if

she dallied any longer. Giving him one last look and seeing the resolute expression on his face, she knew he would be there at five to take her home.

But this would be the last time.

⤲

Seth pulled out of the parking lot, fairly pleased with himself.

Carrying Miriam to work this morning had been pleasant. Far more pleasant than the trip on Tuesday, when she'd done everything in her power to be as bland and uninteresting as possible, but he'd seen right through her. She wasn't the type of girl to run at the mouth over nothing. This morning proved that.

It had taken him a while, but he had finally realized his mistake. He'd overdone it. He'd been too charming, too earnest. He could only imagine how he'd appeared to her. While that tactic had worked with girls in the past, he should have known it wouldn't with her. He didn't have to be an extra-strength version of himself to pique her interest. With other girls he'd always felt the need to be "on." To be the center of their universe, at least until he was tired of them. But maybe it hadn't been the girls he'd been weary of. Maybe he'd just been sick of the false version of himself.

With Miriam, he didn't have to worry about that. She responded to the real Seth. From now on he intended to be as real with her as he possibly could.

Chapter Eight

"Is everything all *RECHT*, Miriam?"

Miriam looked at her mother. "*Ya*. Why do you ask?"

"Because you just sewed the tie of your *kapp* to the quilt."

Glancing down, she saw her mother was right. She hadn't even noticed that the ribbons of her *kapp* had been dangling on the quilt laid out on the kitchen table in front of her. Carefully she removed the needle and pulled out the three tiny stitches, then took the flat, white ribbons and tucked them into the front of her dress.

"You seem preoccupied tonight." Mary continued with her own stitching.

They were repairing one of *Grossmammi* Emma's quilts, a navy blue and cream–colored Amish star design. It was one of the first quilts her grandmother had made as a young girl, and after almost ninety years some of the stitches had loosened.

Miriam rethreaded her needle with navy blue thread. "*Nee.* Well, maybe just a little."

"Anything you'd like to talk about?"

She looked at her mother, who had her head bowed as she formed small, perfectly even stitches. Perfectly parted gray hair peeked out from her *kapp,* and she paused to adjust her eyeglasses before she resumed her stitching. There was a considerable age gap between her parents and Miriam, their youngest child— over forty years. Still, while she had a close relationship with both of them, she had never confided in her mother about Seth. She wasn't sure she ever wanted to.

The back door to the kitchen opened, and Lydia stepped inside, saving Miriam from having to answer *Mamm*'s question.

"Hello," her sister said, holding a large wicker basket by its handle. She set it down on the kitchen counter. "Here are the soaps you asked for."

Mary put down her needle and rose from her seat. "*Danki*," she said, peering into the basket and examining the contents. "These will make lovely Christmas presents for the family."

Lydia gave her a satisfied smile, then glanced down at the quilt. "Making repairs?"

"*Ya*," Miriam replied. "We're starting with this one, since it's the oldest. I'd like to reinforce as much stitching as I can on all her quilts."

"They certainly are beautiful," Lydia said, nodding. "You really are taking *gut* care of them, Miriam."

"Can you stay for some coffee?" Mary asked. "I've got a few cookies and half a pumpkin pie left over from Sunday's potluck."

Lydia shook her head. "*Nee*. I'm sorry, *Mamm*, but I can't. I just came by to drop these off. I know you want to get them wrapped to take on First Christmas." She looked at Miriam. "I have to go into Paradise tomorrow morning. I can give you a ride to work, if you need one."

Miriam hesitated. Seth had offered to pick her up again in the morning, and again her resolve melted and she'd said yes. They'd had another pleasant ride home, and she found she really enjoyed his company. Yet she knew this had to end. Soon

Seth would find something—or someone—else to pay attention to, and he'd forget about her. But a tiny part of her desperately wanted to enjoy his interest as long as it lasted.

"*Danki* for offering, but Seth's picking me up in the morning."

"Seth?" Lydia's brow lifted with interest.

"A friend," she responded, wishing she hadn't said his name.

"He's been nice enough to pick her up and take her to work the past couple of days," Mary added. "He's also been bringing her home. It's been a big help."

Lydia gave Miriam a pointed look, but Miriam purposely blanked her expression. She didn't need her sister's well-intentioned interference.

Lydia just shot her a knowing smile, then gave their mother a hug and turned to leave. "I probably won't see you until we go to Sarah and David's. Tell Pop I said hello."

"I will. He's at a church meeting, but when he gets home I'll tell him."

After Lydia left, Miriam tried to focus on the quilt again. All night she'd been chasing away thoughts of Seth—romantic thoughts, to her dismay—with little success. Actually saying his name aloud made his image in her mind more real and harder to dispel.

Mary sat down at the table, but she didn't pick up her needle. "Is Seth the reason you're so pensive tonight?"

Miriam looked up, ready to deny it, but unable to do so. She nodded.

"Do you like him, Miriam?"

"He's a . . . friend."

"Are you sure that's all?"

Miriam glanced up. "Of course. Why would there be anything else?"

Mary smiled. "He's going to a lot of trouble to carry you to and from work."

"I know. I told him not to, but he keeps insisting."

"Seems to me like he wants to be more than friends."

Miriam shook her head. "That's impossible."

"Why?"

Miriam suddenly felt transported back to eighth grade. She closed her eyes, wishing away the past. "Because it just is."

"Oh, honey." Mary placed her hand over Miriam's. "I don't know why you find it so hard to believe Seth is interested in you."

"You don't understand."

"Then help me to."

Miriam hesitated. She'd never told anyone what happened on the playground long ago. But her mother's genuine concern tugged at her, untying her pain until she couldn't hold it in any longer.

Saying it out loud made her feel slightly foolish, but also a bit relieved. When she finished, she looked down at the table as she smoothed a wrinkle in her *grossmammi*'s beautiful quilt.

"Miriam," her mother said softly. "I'm so sorry. You're right, Seth was cruel. But he was fourteen. Everyone knows fourteen-year-old boys do stupid things."

"Except for fourteen-year-old girls."

"True, but they eventually figure it out. And the best thing is that no one stays fourteen forever. We make mistakes. We grow up; we learn from those mistakes; we mature." She dipped her head to look at Miriam. "Do you really think Seth is still that thoughtless teenager?"

"*Nee* . . . well, maybe?"

Mary laughed. "As long as you're sure."

Miriam couldn't help but smile.

"Seth's not the same boy he was back then. A lot has happened to him, especially the accident. Trauma has a way of changing people. Some for worse, and some for better."

Miriam thought about that for a moment. Seth had told her he was different, and she'd seen glimpses of that. But had he really changed? Even if he had, that didn't explain his sudden interest in her.

Mary looked at Miriam for a moment, her blue eyes softening. "I'm thinking your problem with Seth has more to do with you than it does with him."

Miriam frowned. "What do you mean?"

"You're letting a comment made by a young boy several years ago dictate your behavior today. You've kept most people, especially young men, at arm's length."

"Can you blame me? What he said is true." Miriam sighed. "I am a four-eyed beanpole. Still."

Mary lifted Miriam's chin. "Let me tell you what I see. I see a young woman who is intelligent and good with people. I see a fantastic quilter who has skills and artistry I could only dream of. I see someone who cares for her family and who takes her job seriously. I see someone with a big heart she's just waiting to share with someone."

Tears came to Miriam's eyes. She should deflect her mother's compliments, reflect the humility she knew was expected of her. But at that moment, she really needed to hear those words.

"Those are the qualities you need to focus on, Miriam. Not what's on the surface. Look at Seth. He has the body of a young man, but he can't walk without his stick. He has a beautiful face, but it's forever scarred. Yet he carries himself with confidence. He's not letting his physical imperfections keep him from being himself, or from getting what he wants. And though you deny it, you might have to accept that it's you he's wanting."

Wiping her eyes with her fingers, Miriam said, "But I don't understand why. He could have his pick of any girl. Any *pretty* girl. Why would he choose me?"

A small smile formed on Mary's face. "Because he sees what I see. He sees you for the wonderful woman you are. If you ask me, I think he's a smart *mann*."

Miriam chuckled through her tears. "*Danki*. I really needed to hear that."

Taking her daughter's hand, Mary said, "Maybe I've been neglectful in telling you."

"*Nee*, I've just been prideful."

"Listen to me, Miriam. We're all prideful; it's something we fight every day. It's a battle we can't win without God's help. Remember—God doesn't care what you look like on the outside. What he cares about is your heart. And you have a beautiful heart, *dochder*." Tears glistened in her eyes. "Don't ever forget that."

Miriam smiled and wiped a tear from underneath her glasses. Both women resumed working on the quilt. While Miriam concentrated more carefully on repairing the stitches, her mother's words remained in her mind. Was it possible? Had the boy who thought she was a four-eyed beanpole grown into a man who truly liked her? Her mind couldn't grasp the concept.

But her heart was willing to try.

❧

Something was different about her.

Seth couldn't put his finger on it, but Miriam seemed more lighthearted the next morning when he picked her up. When he opened the buggy door, she *almost* smiled at him. He wanted to ask her what was making her happy, but they hadn't gotten to that point in their relationship yet, where he felt he could pry.

Relationship. When had he started thinking about Miriam in terms of a relationship? He couldn't pinpoint the exact moment, but he took her agreement to let him take her to work as a sign that he was making some headway. Right now he would be happy to move past acquaintance to friendship.

And maybe something more.

She didn't say anything until they were well on their way to Paradise. They had just passed a large field of grazing black-and-white dairy cows when she said, "Tell me about your accident."

Seth's hands tightened on the reins. It was an inevitable question; he just hadn't expected her to ask it so soon. Or so bluntly.

"Not much to tell. I got drunk, got in my car, and hit a tree."

"Why?"

He turned and looked at her. "What do you mean, why?"

"Why would you do something like that?"

"I didn't do it on purpose," he said, flustered.

"Somebody forced you to drink and then made you drive?"

"*Nee!*" He pulled on Gravy's reins, slowing the horse down. The road was clear of cars, so he took the opportunity to face Miriam.

She glanced down at her hands, her glasses slipping down her nose a bit. "I didn't mean to make you mad. You said yesterday that you were different. I just wanted to know how that happened."

He blinked. She'd never expressed an interest in knowing anything about him before. But why did she have to ask about that? Because he knew that he couldn't sidestep the truth. Not with her.

Seth swiveled around and faced the road, but he kept Gravy moving at a slow pace. Let the *Englisch* drivers honk their horns. He didn't care. They hogged the road anyway.

"After I finished school, I went to work with my *daed*. That didn't last very long. We fought all the time, mostly about stupid stuff. I see now that I wasn't doing my share, but at the time I thought he was being too critical, too harsh. At the same time I'd made a few *Englisch* friends from the local high school. They invited me to their parties, and I brought them to some of ours." He glanced at her. "I'm not talking about the frolics and singings. I'm talking about the drinking parties."

"I know. I never went to those parties, but I knew a few girls that did."

"I'm glad you didn't go. Because if you had been there, you would have likely seen me. And it would be hard to look you in the eye right now if you had. I'm not proud of the way I was back then. But at the time I thought I was living the life. Finally my *daed* got fed up with me and fired me, with *gut* reason. That's when I left for Lancaster, got a job in a factory, and bought the car. I honestly thought they had given up on me, especially my *daed*. So if they didn't care, I didn't. One thing I knew for sure, I couldn't stay in Paradise. I couldn't join the church and be Amish."

"But you did," Miriam said. "You came back."

"It's only by the grace of God that I'm here. And I found out after my accident that my parents had prayed for me every day while I was gone. They hadn't given up on me. They had given me to the Lord."

A chill ran down Miriam's back as she thought about how difficult that must have been for Seth's parents.

"I really screwed up, Miriam. I didn't even have a driver's license at the time. I bought the car used off a friend of one of my *Englisch* buddies. I paid cash and drove it illegally. I got my hair cut; I wore *Englisch* clothes. I tried to strip away everything about me that was Amish."

The loud blast of a horn blared in their ears, making Miriam jump. The car whizzed by, but Seth didn't look at the driver. "Sorry," he said to her. "I'll go faster."

She shook her head. "We're fine."

"Okay." It pleased him that she wanted to lengthen their time together. But he hadn't told her all the details. What would she think of him then?

Chapter Nine

MIRIAM FOUND HERSELF DRAWN IN TO SETH'S EXPLANATION. SHE had never felt the pull of the world, and she didn't have a *rumschpringe* the way some kids did. She joined the church when she was eighteen and had never had any doubts about her faith. Listening to Seth's story only reaffirmed that she had made the right decision. The outside world held nothing but trouble.

"As I said before, my parents were praying for me," he continued. "And not only them. My brothers and sisters, they were all praying. And God must have heard them, because the night of the accident, I was so down on myself I didn't know what to do. I was tired of the partying, tired of my so-called friends who were only interested in what they could score—booze, women, drugs."

As he spoke, he mixed in more English with his Pennsylvania *Deitsch*, as if he were being transported back to relive his time with the outlanders. "I felt like I was divided in two—the wild part of me that longed for worldly things, and the Amish part that longed for my family. I missed them so much, more than I ever thought I would. I wanted to come back, but I didn't want to admit that they were right and I was wrong.

"That night I was staying at some guy's apartment—I didn't even really know who he was, but I needed a place to crash—and I drank more than I ever had before. I knew I couldn't stay, not just in that apartment, but in that world. I didn't belong there. But I couldn't go home either. I didn't know where I belonged, and that scared me more than anything."

They had reached Lincoln Avenue, and Seth steered Gravy to the left, toward the fabric shop. People, both *Englischers* and Amish, were already walking up and down the sidewalks, looking into the candle, quilt, and handicraft stores, waiting for them to open. The contrast between the two peoples was striking—the *Englischers* with coats and jackets of bright colors and modern styles alongside the Amish in their dark cloaks, coats, bonnets, and hats.

When Seth completed the turn, he continued talking. "One thing I did know is that I couldn't stand to be in that apartment another minute. So I got my keys, somehow made it to my car, and got in. I hadn't gone very far when I swerved off the road and hit the tree. I don't remember much after that, until I woke up in the hospital after I'd had surgery on my leg."

He paused, casting a glance at Miriam. She stared at his profile, the scar on his face so prominent when they were this close to each other. She could only imagine the pain he'd gone through, not only physical, but inside too.

"They had given me a lot of painkillers, so everything was pretty fuzzy for a couple of days. But once the haze had cleared and I could think straight, I realized what a gift God had given me. The gift of life, along with a second chance. I wasn't about to disappoint him."

"But what about your *Englisch* friends? Didn't they want you to come back with them?"

"That's just the thing, Miriam. There was no bond between us, other than hanging out and having fun. I think the accident probably scared a few of them, too, because it could have easily been one of them that smashed into a tree. Whatever the reason, they didn't visit. But you know who was there? My family. My *mudder* came every day and stayed as long as she could. You know how far away the hospital is. She had to hire a taxi to take her there. My *daed* would come when he could, as well as my brothers and sisters. They never gave up on me. Not when I strayed, and not when I got hurt because of my own dumb choices. That's when it became clear. I belonged with my family. I belonged in the church. I was Amish, and for the first time in my life, I was glad to be."

Miriam sat there for a moment, taking in everything he'd said. Then she spoke. "I don't understand."

His head whipped toward her, surprise etched on his features. "You don't? What part confuses you?"

"I understood what you said. What happened to you. I guess what confuses me is why you felt so divided. I've never experienced that myself. I always knew where I belonged."

"I can sum it up in one word. *Hochmut.*"

"Pride?"

He nodded. "I was overflowing with it. I don't know how people stood me back then. From the time I was small I'd been able to manipulate a situation to get what I wanted. I thought I was too *gut* for the Amish. I wanted to be cool, like the *Englisch* I hung around with. With them I had no rules. I could wear anything, say anything, do anything.

"I had a lot of time to think in the hospital, and then when I came home to finish my recovery. I also had a lot of time to pray. God showed me some things about myself over those five months. How I had put my family through so much pain because of my selfishness. That I had treated so many people so badly. I wasn't going to do that again. I had a lot to make up for, and as soon as I was able to walk without crutches, I got started."

As he spoke his last words, a sinking feeling came over Miriam. "I see."

He pulled into the parking lot and stopped the buggy. Turning to her, he smiled. "Well, we're here, and I talked your ear off. I'll be by to pick you up this afternoon, *ya?*"

She shook her head. "I have a ride already." She didn't, but she would find one. He had finally given her the strength she needed to turn him down. For good.

His smile dimmed. "Okay. Then I'll pick you up tomorrow morning."

"I don't think so." She opened the door and hurried out, keeping her head down so he couldn't see her face. Because if he looked at her one more time, the tears she was holding on to so tightly would fall. She scurried to the fabric shop, yanking her key out of her patchwork bag as she did, blinking back the tears stinging her eyes. She wouldn't cry. Not now, when they would have customers in a few minutes.

It took her more than three tries to unlock the door. When she finally did, she ran into the store and headed straight for the back room, not turning on the lights. She went into the bathroom and slammed the door, taking a deep breath as she leaned over the sink.

Now she knew why Seth had talked to her at the singing. Why he had bought her raspberry fudge. Why he was taking her to and from work.

Guilt.

He was paying penance for his sins. How could she have been so stupid as to believe her mother's words? Or to let herself entertain romantic feelings for him? Seth didn't see anything special in her. All he saw was a way to assuage his guilt. If only she had discovered it sooner. Before she had let him back in her heart.

∽◠◡◠∾

Seth sat in the buggy, stunned. He couldn't move. He couldn't do anything, not when his mind and emotions had been knocked so far out of whack. He had worried about what Miriam's reaction might be to his confession, but he hadn't thought she would be so cold. So harsh. So unfeeling.

But that wasn't exactly true. When she got out the buggy, she tried to hide her face from him, but he caught a quick glimpse of her expression before she ran inside.

She was upset. Deeply upset. That wasn't his intent at all.

It hadn't been easy, laying himself open like that. But it had been cathartic, and until she had shot out of his buggy like a bullet out of a rifle, he had felt better. He hadn't told anyone the things he told her. He had trusted her. If anyone would understand what he'd gone through and what he had learned, he thought she would. She was smart and compassionate. But he'd also thought she was nonjudgmental, and clearly he'd been mistaken.

He had half a mind to go into the shop and see her. Ask what she was so upset about.

But why should he? She had told him yesterday she had

feelings. Well, he had them too, and right now they'd taken a beating. Grabbing the reins, he steered the buggy around and left.

His mind whirled as he drove back to his house. The sun was glowing bright in the morning sky, but he barely noticed. Why was he bothering with her anyway? She had been nothing but trouble since he'd had the stupid idea of getting to know her better. He'd spent the rest of his Christmas money on her. He'd gone out of his way to take her to and from work—it wasn't as if he lived down the street from her; his house was a good four miles away. And what did he get for his trouble?

The buggy door slammed in his face.

Fine. He was done. He had better things to do than chase her around. There were a dozen other girls who would welcome his attention with open arms.

But none of them were like Miriam.

He sighed, all his internal bluster gone. One word kept piercing through the mixed-up scramble of emotions consuming him.

Demut.

Humility. He'd rejected the trait years ago, preferring to embrace his pride instead. Taking that road had led to near destruction.

He had told himself that he was through with being proud, done with making sure his ego was intact. He wanted to be clothed in *demut*, to be humble, to follow Jesus' perfect example. Today had been his first true test of that new resolve, and he had failed miserably.

The path was before him, divided in two. He could leave

her alone while he pursued someone who didn't make him feel like the bug on the bottom of a boot. Or he could scrape off all remnants of his pride and find out why she got upset so suddenly. He had no idea which road to choose.

◯

"You sure you don't want anything to eat before you go to work?"

Miriam nodded. "I'm sure."

"But you didn't eat much last night." Mary set the plate of pancakes on the table. "Are you ill?"

"*Nee.*" Only heartsick.

All through the night and this morning she tried to leave Seth in the dust of her memories. A small part of her hoped he might ignore what she said and pick her up after work anyway, but he didn't. Not that she was surprised. Guilt stabbed at her, but she pushed it away. Seth wasn't the hurt party here; she was.

But as much as she tried not to think of him, he kept stubbornly popping back up, like a jack-in-the-box with a broken lid. She should never have gone to the singing Sunday night. If she hadn't, she wouldn't be trying to fit the shattered pieces of her heart back together. The next time Lydia tried to force her to do something she didn't want to do, she would stand her ground.

"I wish you'd eat something, Miriam. You're thin enough as it is."

She'd heard that comment all her life, from various family members and friends who had good intentions when shoving food in her face. She couldn't help being thin. Just like she couldn't help being unattractive. That was how she was.

That was who she *really* was. A four-eyed beanpole. Despite what her mother said.

"All right," Mary said. "If you're not eating, then go ahead and tell Pop you're ready to go. He's on a tight schedule today." Normally a very placid woman, Mary gave her a stern look. "Next time don't wait until the last minute to ask for a ride."

"I won't. I promise."

"Too bad Seth couldn't pick you up today. He's freed up your *daed* to finish up some projects around here. Ah, well." Mary scooted away to finish cleaning up the rest of the dishes.

Miriam stared at the short stack of pancakes before her. Her stomach turned at the sight of them. She rose from the table and smoothed the skirt of her sky blue dress, adjusting the apron she wore over it. Checking to make sure the pins were secure in her *kapp*, she donned her cloak and put on her gloves. After slipping on her black shoes, she went out the back to find her father, who was hitching up the horse in the barn.

"*Danki*, Pop," she said, the cold morning air seeping through her black cloak. She shivered. "I appreciate the ride."

He gave her a curt nod, his gray beard bobbing against the collar of his black coat. She could see that both her parents were put out with her, and for good reason. But she was willing to deal with her guilt and her father's gruff demeanor if it meant she wouldn't have to see Seth Fisher again.

"*Herr* Herschberger?"

Both Miriam and her father turned around at the sound of his name. She drew in a sharp breath. Seth was standing there, leaning on his walking stick, looking her straight in the eye. His expression was inscrutable.

"May I take Miriam to work?" he asked.

It was as if her feet had been nailed to the ground. She couldn't move; she couldn't say anything. Only silently pray her father would say no.

"*Ya*, Seth," he said, sounding relieved. He let go of the horse's reins and adjusted his glasses. "And *danki*. I have a generator to repair, and I promised the woman I'd have it done by noon."

Miriam closed her eyes. Was it too much to ask God to answer her prayers just once?

"Miriam, go with Seth," her father said, hanging up the horse's reins on a peg on the barn's wooden wall. He walked past them toward the house. "Oh, and can you bring her home too? I can pay you for your time and trouble."

"That won't be necessary. I'll bring her home, but I'll accept no payment."

After her father left, the two of them stood in the barn, neither of them moving. Seth's expression seemed set in stone. It dawned on her that she'd never seen him angry before. But if he was mad at her, then why was he picking her up? As long as she lived she would never understand this man.

"Ready?" His tone wasn't the least bit friendly.

"You don't have to do this," she said. "I don't want to bother you."

His blue eyes softened a bit, and he tilted his head to the side. "It's not a bother."

Her heartbeat doubled. With a tiny shake of her head she steeled her resolve. "I don't *want* you to pick me up."

His expression hardened once more. "And why is that?"

"Because . . . because . . . " She couldn't bring herself to say the words.

He scrubbed his hand over his face, then pulled on his clean-shaven chin. "Miriam, are you trying to drive me *narrisch*?"

"I'm trying to drive you away!"

"Fine, but you at least owe me a reason. And an explanation as to why the minute after I poured my heart out to you, you shut the door in my face."

"You want to know why?" She could feel her mouth trembling with ire, but she was powerless to stem the emotion. "I don't like being used."

"Used? How have I used you?"

"You think I don't realize what you're doing?"

"Miriam, stop answering questions with questions. Would you just tell me what you mean?"

She licked her dry lips. "I'm not a balm for your guilt."

⁓

Seth couldn't believe this. Here he was, standing in her parents' barn in the freezing cold, trying to be a nice guy and give her a ride. Instead, he found himself on the receiving end of her accusation. He shoved his hat off his forehead and stared at her. "Unbelievable. You think I'm doing this because I feel guilty?"

She nodded. "Why else?"

His hand fisted tightly around his walking stick. Again he asked himself why he was here. He'd gone home last night, determined not to see her again, choosing pride over humility. Then he had prayed and asked God for direction, only to discover the

Lord's ideas were the opposite of his own. When he woke up, he headed straight for the barn and hitched up the horse. Now he was here, trying to figure out how everything got so complicated. Relationships weren't supposed to be this hard.

There was that word again. *Relationship.* Right now they could barely look at each other. This was as far from a relationship as two people could get.

The air between them was as frigid as the temperature in the barn. In one of the stalls he could hear the rustle of the Herschbergers' horse. Seth's hand relaxed, but only because it couldn't stay in that stiff position.

"Miriam, it's true; I do feel bad for a lot of the things I did back then, including what I said to you. But I thought when I told you I was sorry I had paid for that transgression."

She didn't say anything, merely pressed her lips together in a thin line.

Why wasn't she responding?

Moisture suddenly collected in her eyes.

Then he knew. He'd hurt her more than he realized. Had she been carrying around that pain for five long years?

"Miriam," he said again, softening his voice. "I was so young back then. So stupid and full of myself. It was a throwaway comment from a dumb kid trying to make his friends laugh. I didn't mean it."

"*Ya*, you did." She looked at him, and his heart shattered. "Because it's true. Now, if you'll please take me to work. I'm going to be late."

Chapter Ten

Seth was tempted to curse. Salty language had filled his mouth during his *rumschpringe*, but he had put that, and so many other things, behind him. Yet old habits died hard, and he had to bite his bottom lip to keep from swearing.

Miriam didn't say a word on the ride into Paradise. More than once he thought about drawing her into conversation but decided against it. He needed more time. They needed more time. Pat answers weren't going to solve this problem or convince Miriam that her words were so, so wrong. That she thought that way about herself broke his heart. Knowing he was the source of it just about killed him.

Seth pulled up to the parking lot. Miriam grabbed her bag, that quirky bag made of so many colors and patterns it should hurt his eyes, but somehow looked like a work of art.

"Miriam." At first he thought she would ignore him, and he was grateful when she paused. "We'll talk more when I pick you up this evening."

She hesitated one more moment, then left.

He wanted to go after her, but he held back. Not only did he know it wouldn't do any good; he wouldn't have been able to catch up to her with his bum leg. He hung his head, trying to stem his frustration at being so physically limited. If it weren't for his injury, he could have tracked her down and at least made another attempt at settling things.

He stared at his leg. It was thinner than the other one, but the difference wasn't noticeable through his trousers. Still, he knew, and it would be a long time before he would gain his full strength. Some days he handled that knowledge better than others. And sometimes, like right now, he hated his crippled body.

He took a deep breath. If it weren't for his injury, he wouldn't be here, dealing with the past and trying to forge a new future. The somber thought yanked him out of his brooding.

He looked up and slapped the reins against Gravy's flanks, guiding him toward the road. He couldn't go after Miriam, and he didn't think he should. The only thing he could do was go home. And wait. For what, he didn't know.

On the ride home he thought about what she'd said. How she felt about herself. Granted, there were women out there with curvier figures and prettier faces, but now that didn't matter to him. At one time it had; he couldn't deny that. There was only one woman he was interested in, one woman who could drive him crazy one minute then sneak into his heart the next.

Miriam Herschberger.

He had thought he had his work cut out for him before when he just wanted to be friends with her, but now that he admitted his feelings, the challenge seemed insurmountable. Not only did he have to battle his own demons; he had to help Miriam fight hers.

✧

"Aww, honey. You should have stayed home today." Tammy ushered Miriam to the back office soon after Seth had dropped her off.

Miriam fought to gain her composure. "I'm so stupid," she said. "I'm stupid for thinking he had changed, stupid for hoping he liked me."

"You're not stupid. You're human. And unfortunately we were created to love and be loved. It's just hard to find the right person. Trust me, I know. I had to learn the hard way."

"I'm not in love with Seth." Miriam sniffed and reached for a tissue.

"You can say that, but a girl doesn't melt into tears over a guy unless she feels something for him."

"I'm not crying."

"Not *yet*." Tammy gave her a sympathetic smile.

Miriam sighed. If he had said something, just one word of denial after she admitted she was ugly, things would have been different. Instead he just looked at her. The silence spoke volumes.

"He's supposed to come back for me after work," she said.

"Do you want him to?"

She shook her head vehemently. "*Nee.*"

"All right. We'll close up a little early today—"

"But—"

"And I'll take you home."

When Miriam tried to protest again, Tammy waved her off. "We've both been working hard enough lately. We deserve a little reward, okay?"

Miriam nodded. Tammy was resolute, and when she set her mind on something, she couldn't be persuaded off course. Besides, if the shop closed up early, she would surely miss Seth. And that was all she cared about.

The day went by quickly, as they had a steady stream of customers. Christmas was a little over a week away, and people were buying last-minute gifts such as sewing supplies, stitchery kits, and skeins of yarn. After Miriam had checked out the last customer, Tammy went to the door and turned the sign to Closed.

"Are you ready to go home?" she said.

"But the store's a mess."

"It will wait until morning. Who's the boss here?"

Miriam allowed a little smile. "You are."

"So I make the rules, and I say when we can bend them. And we're bending them backward today. Let's go."

Closed?

Seth tilted his hat back a little. The shop was closed? He checked his timepiece. No, he was on time. Even a few minutes early. He looked at the sign again and grimaced.

He'd missed her.

He'd spent the entire day thinking about what he would say to her. How he could reassure her that what she thought of herself wasn't true, and it wasn't what he saw when he looked at her. He even practiced some of his points out loud as he drove to town to pick her up. Now he couldn't say anything to her, because she was gone.

Turning around, he walked back to the buggy, trying to figure out what to do. The businesses lining Lincoln Avenue were adorned on the outside and inside with beautiful gold, green, and red ribbons and ornaments, holly boughs, and wreaths, and other silver sparkly things, but he barely noticed the frippery. Instead he focused on what had happened to Miriam. Her boss probably took her home, since they'd closed up early. The thought of driving back to her house popped into his mind, but there was no guarantee she would be there. It probably would be a wasted trip.

It seemed like he was spinning his wheels in a mud pit, and not for the first time.

He untied Gravy, then threw his walking stick inside the buggy, hurled himself in, and set off. He scratched an itch on his cheek, feeling the scar. Then he looked at his walking stick. What a pair they were. *He* was the damaged goods, not her, no matter what she thought of herself. But maybe they were both too broken—him on the outside, her on the inside.

Thirty minutes later he was back home and heading for his *daed*'s shop. Officially he was supposed to start work next week, but he had been filling his time in between chauffeuring Miriam with a special project. He didn't want to work on it today, but if he didn't it wouldn't be finished by Christmas.

Entering the shop, he saw his father hunched over a table, a chisel in his leathery hands. With speed and precision gained over years of carving, *Daed* made wide, shallow cuts in the dense wood. Usually he worked with oak, but Seth saw that today he was using cherry. Melvin pushed on the chisel a couple of times, then brushed away the thin strips of excess wood.

Not wanting to interrupt him, Seth limped over to another table where his project lay. He ran his hand over the wood he had sanded smooth yesterday. If only he could sand away the rough edges of his life so easily.

KATHLEEN FULLER

"Didn't hear you come in."

Seth turned to see his father rising from his chair. He arched his back a bit, then shook out his arms, stiff from being in one position for so long.

"I didn't want to disturb you," said Seth.

"You're not." Melvin strolled over to Seth's workstation. He picked up the sanded wood and examined it. "Looks good." He put it back down.

"*Danki.* Where's Noah?"

"Making a delivery. He'll be back in a bit."

Seth nodded, then turned to stare at the wood. He looked at it for a long time, not really seeing it, as he tried to figure out what to do about Miriam, if he should do anything at all.

"Something on your mind?"

He started, not only at the sound of his father's voice, but at the interest in his tone. His first reaction was to tell him nothing, to say everything was fine. He'd never revealed his personal problems to his father before.

But maybe this time he should. Maybe that had been one of their problems all along—he and his *daed* had never really talked *to* each other. Sure, they'd talked *at* each other, and had done a lot of yelling along the way. But now, for the first time ever, Seth wanted his father's counsel.

"*Ya*," he said. "There is something on my mind."

"Anything to do with that gal at the fabric shop?"

"*Ya*," he repeated.

Melvin shook his head. "Womenfolk."

With a small smile Seth said, "They never used to be this complicated."

"I reckon you never cared as much before."

Seth nodded, unable to deny the truth and surprised by his father's flawless assessment. "Exactly. I do care, more than I realized."

"I take it you're courting her."

"*Ya, Daed*. I am. At least I'm trying to. But I'm not sure I want to bother with her anymore. I've tried everything I can think of to get her to just like me. I charmed her, bought her a gift, gave her rides to and from work, but she doesn't want to have anything to do with me. I don't understand it."

His father tugged on his nearly completely gray beard, which hung past his throat. Then he ran his fingers through it, something he always did when he was deep in thought. He peered at Seth, tilting his head, as if he were sizing up his son. "Sounds like a problem."

"It is."

"Leave her alone."

Seth's eyebrows shot up. "What?"

"Leave her be."

"I–" He looked at the pieces of wood on the table, suddenly regretting being so open with his *daed*. His father didn't understand at all. "I can't do that."

"Why not? You just said you didn't want to be bothered."

"*Ya*, but . . . I didn't mean it to come out that way . . . I . . . I don't know." He sighed. "I don't know anything anymore."

"*Ach*. That's a first for you."

"*Ya*, it is." His leg was aching, so he pulled up a stool and sat down.

"You've always gotten what you wanted, Seth." Melvin put

his hand on his son's shoulder as he walked past him. "Things have come easily to you. Too easily, I'm thinkin'. Maybe now you've finally found something you can't have. That's where your real trouble is. Accepting that something you want real bad is out of reach."

"So I'm just supposed to forget about her?"

"Maybe." He cocked his head to the side. "Or maybe you just have to work harder, harder than you ever had to in your life. Guess you need to figure out if she's worth it." Melvin paused. "What did God tell you to do?"

His cheeks heating, Seth said, "I don't know. I didn't ask."

"Then ask him." Removing his hand, he turned, walked back to his table, and went back to work.

Seth pondered his words. Was *Daed* right? Was his dogged pursuit of Miriam fueled by the need to attain, instead of a true attraction? He wasn't sure. One thing was clear, however. His father said to leave her be, and that was a wise recommendation. He also said to talk to God, something Seth should have done in the first place.

He glanced across the room at his *daed*, who was once again engrossed in his carving. Rising from his stool, he went over to him, swallowing the lump that had suddenly appeared in his throat. So many times he had dismissed his father as a fool, a stubborn old man who didn't understand anything. How wrong he had been.

"*Danki*," Seth said quietly when he reached him. "I appreciate the advice."

Melvin looked up, his face remaining as placid as it always did. But his eyes reflected something else. *Respect*. Seth had never seen it before, at least not directed toward him. The two men didn't say anything else, and after a moment Seth turned away and went back to working on his project, silently praising God that at least one of his strained relationships was moving in a positive direction.

◦◦◦◦◦

Miriam was relieved when Seth didn't pick her up for work on Saturday morning. Her father hadn't needed the buggy, so she drove herself to work, picking up extra hours because of the Christmas holiday. Near closing time her stomach twisted in knots as she expected Seth to show up and ask to take her home. He didn't. She didn't see him at church on Sunday, and he never made an appearance at the shop on Monday. Apparently, she had gotten through to him. She wouldn't have to deal with Seth Fisher anymore. She should be pleased.

Instead, she felt more miserable than before.

On Wednesday morning Tammy came into the shop, clad in jeans and a green and red–striped sweater. Red metallic jingle bells hung from her ears, and a strand of tiny, blinking Christmas lights were around her neck. She rivaled some of the Christmas trees in the shop windows. Miriam looked at her, not knowing what to think.

"Time to get into the Christmas spirit!" Tammy set down her large tote bag on the counter and pulled out another strand of gaudy lights. "Here's one for you."

"*Danki*, but I can't take them."

"Oh." Her cheeks flushed. "Can't believe I forgot that."

"It's all right."

"What do you all do for Christmas? Do you have a tree? Presents?"

"A tree, *nee*. We do exchange presents, usually the second day after Christmas. The day of Christmas we gather with friends and family and celebrate Christ's birth."

"Sounds nice." Tammy smiled.

"It is." Miriam put the cash drawer in the register and went to the front door. They had a few minutes before the store opened for business. She paused and stared out the glass door, watching as cars, buggies, and people, both Amish and *Englisch*, passed by.

"Looking for someone?" Tammy came up from behind.

Miriam stepped back. "*Nee*." Casting her gaze to the ground, she slid by Tammy and went to straighten a shelf that didn't need straightening.

"Is he coming today?"

"Who?" Miriam adjusted several bolts of flannel.

"You know who I'm talking about. Seth."

Miriam shook her head, hoping she appeared more nonchalant than she felt. "Matthew is picking me up."

"So you're back to having your cousin provide your transportation."

"*Ya*. It's easier that way."

"You mean it's safer that way." Although Tammy was dressed comically, her expression was serious.

Miriam turned around and looked at her, dumbfounded. "Matthew is a *gut* driver, *ya*."

Tammy shrugged. "Suit yourself."

Frowning, Miriam turned away, not appreciating the

disapproval in her boss's voice. She said very little for the rest of the day, and nothing on the ride home. Fortunately Matthew wasn't much of a conversationalist, and Miriam didn't feel the need to make small talk. She was free to focus on her last encounter with Seth. He had said he poured his heart out to her. And all she had cared about was whether he thought she was pretty or not.

No wonder he didn't come back.

For the first time she realized how self-centered she had been. She'd always thought of Seth Fisher as being so full of himself, but he was nothing compared to her. He talked about how his pride had led him on a path of destruction. Where was her self-absorption leading her?

To loneliness. Resentment. Even envy when she saw other couples together.

"I'll pick you up tomorrow, *ya?*" Matthew slowed the buggy in front of their driveway. He didn't drive to the house like Seth always did.

"*Ya,*" she said, almost as an afterthought. In a haze, she walked up the driveway and entered the house, heading straight to her bedroom. Dropping her bag on a nearby chair, she sat down at the edge of her bed.

A soft knock sounded at the door. "Miriam?" her mother asked. "Is everything okay?"

"*Ya,*" Miriam said.

"Can I come in?"

Miriam hesitated. She really didn't want to talk to her mother right now, but she knew *Mamm* wouldn't relent until they spoke. "Okay."

Her mother walked in and sat down next to her. "I noticed Seth hasn't been around lately."

Looking away, Miriam shrugged. "I guess he's busy."

"That might be so, but I'm guessing there's another reason why Matthew is driving you to work again."

When Miriam didn't respond, her mother continued. "I don't understand, Miriam. You fret that no one is interested in you, and when a young man shows interest, you push him away."

Miriam blanched. "It's not that simple."

Mary put two fingers above her gray eyebrow and frowned. "I thought when we had that talk the other day you two were going to work things out. Instead your cousin is dropping you off, and you've been sulking around here for two days. I can see this is tearing you up inside, and I'm sure he's going through the same thing."

"I doubt it."

"Honey, don't slam the door without looking at what's on the other side." She took Miriam's hand in hers. "What do we value above everything else, except of course the Lord?"

Miriam frowned at the unexpected question. "Faith, family—"

"Let me stop you there. Do you want a family?"

"I have a family," Miriam said, confused.

"I mean one of your own. A husband. Children."

Miriam paused, tempted to shake her head. But that would be a lie, one her mother would see right through. "*Ya*," she said quietly. "I do."

"How will that happen if you don't let anyone get close to you?"

"But I'm—"

"What? Unattractive?" Mary ran her hand over Miriam's cheek. "Miriam, self-pity is unattractive. Low confidence is unattractive. Pushing people away is unattractive." She softened her tone. "Your attitude is standing in the way of what you want. That and your fear of getting hurt. But can't you see, you're already hurting? You will be for the rest of your life if you don't change how you feel about yourself." She leaned forward and kissed her cheek. "I could sit here all day and tell you what a beautiful *maedel* you truly are. Yet it won't mean anything if you don't believe it yourself." She rose from the bed and left the room.

Miriam sat for a moment, frozen. Were her *mamm*'s words true? Was she pushing Seth away not because of him, but because of herself?

Her grandmother's beloved quilt hung over the back of the chair. She stared at it, wishing her grandmother were here. Miriam knew what she would say. She could even hear her gentle voice speaking the words.

Take it to the Lord, mei kind. *Take your problems to the Lord.*

Her grandmother was right. She should have been praying all along.

Rising from the bed, Miriam turned around and knelt on the floor, folding her hands and closing her eyes. She prayed for forgiveness for her pride and her self-centeredness, she prayed for wisdom about Seth, and she prayed for healing—not just for her own hurt, but also for Seth's. She poured out her heart to the Lord and admitted to him all of her fears and insecurities. There were so many of them, and it took a long time before she felt the healing spirit of God flow through her. But when it did, when God's peace descended upon her, she realized what she had to do.

Chapter Eleven

SETH CONTINUED TO RUB HIS THIGH AS HE GLANCED ACROSS THE room at his father. After supper they had both retired to the living room—his father to read, and Seth to think more about his situation with Miriam. His mother had remained in the kitchen, peeling apples to make filling for the shoestring apple pies she would be taking to Sarah and David Fisher on First Christmas. Seth looked forward to spending some time with his cousin and his wife, along with other friends and family. He used to find First Christmas boring, as it involved Bible reading and hymn singing instead of opening presents. But this year the holiday held special meaning for him. For the first time he recognized its holiness, and he wanted to show his reverence for the birth of the Savior.

Melvin turned the page of the newspaper he was reading, the newsprint crackling with the movement. "Leg bothering you?"

"A little."

"Got some of that salve left from when you came home."

Pinching his face at the thought of using the smelly goop his mother and father swore took care of all their aches and pains, Seth said, "It's fine, *Daed*. Just a twinge." Actually it was more than a twinge, but he could live with it. Still, he appreciated his father's concern. "Think I'll help *Mamm* with the apples."

Melvin nodded, but kept his nose buried in the paper.

Seth looked at his walking stick. Lately he hadn't been using it as much in the house, although he did rely on it when he went out and while he was in the woodshop.

He limped to the kitchen without it, inhaling the mild, fruity scent of fresh apples. He looked at his mother, who was seated at the square table, slicing an apple in half. "Need some help?"

Rachel smiled. "*Ya*. That would be nice. You can peel while I cut."

After retrieving another paring knife from the utensil drawer, he went and sat down next to his mother. A tall gas lamp stood in the corner of the room, flooding the room with plenty of light. They peeled apples in silence for a short while.

Rachel dropped several pieces of cut apple into a large bowl. "You used to help me a lot when you were younger." She glanced at him. "I missed that."

"You know, I do too." Looking at her, he smiled. "I didn't realize how much until right now." Applying the blade to the top of the apple, he broke the green skin, then slid the sharp blade beneath the peel until he had removed it from the apple in one strip. Setting the peel aside, he grabbed another Granny Smith.

"When you were little, you used to eat the peels," his mother said, working her knife with her plump hands through the middle of an apple, this time a Jonathan. "They're yours if you want them."

He grabbed a short piece of green peel and put it in his mouth, letting the tart sweetness coat his tongue. "Don't think I can eat all these, though."

"We'll give the leftovers to the pigs."

"I'll take them out there when we're through."

His mother put down her knife, worry instantly appearing on her round face. "I don't think that's a good idea."

"I have to start doing my share around here."

"But you're still healing."

"I'm healed enough to feed the pigs. Don't worry, I'll be careful, and I won't go inside the pen."

She picked up her knife and started slicing again. "A mother never stops worrying about, or loving, her children."

He glanced down at the pile of peelings in front of him. "I haven't always deserved it."

"Seth," she said, stilling the knife and looking at him again. "A mother's love isn't earned. It's freely given. Don't ever forget that."

Swallowing the lump that suddenly appeared in his throat, he said, "*Danki*."

"Seth."

At the sound of his father's voice, he turned around. Melvin was standing in the kitchen doorway.

"*Ya?*"

"Someone's here to see you." His *daed* stepped to the side. A slender woman walked into the room, an unsure expression on her sweet face.

"Miriam?"

She gazed down at the floor, as she so often did when she was around him. "I hope I'm not interrupting anything."

"*Nee*, you're not." Seth stood from his chair and gestured toward his mother. "*Mamm*, this is Miriam Herschberger."

Rachel smiled, dimples forming on her plump cheeks.

"Hello, Miriam. I've known your *mudder* for a long time. How is she faring?"

"She's well. *Danki* for asking." She looked at Seth for a fleeting moment, then back at Rachel. "If this is a bad time, I can talk to Seth later."

"*Nee.* I won't hear of it. Seth and I have just finished our conversation."

He caught his mother's knowing look and gave her a small smile of appreciation.

Rachel put down her knife and stood. "If you don't mind, Miriam, I could use some help with these apples. If you and Seth could peel and cut them, then I can finish the present I'm working on for Sarah and David."

"Sarah and David Fisher?" Miriam asked.

She nodded. "David is my nephew, my youngest brother's *sohn.* We're going to their house for First Christmas."

Seth thought he saw something flicker across Miriam's face, but he wasn't sure, as she still wore her uncertain expression.

"I'm putting the last few touches on a lap quilt for them," Rachel explained. "I've made one for all my nieces and nephews and their families. It's taken a while, but David and Sarah are the youngest, so they had to wait to get theirs." She smiled. "I hope they'll be pleased with it."

"I'm sure they will," Miriam said. "I'd love to see it when you're finished."

"Of course. Seth says you like to quilt."

Miriam looked at him, surprise in her eyes, as if she couldn't believe he would talk about her to his mother. "*Ya,*" she said quietly, still keeping her gaze on him. "I do. Very much so."

"Hopefully I can see some of your work one day. He told me you're very talented."

A flush heated her cheeks, and she cast her eyes to the ground. "*Danki*," she said in a nearly transparent voice. "I would be happy to show you some of the projects I've been working on."

"*Gut.* Before you leave, we'll figure out when we can do that." She looked at Seth, a small smile teasing her lips before she addressed Miriam again. "Would you mind helping him with the apples?"

"*Nee.*"

"You can use that knife right there. *Danki*, Miriam. I appreciate it."

At some point during the conversation, his father had disappeared, and after thanking Miriam, his mother beat an equally hasty exit.

Cautiously, Miriam pulled out the chair and sat down. She reached for a peeled apple and picked up the knife. He noticed the slight shake of her hands, but she still handled the knife with expertise as she cut the fruit into medium-sized chunks.

Seth peeled an apple and handed it to her, waiting for her to say something. What was she doing here? It was on the tip of his tongue to ask her, but he remained silent, letting her take the lead this time. Obviously she wouldn't be here unless she had a specific reason, and he would bide his time until she decided to talk.

But instead of speaking, she kept cutting. So he kept peeling, his patience wearing thin. After they went through four apples, he couldn't take it anymore. When she reached for another apple, without thinking he took her hand in his. "Miriam, what are you doing here?"

She glanced at his hand, which had covered hers completely. Quickly she slid it out from beneath his grasp. "I—I . . ." Taking a deep breath, she started again, this time looking at him while she pushed up her glasses. "I came to apologize."

"Apologize?"

"For being so selfish."

"Selfish?"

"You were right. You were open and honest with me, and I didn't appreciate that. I was too caught up in my own problems that I wasn't there for you. I'm sorry for that." Her gaze shot down again, as if her nerve had suddenly drained from her. She grabbed another apple and started chopping.

"Miriam," he said, watching her slice the apple with even more zeal than before. "*Miriam.*"

Finally she stopped and looked at him, as if exasperated that he would interrupt such an important task. "What?"

He pointed to the apple pieces. "I was supposed to peel it first."

She looked down at the apple she'd been cutting, the peel still completely on the fruit. Her shoulders slumped, and suddenly she laughed.

The sound both surprised and delighted him. "You have a great laugh."

Looking up at him, she smiled.

"And a great smile." He grinned. "You need to smile more."

Her face flushed, almost matching the color of one of the Jonathans he'd been peeling.

He picked up another piece of apple peel and put it into his mouth. Then he offered her some. "You don't have to take it," he said. "Most people don't care for the peel on its own."

"Not me. I like the peels." She accepted a piece and took a small bite. "*Gut* apples," she said.

"*Ya.* They'll make *gut* pie, although my *mudder* could probably make bad apples into something delicious." Seth watched as she took another bite, savoring the taste, the light brown freckle above her lip moving up and down as she chewed. He could watch her eat for the next lifetime or so, but they needed to finish or his mother would have his head. "We better get this done or there won't be any pies."

They went back to cutting and peeling. "I accept your apology," he said after a short stretch of silence.

"*Danki.*"

"Do you accept mine?"

"Yours?"

"About what I did in school. I'm really sorry, and I'm not just saying that out of guilt."

She looked at him. "*Ya.* I see that now." Once again, her lips curled in a smile.

His heart slammed against his rib cage. How could he have ever thought she wasn't pretty? Her smile made all the difference, bringing a light to her chocolate-brown eyes. Somehow he'd find a way to make her smile as much as possible.

"Do you think we could start over?" Her smile faded, replaced by insecurity again.

He quickly reassured her. "I'd like that, Miriam. But I have one condition."

Alarm lit her delicate features. "What?"

"No games. Don't make me guess what you're thinking. What you're feeling."

She expelled a deep breath. "I'll try. It's just that . . ."

"What? Miriam, you can tell me."

"I'm scared."

Her admission touched a chord in his heart. "Scared of what?"

"Of everything." She wiped her damp hands on the light blue kitchen towel lying near the cutting board.

"You mean like spiders and the dark?" he teased. When she chuckled, he knew he'd struck the right tone.

"*Nee*. Although I used to be afraid of the dark when I was little."

"Me too."

"Really? I didn't think you had ever been afraid of anything."

"Well, I got over it pretty quickly. That's the thing with fear: you can't let it rule your life. You have to put it behind you as fast as you can."

"I wish I could."

"I'd like to help you try. If you'll let me." He knew it was a risk, but he held out his hand to her anyway. His heart soared when she tentatively slipped her small hand in his.

Her skin was soft, just as he'd imagined it would be. And just as he'd expected, his hand dwarfed hers. Yet holding it was so natural and seemed so right. He squeezed her hand, and even though he didn't want to, he let her go.

Without speaking they resumed their task of peeling and

cutting, but this time the silence between them wasn't as awkward. Her coming here had taken a lot of courage; he could see that now. She had finally let down her defenses a little bit. He would take anything she offered.

"Do you mind if I ask you something?"

He popped another piece of peel into his mouth and chewed. "Sure. Go ahead."

She hesitated, glancing down at the table again. He hoped she eventually wouldn't be so shy around him.

Finally she looked up. "Your scar . . . it doesn't seem to bother you."

"Not anymore. The cut healed really well, considering I had forty stitches." He touched the upper part of his cheek. "A few more inches and that glass would have pierced me in the eye." When he saw her blanch, he said, "Sorry. Didn't mean to be so graphic."

"That's okay. I just feel bad you had to go through something like that. It must have been very painful."

"It was, but my leg was worse, so it kind of took my mind off my face."

"But aren't you worried about what other people might say? That they might . . . "

"Make fun of me?"

She nodded.

He shrugged. "Once that would have bothered me. A lot. But what I am on the outside is insignificant. I realize that now. What counts is what's in here." His hand went to his heart. He paused. "Now let me ask you something."

"What?"

An unexpected attack of nerves assaulted him as he realized how much her answer meant to him. "Does my scar bother you?"

She put her elbow on the table and rested her chin on her hand. After studying his face for a few torturous moments, she said with a smile, "What scar?"

At that moment he knew he could never let her go. If he had to fight to win her heart until he took his last breath, he would, just for the privilege of seeing her gaze at him with stars in her eyes the way she was looking at him now.

After she sliced the last apple, she spoke again. "I should be going." She stood. "I told *Mamm* I wouldn't be long."

"Do you need a ride home?" He scooted his chair from the table and rose.

"*Nee*. I brought our buggy."

"How's your horse's foot?"

"Getting better. That's nice of you to remember."

While he was still in her good graces he asked, "May I take you to work in the morning?"

"Matthew is giving me a ride."

"Oh." He kept the disappointment out of his voice. Maybe he'd misread her. Perhaps she wanted to take things slower than he thought.

"Seth?"

"*Ya?*"

"I will need a ride home tomorrow, if you're able."

He grinned, feeling like he'd just struck gold. "I'll be there."

After she left, he picked up his walking stick and went out to his father's woodshop next to the house. He turned on the gas lamp, and the hissing sound coming from the lamp filled the large room. The shop was cold, but Seth didn't care. He limped over to the table and sat down. The block of wood he'd been working on was starting to take shape, and he tackled the project with new enthusiasm.

"Need some help?"

He turned around and saw his *daed* standing in the doorway. Grinning, Seth said, "You bet."

Chapter Twelve

"Wow, you're in a much better mood today." Tammy lifted up the small lid on top of the cash register and replaced the receipt tape with a fresh roll. First Christmas was two days away, and again they had been very busy. She looked at Miriam and smirked. "But I noticed you haven't taken your eyes off the front door for the past hour. Expecting someone? Someone who might be the reason for your jolly mood?"

Had she been that obvious? All day long she tried to suppress a smile but found it difficult to do. After talking to Seth last night, it seemed that not only had her heart changed, but so had everything else in her life. The shimmer and sparkle of the Christmas decorations were more beautiful than she'd ever noticed before. The tinkling of the bell over the front door was sharper; the colors of the fabrics more vibrant than ever. It was as if the moment she opened her heart to Seth, the world had opened up to her in return.

Miriam would have never had the courage to go see him if God hadn't prodded her. He had given her the strength to bring down her defenses, to take a chance that Seth would accept her apology and not send her away. He would have been within his rights to do just that, but instead he, and his parents, had been welcoming. Her stomach did a tiny flip as she remembered holding his hand. Even though the moment had been brief, their hands seemed to fit perfectly together, her small one in the protective cocoon of his large grasp.

But she tempered her excitement. Holding her hand had been a gesture of friendship, not of any romantic interest. He had never indicated that he was interested in her that way. She had to be content with that. To wish for anything more would be foolish.

Yet she couldn't completely extinguish the flicker of hope in her heart that someday, somehow, he might see her as more than a friend.

She checked the digital clock Tammy kept near the register and tried to keep her mind off impossible things. Nearly five o'clock. Her gaze kept straying to the front door, expecting to see Seth standing there, waiting for her. He'd always arrived a few minutes early, but when she came back from retrieving her cloak and bag, he still wasn't there. She stood by the door and peered outside.

Tammy dimmed the lights and put on her heavy winter coat. "Have you got a ride, Miriam?"

"*Ya,*" she said. Where was he?

"If you need me to, I can run you home." Tammy swirled a red and white–checked scarf around her neck.

"*Nee.* He'll be here."

"Matthew?"

"Seth." Miriam tried to hide her smile, but couldn't.

Tammy's mouth broadened in a wide grin. "Good for you guys! I'm glad you were able to work things out. I always thought you made a cute couple."

"We're just friends. Friends," she repeated, needing the verbal reminder.

With a wink Tammy said, "Whatever you say, Miriam. See you tomorrow. Just make sure to lock up before you go."

"I will."

Tammy left, and after waiting a few minutes more, Miriam stepped outside. The temperature had dropped considerably since the sun had set, and an intermittent breeze cut right through her cloak and dress, chilling her skin. She'd overheard some customers talking about the weather forecast. There was a possibility of snow over the next few days, and they might just have a white Christmas after all.

Another breeze whipped her cloak about her calves and shot through her black kneesocks, chilling her legs. She thought about going back inside to wait. But she was positive Seth would be there any minute. Locking the door behind her, she then turned around, hugging her arms around her body underneath her cloak.

Lincoln Avenue, the main road in Paradise, was still pretty busy, with several people strolling up and down the sidewalks that lined the street. But most of the shops were closing for the night. As more and more and more lights went out inside the stores, her confidence that Seth would arrive started to wane. He should have been there by now.

Darkness descended, and she couldn't wait any longer. Her hands and feet were freezing, and the longer she lingered, the colder she would be. She didn't want to walk home, but she had no choice.

"Miriam!"

Seth! Following the sound of his voice, she turned and looked up Lincoln Street. He stood by the parking lot, waving his hands at her. Relieved, she hurried to meet him halfway.

"I'm so sorry," he said, his breath exhaling in big, white puffs. A mix of panic and remorse filled his eyes. "How long were you standing out here?"

"Long enough." She hugged her arms around her frigid body.

"I didn't mean to be late." He moved closer to her. "I'm really, really sorry."

"Seth," she said, her teeth close to chattering. "It's okay. I'm just glad you're here now."

His brows lifted with surprise. Then he took in her shivering frame. "You're freezing. Let's get you inside the buggy."

They walked to where he had tethered the horse. He went to the passenger side, opened the door, and reached into the backseat. "Here," he said, putting a quilt around her shoulders.

Warmth immediately seeped into her. Then he did something completely unexpected. Her heart stopped as his hands slowly rubbed her arms through the quilt.

"Better?" he asked, his voice close to her ear.

"*Ya.*" She could barely hear herself speak. His large hands covered almost all of her upper arms. He'd never been this close to her, and they were almost in an embrace. If she turned around she would be only inches from his chest. She fought a strong desire to lean against him, to take advantage of his kindness and indulge her own dream. But she stopped herself. They were just friends. But oh, how she wished they could be more.

Seth inwardly groaned as he continued to rub Miriam's arms. He told himself he was just helping her get warmed up. But being this close to her, where all he had to do was bend down a couple inches and he could easily nuzzle her neck . . .

He cleared his throat, then stepped away. Those were definitely thoughts he had no business entertaining. In the past when he had made a move like that on a girl, she had happily accepted it, and usually wanted to do more. But he fought those feelings, not only for Miriam's sake, but also because it was the right thing to do.

She climbed into the buggy, seemingly unaffected by his attempt to warm her. He hobbled around the front and settled in his seat, trying to calm his emotions. Once they were on their way, he said, "Are you warm enough?"

"I am now." Turning, she gave him a small smile before pushing up her glasses.

"*Gut*. I feel really bad about you standing out in the cold. I want to make it up to you."

"You've been kind enough to give me so many rides, Seth. You don't have to make anything up to me."

"But I want to. Are you hungry?" When she didn't respond right away, he said, "Miriam, be honest. I know I'm starving."

"*Ya*. I am a bit hungry."

"Then it's settled. Let's go get something to eat. My treat." His father had given him a few dollars earlier in the week. He hadn't wanted to accept the money, but his *daed* insisted, saying that Seth would more than make up for it when he returned to work after Christmas. "Dienner's is just ahead. That sound okay?"

"Sure."

Over and over Miriam reminded herself that she was *not* on a date with Seth Fisher. They were both hungry, and it was suppertime. It made perfect sense for them to stop and get a bite to eat. Sure, he had offered to pay, but she wouldn't let him. They would go Dutch, just like friends do.

But when he held the door of the restaurant open for her, and then walked behind her, putting his hand on the small of her back for just a split second, she was finding it harder and harder not to wish they were on a real date.

Dienner's Country Restaurant specialized in Amish and German food. Miriam scanned the small dining room while they waited for a hostess to seat them. She didn't see any empty seats, even though it was forty-five minutes until closing time.

"Table for two?" A diminutive woman with platinum blonde hair and purple-framed glasses picked up two menus from the stack near the front door.

"*Ya*," Seth said, over Miriam's shoulder.

"Would a booth be all right? We don't have any empty tables right now."

"That will be fine," he told her.

"Right this way."

Miriam followed the hostess to the back of the dining room, noticing that Seth was right behind her. He had stood near her since they walked into the restaurant. They passed by a table where two Amish girls were eating dinner. One looked up and caught Miriam's gaze.

"Hello, Miriam," Martha Yoder said.

"Hello, Martha." She didn't know Martha very well, as the

girl was a few years younger than she was. Martha's other companion smiled in greeting, but Miriam didn't recognize her.

When they reached the table, the hostess set down the menus. "Your waitress will be here shortly."

"Thanks," Seth said as they both sat down. He slid his walking stick underneath the table, then took off his black coat and set it down next to him. Removing his hat, he slid his long fingers through the thick locks of his dark-brown hair. He'd always worn a hat, and Miriam never noticed how rich the color was until now.

She tried not to gape, but she couldn't help it. A quick glance around the dining room showed that she wasn't the only one who noticed him. Martha and her friend kept looking at Seth, then whispered between themselves. They didn't do much to hide their appreciation for his looks.

Oblivious to their attentions, he grabbed a menu and opened it. "Everything looks great. Have you been here before?"

"*Ya*, a couple times." She removed her cloak and folded it neatly, placing it beside her on the bench seat. Then she picked up her menu and tried to focus on the variety of food listed inside. How could she focus on food with him sitting right across from her?

"All right, I know what I want." He put the menu down on the table. "I'm warning you, I've got a big appetite."

"Uh-huh." She didn't know why her cheeks suddenly flushed, but she didn't want him to see her blushing.

"Have you decided?"

"Uh, not yet."

He reached across and pulled the menu down so they were face-to-face. "Order what you want. I've got it covered."

She shook her head. "I can't let you do that, Seth. I'll pay for my own meal."

"Miriam, relax and don't worry about it. Let's just enjoy ourselves, okay?"

His words were spoken in a gentle tone that had an immediate calming effect on her nerves. He was right; she was too uptight. Lifting up her menu, she perused it for another minute, then settled on her order. "Chicken noodle soup and a side salad." She folded the menu and laid it to the side.

"That's all you want?"

"It's enough for me. My appetite isn't as big as yours."

He chuckled. "Not many are. *Mudder* always made sure she had made enough food for me to have seconds *and* thirds. I always out-ate my *bruders*."

"The woman you marry will have to be a great cook." Her eyes grew wide, and she nearly clapped her hand over her mouth.

"She'll have to like to cook, at the very least." He leaned forward, a teasing spark dancing in his gorgeous blue eyes. "What about you, Miriam? Do you enjoy cooking?"

She licked her lips. "*Ya.* I do."

A grin spread across his face as he leaned back, his gaze holding hers, causing a pleasant jolt to flow through her.

Their waitress suddenly appeared at the table. Miriam placed her order, hiding her disappointment at being interrupted. Once she scribbled down what they wanted, the waitress left, returning shortly after with glasses of water.

Seth picked up his water and took a big drink. As he set down the glass, he said, "You haven't asked me why I was late."

She shrugged. "I figured you had a good reason."

"I do." His lips twitched in a semi-smile.

Tilting her head to the side, she asked, "What is it?"

"Can't tell you."

"What?"

"Can't tell you. At least not now." He was full-blown grinning now.

She couldn't help but smile in return. "Now you're keeping secrets from me?"

"Just one." He lowered his voice. "But something tells me you've been keeping a few from me."

Her face flushed, and she glanced at her water glass. "What makes you say that?"

"You have an air of mystery about you, Miriam Herschberger. I knew that the first time I saw you at the Lapps'."

She scoffed. "There's nothing mysterious about me, Seth. You know everything about me."

He leaned forward, putting his elbows on the table and folding his arms. "I disagree. Sure, I know where you live. Where you work. That you like to quilt. What you do on Sundays. But I don't know your hopes. Your dreams. Your plans for the future."

The lightness of his tone had disappeared, replaced by absolute seriousness. The intensity in his eyes threatened to take her breath away. Suddenly she no longer heard the voices of the other restaurant patrons, or the bustling of the waitresses and bussers. In this crowded restaurant, they were the only two people there.

"Miriam, I want to know everything about you."

Forcing herself to look at him, she said, "There's not much to know."

KATHLEEN FULLER

"I don't believe that."

"Then you'll be disappointed."

"Miriam." His voice was nearly a whisper. "I hate when you put yourself down like that."

Her *mamm's* voice suddenly entered her head. *Self-pity is unattractive. Low confidence is unattractive. Pushing people away is unattractive.* Here she was with the man of her dreams expressing an interest in getting to know her, and she was putting him off. She wasn't being fair to him, or to herself.

The waitress appeared with their food, saving her from having to answer him. After a short prayer of thanks, they both started on their suppers. Seth had half of his wolfed down before she had finished her small salad. He was right; his appetite was voracious.

They made small talk during the meal. Seth expressed his satisfaction with his chicken dinner, and she said the soup was delicious. But in the back of her mind, she kept thinking about what he had said before their food arrived. Seth wanted to know her hopes and plans for the future. How did she tell him that she only hoped for one thing—marriage and a family? And how did she admit that out loud, especially to him, when she could barely acknowledge it herself?

She had finished the last sip of her soup when the waitress returned, asking if they cared for dessert. To her surprise, Seth declined, and Miriam was full.

"Then I'll just take this when you're ready." The waitress tore the check off her pad and put it on the table, then left to tend to other customers.

Miriam reached for the slip of paper, but Seth was too fast for her. "You're stubborn, you know that? I told you that this is my treat."

He folded the bill and tucked it into his hand. "Now, if you still insist on paying your share, you'll have to fight me to do it."

She looked at his huge hand, knowing she was no match. Still, she couldn't resist a little teasing in return. "I may just do that. But I feel it's my duty to let you know that I don't always fight fair."

"Oh, I'm counting on it."

Unable to resist, she moved to touch his fist when he suddenly grasped her hand with his free one. "Gotta be faster than that."

They both laughed, and she loved the way he put her at ease. She also loved how he held on to her hand. Really, there was so much to love about him.

Love? She shoved the thought out of her head. She couldn't afford to think about Seth and love in the same context. Loving Seth would be easy, but pointless. He would never return it.

But then again . . . what if he did? Was it even possible? His smile, his touch, his interest in her thoughts and feelings, gave her a glimmer of hope. And as her mother, Lydia, and even Tammy had been telling her, she deserved happiness. She deserved love. Was it so impossible to believe she could have both with Seth?

He let go of her hand, a little reluctantly, she thought. "You ready to go?"

She nodded. "I just need to stop by the ladies' room."

"No problem. I'll meet you up front."

Excusing herself, she passed by Martha's table, but she paid the girls no notice. Her thoughts, and heart, were consumed with Seth. Unable to stop smiling, she went into the bathroom and went inside a stall. When she finished, she was moving to open the stall door when she heard someone enter.

"I feel so sorry for Seth Fisher." Martha's voice echoed against the walls.

Miriam paused, listening. Why would Martha feel sorry for him?

"I heard he almost died in that accident," the other girl said.

"*Ya*," Martha said. "He's lucky he only has a limp."

"And the scar."

"But even with the scar he's still *gutguckich*. Those eyes are to die for."

Miriam smiled. Martha and her friend had echoed her own thoughts. She opened the stall door a crack. The two young women were checking their reflections in the mirror, making sure their *kapps* were well secured. Martha tucked the ribbons of her *kapp* into the front fold of her dress. "What I don't understand," she said to her reflection, "is what is he doing with Miriam?"

"That's your friend's name?"

"She's not really my friend. I just know her in passing." She lowered her voice. "Talk about homely."

Miriam sucked in her breath.

"I mean, they surely weren't *together* together. Like, courting together," Martha said.

"But he was holding her hand," her friend pointed out, slipping on her black cloak.

"*Ya*, but probably because he felt sorry for her."

Miriam slumped against the stall, her confidence slashed to

ribbons. Is that how they looked to other people? Beauty and the beast, like the fairy tale she had read as a child—only in her story the woman was the beast? Thoughts assaulted her like hailstones hitting the pavement. What would his friends say if she and Seth did start dating? Would they point out how ill suited they were for each other? Probably. Would she have to compete with other girls for his attention? Absolutely.

Tears burned in her eyes; pain clogged her throat as she heard the girls finally leave. She stood there for a few more moments, unable to move, wishing she had never agreed to go to supper with him. He was waiting for her, and she couldn't hide in the bathroom forever.

Lord, help me!

Drying her eyes, she went and washed her hands, unable to bear looking in the mirror. But it was as if it had a magnetic pull, and she couldn't help herself.

Her eyes were red-rimmed behind the lenses of her glasses. Her skin was pasty white, and her lips were trembling. She couldn't go out there looking like this. Seth would notice and want to know what was wrong.

Taking a deep breath, Miriam sucked in all her negative emotions. She tried to force a smile, realized she couldn't do it. She couldn't fake how she felt, and she couldn't hide her emotions anymore. Seth said he wanted to know her, and now he would. The real her. The insecure her. And if he couldn't handle it . . . then she would have to accept that. Somehow.

Chapter Thirteen

SOMETHING WAS WRONG WITH MIRIAM. SETH COULDN'T PINpoint what it was, but she wasn't the same woman that he'd just shared a wonderful meal with. During supper she had been more relaxed than he'd ever seen her, open to his teasing, even kidding him in return. He hadn't enjoyed himself so much in a very long time.

But now, as she approached him from the restroom, he could see something was wrong. Her shoulders were slumped, and when she neared him he could see her eyes were a bit bloodshot. Had she been crying? What in the world could have upset her so much in such a short period of time?

He was determined to find out.

"You forgot these," he said. He held out her quilted bag and her cloak.

"*Danki.*"

Not missing the melancholy tone in her voice, he handed her the bag, then moved to help her with her cloak. But she shook her head and took the garment from him. "I've got it," she said.

"All right." Puzzled, he watched her as she put on the cloak, but she refused to look at him. Without a word she headed for the front door and walked briskly in front of him. He couldn't limp fast enough to keep up with her. Annoyed, he said, "Hey, Miriam. Could you slow down a bit?"

"Sorry." She did slow her steps, but she didn't turn around and look at him.

When they reached the buggy, he was truly concerned. He slid between her and the buggy's passenger door. He wasn't graceful to say the least, but he didn't care. He had her attention and that was all that mattered. "Miriam, tell me what's wrong. We were having such a good time a little while ago—at least I was, and I thought you were too." When she tried to look away from him, he reached out and touched her chin, gently forcing her to face him. "Don't shut me out. Talk to me."

"I—I can't." Tears sprang to her eyes.

At the sight of her sorrow, he wanted to grab her in his arms. But he resisted the urge. Embracing her now would either scare her or put her off, and he didn't want either. What he wanted was for her to share her burden, whatever it was, with him. "Miriam, please."

She slid her finger underneath the right lens of her glasses and wiped her damp eye. "Just take me home, Seth."

"*Nee*. I'm not taking you anywhere until you explain yourself. You promised me you'd be honest. Now's the time to honor that promise."

Rivulets of moisture flowed down her cheeks, each drop piercing his heart like a shard of glass. "Please," she said. "Just take me home."

He grasped her shoulders, thankful for her sake they had parked at the far end of the lot and were secluded from any passersby. "Miriam," he said softly, trying to reassure her. "You can tell me anything. I just want to help you." Unable to resist, he took her face in his hands, wiping her tears with his thumbs. "Trust me. That's all I ask. Just trust me."

⸎

Seth's hands were so warm, his touch so gentle that she thought she might melt in a puddle right there in front of him. The lights illuminating the parking lot were strong enough that she could see his face clearly. She read the sincerity in his eyes. But something still held her back.

"Don't be afraid, Miriam," he said, his thumbs grazing her cheeks again. "I said I wanted to help you fight whatever you're scared of. I meant those words."

She put her hands over his and removed them from her face. "Seth, why are you pushing so hard?" Turning from his embrace, she put her back to him. "Why are you even bothering with me?"

She felt the heavy weight of his hands on her shoulders. "You want to know why?" He let out a heavy sigh as he guided her to face him. "I've been lying to you, Miriam. I should have been honest with you from the beginning."

Fresh tears sprouted from her eyes. This was an awful, confusing mess, and she didn't understand any of it. "You want me to trust you, but now you're telling me you lied?"

"I'm telling you I lied so you *can* trust me. Miriam, we can't be friends. That's the absolute truth."

Closing her eyes against the words, she swallowed. "I see."

"*Nee*, you don't." He dropped his hands from her shoulders, then rubbed his hand over his face. "I care for you, Miriam. A lot. And *not* as a friend." He leaned down until he was looking her straight in the eye. "Do you understand what I'm saying? When I'm not with you, I'm thinking about you, and wishing we were together."

Her eyes widened. "You are?"

"*Ya*, I am."

This still seemed beyond her ken. "But why? There are so many other *maed* you would be better . . . " She bit her bottom lip.

"Better what?"

"Better suited for." There, she said it out loud.

"Better suited?" He scoffed. "I can't think of a single *maedel* I'd rather be with than you."

"You say that now, but what about next week? Or the week after that?" She pushed up her glasses. A chill entered her bones, but she wasn't convinced it was totally due to the frigid weather. "Seth, you've been through a lot. You say you've changed, and I see that you have. But just because you want to have *demut* doesn't mean you have to be with an ugly duck like me."

"Is that what you think? Miriam, you are so wrong."

He moved closer to her, but she stepped away. She couldn't handle being near him. It made what she had to say next that much harder. "Think about what your friends will say when they see us together. You don't think they'll ask you why you settled for something less than you deserved?"

He grabbed her shoulders again. "*Stop* this! I don't care one whit about what anyone else thinks about me, or about us. Miriam, here's another bit of honesty. I've dated a lot of girls. A *lot*."

"That's supposed to make me feel better?"

"Just let me finish. I'll admit those girls were beautiful on the outside. But inside, they left much to be desired. Then I met you. Again." He stepped toward her, his eyes glistening. "You showed me what true beauty is. It's what's in here." His hand covered his heart. "You're so full of beauty inside it overflows. You might not be able to see it, but I can." He touched her face, then cradled her cheek in his hand before drawing her into a kiss.

Shock coursed through her as his lips caressed hers, at first insistently, then with such gentleness it made her cry. Her arms automatically went around his waist as the tears flowed down, wetting both their cheeks. He pulled away for a moment, only to press his lips to hers once again.

Finally, he broke the contact. "It's me who doesn't deserve you," he said, sounding breathless.

She fought to catch her own breath. His kiss had washed away every doubt she had.

He slowly slid off her tearstained glasses. "Do you understand now?"

She nodded, unable to speak.

"Miriam, you are so beautiful to me. And I will always think that, no matter what anyone else says." He wiped her cheek with the back of her hand. "Do you believe me?"

"I—I want to."

"Well, that's a start." He grinned and replaced her glasses. "I'll spend every day showing you how much you mean to me, Miriam Herschberger, until you do believe it."

"But Seth," she whispered. "What if I can't? I've never

been as self-confident as you."

He took her hand in his. "Then we'll find our way together."

Her heart soared. "Are you saying you want to date?"

He looked up to the sky. "Finally, she gets it." Looking back at her, he said, "*Ya*, I want to court you. As soon as possible. What are you doing on First Christmas?"

She smiled. "The same thing you are. I'm going to the Fishers' house."

"*Sehr gut*. Can I offer you a ride, then? I think I know where you live." He chuckled. Leaning in close to her, so close she thought he might kiss her again, he said, "Just remember that I won't take *nee* for an answer."

Miriam hesitated, looking into Seth's handsome face. His tender words and gentle kiss were almost too good to believe. But she had to believe. Not only in him, but in herself. She suspected the journey wouldn't be easy, but with Seth by her side, and with lots of help from the Lord, it was one she was willing to take.

Chapter Fourteen

MIRIAM PULLED BACK THE CURTAIN AND PEERED OUTSIDE IN THE darkness. It was First Christmas, and she was at home, waiting for Seth to pick her up. Just thinking about him brought a smile to her face. Touching her lips, she remembered his kiss. They had seen each other one time since, but he had been a perfect gentleman, not even kissing her on the cheek when he brought her home from work last night. But she saw in his eyes that he wanted to kiss her, just as badly as she wanted him to. Knowing that was enough.

Her hand went to her stomach, trying to calm the butterflies that were steadily growing there. The news that she and Seth Fisher had started dating had run quickly through her family, who had all given their approval—especially Lydia.

"See, I was right about you going to that singin'," she had said. "You should listen to me more often."

When she saw Seth's buggy pull into her driveway, Miriam dropped the curtain and retrieved her cloak. Her parents were already at the Fishers', so she turned off the gas lamp and stepped out on the front porch, using a small battery-powered flashlight to illuminate her steps. Feather-light drops of moisture landed on her skin, and she realized it had just started snowing.

Seth came out of the buggy and walked toward her. She noticed there was something different about him right off. Then she realized what it was as he neared the house. "Where's your walking stick?"

"Don't need it. Are you ready to go?"

She nodded and walked in step with him. He opened the door to the buggy and helped her in, then entered on the other side. But instead of grasping Gravy's reins, he just sat there.

"Is something wrong?" she asked, a tiny thread of alarm winding through her.

"*Nee.* Nothing's wrong."

Then she realized the buggy had an extra light inside, making it easier to see the interior, along with being able to see him. Curious, she said, "It's brighter in here tonight."

"*Ya.* There's a reason for that." He pulled a small rectangular package out of his pocket. "I wanted to see your face when I gave you this." It was wrapped in brown paper, with a silver bow on top. He held it out to her. "*Frehlicher Grischtdaag.*"

Slowly she took the gift from him. "Merry Christmas to you." She flushed. "I'm sorry, but I didn't get you anything."

"You're present enough for me."

She rolled her eyes. "That's laying it on a bit thick, don't you think?"

He laughed. "Sorry, it's a habit. Go ahead, open it."

She removed the silver bow, then carefully unwrapped the paper. Inside the package was a tiny wooden chest, a small replica of a large one. The letter *M* had been burned into the lid, along with dainty ivy leaves. The entire thing had been stained and lacquered to a smooth sheen.

"It's beautiful," she said, running her finger over the grooves in the *M*. "Did you make it?"

"*Ya.* That's why I was late the other night picking you up. I was working on it in *Daed*'s shop, and time got away from me. It isn't much. Most of my money from now on is going toward paying back the community for taking care of my medical bills." He took her hand and looked at her. "But I want you to know that someday, as soon as I'm able, I'm going to make you the real thing. You'll have a beautiful hope chest fit to hold your grand-mother's quilts."

"Oh, Seth." She squeezed his hand, barely able to believe she could be this happy.

He grinned. "Ready to go?"

"*Ya,*" she said. "I'm ready." And she wasn't just referring to going to the Fishers' to celebrate the birth of the one true King. Instead of hiding in the past, she was ready to face her future, with Seth, God willing.

She had always thought having Seth Fisher in her life would take a miracle. As she glanced at his profile, she realized that the Lord, in his merciful grace, had given her just that.

A Place of
His Own

To Trish,
my everlasting friend.

Chapter One

"AMANDA, THOMAS PINCHED ME!"

"I don't wike peas."

"*Waaaah!*"

Amanda Graber surveyed the chaos swirling in the kitchen as she tried to get supper on the table and corral her six much younger brothers and sisters. None of them were cooperating.

"Thomas, leave Andrew alone." She set down a warm loaf of freshly baked bread in the center of the long oak table. "Christopher, you only have to eat four peas. You can manage that." She bent down and picked up her youngest sibling, Jacob, kissing the small red mark where he had bumped his forehead when he fell on the kitchen floor. "All better?"

He nodded, then sniffed.

Amanda wiped two big teardrops from underneath his large blue eyes, then handed him to Rachel. "Put Jacob in his high chair," she said, giving the tot a quick tap on his chubby cheek. She leaned against the counter and wiped her damp forehead with the back of her hand despite the cool fall breeze wafting through the open window.

The clip-clop of their father's horse and buggy reached her ears. Turning to Andrew and Thomas, she said, "*Daed*'s home. Please go outside and help him with the horse. And, Thomas, no more pinching!"

Twenty minutes later everyone, including *Mamm*, settled down to eat. Amanda placed a bowl of steaming mashed and buttered potatoes on the table, then took her place next to her sister Hannah.

Daed cleared his throat, the signal for everyone to quiet down and bow their heads.

Amanda listened and prayed along as her father blessed the meal. After saying amen, she sat back and watched her family pile their plates with the food she'd prepared for supper. Thick slices of meat loaf and the vegetables, along with bread and butter, quickly disappeared from the serving dishes.

"Amanda?"

She turned at the sound of her mother's voice. *"Ya, Mamm?"*

"Aren't you going to eat?" Dark shadows underscored Katharine Graber's brown eyes.

"*Ya*, I'll have something in a minute." She regarded her mother for a moment. "Are you feeling all right?"

"I'm feeling fine. Just a little tired."

Amanda glanced at her mother again before looking at the empty white plate in front of her. Lately her mother had seemed more than a little tired, and she couldn't help but worry about her. As she neared the end of her pregnancy, her *mamm* seemed to be having a more difficult time with this baby than she'd had with the other ones. Amanda silently prayed for both her mother and the unborn child's safety.

Mamm gave her a weary smile. "Everything looks and smells delicious, Mandy. *Danki* for making supper tonight. I don't know what I'd do without you."

Amanda smiled back. She enjoyed cooking, just as she enjoyed taking care of her brothers and sisters. Sure, they were a handful, but they were also a lot of fun and brought tremendous joy to her life. Some of her friends complained about having to care for younger siblings, but not Amanda. As an only child until the age of fourteen, she had always longed for a brother or sister. Now that she had them, she counted them as blessings. She was twenty-four, plenty old enough to be thinking about a family of her own. And while she stood only five-foot-three and possessed a thin frame, she hoped she would follow in her mother's footsteps and have a large brood of her own, God willing.

Although a couple of young men had shown interest in her, Amanda had yet to meet the one she wanted to marry. One man in particular, Peter Yoder, didn't seem to get the message. Each time he asked her to a singing or expressed an interest in courting her, Amanda firmly told him no. Still he doggedly pursued her.

God would bring the right man into her life. Until then, she kept her focus on helping her mother with the younger children.

"*Sehr gut, Dochder.*" David Graber shoveled a forkful of mashed potato and meat loaf into his mouth, then wiped his brown beard with a napkin. Threads of gray were starting to show through, but her father still looked several years younger than forty-four, and acted at least a decade younger than that.

"Yuck." Christopher picked up a green pea and made a face.

"Christopher." *Daed* gave the boy one of his infrequent stern looks. "Mandy went to a lot of trouble to make us a *wunderbaar* supper. Eat your peas without complaint."

Frowning, Christopher nodded, then put the pea in his mouth and chewed, wrinkling his nose.

Daed remarked that business was booming at Yoder's Lumber, where he worked as a sawyer and foreman. Being in charge of the first shift of workers, he made very good pay. "God has blessed me, Katharine," he said, looking at his wife, then panning his gaze over his family before returning to her. "He has blessed us all."

Taking in the tender look her parents exchanged, Amanda sent up another silent prayer of thanks for her father's job and for being a part of such a wonderful family. Even though they sometimes fought among each other and life didn't always run smoothly, they were all satisfied and happy.

"Rachel, please clear the table," *Mamm* said after everyone finished eating. "Hannah, it's your turn to wash the dishes. Andrew can help you dry."

"Aww." Andrew scowled. "That's women's work."

"*Nee*, it's not just women's work." *Daed* shoved away from the table. "And for that remark, *mei sohn*, you can dry the dishes for the rest of the week." He rose from the table, tapped Andrew lightly on his sandy blond head with his fingertips, then ruffled Christopher's dark brown hair. "I'm sure the animals are hungry by now. Thomas, come with me."

They left the kitchen to go to the barnyard and feed the family's six pigs and three cows, which would be slaughtered in a couple weeks to provide the family with more than enough meat for the following year. They would share the extra with other families in the community.

Andrew continued to scowl, but he scampered from his chair and headed to the sink to do his assigned chore.

Mamm rose from her chair, picked up a napkin, and wiped mashed potatoes from Jacob's face. "*Danki* again, Amanda. You may be excused."

With a nod Amanda rose and headed upstairs to her room. Her mother and father would put the younger children to bed with Rachel and Hannah's help, leaving Amanda free to do whatever she wanted. Usually in the evening she worked on her sewing, making Amish dresses, lightweight spring coats, and shawls to sell at Eli's Country Store and Dry Goods just outside Paradise. Sometimes she read, and during the warm spring and summer evenings, she liked to go outside to walk, pray, and be alone. After a busy afternoon watching her siblings and making dinner, she definitely needed to spend some time with the Lord.

She paused and looked out the window of her bedroom, her reflection obscuring the view outside. Noticing the awkward tilt of her white *kapp*, she straightened it, then adjusted one of the bobby pins holding it in place against her light brown hair. She pushed open the window, allowing the fresh evening air into her stuffy room.

As she looked around her family's property, she again thanked the Lord for His abundant blessings. Her parents had purchased the house and its attached five acres when Amanda was two years old. Their barn sat to the left of the house, set back about two hundred yards. There they kept the pigs and cows and their two horses. A wooden play set, complete with a slide and three swings, was situated closer to the house. Three acres beyond that were woods, where Amanda and her friend and only neighbor, Josiah, used to play when they were young.

She sighed as Josiah's image came to her mind. She had thought of him often over the years, since he'd moved away a decade ago at the age of fourteen. He'd been an only child, as she was for so long, and the two of them had spent nearly all of their time together, hiking in the woods, building forts, and sometimes, to Josiah's great misery, playing house. Amanda smiled at the memory. Josiah had been a nice boy, and even though she knew he hated pretending they were married, he went along with it every once in a while.

Then when he turned thirteen, his *mamm* had died. What a horrible day, not only for him but for the community. Emma Bontrager had been a sweet woman, beloved by many. After her death things had changed. Amanda didn't see Josiah as much, and when she did there was an underlying sadness in his green eyes that never completely disappeared.

Then one day he was gone. There had been no explanation, no good-bye. She had waited for him at their special place in the woods, a small clearing where they had often played. He never showed up. That evening, when her parents told her Josiah and his father had moved away, she had burst into tears. How could he leave without telling her? Without even saying good-bye? It had taken her a long time to get over his leaving.

She often thought about him. Was he married? Did he have any children? Had he even stayed in the Amish faith? She prayed that wherever he was, he had found the happiness he deserved.

"Amanda? Would you read me a story?"

She turned around to see Christopher standing in the doorway, clutching his favorite book to his chest with both hands. From the way he kept looking over his shoulder, she had a feeling he had sneaked upstairs without their mother's knowing. If she had, she would have called him back down to the family room and told him to leave Amanda alone for the evening.

Smiling, she went and knelt in front of him. She plucked the book out of his hands and turned it over, glancing at the orange and green cover. "Aren't you tired of hearing this one?"

He shook his head. "'I do not like green eggs and ham,'" he quoted. "'I do not like them, Sam I am.' You know, Mandy, I don't like green eggs and ham neither. They look yucky."

"You don't like any food that's green, Christopher." Laughing, she grasped his hand and led him downstairs to the bedroom he shared with Andrew and Thomas. "You know what," she whispered to him a few moments later as she sat on the edge of his bed and settled him on her lap. "I don't think I'd like them either."

❦

Josiah Bontrager gripped the horse's reins until his knuckles turned white. He fought an onslaught of memories as he stared at the decrepit house before him, a house he hadn't seen since he'd left Paradise ten years earlier. Long curls of white paint stuck out from the siding and littered the surrounding tall, brownish grass. A crack ran down the middle of one window, and he spied a couple of missing panes. The porch that spanned the front of the house tilted, and he suspected there were more problems with it than splintered boards. A decade of neglect loomed before him.

He loosened his grip on the reins and guided the used buggy—new to him, along with the horse—onto the rut-ridden dirt driveway. When he glimpsed the barn behind the house, he groaned. It was in even worse shape than the house. He took off his hat and ran his fingers through his sweat-dampened hair. Why had he bothered to come back here?

But he already knew the answer. He'd returned to Paradise because he'd had no choice. Even now he wanted to turn around, take what little money he had, and head for Holmes County, Ohio. No one knew him there. A perfect place for him to start over, to leave this mess and the pain of the past behind. But he couldn't do that just yet. He couldn't ignore this place any longer, although God knew he'd tried many times over the years.

The horse whinnied, signaling her hunger to Josiah. He steered the mare toward the entrance of the barn. After he jumped out of the buggy, he stroked the horse's brown nose, then dragged the sliding door open. The musty, stale scent of old hay and decaying manure hit him full force. He walked into the dim, cool barn, autumn sunlight spilling through the open slats and holes in the weathered wood. Everything remained as he remembered, though covered with cobwebs and dust.

He spied the back corner of the barn, his gut tightening. Unwilling to fully contemplate the memories of what had happened there, he scanned the rest of the structure, focusing on the list of things he would have to do to get the barn and the house back in shape. Anything to keep his mind off the past.

The horse whinnied again, and he moved to take care of her. He went to one of the three stalls and found an upended, rusty metal tub. Not the most sanitary water container, but it would have to do until he bought a new one. Flipping the tub over, he set about preparing the stall so the horse would have a fairly decent place to spend the night.

Thirty minutes later he had filled the tub with fresh water from the pump. The water had been rust-colored at first, but once he'd let it run awhile, it had turned clear. He also turned over the matted-down hay and poured a small bag of feed into the trough. Tomorrow he would pick up fresh hay, paint, and a few other things he needed to get started on the repairs. The sooner he finished, the sooner he could leave.

He watched the good-natured mare as she munched on her feed, apparently indifferent to her less-than-ideal surroundings. "You're a *gut* girl," he said, though he missed his old horse, Patches. He wished he could have brought the gelding with him, but he had no way to transport the animal. Everything about coming back to Paradise had been hard. He'd been a fool to think it could be otherwise.

The sun had already set, and he needed to get things set up in the house. Making his way through nearly waist-high grass, he reached the two concrete steps leading to the back door. He yanked on the screen door and nearly stumbled backward when the rusted metal frame immediately separated from its hinges. Grimacing, he tossed the door to the side, and it hit the side of the house with a dull clang. Tomorrow morning he would fix it. He pushed open the solid wood door, not surprised to find it unlocked, and stepped inside the dark kitchen. As his eyes adjusted to the darkness, he saw the shadow of the old battery-operated lamp his mother had always kept on the counter. No use turning it on; he knew the batteries would be dead by now. He'd put new ones in the lamp in the morning.

Using his flashlight, Josiah guided himself to his old bedroom upstairs. All he wanted was a decent night's rest. He was too tired to do much else.

But as he continued to inhale the stale yet familiar smell of his childhood home, he wished he were too tired to feel.

∽◯∽

Amanda finished reading to Christopher and tucked him into bed. Then she ran back upstairs to her room and grabbed a flashlight before leaving the house, prepared to enjoy the pleasant October evening. The sun had just dipped past the horizon, bathing the sky with pale swaths of color. Taking a deep breath as she stood on the back stoop, she inhaled the sweet scents of grass and freshly cut hay and the pungent odor of livestock.

Something soft and furry brushed against her legs. She glanced down to see Lucy, their pregnant calico cat, weaving around her ankles. "How are you, sweetheart?" she said, bending down to scratch behind the cat's ears. Lucy starred to purr, but another sound interrupted the cat's contentment, making her perk up her ears.

Amanda stilled her hand and listened. "I hear it too." The sound recurred. A horse's whinny. Soft, and sounding far away. "Probably Jack," Amanda said, rising to a standing position. She pulled her plain navy blue sweater closer to her body. Sometimes her father's horse had trouble settling in for the night, so she decided to go check on him.

She went to the barn and slid open the door. The pigs jumped up immediately, all snorting at the same time, even though her father had fed them little more than an hour ago. The cows lowed but didn't move toward her, content to chew their cuds.

"*Nee*, I have nothing for you," she said, laughing at their eagerness. She walked over to the horse stalls. Nelly and Jack both seemed all right. As she nuzzled Jack's gray nose, the pigs settled down and stopped their grunting. She had just turned to give Nelly some attention when she heard it again.

Another whinny. Louder and more urgent. Confused, Amanda walked out of the barn and listened again. By this time the sky had darkened considerably. She flicked on her flashlight and listened again. A third whinny broke through the silence. Turning, she realized it came from the Bontragers' barn. Her brow furrowed. The old building had been abandoned for a decade. How did a horse get inside?

She looked in the direction of Josiah's barn, and a wave of sadness washed over her, as it normally did when she saw the poor state of both barn and house. Theirs and the Bontragers' were the only two homes on their small road, and for a while after Josiah and his *daed* moved away, her father tried to keep the place up. He mowed the lawn, fixed a shutter when it blew off during a particularly strong thunderstorm, and generally tried to maintain the property. But the demands of his own growing family made it difficult for him to work on both properties. No one knew where the Bontragers had gone, and no one had heard from them after they left. They had just disappeared.

Amanda walked to the barn, determined to find the horse. The tall grass whipped against her bare calves and ankles, both tickling and scratching her skin. When she reached the shabby building, she hesitated for a moment, waiting to hear the whinny again. The only thing she heard was the faint sound of crickets chirping. With fall in full swing, their night music would soon fade away during the cooler evenings.

Maybe she was hearing things. She was about to turn around when she heard a rustling movement coming from the inside. Her curiosity getting the best of her, Amanda grabbed the rusty handle of the door and pulled. The door slid open with surprising ease, considering it hadn't been used for such a long time. The cloying odor of moldy hay hit her immediately.

She shined her flashlight around the nearly pitch dark barn. Cobwebs covered the corners and walls, and in the right corner she saw a short wooden stool lying on its side and the black outline of a horse whip resting next to it. Shifting the light over to the other side of the barn, she saw the stall. Sure enough, a horse stood inside it. Puzzled, she took a few steps forward.

Then someone grabbed her shoulder.

She screamed and spun around.

Chapter Two

JOSIAH NEARLY JUMPED OUT OF HIS SKIN AS THE WOMAN'S shriek pierced the air. He dropped his hand from her shoulder, then shielded his face when she pointed the flashlight directly in his eyes.

"Who are you?" she asked, sounding breathless.

He shut his eyes against the blinding light. "I should ask you the same thing. What are you doing in my barn?"

"*Your* barn? Listen, I don't know who you are, but this property belongs to the Bontragers. You're trespassing."

"Look, can you put down the light?"

She complied, and Josiah dropped his hands.

"*Danki.*" Green and yellow spots danced in front of him, rendering him sightless for a moment. But his relief was short-lived when she shined the light in his face again.

"Josiah?"

It was a soft, familiar voice. His heart tripped as he groped for the flashlight and plucked it from her hand.

"Hey, that's mine! What are you doing?"

"Keeping you from blinding me, that's what." He shined the light on her, although not directly in her face. When he got a good look at the woman standing in front of him, he nearly lost his breath. "Mandy? Is that you?"

"*Ya.*" Her full lips slanted upward in a smile that lit up her entire face. "Oh, Josiah! I can't believe you're here!"

He almost lost his footing when she threw her arms around him. The top of her head brushed against his stubbly chin, and he inhaled the sweet scent of her hair, neatly secured beneath a white prayer *kapp*. When her cheek touched his chest, all the air pushed out of his lungs. He wasn't prepared for this or for his reaction to her nearness. He hadn't thought he'd see her so soon after his arrival. He wished he didn't have to see her at all. Yet his body betrayed his thoughts, and his arms automatically started to go around her slight frame until she stepped away and slapped his arm.

"Hey!" he said. She had just hugged him, after all. "What was that for?"

"Scaring me to death. You shouldn't sneak up on people like that."

"And you shouldn't be snooping around someone else's property." He held the flashlight at an angle so he could see her face without aiming the light directly on her.

"I heard a noise. I wanted to see what was going on."

"That wasn't very smart of you. You don't know who could have been hiding in here."

"Well, I certainly wasn't expecting *you*." She crossed her arms. "I thought you'd disappeared completely."

He only wished that were true. "*Nee*. I came back."

"I see that." She tilted her head in the direction of the mare's stall. "I heard your horse whinnying. Is he all right?"

"*She* should be fine." He shined the light toward the stall. Everything seemed in order. "Probably getting used to her surroundings." He could certainly relate. He looked back at Amanda. "She's okay."

"*Gut*."

They stood there for a moment in the dark barn as he held her small flashlight between them. The light cast her face in shadows, but he could still make out her features. She had changed a lot since he'd last seen her, when they were both fourteen. Even then she had been pretty, a fact that had struck him full force the year he turned twelve. But the word hardly did her justice now. Her eyes were large and round, her nose small and pert, and her lips full and lovely. Unable to help himself, he took in the rest of her slender frame, immediately noticing she had become a beautiful woman.

He turned away, not liking one bit the unstoppable attraction flowing through him. Despite his efforts, he'd never gotten over his boyhood crush, one he had kept a secret from everyone, especially her. Even at that time he knew he was tainted.

"Josiah?" she said, stepping toward him. She put her hand on his arm. "Please don't be upset with me. I'm sorry. You're right, I shouldn't have been snooping. I didn't mean to make you mad."

Now that was the Amanda he remembered. A people pleaser through and through, always worried about other people's feelings, never wanting them to be uncomfortable or, God forbid, angry.

He looked at her, eager to give reassurance. "It's all right, Mandy. I reckon I should have let your parents know I was here. Didn't mean to scare you, either."

She grinned, and his heart skipped several beats. *Not a good sign.*

Slipping her arm through his, she guided him away from the stall. "You must come over and see them right now. I know they'll be happy to see you, just as I am. Your father can come too."

"He's not here."

"Oh. Is he coming later?"

"*Nee.*"

"Okay. Well, then you can tell us where you've been all these years." She looked up at him. "I'm dying to know."

But he wasn't dying to tell her. In fact, he didn't want to explain anything to her or her parents or anyone else in Paradise. But that wasn't realistic. People would have questions, and they would want answers. He would tell them a few things, enough to satisfy their curiosity, but no more than that. Better to let the past stay buried.

He glanced down at her arm in his. Amanda had always been demonstrative, a stark contrast to many of the Amish, who were much more reserved. Her walking arm in arm with him seemed so natural, just as it had when they were kids. His life in Paradise up until the day his mother died had been carefree and happy, and Amanda Graber had a lot to do with that.

"I made chocolate chip cookies yesterday," she said as they exited the barn. "We can have some cookies and milk and catch up on old times."

Reluctantly he stepped away from her. "*Nee*, I can't. Not tonight."

Disappointment seeped into her eyes. "Then maybe tomorrow. I'll let *daed* know you're here. I'm sure he'll want to talk to you."

He nodded, remaining noncommittal. "It's been a long day, and I just got here a couple hours ago."

"Of course. I'm sure you had a long trip from . . ." She hesitated. When he didn't respond, she simply shrugged and smiled. "Josiah, I'm so glad you came back home." Whirling around, she started to walk away, then called over her shoulder, "See you tomorrow!"

He watched as she headed for her house, a house nearly as familiar to him as his own. The glow of gas lamps burned like welcome beacons through several of the windows on the bottom floor. He'd spent many hours inside, sharing lunches and dinners with Amanda and her parents, who treated him like their own child.

For the first time since he'd stepped back in Paradise, his mind opened to the pleasant memories from his childhood. His life hadn't always been a living nightmare.

Only after Amanda had gone inside did he glance down and realize he still held her flashlight. He thought about returning it. He could imagine her inviting him inside and his being enveloped by the warmth of a family who cared about each other and also cared about him. His soul ached for that, yet he knew he would never have it. He couldn't. Just like he couldn't walk the hundred yards or so to Amanda's house. Not tonight.

Because if he did, he would never want to leave.

∽

Amanda practically floated up the stairs to her bedroom. She couldn't believe Josiah Bontrager had come back to Paradise! She also couldn't

KATHLEEN FULLER

believe how much he had changed. Her last memories of Josiah were of a scrawny boy who had a crackly voice and was at least three inches shorter than she.

He certainly wasn't that scrawny boy anymore. Josiah had grown into a tall, fit man with a deep, smooth voice she could listen to all day. Even in the low light of her flashlight, she could see how handsome he'd become.

Her flashlight. She had forgotten to get it back from him. For a brief moment she considered walking back to retrieve it, but she decided not to. He seemed eager to go inside his house. He looked tired, weary even, and she didn't want to bother him again. Besides, she would see him tomorrow. Then she'd not only get her flashlight back but find out where he had been all these years.

Slipping the bobby pins out of her *kapp*, she removed it and laid it on her dresser, then opened the drawer and pulled out her nightgown. She had her own room, another added benefit to being so much older than her siblings. Small, but the perfect size. She didn't need much space.

After she put on her nightgown, she knelt beside her bed and said her evening prayers. Once she finished, she slipped between the cool sheets and pulled the green-and-white basket-patterned quilt over her body. Despite the fatigue from putting in a long day of work, helping her *mamm* with the children and chores, she still couldn't get Josiah out of her mind.

Obviously he had changed physically, but she sensed something else different about him, something intangible and mysterious. She smiled in the darkness. Tomorrow she would find out exactly what that was. She rolled on her side and hugged the extra pillow she couldn't sleep without, Josiah Bontrager still filling her mind.

❦

"Josiah Bontrager's back," Amanda announced as she bounced into the kitchen the next morning.

Her *mamm* paused as she pulled nine white plates out of the cabinet, a surprised expression on her face. "He is?"

"*Ya*." Amanda took the plates from her *mamm* and started setting the table. "Last night while I was outside, I heard a sound coming from the Bontragers' barn. When I went inside, I saw a horse in one of the stalls."

"Really?"

"*Ya*. Then Josiah came up behind me. Practically scared me to death at first, but I was so happy to see him I didn't care."

"You shouldn't be nosing around someone else's property, Amanda. Especially by yourself." *Mamm* gave her a somber look as she cracked an egg into a skillet on top of the propane stove.

Amanda smirked. "He said the same thing."

Rachel yawned as she entered the room with Hannah. "Who's 'he'?"

"Josiah." At that point the kitchen filled with children, some wide awake and full of energy, others still dragging. Amanda scooped up Jacob in her arms before Thomas accidentally trampled him.

"Who's Josiah?" Hannah asked.

"The young man who used to live next door."

"You mean someone actually lived there?" Andrew said. "In that dump?"

"Thomas, come butter the toast," *Mamm* said, scooping the fried eggs onto a platter. "Andrew, that's not nice. Josiah and his *daed* moved away nine years ago."

"Ten," Amanda corrected, helping her younger siblings get settled at the table. "Josiah moved away ten years ago, *Mamm*."

Just as she went to pick up the platter of cooked eggs, her father walked into the room, pulling his black suspenders over his shoulders. "Did I hear you mention Josiah?"

Amanda grinned. "*Ya, Daed*. He's back. Came in sometime yesterday."

Daed looked at her. "How do you know that?"

"I saw him last night. For just a few minutes."

"Was he alone?"

"David," *Mamm* said in a low voice.

Amanda didn't miss the look that passed between her parents, but she thought she should answer her father's question. "I think so. He didn't say anything about his *daed*."

Daed nodded and sat down at the table.

When everyone finished eating and her father left for work, Amanda picked up Jacob out of his high chair. "I invited Josiah over, *Mamm*. I thought you would like to see him again."

"Hannah, it's your turn to clear the table." *Mamm* looked up at Amanda as Hannah began to remove the dirty dishes. "Of course I want to see him. So would *Daed*. He was like a *sohn* to us, and a brother to you."

Amanda's face reddened. What would her mother say if she knew that last night her thoughts about Josiah Bontrager had been anything but sisterly?

"When is he coming over?" *Mamm* asked, slowly rising from the chair. She laid her hand over her swollen belly.

"I don't know."

Jacob squirmed in Amanda's grasp, and she set him down, watching him as he toddled over to the living room to the large toy box in the corner. Flipping open the lid, he bent over, his head disappearing inside the box as he searched for his toys.

"Josiah didn't say. We didn't talk very much. He seemed pretty tired. I thought I might take some lunch over to him, if we don't see him before then."

"I'm sure he would appreciate it. Now, if you could start the wash for me, Amanda . . . It's such a nice, breezy day. The clothes should dry quickly on the line. Get Rachel to help you."

Amanda nodded and searched for Rachel. She found her sister swinging outside while Andrew and Thomas chased each other into the woods. As she breathed in the fresh spring air and let the warmth of the sun seep into her skin, she agreed with her *mamm*. The Lord had blessed them with a beautiful day. Before long autumn would end and winter would set in, and days like this would be a memory.

An hour later she and Rachel were putting the second load of laundry on the line that stretched between the house and the barn, when she saw Josiah emerge from his house. He stood on the back stoop and leaned backward, stretching. She couldn't help but stare at him. Even though he stood some distance away, she could see him clearly enough, more clearly than she had in the dim light of the barn last night. He didn't have his hat on, and she took in his hair—thick, brown, and wavy, with coppery, sun-streaked highlights. A little long for the traditional Amish hairstyle, but she didn't mind. In fact, she liked it that way, noticing how the ends brushed a little past the top of his shirt collar.

A light breeze rustled the colorful leaves of the oak trees surrounding Josiah's property, causing a few to release and flutter to the ground. The movement lifted a couple of locks of his hair. Amanda squeezed the light blue dress she held in her hands.

"Mandy, are you gonna hang up that dress or what?"

Amanda looked at her sister, who held up a damp pair of Christopher's small trousers. Quickly she clipped the dress to the line and took the trousers, all the while unable to keep her gaze off Josiah. They had been the best of friends, and now he'd come back into her life after all this time. No wonder she couldn't get enough of looking at him.

As she finished hanging the wash, she peered over the line of clothes and watched Josiah heading for the barn. Disappointment threaded through her when he didn't even look in the direction of their house. Hadn't he heard Rachel and her talking? If he had, he must be purposely ignoring them, and she didn't know what to make of that. He had never ignored her before.

Josiah disappeared into the barn and emerged with his horse a few moments later. He led the horse to the buggy parked next to the barn and hitched it up. As Amanda hung the last item of clothing, he jumped into the buggy and steered it down the dirt driveway.

"Is that Josiah?" Rachel asked, turning around to see the buggy turn onto the road and disappear in the distance.

Amanda ducked underneath the line. "*Ya*, that's Josiah."

"Were you two friends?"

"We were *sehr gut* friends," Amanda said, remembering that her sister was just days old when Josiah left.

"Are you still?"

She looked at Rachel. Doubt pressed at her, but she shoved it away. Their encounter in the barn had been awkward. Maybe it would take time for Josiah to pick up where their friendship had left off. While she had several good friends and many acquaintances, no one had ever taken Josiah's place.

"*Ya*," she said, grabbing the laundry basket and motioning for Rachel to follow her. "We're still friends."

Chapter Three

"As I live and breathe," Josiah's Aunt Vera said, slowly rising from her kneeling position at the back edge of her almost completely harvested garden. She wiped her hands on her apron and walked toward him, then placed a soft, wrinkled hand on each side of his face. "Josiah." Tears filled her brown eyes. "I didn't think I'd ever see you again, *kind*."

He smiled, and the knot that had formed in his stomach as he drove to his aunt and uncle's house loosened a tiny bit. After finishing up in town and making a stop at his mother's gravesite, he'd decided at the last minute to stop by Vera and John Yoder's home on his way back from town. He had spent a lot of his childhood here.

"You look like your *mamm*," Aunt Vera said, swiping a thick finger underneath her lower lashes. "Heavens, I miss my sister. It's *gut* to have you back, Josiah." She drew him to her and enveloped him in her fleshy arms, then released him. "John's in the shop. I'm sure he'll be just as excited to see you. *Geh*, and I'll bring you some fresh iced tea."

"*Danki*," Josiah said, then left the expansive front porch and walked around the back of the house to his uncle's buggy and harness shop. Glancing around at the well-kept property with its large white house, barn, huge storage shed, and attached shop, he realized not much had changed here. The Yoders' property remained in its usual pristine condition. Not a single leaf or twig could be found on the black asphalt driveway that connected all three buildings, which were surrounded by perfectly manicured grass. A stab of envy went through him. Even when things hadn't been so bad at home, his family's property had never looked like this.

The knot in his stomach re-formed as he approached the door to the shop. He hoped his uncle would react with the same welcoming attitude as his aunt, but he couldn't be sure.

As he pulled open the door, the familiar tinkle of the bell above the door frame rang out. He scanned the room, which, like everything else he'd seen since his return, seemed to stand still in time. The shop had two sections. He stood in the front "office" where his uncle and cousin dealt with customers and showed them pictures of buggies and samples of paint, leather, and upholstery fabric. In the larger back room, secluded from the public, the buggies and harnesses were made.

The office was empty, and Josiah assumed they were all working in the back. He walked over to a small counter and ran his hand over the binder that held the pictures of his uncle's handiwork. Flipping it over, he glanced at the photos of a variety of Amish buggies, memories once again flooding over him. He recalled the times he had been allowed to help his uncle in the shop.

"Can I help you?"

Josiah looked up to see a tall, broad-shouldered young man walk into the office, wiping black grease off his hands with an old rag. The man's blue eyes narrowed. Josiah stood face-to-face with his cousin Peter, the one person in Paradise he knew for sure wouldn't welcome him back.

Peter's expression reflected the wariness Josiah felt. "What are you doing here?" Peter asked, tossing the rag on the counter. "We all thought you were gone for *gut*."

"Nice to see you too." Josiah held his temper, not an easy thing to do since there was no love lost between the two cousins. As far back as he could remember, Peter had seemed to resent him. Apparently time hadn't softened those feelings.

"Peter, do you need some—"

Josiah focused his attention on the man who entered the room. The short, stocky Amish man held his gaze for a moment before his face broke into a wide grin. "Josiah!" He crossed the room and wrapped his nephew in a big hug.

The knot of tension completely released as he embraced his uncle.

Uncle John stepped away, his gaze taking in Josiah from head to toe. His smile remained in place, causing deep crinkles to form around his light blue eyes, eyes that were identical to Peter's. "I've missed you, *sohn*."

Josiah thought he saw tears behind the man's large, wire-framed glasses. "I missed you too."

"Peter, watch the shop for me." Without looking at his son, John clapped an arm around Josiah's shoulders. "Your cousin and I have a lot of catching up to do."

Josiah didn't miss the resentment in Peter's eyes. But to his cousin's credit, he simply nodded and said, "*Ya, Daed.*"

John led Josiah to the main house. Once inside they went to the kitchen and found Aunt Vera placing amber-colored glasses of iced tea on a wicker tray. "We can talk here," John said, gesturing to one of the wooden chairs at the polished kitchen table.

Josiah sat down, and Aunt Vera placed a glass of tea in front of him. She put her hand on Josiah's shoulder and squeezed. He glanced up and met her soft gaze. "*Danki, Aenti* Vera."

She smiled. "Are you hungry, Josiah? I can whip you up something for breakfast. Or since it's close to lunch, perhaps you'd like a sandwich. I have some honey-roasted ham in the icebox, and the most delicious Swiss cheese you've tasted in your life. We picked it up at the Stoltzfuses' when we were there last week."

Although Josiah had skipped breakfast, he shook his head. "*Nee.* The tea will be enough, *danki.*"

She nodded and handed her husband his drink. After giving Josiah one last smile, she left the room.

Josiah took a long swallow of the perfectly sweetened tea, letting the cold liquid slide down his throat. John leaned forward, his eyes filled with intensity. "I guess you got my letter?"

"*Ya*. It came a couple weeks ago."

"When did you get back?"

"Last night."

"Took me awhile to find you, Josiah. We haven't heard from you since you left. I suppose there's a *gut* reason for that."

Josiah nodded but didn't say anything. He had his reasons for not contacting anyone after leaving Paradise, reasons he wouldn't share with anyone, not even his uncle.

"There's been a couple people interested in the property. David Graber mentioned a real estate agent snooping around a few months back, asking questions about it. As I'm sure you know already, it's a sight. David tried to keep up with it, but it became too much for him after a while. He has his own family and property to mind first, and I haven't had much of a chance to go over there like I wanted."

"I appreciate David's help," Josiah said. "And I'm glad you contacted me. To be honest, I hadn't thought about the house in a long time."

John removed his straw hat and placed it on the table, revealing his salt-and-pepper hair, molded in the shape of the crown of his hat. "What did your *daed* say about you coming back here?"

"He passed away two years ago."

"*Ach*, Josiah." John sounded distressed. "I had no idea. I'm so sorry for your loss."

Josiah stared at his hands cupping the glass. "*Danki*," he said, his voice barely audible.

"What happened?"

"Got sick. How do I get in touch with the folks interested in the house?"

John hesitated, then finally said, "David might know the name of the realty company. You could ask him. You could probably sell it as is, but I thought you might want the opportunity to get what the house and land are worth. If it's your intent to sell."

"It is."

"All right. If you need any help, let me know. If I can't be there, I'll send Peter."

"I'm fine. I'm not afraid of a little work."

"A little?" John shook his head, letting out a chuckle. "I'd say a little is a huge understatement. But then again, you always were a hard worker. Dependable, always did a *gut* job for me when you helped out here in the shop."

Josiah warmed at the compliment. It had been so long since someone in his family had given him one. "I appreciated the opportunities you gave me to work here."

John nodded. "Do you need any money, Josiah? To help pay for materials?"

"I'm *gut*. I have all the money I need."

"How about a place to stay, then? We have plenty of room here. Can't imagine that place is fit to sleep in."

"It's not that bad," Josiah said. "Really, I'm fine."

"Well, if you need anything, let me know." He clapped Josiah on the shoulder. "We're family, *sohn*. Sometimes that's the only thing you can depend on."

Josiah nodded, but he didn't share his uncle's view. If anything, family was the last thing he could depend on.

∽

Amanda sprinkled powdered sugar over the pan of brownies she had baked earlier that day. She slid a sharp knife through the soft, chocolatey dessert, cutting it into even portions. Putting four pieces on a plate, she covered them with plastic wrap and placed the dish on the counter, then she walked over to the kitchen window and peered outside. From here she had a good view of Josiah's house. Dusk had arrived, and he still hadn't returned.

Through the window screen she could hear her family laughing and playing outside. Her *daed* had come home from work early and was outside with the rest of the children, playing a game of catch with the boys while the girls played on the swing set. Her *mamm* sat on a chair and watched the ruckus while she knitted a small, pale yellow cap for the baby. Taking advantage of the evening, the entire family had enjoyed a simple picnic outside with turkey sandwiches, homemade sweet pickles, and potato salad.

Taking one more glance at Josiah's house, she stepped away from the window. After covering the rest of the brownies, she quickly washed the dishes. She had hoped Josiah would be back by now. All day she had looked forward to his coming home so they could talk. They had ten years of conversation to catch up on. But as the hours passed, her disappointment and frustration grew. To be honest, her pride was a bit pricked as well. Maybe he wasn't as eager to catch up on things as she was.

After she dried the last dish and put it away, she wiped down the counters, intending to join her family outside. It was a beautiful evening, although slightly cool. She slipped on her sweater but decided not to wear shoes, anticipating the feel of the soft earth and cool grass between her toes.

Suddenly she heard the sound of a buggy approaching. Peering out the window again, her grin grew to full size. Josiah. He'd finally come home. She picked up the plate of four brownies and walked outside toward his house.

"Amanda!" From her seat in a white plastic lawn chair, Katharine motioned for her daughter to come toward her. When Amanda reached her, she asked, "Where are you going?"

"To take Josiah some of the brownies I made earlier." She held up the plate.

"But he just got home. Maybe you should wait until tomorrow?"

Amanda frowned. "I won't be gone long, *Mamm*. I'm sure he would appreciate the treat."

"Is that the only reason you're going over there?"

"What other reason would there be?"

Mamm tilted her head. "To be nosy?"

Amanda sighed at her mother's knowing look. "Aren't you the least bit curious as to what he's been doing all this time? Where he moved to? How his father is doing?"

Her mother's expression grew serious. "Sometimes it's best to let things be, Amanda. If Josiah wants you to know those things, he'll tell you. On his own."

"What do you mean?"

"I know you, Amanda Marie. And while you mean well, sometimes you can push too hard."

"*Mamm*, I'm just going to take him some brownies, not give him the third degree."

Katharine gave her a weary smile. "All right. Then you'd better get on over there, if you're going to go."

Amanda nodded and turned. This wasn't the first time she'd been told she could be too pushy. It was a flaw she worked to correct, with varying degrees of success.

She strode over to the Bontragers' barn, the small rocks and dirt clods on the driveway poking into the bare soles of her feet. Josiah had his back to her as he unhitched his horse, the sleeves of his pale blue shirt rolled up a few inches above his elbows. His movements were efficient, and she could hear him speaking in low tones to the horse as he took a moment to stroke her nose. She approached him quietly so as not to disturb the horse, then tapped him on the shoulder.

He jumped and spun around, nearly dropping the horse's reins. "Amanda! Don't sneak up on me like that!"

Amanda opened her mouth to speak, but the words fled her lips. She had thought him good-looking in the dim light of the barn last night and at a distance this morning, but now that she stood close to him, in the full light of evening, he was twice as handsome. His yellow straw hat was positioned low over his forehead, the brim shading his eyes but not obscuring them. She didn't remember their being that bright shade of green, a lighter shade than the grass tickling her toes. His tan face had a dark shadow of whiskers above his lip and on his jaw.

"Did you need something, Amanda?"

His impatient tone startled her. She looked up into his eyes again, which were flat, almost lifeless. An ache appeared in her chest. She had never seen anyone look so . . . empty.

"Here," she said, holding out the plate of brownies, struggling to keep her tone steady. "I remembered how much you liked my brownies, so I made a pan today. Of course, I had to save most of them for my brothers and sisters, but I was able to spare a few." She smiled, hoping to lighten his somber mood.

Instead, he frowned. "Brothers and sisters? I thought you only had one sister. She was born right before we left, I think. What was her name?"

"Hannah," she said, a little hurt he didn't remember. "After you left, *Mamm* and *Daed* had five more children, and *Mamm*'s expecting another one soon."

His flat expression softened, but only a bit. "Seems they've been busy."

She blushed. "*Ya.*"

He took the plate from her hand. "*Danki,* Amanda. That was mighty kind of you."

"Don't mention it. I like to cook. Have you had supper yet?"

"*Nee,* but I'm not really hungry."

"Josiah, you can't go without dinner. Tell you what, while you take care of the horse, I'll go inside and fix you something to eat." Her anxiety lessened. The kitchen had always been her comfort zone.

"You don't have to do that—"

"It's no bother at all," she said over her shoulder, already heading to the house. When he called out her name again, she ignored him, determined not to let him turn down her offer. He'd been out all day, and he shouldn't have to fix his own supper. Not when she could easily do it for him.

Tall weeds and grass tickled her bare legs as she made the way to the back door. She skipped up the two concrete steps and noticed the screen door missing. Glancing around, she saw it lying on the ground next to the house. She picked it up and leaned it against the house before going inside.

She hadn't been in the Bontragers' home since they had moved away. Although her *daed* had tried to take care of the outside, no one had ventured in as far as she knew. The dank, stuffy smell confirmed her suspicion. Stepping inside the small mudroom, she opened another door, which led into the kitchen. She couldn't see much more than shadows in the darkened space, so she searched for a battery-operated lamp or gaslight. Finally, she found a small battery lamp next to the metal sink and flipped on the light. The glow illuminated a thick layer of dust on the counter.

Cobwebs decorated every corner, from the ceiling to the wood-planked floor. Some of the nails had come loose, and the planks themselves were rough and dirty. Grime covered the stove, and two of the cabinets were missing doors.

"Not much to look at, is it?"

She turned around at the sound of Josiah's voice. He stood in the doorway, his expression shadowed from her view, his tone expressing his displeasure. Not that she could blame him. The kitchen, and probably the entire house, was a mess.

Still, there was a stove—and running water, she hoped. She started opening cabinets, looking for any kind of ingredients to prepare what would surely be a simple meal. The first two cabinets revealed only more cobwebs.

The thud of his shoes sounded against the floor as he came up behind her. He put his hand on one of the cabinet doors, his arm hovering over her shoulder. "Don't."

Twirling around, she looked up at him, their faces only inches from each other. Her breath hung in her throat at his nearness, and her heartbeat accelerated. But not out of fear or even anxiety. Attraction crackled between them, pure and simple.

Her reaction to him didn't make sense. This was Josiah, her best friend from childhood. Yet the person standing before her wasn't a child anymore, but a man.

Licking her suddenly dry lips, she asked, "Um, do you keep your food somewhere else?"

"I don't want you making me anything."

His words were low, with a tinge of anger in them. Hurt pricked at her. When did he develop such a short fuse?

They stared at each other for a moment. His hand didn't move, and suddenly her confusion at his tone melted into something else. The last remnants of sunlight shone through the kitchen window, blending with the stark light of the lamp. She could see his face clearly now, saw the darkening of his eyes as he continued to hold her gaze. Then he suddenly dropped his arm and stepped away.

"Best if you go home now, Amanda." His voice sounded slightly hoarse, and a shiver passed through her at his raspy tone.

"But—"

"*Geh!*"

She shrank back. "All right." Spinning around on the balls of her bare feet, she turned to leave. She'd taken no more than three steps when she felt something sharp pierce the bottom of her foot. "Ow!" Lifting up her foot, she spied a dark streak of blood on the bottom of her heel.

"What?" Josiah said, striding toward her. His harsh tone had softened into concern.

"*Nix.* I just cut my foot." As the stinging pain traveled through the bottom of her heel, a drop of blood landed on the floor.

He hesitated, then sighed. "Let me see." He pulled out a chair from the kitchen table and gestured for her to sit.

"It's nothing, Josiah." Her voice held more of an edge than she meant it to. "Just a little cut. I'll go home and put a bandage on it." She didn't want to stay here any longer, especially when he didn't want her to, something he'd made very clear. But when she put her foot down to walk out, she couldn't hide her wince.

He grabbed the lamp from the counter and set it on the table. "Sit down, Amanda."

His sharp tone brooked no argument, and neither did the resolute expression on his face. She sat.

Chapter Four

"GIVE ME YOUR FOOT," JOSIAH SAID, CROUCHING IN FRONT of her.

"Josiah, it's not that bad. You don't have to—"

He grabbed her ankle, effectively cutting her off. Gentling his grip, he balanced the back edge of her heel on his knee and examined the wound. "Cut's about an inch wide. Not bleeding too much."

"See, I told you."

"But you have a big splinter stuck in it." He put her foot down and left the kitchen.

"Josiah?" She frowned when he didn't answer her. Josiah hadn't only changed physically. He had a completely different personality than she remembered. He'd never behaved like he didn't want to be around her, or that she was in his way.

Disappointment threaded through her. She'd been so excited to have her best friend back. Now she wondered if they would ever be friends again.

She looked up as he entered the room carrying a bandage, tweezers, and a brown bottle of peroxide. At her questioning look he said, "I always keep a first aid kit around. Never know when you might need it."

Setting the supplies on the table, he knelt in front of her again and took her foot. He hesitated for a moment, and a wave of embarrassment flowed through her. She'd never been too concerned about her feet before. But with him crouched in front of her, holding her foot in a surprisingly gentle grip, she suddenly became self-conscious.

Silently he took the tweezers and yanked out the splinter so quickly she barely felt it. He unscrewed the white cap of the peroxide and poured it over her heel, apparently not caring that the antiseptic dripped on his pants. A glimmer of hope sparked inside her. Maybe he hadn't changed completely after all.

Her heel still damp, they stayed motionless for a few seconds. Her foot twitched, and he grabbed it, as if worried it would fall off his knee. But instead of letting go, his thumb brushed the instep. An accidental movement, yet so featherlight she shivered.

Clearing his throat, he let go of her foot, snatched the bandage off the kitchen table and used his teeth to open the wrapper. He quickly affixed the bandage on the bottom of her heel, smoothing out the adhesive. "Done," he said, his voice brusque.

"*Danki.*" She put her foot down.

The moment she moved, he jumped up and took several steps backward, not looking at her, erecting a noticeable wall between them.

Inwardly she sighed. He really didn't want her here. She stood and turned around, being more mindful of the splintery floor, and walked toward the door, ready to be gone. But instead of leaving, she hesitated at the doorway. Facing him, she asked, "What did I do wrong, Josiah? Why are you so upset with me?"

✐

Josiah couldn't answer right away. He had fully expected her to leave, and a part of him had wanted her to. But another, stronger part wanted her to stay. Confusion and hurt were displayed on her lovely face. He had no idea how to soothe them away.

Over the years since he'd left Paradise, Josiah had thought of Amanda often. They'd had more than a close friendship, at least from his standpoint. At the tender age of twelve, he had decided to marry her, but of course he didn't tell her that. There would be time for that, he had thought. Plenty of time for him to make her fall in love with him.

Then his mother died, and everything changed. Amanda had been there for him during that dark time, more than she realized. And after he left Paradise, he had dreamed of the day he would see her again. But as time passed, he realized how impossible that would be. So he tried to push her out of his mind. He'd even tried dating a couple of girls, hoping to quash his feelings for Amanda, but the idea of courting anyone else felt like a betrayal. Then his life had gotten so out of control he refused to allow himself to have feelings for anyone. Even so, Amanda had never been all that far from his thoughts, or his heart.

And now he was back in Paradise, and Amanda was back in his life. Before leaving his house that morning, he had seen her putting out the wash, and it had taken everything he had to keep from staring at her. He'd had to dig deeper still when he tended to her foot. He couldn't let her leave with a bleeding foot, especially since she had injured it on his pathetic excuse for a floor. When he knelt in front of her, trying to ignore her small, delicate foot, he had to fight for the resolve to keep his feelings from breaking the surface.

Then he had stroked her instep. The movement had been instinctive, and it was done before he could stop himself. At that point he knew he couldn't be that close to her again. He'd spent more than a decade smothering any feelings and tightly controlling his reactions. Yet in the span of a few minutes, Amanda Graber had threatened to undo all of that, without even knowing it. He couldn't afford to let that happen.

"Josiah?" Her steps were tentative, and not only because of the sad state of his kitchen floor. He'd been so cold to her, no wonder she was skittish. "Josiah, I don't understand. I thought after all these years you would be happy to see me."

"I am." The words were out before he knew it. Clamping down his lips, he didn't say anything else. Then she smiled, and his knees almost buckled.

"I'm so glad to hear that," she said as she moved toward him. She sighed, a light, pleasing sound that sent a ripple down his spine. "I thought maybe I'd somehow made you mad without knowing it."

He shook his head, unable to let her believe she was at fault for his keeping his distance. "It's just that . . . I'm tired, I guess. It was a long trip here, and as you can see"—he held out his arms wide—"I have a lot of work to do on the house and barn."

"I can help you."

She was now standing only a few feet away from him. Close enough that he could see flecks of green in her hazel eyes, which were rimmed by thick lashes. Another detail he either had forgotten or had been too young to pay attention to. But now he couldn't stop staring at her. "I appreciate the offer, Amanda, but I won't be needing help. It'll take me awhile, but I'll get it done."

"Well, that doesn't make any sense to me." She put her hands on her hips. "I'm as able-bodied as you, and you said yourself you have a lot of work to do. You know what my *grossmammi* used to say when I was little?"

He crossed his arms over his chest. "Many hands make light work?"

"*Nee*, although that's true too. She used to say that only a fool refuses a neighbor's outstretched hand. I remember a lot of things about you, Josiah Bontrager. But I don't remember you being a fool."

His father would have begged to differ, but he didn't say that out loud. "I don't think it's foolish to not want to put you to any trouble."

"It's no trouble. Besides, my sisters and brothers can help. They're out of school on the weekends. Actually, they're out of school for the rest of the week because their teacher has the flu, so we can start right away."

"How many brothers and sisters did you say you had?"

"Six." She ticked their names and ages off on her fingertips. "Hannah is ten; Rachel, nine; Andrew turned eight last month;

Thomas is six, although he'll insist he's six and a half; Christopher is four; and Jacob is eighteen months. *Mamm*'s expecting number eight in July."

Josiah's eyes widened. "That's incredible."

"I know. They really thought I would be the only one, especially after trying for so long, but then once she got pregnant with Hannah, the babies kept coming."

"So what's it like having all those brothers and sisters underfoot?" He couldn't hold back his fascination or his wonder at Amanda's enthusiasm as she talked about her brothers and sisters. When he'd left Paradise, he and Amanda had been only children. He couldn't fathom having so many younger siblings.

"*Wunderbaar!*" She clasped her hands together for emphasis. "Sure, it's a lot of work, especially since *Mamm* doesn't feel well right now. She usually gets extremely tired in the last trimester. But I help out as much as I can, and I really love taking care of them. I hope to have a large family someday."

Josiah bit the inside of his cheek. He remembered playing house with Amanda when they were kids, at her insistence, of course. A stupid game, he'd thought at the time, but he gave in because she would always agree to climb trees with him afterward. So it didn't come as a surprise that she would want a large family. And while as a boy he'd felt dumb playing house, now he longed to have a wife and children of his own. No, scratch that. He had longed to have a family of his own with Amanda. But as he did with every other yearning, he suffocated it. Marrying Amanda wasn't in his future. Not out of choice, but out of necessity.

"I know Andrew and Thomas are young, but they're hard workers," Amanda said. "They've been helping *Daed* around the house since they were small. And I'm sure Hannah and Rachel won't mind working in here with me." She strolled around the kitchen, ideas obviously rolling around in her mind. She ran her fingertips over the dusty countertops. "First we'll need to scrub everything down. Then we can fill the pantry with food and figure out a place to put the cooler so you can keep ice and the cold stuff. And you'll need some sort of stove." She opened up the rusty gas oven and peered inside, then coughed. "We'll clean this out too." Standing, she looked at him, her mouth curved in a lovely smile. "Before long you'll smell the sweet aroma of apple pies baking."

"I don't bake." This was getting out of hand. He had merely wanted her not to feel bad; he hadn't meant to open the door for her to do all this for him.

"Silly, I know that. Remember the time we made cookies together at my house?"

He nodded, his mind transported to the past. They had been ten years old, and although he'd followed the recipe and done everything Amanda's mother had said, his cookies were hard and tasteless, while Amanda's had been delicious. He had never baked before—his father believed only women should cook and would get angry when he'd catch Josiah helping his mother in the kitchen—and after that failure he never attempted it again.

"I'll make the pies," she volunteered. "Is apple still your favorite?"

He hesitated before answering. The idea of coming into this desolate house and having a fresh-baked pie waiting greatly appealed to him, wearing down his already thinning resolve. Perhaps one pie wouldn't hurt. "*Ya*."

"Then it's settled." She brushed past him, giving him another one of her wonderful smiles, the kind that not only brightened her face but lit up the entire room. "The kids and I will be here tomorrow morning," she said over her shoulder as she headed for the door.

"Amanda, wait."

She turned around.

He almost told her no. He could repair the house and barn by himself. He had the tools, the skills, and—after selling his horse and the tiny mobile home he and his father had shared in Indiana—he had enough money for materials. But it would take him twice as long to complete the renovations if he did them alone. That would make it twice as long before he could sell the house and leave Paradise for good. If he had Amanda and her siblings' help, he would finish much sooner and finally be on the road to Ohio.

"Did you want to tell me something, Josiah?" Amanda asked.

"*Ya*," he said, finally making up his mind. "I . . . I'll see you in the morning."

With another smile and a wave of her hand, she disappeared outside.

He leaned against the countertop and blew out a breath. Deep down he appreciated the help. If only it hadn't come in the form of Amanda Graber. At least she would be inside most of the time while he worked on the exterior of the house. The less contact they had with each other, the better off they both would be.

The next morning Amanda awoke well before sunrise. She had to get all her chores done before she went to Josiah's and got started on the kitchen. What a mess! She had assumed there would be some problems with the outside of the house after ten years of neglect, but she hadn't thought the inside would be so bad. It made her wonder if the interior had been in bad shape before Josiah and his father had moved away.

But that didn't matter anymore. She had discussed her plan to help Josiah with her *mamm* and *daed* the night before, and they both agreed it would be a good idea. Not only was it the neighborly thing to do, but it would be good for Andrew and Thomas to learn a little about repairing a house—not to mention that it would keep them out of trouble. Hannah would stay home and help with Christopher and Jacob, but Rachel would be allowed to assist Amanda, who had spent the rest of the night creating a long list of what needed to be done.

Amanda put on her *kapp* before retrieving her shoes from the closet. She'd learned her lesson about going barefoot at Josiah's, and she would make sure her siblings also protected their feet when they went over there. As she slipped on her black shoes, she felt a tiny stab of pain on the bottom of her heel, reminding her of Josiah's tender care of her foot. While she didn't completely understand why he behaved so strangely toward her, she was glad he had agreed to let her help. She didn't think she could stand seeing him working so hard by himself when he didn't have to.

She dashed down the stairs, careful not to trip in the dark. When she reached the kitchen she turned on the lamp and started breakfast. Before long everyone in the house had awakened and settled down for a morning meal of flaky biscuits, flavorful sausage gravy, and lightly scrambled eggs.

After everyone had finished eating, and Hannah and Rachel had cleaned the kitchen, Amanda drew Rachel, Andrew, and Thomas to the side. "We're going over to Josiah's house today," she said, bending down in front of them so she could meet their gazes.

"We are?" Andrew asked, tugging on one of his black suspenders. "Why?"

"To help him fix his house. He has a lot of repairs to do, and it would be hard for him to do them on his own."

"Will I get to use a hammer?" Thomas asked, his eyes filling with excitement.

"As long as you don't hit his thumb with it like you did *Daed*'s, then I'm sure you can."

"That was an accident," Thomas said, guilt crossing his cherubic features.

"I know, honey. And *Daed* did too. Just be careful, and do what Josiah tells you to." She eyed her brothers directly. "Without argument."

"We will," they said in unison.

"What am I supposed to do?" Rachel asked.

"You and I will be cleaning the kitchen. It needs a lot of work."

Rachel nodded. "Are we going over there now?"

"As soon as you get your shoes on."

"Aww, I don't wanna wear shoes," Thomas said.

"You have to." She pointed to her foot. "I have them on, and with good reason. Yesterday I got a splinter in my heel. There's also rusted nails and broken glass in the yard. You don't want to cut open your feet, do you?"

Thomas and Andrew both ran to get their shoes.

She waited for her siblings to get ready and watched Hannah take Jacob out of his high chair, knowing her sister was probably glad she didn't have to help Josiah. Hannah had never been keen on doing chores, but she didn't mind watching her baby brothers.

"We're ready." Andrew and Thomas ran from the living room to the back door of the kitchen, skidding to a stop in front of her. Rachel, more mature at age nine, ambled a bit more slowly.

"Okay, let's go!" As Amanda trailed behind her sister and brothers, carrying a blue bucket filled with rags and cleaning supplies, a strange feeling formed in the pit of her stomach. She couldn't shake the feeling that Josiah had agreed to this reluctantly. What if he had changed his mind overnight? The boys would be disappointed . . . and so would she.

Andrew and Thomas chased each other in the tall grass while she and Rachel went to the back entrance. The rusted screen door still leaned against the house, and in the early morning light she noticed a fist-sized hole in the screen. She knocked on the wooden door. Once, then twice. After the third time she turned the knob, finding it unlocked.

"Stay out here for a minute," she instructed Rachel, then tilted her head in the direction of her brothers. "Keep an eye on them, make sure they don't go into the barn. We shouldn't disturb Josiah's horse."

Rachel nodded and walked toward Andrew and Thomas, who were now playfully pushing each other.

Amanda opened the door and stepped inside, once again greeted by the musty, dank smell. None of the lights were on, and she didn't see any sign that Josiah had been in the kitchen since she'd left last night. She turned on the lamp, then went to the window over the kitchen sink. With a few strong pushes she opened it, breathing in the welcome fresh air.

Aided by the steady stream of sunlight through the window and by the lamp, she could see that she had underestimated the amount of work she and Rachel would have to do. The light blue paint on the walls underneath the wood cabinets had peeled off in spots, and dust and cobwebs coated everything. Further examination showed several piles of small black pellets, a clear indication that mice had taken up residence. Rodents and bugs outdoors had never bothered her, but vermin had no place in a house, especially the kitchen. A good scrubbing down of everything would help, but she suspected Josiah would have to set out a few traps to get rid of them completely.

The squeak of a floorboard sounded, and she whirled around to see Josiah entering the kitchen. His streaked hair stood up in tufts all over his head, his suspenders were dangling around his waist and legs, and his shirt was buttoned partway. Clearly he had just woken up.

He rubbed his eyes and looked at her. "Amanda?"

"*Guder mariye!*" she said. "I knocked a few times, but no one answered, so I decided to go ahead and get started."

"Guess I was more tired than I thought." He looked at her for a moment, then he quickly buttoned up the rest of his shirt and slid on his suspenders.

"Andrew, Thomas, and Rachel are outside," she said. "The boys are excited to help."

Josiah ran a hand through his hair, trying unsuccessfully to tame the tufts. His wavy hair looked so thick and soft. As he continued to thread his fingers through the unruly locks, she wondered what the texture felt like.

KATHLEEN FULLER

She blushed and looked away. She had no business thinking about touching Josiah's hair. Still, she had difficulty getting the temptation out of her mind. Hoping the flaming color on her cheeks had ebbed, she looked at Josiah. "I thought I'd start by wiping down the counters."

He shrugged. "Whatever you want to do."

Her shoulders sagged. Back to treating her like a stranger. In fact, now he wouldn't even look at her. Instead he went to the back door and grabbed the pair of work boots that had been placed nearby. He sat down on one of the wooden kitchen chairs and pulled them on. "You say your brothers are outside?"

"*Ya*," she said, trying to hide her disenchantment at his mood.

"I'll send your sister in to see you." He grabbed the yellow straw hat hanging on the peg near the door and walked outside.

Amanda frowned, crossing her arms over her chest. Not a thank-you or a good-bye or even a see-you-later. He could at least show a little appreciation. She was half tempted to walk out of the kitchen and take her siblings back home.

But that wouldn't be right. She had told him they would help, and she would keep her word. Closing her eyes, she prayed aloud, as she often did when she as frustrated. "Dear heavenly Father, I don't know what's going on with Josiah, but You do. He's changed so much, and I don't know why. I have no idea where he's been all these years, and for some reason he doesn't want to tell me. Help me to help him with whatever he needs and to do it with a selfless heart."

Chapter Five

FOR MOST OF THE MORNING JOSIAH FELT LIKE HE HAD
two little shadows. Andrew and Thomas were more than eager to
help. Whatever task he gave them, no matter how mundane, they
did without complaint. So far they had picked up all the sticks in
the backyard and put them in a pile a few feet from the house.
They also collected as much small debris as they could and put it
in a glass mason jar. Surprisingly, there weren't too many rusty
nails or shards of glass, and those were mostly near the house
where a window had been broken and a couple of shutters had
fallen off. Undoubtedly there had been a few storms over the
years, and heavy winds could do a lot of damage. He should be
grateful the house wasn't in worse shape. But when he took a look
at all the work he needed to do, gratitude was far from his mind.

"Here, Mr. Josiah." Andrew held the half-filled quart jar out to
him. "What else you want us to do?"

He glanced around the yard, pushing back the brim of his hat
and letting the air dry his damp forehead. Most of the morning had
been spent cleaning the front and back yards enough so he could
use the push mower on the overgrown grass. He sized Andrew up.
For eight, the boy seemed tall, reminding him of Amanda's father.
He also seemed to possess his *daed*'s work ethic, something Josiah
had appreciated in David Graber even as a boy. "Ever use a push
mower?"

Andrew nodded. "For a long time. Since I was seven."

Josiah hid a smile. "Sounds like you have some experience, then."

"*Ya*, I do. Lots. And your lawn needs mowing bad, Mr. Josiah."

He let out a deep breath, maintaining the serious tone of the conversation. "I think you're the man for the job. I bought a brand-new push mower yesterday. Want to break it in for me?"

Showing a grin that featured two gaping holes, one on the top and one on the bottom, Andrew bobbed his head up and down. "I sure would."

"It's in the barn. Wait here and I'll bring it out to you."

"What about me, Mr. Josiah?" Thomas wiped his nose with the back of his hand.

Josiah squatted down in front of him. "What would you like to do?"

"Use a hammer," Thomas said matter-of-factly.

Rubbing his chin, Josiah said, "All right. I've got some rotted boards on the front porch that need replacing. You can pull the nails out for me. How does that sound?"

Thomas nodded. "Sounds *gut*, Mr. Josiah."

Josiah chucked the boy under the chin and stood, his mood lighter than it had been in days. Something about being around these boys, with their earnest and genuine eagerness to help, combined with the beautiful, crisp fall weather, elevated his spirits. "Be right back," he said and went to get the mower. A few moments later Andrew went to work on the lawn while Josiah and Thomas tackled the front porch.

Josiah held up the hammer and pointed to the claw. "Have you ever used this end before?"

The boy shook his head. Unlike Andrew, Thomas said few words, something Josiah could relate to.

"See that nail sticking up over there?" Josiah pointed the hammer at the flat head of a bent, rusty nail poking through the end of a long plank of wood. A soft breeze kicked up, and a few brown leaves danced across the porch. "You get it out like this." He demonstrated how to use the hammer to remove the nail, then handed the tool to Thomas. "Now, find another one and try it yourself."

Thomas searched the porch until he found a second protruding nail. He squatted down and tilted back his small yellow straw hat. After a few attempts he slid the claw around the nail. With a couple of tugs, the nail slid free, due more to the softness of the rotted wood than to Thomas's natural strength.

"*Sehr gut*," Josiah said, happy to see the surprise in the boy's blue eyes when the nail gave way. "Ready to do some more?"

Thomas grinned. Unlike his older brother, he still had all his baby teeth. "*Ya*. This is *schpass*."

For the next hour or so Josiah and Thomas removed nails while Josiah kept one ear out for Andrew and the mower. He wasn't used to being responsible for anyone but himself.

When he'd removed the last nail, the front door opened with a loud squeak. He turned to see Amanda standing in the doorway behind the screen door. Hopping to his feet, he opened it himself, in case it fell loose from its hinges like the back door had.

"You *buwe* hungry?"

When Thomas nodded enthusiastically, Josiah inwardly cringed. He had nothing to eat in the house. Most times he ate fast food or sandwiches and chips, and he hadn't even planned for either of those today. He stepped forward and looked at Amanda. "Give me a minute to hook up the buggy, and I'll go into town and get us something."

She waved him off. A damp lock of light brown hair had escaped from beneath her *kapp*, and she tucked it behind her left ear. That and the rosy glow of her cheeks were a testament to how hard she'd been working. "Don't bother. I already have lunch prepared."

"You do?"

"*Ya*. Rachel ran home and brought over a few things. It's nothing fancy, but it's food."

Thomas dashed past Amanda, not waiting for an invitation to go inside. She turned around and called, "Wait on the rest of us, Thomas. And don't forget to wash your hands!"

"I'll need to go to the pump," Josiah said, moving to leave. "I haven't had the water hooked up to the house yet. *Daed* had it disconnected when we left."

"Took care of that too. There's a bucket with clean water by the sink, along with some bar soap." She glanced down at his hands. "Don't forget to clean yours too." She winked at him, then turned around and went inside.

This time Josiah couldn't stop his smile as he followed her inside the house. When he reached the kitchen, he blinked. How she had managed to do so much in such a short period of time amazed him. All the cobwebs were gone. The table and chairs were wiped clean, along with the countertops and cabinet doors. He glanced down at the uneven wood floor. Despite looking in desperate need of repair, he couldn't detect a speck of dirt on it.

"Thomas, I know you're a big boy, but let me help you anyway."

He glanced at Amanda, who was helping Thomas rinse his soapy hands. A blue bucket—not one of his, he noticed—sat next to the metal double-basin sink, which had been polished to a brilliant shine. A bar of gold-colored soap lay next to the faucet.

Amanda lifted the bucket and poured water over Thomas's sudsy hands, then handed him a towel. "Now, go remind Andrew that he said he'd be in here five minutes ago. I think he's having way too much fun with the lawn mower."

Josiah chuckled, and Amanda turned around and looked at him, her expression soft. "Nice to hear you laugh, Josiah."

Actually, it felt good to laugh. He hadn't laughed in such a long time, longer than he cared to remember. There hadn't been much to be happy about in his life over the past few years.

"Your turn," she said, pointing to the bucket. "Hands. Now."

He smirked. "I'm not twelve, Amanda. You don't have to remind me. Twice," he added.

A flush came over her face. "Sorry. I guess I get carried away sometimes."

"Sometimes?" a female voice said.

Josiah turned to see Rachel placing plastic forks beside the white paper plates on the table. She was several inches shorter than Amanda, with darker brown hair and a more olive tone to her skin. In some ways she reminded him of Amanda at the same age.

"Very funny, Rachel." But Amanda didn't seem to mind her sister's good-natured teasing.

The boys bounded inside as Josiah finished washing his hands. He helped Andrew with the almost-empty bucket. He would take it out after lunch and refill it for Amanda. No need for her to fetch more water, not after everything she'd already done.

They crowded around the small, circular kitchen table. As a family of three, the Bontragers hadn't needed a large table, but it was a tight fit for five. Amanda sat across from Josiah, with Thomas to her left and Rachel to her right. Andrew was sandwiched between him and Rachel.

"Let's pray." Amanda held out her hands, and Rachel and Thomas quickly entwined their fingers with hers.

Josiah swallowed. When had he last prayed, much less said grace before a meal? Since his mother's death, his father had given up on praying, and on God altogether. Josiah hadn't taken his grief that far, but he had come close over the years. And while he had joined the church when he turned twenty, it had been more out of a desire to fulfill his mother's wishes than to become closer to the Lord.

"Mr. Josiah?"

He looked down at Andrew's outstretched hand.

"Aren't you gonna pray with us?"

Josiah glanced at Amanda, who gave him an expectant look. He noticed something else behind her eyes. Curiosity . . . and compassion. He averted his gaze and grasped Andrew's small hand, then Thomas's even smaller one. Regardless of his standing with the Lord right now, he didn't want to keep the children waiting on their food.

"Josiah, will you pray, please?"

He looked at Amanda again, then glanced at the children. Shifting in his seat, he slowly bowed his head, wondering what he would say.

Suddenly a prayer from childhood came to mind. "God is great God is *gut* let us thank Him for our food amen," he said all in one breath, then released the boys' hands.

"We say that prayer at home sometimes, Mr. Josiah," Thomas remarked. "Although we don't say it that fast."

Everyone laughed, and he felt the tension drain from his body. Surveying the food on the table, his mouth started to water. Diagonal wedges of tuna fish sandwiches were piled high on one plate, a bowl of small sweet pickles situated beside it. A bag of potato chips lay open near Rachel, and in the center of the table was a pitcher half filled with lemonade. Either she or Rachel had already poured the drink into everyone's red plastic cup.

Amanda handed him the plate of sandwiches. "Tuna fish. Hope you still like it."

Nodding, he took two halves. "My favorite sandwich."

"I remember."

He met her gaze. Sweet heavens, she was so pretty. And so capable. Another quality he hadn't been old enough to appreciate fully when they were younger. But then again, she had always approached everything with confidence, whether it had been baking cookies, climbing trees, or fishing in the stream two miles down the road. He couldn't remember her ever failing at anything.

He passed the sandwiches to Andrew, who only took one half. Clearly the young boy didn't care too much for tuna fish.

Soon everyone had what they wanted and started eating. Josiah tried to keep his attention focused on his food and not on the woman across the table who kept bringing out so many emotions in him.

But he was finding that impossible to do.

~⌒~

Josiah continued to confound Amanda. One moment she would see a glimpse of the Josiah she used to know—his deep-throated chuckle, his crooked smile, his kindness as he dealt with her brothers. She had watched him and Thomas through the front window in the living room as they had removed the nails, and the gentle yet respectful way he dealt with her six-year-old brother tugged at her heart. A natural with children, something he probably wasn't even aware of. Although she had warned her brothers not to give Josiah a hard time, she knew their compliance had been due more to his treatment of them than to her directive.

With Rachel's help they had made quick work of surface cleaning in the kitchen, which had given her enough time to put together a decent lunch. Remembering how much Josiah had loved tuna fish sandwiches—which she didn't particularly care for—she had asked Rachel to go home and bring her the ingredients for lunch.

Taking tiny bites of her half sandwich, she thought about his discomfort with praying. She had never noticed it before, at least that she could remember. But when they were kids, they said rote prayers, repeating what their parents said at the supper table and what they had heard during church. His rapid-fire prayer had tickled her brothers' funny bones, but it made her curious. Had he joined the church? He dressed and lived as an Amish man, but that didn't necessarily mean he had been baptized. More questions. She wondered if she would ever discover the answers.

Josiah, who had kept his head lowered during most of the meal, pushed the last bite of sandwich into his mouth. After washing it down with a gulp of lemonade from his cup, he looked at her. "*Danki* for the lunch. It was *sehr gut*."

"You're welcome." She left her mostly uneaten sandwich on her plate, planning to throw it in the pig trough before she went home so it wouldn't go to waste.

He pushed back from the table and stood. "I better get back to work." Glancing at the boys, he added, "Andrew and Thomas have put in a full day already. They don't have to help any more if they don't want to."

Seeing the disappointment on their faces, Amanda said, "I think they have enough energy to work a little while longer. Right, *buwe?*"

"*Ya*," Andrew said, standing. "I still need to mow on the other side of the house."

Thomas nodded his agreement.

Josiah stroked his chin, something she noticed he did when deep in thought. She surmised he was still reluctant to accept their assistance. But surely he saw how quickly they completed the work with all of them helping out.

"Okay," he finally said. "Andrew, finish up the lawn. But then you're done for the day. A *bu*'s got to have time to play. Thomas, you can come with me to the barn. I've got to feed the horse."

"Does she have a name?" Thomas asked.

Josiah shook his head. "Not yet. Having trouble coming up with one. Maybe you can help me out with that too."

Thomas smiled, his chubby cheeks puffing up.

Amanda's heart warmed as she watched Josiah and her little brother leave the kitchen together. Josiah had said exactly the right thing to Thomas. Instead of dismissing him, he had included him, making him feel important and needed. Wasn't that what everyone wanted?

She and Rachel cleared the table, which had been easy to do since they had used mostly paper products. "Why don't we work on the pantry and cabinets next?" she said to Rachel. "Tomorrow I'll tackle the stove."

The rest of the afternoon went quickly. By late afternoon Andrew and Thomas had already gone home, presumably to grab a snack and play outside. Amanda planned to finish scrubbing down the inside of the cabinet under the sink before calling it a day.

She climbed practically halfway inside the deep cabinet, trying to reach the very back, when she felt something touch her shoulder. Jerking up, she hit her head. "Ow!" As she backed out of the cabinet, she said, "Rachel, don't scare me like that!"

"Are you all right?"

Looking over her shoulder, she saw it wasn't Rachel who had tapped her, but Josiah. Rubbing the top of her head, she nodded. "I'm fine." Then she chuckled. "We seem to be in the habit of startling each other."

He didn't share her humor. "I'm really sorry." He peered down at her, examining the sore spot. "Are you sure you're all right? Sounded like you smacked your head pretty *gut*."

"No worries. I've got a hard head." She grinned. "Or so I've been told."

His lips twitched, and she thought for a moment he might smile.

She started to rise, and his hand came under her arm to assist her. When she stood, she realized how close they were to each other. That funny tickle in her stomach that seemed to always appear when they were near each other returned. She met his gaze for a moment, unable to pull away. Once again she reminded herself that this was Josiah Bontrager. She had no business having these crazy feelings about him. And once again her heart refused to listen.

He pulled away first. Averting his eyes, he stepped back. "Glad you're not hurt."

"You could never hurt me, Josiah."

His head shot up, and he stared at her again. And in that moment she saw something in the depths of his eyes. Pain. Stark and raw, it disappeared when he deadened his expression again. "You should be getting home. It's near suppertime, and I'm sure your *mamm* and *daed* will want you there."

"*Ya*, they're probably expecting me," Amanda said, still concerned about what he had unwittingly revealed. What could have happened to cause him such pain? Did he still grieve his mother's death so deeply after all these years? Possibly, but she suspected that wasn't all.

He pushed his straw hat farther back on his head. "Then I don't want to keep you."

"Why don't you join us? I don't know what we're having, but *Mamm*'s cooking tonight, and I'm sure it will be delicious."

"I wouldn't want to impose."

"You wouldn't be imposing, Josiah. Even though you've been gone for a long time, you're still a part of our family." She stepped toward him. "That hasn't changed, and it never will."

Chapter Six

JOSIAH FOUGHT AGAINST THE REGRET AND LONGING coursing through him. More than anything he wanted to say yes to Amanda, to take her up on her invitation and have supper with her and her family. Especially with her. No matter how hard he tried to look at her through the filter of childhood innocence, he couldn't do it. He didn't see his friend standing in front of him, or even the object of a schoolboy crush. He saw a woman. A beautiful, kind, caring woman who was everything he wanted . . . and needed.

He never should have agreed to let her help him with the house. Getting the renovations done quickly wasn't worth the pain her presence in his life caused. And spending the evening with the Grabers was the last thing he needed to do. He had gotten a taste of how wonderful being with a real family could be at lunch earlier that day. He didn't want to put himself through that again, being on the outside looking in, knowing they had something he desperately wanted but couldn't have.

"*Danki* for the invitation, but I planned to get something in town," he said, turning his back to her. He couldn't look at those beautiful hazel eyes anymore—eyes filled with invitation and promise. He doubted she realized how she looked at him, how her feelings were revealed so clearly to him. He hadn't imagined the spark that had ignited when they stood so close together in the kitchen.

"You're going to eat fast food? You'd prefer that over a home-cooked meal?"

No, he didn't prefer that at all. But he had no other choice. "I have a couple more things to pick up in town," he said, coming up with the excuse on the fly. And because he couldn't stand there in his kitchen, wanting more than anything to say yes to any request she made of him, he headed toward the door. "*Danki* for everything." Unable to help himself, he glanced over his shoulder.

Her bright expression faltered. "You're welcome, Josiah. But you don't have to keep thanking me. It's a pleasure to help out a . . . neighbor."

He turned and looked at her. The emotion in her eyes was anything but neighborly, and it tugged at his heart. He had to get out of there, fast. "Shops will be closing soon. I need to get to town before five." He stood near the back door of the kitchen, gesturing with his outstretched hand for her to go.

"Oh. Okay." She looked at him with uncertainty one more time before sliding past him and walking out the door.

Her arm brushed his, and he closed his eyes. He had faced challenges in his life—a lot of difficult challenges—but keeping his feelings for Amanda securely wrapped was by far the hardest.

A moment later he followed her outside and surveyed his backyard. Andrew had done an excellent job mowing. The shorn grass was already turning brown, and tomorrow it would need to be raked up. But the boy had done the hard work. Pushing that mower through grass that had in some places reached his waist couldn't have been an easy task.

Amanda faced him, the afternoon sun shining through the rustling branches of the oak trees behind her. He couldn't help but breathe in the sweet scent of the freshly mown grass as he gazed at her. For a fleeting moment he forgot everything, concentrating on nature's beauty as well as the natural beauty in front of him.

"So I'll see you tomorrow morning," she said. "Same time?"

Her words broke the spell. "I don't—"

"Josiah Bontrager, if you tell me *nee* again, I'll . . . I'll . . . well, I don't know what I'll do, but you won't like it! You're making me *ab im kopp*, you know that?" Striding toward him, she stopped barely a foot away. "You never used to be like this, Josiah. Stubborn. Bull-headed. Cold. And above all, frustrating."

He looked away, not liking her description of him even though it was accurate. "People change, Amanda."

"*Ya*, but they don't change into completely different people. Not unless . . ." Her tone softened. "Not unless something happened to them." She moved closer. "What happened to you, Josiah?"

His jaw jerked, and he couldn't face her.

She laid her hand on his shoulder. "Josiah, we're friends. Whatever you went through, you can tell me. I want to help."

The warmth of her hand seeped through the cotton cloth of his shirt. Stepping back, he forced her to drop her hand. "You can't help me, Amanda. You can't change the past."

She sighed. "*Nee*, I can't. But you don't have to live in the past either."

The soft sigh she expelled covered him like a warm blanket on a cold winter's night. He looked at her. So sweet, so innocent. She had no idea what she had asked of him. He had made a vow to himself not to reveal those deep secrets, and he wasn't about to break that promise.

She moved toward him, placing her hand back on his arm. "Talk to me, Josiah. You never had trouble doing that before. Remember how much time we spent just talking? Lying on a soft bed of grass on a summer night, looking at millions of stars, sharing our hopes and—"

"Stop." He grabbed her hand, a little harder than he meant to. But he couldn't help it. Every word she spoke dug into him.

Shock registered on her face, and she tried to twist out of his grip. "Josiah, you're hurting me."

He glanced down at his hand locked around her wrist. Stricken, he released her, not missing the red ring circling her pale skin. He staggered backward. "Amanda, I'm . . ." Unable to finish, he turned and ran to the barn. Only when he reached the inside, away from her view, did he allow himself to breathe.

She had said he would never hurt her. Just now, he had proven what he always knew—he could.

～⌒～

Amanda rubbed her wrist as she watched Josiah flee. It didn't hurt that much, only tingled, and she had been surprised more than anything. Why had he grabbed her like that? She was tempted to follow him but thought better of it. In the old days she would have chased him down and demanded that he talk to her. But his reaction gave her pause, and she remembered her mother's warning about being too nosy. Instead she headed for the house, trying to figure out what to do.

As she passed through the backyard, she barely noticed her siblings running around and playing by the swing set. She had to find a way to help Josiah. But how, when she had no idea what was wrong?

Still thinking, she walked into the kitchen, where the scent of fried chicken filled the air. Her mother stood next to the stove, a hot pot of oil bubbling over the gas burner. She dipped a chicken leg into a shallow dish holding beaten eggs, then rolled it in a separate dish of flour. Grease spattered as the floured piece hit the hot oil. Katharine wiped her forehead with the back of her hand, looking less tired than she had been lately.

Her mother turned her head, apparently noticing her for the first time. "Amanda. I'm glad you're home. I could use some help. I know you've been over at Josiah's all day, but if you could fix the corn, I would appreciate it."

Amanda nodded and walked to the pantry to retrieve two quart jars of home-canned corn. As she dumped the vegetables into a large pot, she continued to consider her dilemma.

"Andrew and Thomas seem to have had a *gut* time today," Katharine remarked, flouring another piece of chicken. "They couldn't stop talking about *Mr.* Josiah. I've never heard them get that tickled from doing a day's hard work."

"He's *sehr gut* with them." Amanda added a soft pat of butter to the corn and stirred. "And they worked really hard. So did Rachel. We got a lot accomplished in the kitchen."

"There's much satisfaction in a job well done." Katharine cast Amanda a sidelong glance. "You always do a *gut* job, *Dochder*."

"*Danki, Mamm.*" She set the pot on top of the stove and turned on the burner, staring at the small yellow kernels as if they held the answers she needed.

"Amanda?"

Her mother's voice jerked her out of her thoughts. *"Ya?"*

"Is everything okay? You haven't said much since you got home." Using a small wire mesh basket with a long wooden handle attached, she fished out three pieces of golden brown chicken and put them on a platter covered with two layers of paper towel. "That's not like you."

"I just have a lot on my mind." Amanda stirred the corn again, which had started to bubble.

"I suspect Josiah's on your mind."

Amanda looked at her mother and sighed. "*Ya*, he is. He's different, *Mamm*. A lot different than he used to be."

"Of course he is, Amanda. You are too. The last time you saw each other you were barely teenagers. Now you're both adults. You can't expect him to be the same *bu* he was back then."

"I don't. But I don't expect him to be a stranger, either."

Katharine dropped two more chicken pieces into the large pot. The cooking oil bubbled and splattered. When she didn't say anything, Amanda took the opportunity to explain.

"I've missed him, *Mamm*. A lot. I didn't realize how much until he came back." She turned the heat down under the corn and faced her mother. "He never said good-bye, you know. I want to know why he left so suddenly. And what he's been doing over the past ten years." She frowned. "But he's built this shell around himself. Like a turtle. And just when I think we're to the point where we can have a real conversation, he ducks inside."

"Maybe he feels threatened."

"But why?" Amanda held up her hands. "How can he feel threatened by his best friend?"

"*Former* best friend. Don't forget that." Katharine checked on the chicken, then placed one hand behind her on the small of her back.

"Here, *Mamm*. Let me finish the chicken. You sit down." Amanda led her to a chair by the kitchen table.

Her mother plopped down. "*Danki*, Amanda. Really, I'm fine. Just a twinge in my back."

"All the more reason for me to finish supper. There're only a few pieces left anyway. You go ahead and rest."

Amanda returned to the stove and dredged the last three chicken legs in flour and dropped them in the oil. Wiping her floured hands on a towel, she turned to her mother, picking up the thread of their conversation. She couldn't let it go just yet. "Do you know why Josiah and his *daed* left so abruptly?"

"Even if I did, it's not my place to say, Amanda. I don't indulge in gossip, and neither should you."

"But this isn't idle gossip, *Mamm*. I can tell there's something really wrong with Josiah, but he won't talk to me."

"Did you stop to think he has his reasons?" *Mamm* looked at her again. "Amanda, I know you care for him. You two were so close when you were young, so it makes sense that you would be curious. But even though you shared that closeness at one time, a lot has happened, in both your lives. Maybe you weren't meant to be friends beyond your childhood."

Amanda shook her head. "I don't believe that. I can't." She

paused. "I think God brought him back to Paradise for a reason, and not just to fix up his house."

Katharine looked skeptical. "Do you really believe that? Or is it wishful thinking?" She rose from her chair and walked over to Amanda, putting her hand on her shoulder. "You have such a beautiful heart, *kind*. You want to solve everyone's problems because you care so much. But there are some things in this world you can't fix. You might have to accept that this is one of them."

A couple of hours later, after they finished eating supper and washing the dishes, the rest of the family gathered in the living room to listen to *Daed* read from the Bible, something they did at least one night a week. Although Amanda usually joined them, she didn't this time, and instead grabbed her jacket from the peg by the back door and slipped outside to the swing set.

The sun had dipped beneath the horizon, cloaking the sky in dusky gray. She sat down on a swing. Stretching her legs in front of her, she dug her toe into the cold dirt and gently pushed the swing back and forth as she stared out at Josiah's house. She didn't see his buggy near the barn.

She thought about her mother's words. Normally she followed her counsel, but she couldn't shake the niggling thought that her *mamm* might be wrong in this case. Somehow she'd find out the truth on her own.

No, she wasn't completely on her own. She had God on her side, just as Josiah did. And while she didn't think she would get him to open up about his past right away, she could do her best to remind him that whatever he had been through, he hadn't been alone. Not then, not now. From the discomfort he had displayed praying over the meal, she had a feeling he had forgotten that.

Chapter Seven

JOSIAH AWOKE TO THE SOUND OF TWO BOYS ARGUING outside. Although the night had been cool, he had slept with the window open to dispel the mustiness in his room. He could hear Thomas and Andrew's voices clearly.

"But you got to help him yesterday," Andrew said. "It's my turn to work with Mr. Josiah."

"But I don't wanna go home," Thomas countered.

"You don't have to. I'm sure there's other stuff you can do around here. Like help Amanda in the house."

"I wanna use a hammer again."

"It's my turn. I just tole you that."

Josiah rubbed a hand across his face. Apparently Amanda hadn't listened to him when he said he didn't need any help today. Throwing back the ratty quilt he had used as a covering, he got out of bed and went to the window. The boys were pushing each other now, and Josiah knew soon they would be rolling around on the ground, half fighting and half playing, as boys were wont to do.

He heard a door slam, and a moment later Amanda stood at her brothers' sides. He couldn't hear her words, but the way she placed her hands on her slim hips expressed her displeasure. Today she wore a black apron over a dark green dress that reached her calves. He forgot about Andrew and Thomas as he watched her, mesmerized. After a few moments, he regained his senses. He clenched his fists and turned away.

He didn't want to deal with this today. Last evening, he'd gone to Paradise, slowly riding down the side roads until long past dark, not wanting to go back home. Even though he hadn't lost his temper with Amanda, he had caused her pain, and he could hardly stand that. Gripping her wrist enough to make a mark served to solidify what he already knew—he couldn't be trusted to keep himself in control.

He pulled on his trousers, then picked up a blue shirt from his duffel bag and slid it over his shoulders. He hadn't bothered to unpack everything, and he didn't intend to. Having to pull everything out of a duffel bag every day served as a reminder that he wouldn't be here any longer than necessary.

It took him only a few minutes to get dressed. He scrubbed his hand over his face one more time. He hadn't shaved in two days, and he couldn't let his beard or mustache grow out any more. For a short time he had tried to live like the *Englisch*, but during that part of his life, he felt that he was turning his back on his mother somehow. Despite his inner struggles, he found a tiny measure of peace living Plain and following the *Ordnung*, even if he wasn't sure about his relationship with God.

He scrambled downstairs and went into the bathroom. Ten minutes later he emerged, clean shaven, but no more ready to face Amanda. How could he look her in the eye after he'd physically hurt her yesterday?

"Josiah? Is that you?"

Her lilting voice filtered from the kitchen to the other side of the modest house. Steeling himself, he headed toward her. He would put a stop to her coming over once and for all.

But then he saw her standing in front of the stove, as if she had always belonged there, in his kitchen, in his house. Once he smelled the tantalizing aroma of bacon cooking, he lost his resolve.

Turning, she told him good morning with a bright smile.

The thought of seeing her beautiful face every morning meandered through his mind, making his breath catch. How long had it been since he'd had someone make him breakfast, other than a cook in a restaurant? Years, since his *mamm* died. He swallowed as more memories overcame him, thoughts of his mother's buckwheat pancakes and homemade maple syrup so sweet and rich he would eat until almost bursting. His favorite breakfast, one she made for him often. What he wouldn't do to taste those pancakes now.

"I hope you're hungry. I'm used to cooking for a crowd, and I think I made too much." The oven door squeaked painfully as she opened it. Reaching inside, she pulled out a platter piled high with—he couldn't believe it—pancakes.

She lightly touched the top one. "The oven's not working yet, but the pancakes are still warm. Can you yell for Andrew and Thomas to come in?"

He hesitated. The scene seemed so strange, like he had gone back in time to when he and Amanda used to play that silly game of house. Only now it seemed almost real.

"Josiah?" She looked at him as she set the pancakes on the table. "If we wait much longer, they'll be cold."

He nodded and walked out the back door. Obviously the boys had made up with each other, because they were both climbing the old oak tree about twenty yards from the house. He cupped his hands around his mouth and yelled. "Andrew! Thomas! Breakfast, *nau!*"

The boys scrambled down the tree and broke into a sprint. He could tell they were racing, and the sight brought a smile to his face. A couple of inches shorter than his older brother, Thomas had a more natural stride. But Andrew had a superior kick, which he employed when they were a few feet from the house. They finished even.

"I . . . won!" Andrew said, gasping for air.

"*Nee*," Thomas said, not sounding quite as winded. "I won." He looked up at Josiah. "Didn't I, Mr. Josiah?"

Josiah cleared his throat, trying to maintain a serious tone. "It was a tie."

"Naw," Andrew said. "I beat him by a mile."

"Mr. Josiah said it was a tie, so it was a tie." Thomas gazed up at him again.

A mix of pride and possessiveness filtered through Josiah as he took in the young boy's admiring gaze. To be considered with such unabashed regard was humbling. Unable to stop himself, he reached out and ruffled Thomas's hair.

"What's taking you so long?" Amanda appeared on the back stoop. She looked at her brothers. "Wash up now. I fixed your favorite—pancakes and bacon."

"Awesome!" Andrew and Thomas gave each other a high five, then ran inside the house.

Josiah turned around and faced Amanda. "You didn't have to make breakfast, you know."

Instead of protesting as he expected, she simply smiled, winked at him, then went back inside the house.

He let out a sigh. Pancakes and a beautiful woman. How could he resist that? Somehow he had to try. But not until *after* breakfast.

⌇⌇

Andrew and Thomas inhaled their food, and Amanda sent them outside to play again until she and Josiah were finished eating. Then they could all get started on the work of the day.

She cut her pancake in half, then in quarters before pouring a small amount of syrup over the pieces. Glancing up, she noticed Josiah had his head down again, eating nearly as fast as the boys had. "Is my cooking that bad?"

He glanced up, one protruding cheek stuffed with food. "What?"

"The food. Is it so bad you can't slow down and taste it?"

A sheepish expression crossed his features. He chewed, slowly, and swallowed. "Just the opposite. It's very tasty."

She smiled. "I'm glad you enjoy it. I think you'll enjoy it more if you don't stuff it down your throat."

"Are you telling me how to eat my breakfast?"

"I suppose I am. Seems to me you need some tutoring in that area."

"Is that so?" Moving in slow motion, he picked up a piece of bacon and brought it to his mouth, then chewed with exaggerated movements. "Is that better?"

She giggled. "Much." Finally. This was the Josiah she remembered. Playful. Funny. Not sullen and somber. She held out the almost-empty platter of pancakes to him. "Do you want any more?"

"Best not." He patted his flat stomach. "I've eaten more than enough."

Clearly it was a compliment on her cooking, and she took it. Rising from her chair, she started clearing the table. She was surprised and pleased when he helped out. After putting the dishes in the sink, she turned around and looked at him. "Rachel was going to come today, but she and Hannah are helping *Mamm* repair a few of the boys' pants. They go through clothes like you wouldn't believe. I thought I'd work in the living room today. That shouldn't take that long. Unless the bathroom needs cleaning first? After seeing the kitchen, I can only imagine what it looks li—"

"Amanda."

The soft way he said her name made her shut her mouth.

He glanced down at his feet, then shifted from one to the other before looking up, all traces of his earlier playfulness gone. "I know I've said this before, and I really, really appreciate your help, but you can't keep doing this."

She tilted her head. "And as *I've* said before, I don't mind. I have *Mamm*'s blessing, and as long as my chores are done at home, it's no problem to give you a hand."

He shook his head. "You're not understanding me. I don't *want* you to help me." His gaze hardened. "I don't want you here."

Leaning against the sink, she crossed her arms over her chest, hurt. "Why not?"

"Does it matter why?"

"*Ya*, Josiah, it does. You can't just say you don't want me here and then not explain."

He threaded his fingers through his hair. "Okay, you want an explanation, here it is. I came back to Paradise for one reason—to fix this house up enough so that it will sell. Once I've done that, I'm putting it on the market. And when it sells, I'm taking the money and going to Ohio."

"You're not staying?"

"*Nee*. I never planned to. So as you can see, there's no point in your being here."

"But our friendship—"

"Look, Amanda. After I'm gone, we'll never see each other again. That's the way it has to be. That's the way I *want* it to be. I'll pay you for the food you brought yesterday and this morning, but after that I don't want you to bother coming over here."

Awareness dawned, and she felt like a fool. He had a girlfriend waiting for him in Ohio. How could she be so stupid? He was already spoken for, and it wouldn't do for him to be spending so much time with another woman, even though they were only friends.

Meeting his gaze, she realized that her mother had been right all along. Nothing was the same between them. Too much time had passed, and too much distance had separated them. Josiah seemed like a stranger to her because he truly was. And he seemed content to keep things that way.

"I understand," she said, turning her back to him. She blinked back tears, unwilling to let him see her mourn as he pounded the last nail in the coffin of their friendship. "I'll finish up the dishes," she said, distressed at the thickness in her voice. "Then the boys and I will *geh*. You don't have to worry, Josiah. We won't bother you again."

Silence surrounded her, and she knew he hadn't moved. After a long moment, she heard him walk out the kitchen door. Only then did she let the tears fall.

KATHLEEN FULLER

"Mr. Josiah!"

Clenching his jaw, Josiah stalked past Andrew and Thomas, ignoring their calling out his name. Bile clawed up his throat as the image of Amanda's stricken expression rewound itself in his mind. He had finally gotten through to her, although it had nearly killed him to do it.

"Mr. Josiah, wait up!"

He continued to walk toward the barn. He had hurt her once again. Not physically, as he had yesterday, but deeply nevertheless. He had seen it on her face, heard it in the tone of her voice. Seen it in the tears she tried to keep from him.

For a split second he had thought to put his arms around her, to apologize for being so harsh. But he stopped himself. She said she'd leave him alone, and that was what he had wanted all along.

"Mr. Josiah!"

He spun around in front of the barn entrance. "What do you want?"

Both Andrew and Thomas shrank back. "We just wanted to know how we could help you today."

"You can help by going home."

"But—"

"*Geh!* Get out of here!"

Andrew turned around and ran back to the house like he had flames licking at his heels. But Thomas didn't move. His lower lip quivered, and his hazel eyes, the same color as Amanda's, filled with tears.

Perfect. He'd made two innocent people cry today.

Thomas looked at him for a long moment, his shoulders slumped. He turned around, but unlike his brother, he didn't run. Instead he walked slowly, each trudging step driving a knife deeper into Josiah's heart.

"How dare you treat them that way!"

He looked up to see Amanda storming toward him. The sorrow he'd seen in her expression had been replaced with anger. Her fists pressed against her sides, she stopped short a few feet in front of him.

"All they wanted to do was help, Josiah. They look up to you, especially Thomas."

"They shouldn't."

"You're right. Not if you're going to treat him like that." She pressed her fingertips to her brow. "If you're mad at me, fine, but they don't deserve your taking it out on them."

The sound of a horse's hooves reached his ears. He looked down the length of his driveway to see a buggy approaching Amanda's house. A superbly constructed buggy, outfitted with as much reflective tape as the *Ordnung* would allow. He knew whose it was.

Josiah had thought this day couldn't get any worse. He had thought wrong.

Chapter Eight

"YOU GOT COMPANY," JOSIAH SAID.

Amanda glared at him, then turned around to glance at the buggy pulling into her driveway. "I'm not expecting anyone. Maybe one of *Mamm*'s friends is dropping by." She faced Josiah, looking as if she wanted to lay into him again. Instead, she frowned. "You look like you know who that is."

"Don't you?"

She turned again. A tall, slender man exited the buggy and tied his horse to the hitching post at the top of the Grabers' driveway. Cousin Peter.

"Oh no," Amanda groaned.

Well, he hadn't expected that reaction from her. "What's wrong?"

Her angry expression had been replaced by one of irritation. "He's been trying to court me for the past year. I've tried to be nice about it and let him know I'm not interested, but he's not getting the message." She glanced over her shoulder. "I wonder what he wants now."

Their argument apparently over, or at least postponed, Josiah moved to stand next to Amanda. "He shouldn't be bothering you like this."

"Maybe he's just dropping off something at the house."

"Has he ever done that before?"

She shook her head. "*Nee*. He's never even visited before."

Josiah wasn't in any hurry for her to leave now, not with Peter walking inside her house. He had a small measure of satisfaction knowing Amanda wasn't interested in his cousin. She'd always had good taste.

Within minutes Peter walked out the door, and Josiah hoped he would get in his buggy and take off. But instead he walked right past the buggy and across the yard, straight toward his house. Great. Just what he needed.

"*Wunderbaar*," Amanda said, lowering her voice and echoing his own thoughts. "He's coming over here."

"I can see that."

"What should I say to him?"

He looked at her incredulously. "You're asking me?"

"He's your cousin." She leaned closer to him. "How do I get him to leave me alone?"

Josiah could think of several ways of convincing Peter to leave her alone, but none of them were appropriate for Amanda to use, or even remotely Christian. He tried to think of a useful response as Peter came toward them with his hat perched low on his head the way he normally wore it, obscuring his eyes.

"Hello, Amanda," Peter said as he reached them. He stopped right in front of her, completely ignoring Josiah. "Your *mamm* said I could find you here."

"Hello, Peter."

Josiah could tell that she was struggling to be cordial, which was unusual for Amanda. He was surprised to find another person in Paradise who disliked his cousin. As the son of one of the most successful businessmen in the area, Peter didn't have to worry about the future. He made good money working beside his father in the buggy and harness shop, and when his father retired someday, the business would be his. He had a lot to offer a woman—a steady job and good stream of income, a nice house, and a secure future. Why wouldn't Amanda want that?

Then Peter opened his mouth, and Josiah realized why.

"I took a break from work to *personally* ask you to the singing at my house two weeks from this Sunday. Even though we're very busy at the shop, I made the extra trip. We've got over a dozen customers on a waiting list, and we're busting our tails to get all the work done." He leaned forward and put his face close to Amanda's, closer than he had the right to. "But you're worth it," he drawled.

Amanda took a step back, clearly unnerved. "Um, *danki*, Peter. You didn't have to go to so much trouble."

"I know." He gave her a haughty smile.

Josiah moved closer to Amanda, his guard up. He didn't like the way his cousin was looking at Amanda, as if he already possessed her. Amanda, for her part, appeared both frustrated and confused.

"I'll come by and pick you up at five," Peter said. He turned to go, still not saying a word to Josiah.

"Peter, wait." Amanda bit her lower lip. "I'm sorry. I can't go with you."

A spark flashed in his eyes. "Why not?"

"Because . . . because . . ." She looked up at Josiah, helplessness in her eyes.

Peter put his hands on his hips. "I'm getting tired of you putting me off, Amanda. There're plenty of *maed* who would jump at the chance to go out with me."

Josiah took a step forward. "Then maybe you should go find all those *maed* you're talking about and leave Amanda alone."

For the first time, Peter acknowledged him. "Stay out of this, Josiah. Better yet, why don't you stay out of Paradise?"

"Peter, how could you say something so terrible?" Amanda said. "And about your own cousin?"

Peter looked down the length of his nose. "He's no cousin of mine."

"Blood says otherwise," Josiah retorted.

"I'm having a private conversation. Do you mind?"

Josiah crossed his arms over his chest. "Since you're on my property, I do mind."

Peter shook his head, then turned his back on Josiah. "Come on, Amanda. We'll continue this at your house."

"There's nothing to talk about." She took a deep breath. "Peter, I already said I can't go with you."

"But you didn't tell me why." He put his arm around her shoulders and guided her away from Josiah. He was at least six inches taller than she was and twice her size in bulk. The gesture seemed innocent enough, but Josiah kept his guard up. When they were a few feet away and in Amanda's front yard, Peter dropped his arm and faced her.

〜⌒〜

Amanda glanced over her shoulder at Josiah, who remained on his side of the property line. Disappointment washed through her when he didn't follow her. Not that she should have expected him to. Peter Yoder was her problem, and Josiah had made it perfectly clear that he didn't want to get involved in her life.

Fine. She would deal with Peter. She didn't need Josiah's help anyway.

"I'm really sorry, Peter," she said, looking up at him. Well, she wasn't all that sorry, but she didn't want to be outright rude to him. "I can't go with you to the singing."

"Amanda, I drove all the way out here to ask you. I took time off from work."

"I know, Peter, but—"

"I don't understand why you keep refusing me. It's not like you've had any other offers. And face it, you're getting old. It's not like you can afford to be picky."

His words stung. "I'd appreciate it if you'd leave, Peter." She moved toward the house, fighting the irritation rising inside her. She wasn't that old. He made her sound like she needed to be put out to pasture.

"Wait—Amanda." He grabbed her upper arm, preventing her from moving any farther. "I'm sorry. It's just that I've liked you for so long." He pulled her toward him. "I don't understand why you don't like me too."

"Peter, let me go." The desperation she saw in his eyes stunned her.

"If you'd only give me a chance . . . please." His head tilted toward hers, and suddenly she realized he intended to kiss her. "You'd see how much I want you—"

"Let her *geh*!"

At the sound of Josiah's booming voice, Peter dropped his grip. Amanda immediately stepped back in shock. Peter had tried to kiss her. Right in front of her house. Had he lost his mind?

Josiah stormed toward Peter. "You touch her one more time and I'll—"

"You'll what?" Peter smirked. "Hit me? Go ahead. I'm sure the bishop will be happy to hear about how you beat up a member of the church, not to mention a member of your own family."

Amanda's gaze darted to Josiah, who remained in place. His fists were clenched at his sides, and his mouth was pressed in a flat line. For a brief moment she thought he might cave in to his cousin's taunt. Then his posture relaxed, but only slightly. "I suggest you leave, Peter. Now."

"Not until Amanda tells me why she can't go to the singing with me."

"I'll tell you why. Because she's going with me."

Amanda's mouth dropped open. Josiah couldn't have surprised her more if he had sprouted wings and started flying around the yard. She should have done a better job at hiding her shock, but she couldn't, not when only moments ago he had made it abundantly clear that he wanted her to leave him alone.

"You're taking her?" Peter scoffed as he looked at Amanda. "Seems to me she had no idea about that."

She met Josiah's gaze. The slightly confused look in her eyes spoke volumes.

"Just as I thought." Peter crossed his arms over his chest. "She's not going with you."

"*Ya*, I am." The words came out before she could stop them. Turning to Josiah, she said, "I'd be happy to go with you. Extremely happy."

Still looking at Peter, he said, "*Gut*. It's a date."

A *date*? Her mouth suddenly went dry. His words were obviously aimed to irk Peter, and from the way the other man's face reddened, it had worked. Still, to proclaim aloud and to his cousin that he had asked her out on a date seemed unreal.

"Fine," Peter said, backing away from them both. "If you want to be with this loser, go ahead. Just remember what you're giving up." He looked past them, gesturing with an upward tilt of his chin at the run-down barn behind them. "He's as worthless as that barn. You'll see." Spinning around, he stalked back to his buggy.

Amanda didn't breathe until Peter and his buggy were well out of sight.

"Are you all right?" Josiah asked.

Her cheeks reddened. "*Ya*. I'm sorry about that."

"Not your fault he's a jerk. He always has been. Comes from being spoiled, if you ask me." He gave her another look. The horse suddenly whinnied from inside the barn. "I've got to feed her. 'Scuse me." He turned and went inside.

Amanda followed him into the barn, squinting as her vision adjusted to the dark interior. She glanced around, seeing the horse in her stall waiting patiently to be fed. There was room enough for three more horses, but she didn't remember the Bontragers ever having more than one at any time.

She watched as Josiah dragged a bale of fresh hay from the other side of the barn closer to the horse's stall. He pulled a small knife out of his pocket, flipped it open, and cut the rough twine securing the square bale. He loosened the hay with his hands, then grabbed what looked like a brand-new pitchfork and tossed fresh hay over the stall door into the horse's trough.

"Josiah."

He didn't stop, nor did he look at her. *"Ya?"*

He wasn't going to make this easy for her. But she wasn't about to walk away. "I appreciate your helping me out with Peter."

"No problem." He shoved the pitchfork into another pile of hay.

"I'm sorry you had to be dragged into it. I wish he would just leave me alone. He's right about one thing: there are plenty of *maed* in the community who would love his attention. Plenty of them that are more his age."

"He's only two years younger than you."

"Two and a half. Besides, twenty-one is too young. For me anyway." She winced, remembering his words about her being old.

Flipping the hay into the stall, Josiah didn't comment.

She clasped her hands together. How could he be so unaffected by what had just happened? She had thought he would at least say something. Instead, he seemed content to ignore the incident entirely.

Stepping forward, she moved until she was almost right beside him, but clear enough away that she wouldn't get the in the way of his work. "Look, Josiah, I know you don't want to take me to the singing. I won't hold you to it." She looked away, suddenly feeling embarrassed and more than a little insecure. "I know you only said that so he would leave me alone."

He moved to grab more hay, but before sliding the pitchfork underneath a large clump, he halted. Turning, he looked at her, his expression resolute. "I said I'd take you, and I'll keep my word."

He didn't have to sound so enthusiastic about it. Also, it wasn't right, not when he was already spoken for. "What about your girlfriend in Ohio?"

His eyes grew wide. "What girlfriend?"

"The one you're going back to once you sell the house." How

painful it was to say that aloud. Why should she be bothered that he had someone waiting for him? She should be more surprised that he hadn't married by now. They were both twenty-four, and most of her friends were already starting families. Even her mother had expressed concern recently about Amanda's lack of a beau.

He resumed working, sliding the pitchfork underneath the last remnants of hay and dropping them in the trough. The crunching sound of hay being mashed between the animal's teeth filled the barn. Slowly Josiah leaned the pitchfork against the wall, then faced her. "There's no one waiting for me in Ohio."

"Oh. She's still in Indiana?" She frowned, confused. If his girlfriend lived in Indiana, why was he going to Ohio?

"Amanda," he said, looking directly at her. "I don't have a girlfriend."

She nearly let out a sigh of relief, but stopped just in time. "Then why are you going there? Why not just stay here in Paradise?"

He kicked at a dirt clod on the barn floor. Dust particles rose and danced in the beams of light streaming through the open gaps in the barn wall slats. "I can't. Not in this house."

"Well, of course not, not with things the way they are. But once you get everything fixed up, this will be a great place to live. Just the way it used to be."

"*Ya* . . . maybe."

She didn't miss the doubt in his voice, and figured he must be tired and overwhelmed. "It will. I promise you that."

Josiah walked to the other side of the barn and leaned against the wall. "Doesn't matter. I'm selling."

Fighting her rising disappointment, she said, "I hate to see you do all this work for nothing, Josiah."

"It's not for nothing. This is a great piece of property and a fairly large house. And look at the barn." He gestured to it with his hands. "Four stalls, a loft, another place to store hay on the ground floor. You can't find barns this nice anymore. Well, it will be nice once I'm done with it. In the backyard there's a place for a large garden, and when I finish with the front porch, it will be a *gut* place to relax at the end of the day."

Amanda could hear a tinge of excitement in his voice as he spoke, and she warmed to it. "In other words, a great place for *you* to live."

He didn't answer her for a long moment as he stared at the horse finishing her meal. Finally he said, "What time did Peter say he was gonna pick you up for the singing?"

His change of subject had been severe, and she had to respect that, even though it frustrated her to do so. "Five. It starts at five thirty. I think we have a problem, though. Peter thinks you and I will be on a date."

"Oh, that." He shrugged, but she noticed he kept his gaze from hers. "I said that for his benefit. I didn't want him to get any ideas that he had a chance with you."

"I see." She hid the disappointment from her voice. "But what if he tells everyone that we're courting?"

Josiah looked up at her. "He won't. The last thing Peter would do is admit he had lost you to me."

"Oh." She didn't know how to respond to that.

He came toward her, his handsome features softening a bit. "Amanda, about this morning. I'm sorry. You're right, I shouldn't have yelled at your brothers that way. They didn't deserve it. I'll make it up to them, I promise."

The sincerity in his eyes touched her. "I know you will."

"And if you still want to help, I can use it. Although I don't understand why you'd want to spend your time working here."

"Because that's what friends are for, Josiah."

"I figured you'd have lots of other things you'd rather do."

She stepped toward him, her heart squeezing at the self-deprecating tone in his voice. Somehow she had to convince him he was worth it. "Remember when we were ten, Josiah? How we promised each other we would always be friends?"

He nodded slowly.

"I intended on keeping that promise. I'm going to keep it now. Nothing you can do or say is going to change that."

The corner of his mouth lifted. "You're stubborn, you know that?"

"I prefer 'persistent.'"

He chuckled. "At least that part of you hasn't changed."

"And what part of me has?"

As soon as she asked the question, she wanted to take it back. It might have been okay to ask such a thing when they were kids, but wholly inappropriate now that they were adults. Still, she held her breath as she waited for him to answer.

"Mandy . . ." His voice, barely above a whisper, sent pleasant waves through her body.

"Amanda! Amanda!"

She whirled around at the sound of Rachel's panicked calls. "In here!" She dashed out of the barn, barely aware of Josiah following closely behind.

Rachel ran to Amanda, the black strings of her *kapp* flying behind her. "It's *Mamm*," she said, taking a big gulp of air, her eyes filled with fright. "There's something . . . wrong." She burst into tears.

Amanda put her arms around her sister's shoulders, fighting the alarm rising inside her. "Let's *geh*," she said, and they rushed to the house. When they burst through the kitchen door, Amanda put a hand to her mouth, her resolve to keep calm abandoning her.

Her mother lay on the floor, unmoving.

Chapter Nine

JOSIAH BLANCHED AS HE ENTERED THE KITCHEN AND SAW Katharine Graber lying on the floor, apparently unconscious. From the large size of her swollen belly, she looked far into her pregnancy. A very young boy sat next to her, confusion on his round face.

Amanda ran to Katharine's side and knelt down near her head. "*Mamm! Mamm*, can you hear me?"

"What's wrong with *Mammi*?" Rachel asked, her voice heavy with tears.

At this point several more children came into the kitchen and started hovering over their mother. They crowded closer to Amanda and peppered her with questions.

"Rachel, Hannah," Amanda said as she looked up, her voice barely controlled. "Take the *kinder* upstairs until I tell you to come back down."

The girls nodded and rounded everyone up. Amid the younger children's protests, they departed the kitchen, leaving Amanda and Josiah alone with her mother.

"*Mamm*," Amanda said, taking her mother's hand. "Please, *Mamm*. Wake up."

Josiah came around the other side. Just as he started to kneel down, Katharine opened her eyes.

"Amanda?" Her eyelids fluttered.

Amanda's shoulders slumped with relief. "How do you feel?" she asked, still holding her hand.

"Okay," Katharine replied, trying to sit up. She looked pale, but otherwise fine. "I guess I must have fainted. One minute I was standing near the stove, the next I'm looking at you."

Amanda put her other arm around Katharine's shoulders and tried to assist her. "You need to lie down on the couch."

Seeing Amanda struggle to help her mother spurred Josiah into action. He crouched down and assisted Katharine to her feet.

"*Danki*, Josiah."

He nodded and put a supporting arm lightly around Katharine's shoulders as Amanda left the room. By the time he and Katharine reached the couch, she had returned with a damp white washcloth.

"Honestly, I'm fine." Katharine waved off Amanda's offer of a cold cloth and sat down. She shifted awkwardly on the couch until she settled in a lying down position, smoothing out the skirt of her plum-colored dress. "I just got a little light-headed, that's all. I don't think I drank enough water today, and it's warm in the kitchen."

Standing next to Amanda in the Grabers' living room, Josiah was sent back into the past. The interior of the house hadn't changed much over the years, and he clearly remembered the light blue, rosebud-covered couch Katharine lay on now. He looked down at her, glad to see some color return to her cheeks.

When he'd entered the kitchen with Amanda and Rachel and seen her lying motionless, a stab of terror had gone through him. His own *mamm* had passed away in a hospital, and that had been traumatic enough. He imagined how frightened the young children were to see their mother lying on the floor.

"*Mamm*, please, just put this on your head for a minute." Amanda placed the washcloth on Katharine's forehead. "You might have gotten overheated too. This will help cool you off."

"All right." Katharine leaned back and closed her eyes, holding the cloth against her forehead. "Where are the *kinder*?"

"I sent them upstairs with Hannah and Rachel."

Katharine opened her eyes, revealing her regret and concern. "I bet they're scared to death. Tell them to come downstairs so I can tell them I'm all right."

"But I don't want to leave you. I'm sure Rachel and Hannah are letting them know everything's okay."

"Amanda, nothing is more reassuring than hearing a mother's voice, especially to a young *kind*. Now, I told you I'm fine. I don't feel dizzy anymore, and certainly nothing is going to happen to me on this couch if I'm alone for five seconds."

"But—"

"I'll get them," Josiah said. "You stay with your *mamm*."

"*Danki,*" Amanda said, giving him a grateful glance.

As a child Josiah had visited the Grabers so many times he knew their house as well as his own. He went down the short hallway to the staircase, then took the stairs two at a time. He'd made it halfway up when he heard the children's murmurs, although he couldn't make out what they were saying.

There were three bedrooms upstairs. He followed their voices to the room at the end of the hall, the heels of his shoes clomping against the wooden floor. The door was partially open, but he knocked anyway.

A girl answered the door, one he hadn't met before. Hannah, he assumed. Like Amanda and Thomas, she had bright hazel eyes and light brown hair. Right now those eyes were filled with anxiety, even though he could tell she was trying valiantly to keep her composure.

"Did *Mamm* say we could come downstairs now?" she asked. Hannah wore a prayer *kapp*, black in color to symbolize that she was under age sixteen. She tugged on one of the ribbons as she spoke.

"*Ya*, your *mamm* wants to see you." Josiah peeked inside the small room, taking in the two single beds on opposite walls, which were painted a light green color. A faceless Amish doll lay on one bed, while the other was covered with a brightly patterned quilt in pinks and blues.

Rachel sat on one bed, holding a young boy in her lap. The child was sucking his thumb and trying to squirm out of his sister's arms, but he wore a playful expression. Fortunately he seemed unaware of what had happened to his mother. Another boy, the one Josiah had seen by Katharine when she fainted, sat on the floor moving a small wooden train engine back and forth over the circular rag area rug. He looked to be a couple of years older than the toddler but younger than Thomas. He, too, appeared oblivious of the worry shared by his siblings.

Andrew and Thomas sat on the other bed, the one with the colorful quilt. Andrew wouldn't look at Josiah, and he didn't blame him. Somehow he had to make it up to the boy. But Thomas caught his gaze, scooted off the bed, and walked over to him.

"Is *Mamm* gonna die, Mr. Josiah?"

Pain lanced him. He had been only a few years older when he'd asked his father that same question, after seeing his mother at the hospital for the last time. His *daed* had refused to answer him, just stared straight ahead, his face blank. From that day forward his father only had two expressions: blankness and fury.

Josiah shook his head, clearing his mind of the memory. Kneeling down in front of him, Josiah said, "*Nee*, Thomas. Your *mamm* is gonna be fine. She wants all of you to come downstairs so she can tell you that she's all right."

The anxiety melted from Thomas's face. "*Danki*, Mr. Josiah. I was really scared."

"We all were," Rachel added, letting the toddler down from her lap.

What did Amanda say his name was? Jacob, that's right. As Josiah stood, Jacob came over to him with arms outstretched. Josiah stared at him, unsure what to do.

"He wants you to hold him," Hannah said, smiling. As with Thomas, the tension seemed to have drained from her body. "That's a *gut* thing, as he normally doesn't take to strangers."

Josiah lifted the boy, who couldn't have weighed more than

thirty pounds. He looked at his face for a moment, noticing a small smear of something above his lip. Chocolate, maybe. He didn't know much about kids, and even less about babies and toddlers. Was this child even old enough to eat chocolate?

"Christopher," Hannah said, holding out her hand to the young boy playing on the rug. "Let's go see *Mamm*. She's feeling better now."

Without a word Christopher stood up, his train engine clutched to his chest. They all filed past Josiah, including Andrew, who still didn't look at him.

Josiah turned and followed the children, carrying Jacob downstairs.

"Mammi!" He heard Christopher's high-pitched voice as he rounded the corner. By the time he reached the living room with Jacob, the children were seated on the floor in front of Katharine. Amanda knelt beside the couch, near her mother's head. She removed the rag as Katharine moved to sit up.

"You should lie back down," Amanda said, sounding more like Katharine's mother than her daughter.

"Nee, I don't need to." She looked at Amanda, her blue eyes reassuring. "The same thing happened to me when I was pregnant with you, Mandy. It was on a Saturday, and your *daed* was here at the time, which was a *gut* thing. I about scared him to death, too, but it never happened again. Not until today." She smiled. "I promise, I'm all right." She looked at the children, her gaze landing on each of them briefly, individually reassuring them that she was fine. Then she glanced around. "Where's Jacob?"

"He's right here." Josiah walked farther into the room. But when he tried to hand Jacob to his mother, the little boy grabbed hold of Josiah's suspenders. Gently Josiah extracted the child's small hand from the black strap and set him on the ground. The boy immediately toddled to his mother, putting the index finger of his right hand into his mouth.

Amanda intercepted him and set him on her lap. "*Mamm* needs her rest, Jacob," she said, her voice low and soft. "She can hold you later."

Josiah stood in the middle of the room, watching the scene before him, feeling like an interloper. His arms felt empty after he had released Jacob, and jealousy stabbed at him as he surveyed the family gathered together. The love they all had for each other flowed throughout the room.

Fortunately the children all seemed all right. A little shaken up, but they appeared to take Katharine's reassurances to heart and had already started getting fidgety.

"Can we go outside now, *Mamm*?" Andrew asked, rocking back and forth on his knees. Josiah could relate to his desire to be outside.

"Sure," Katharine said with a laugh. "Why don't you all go outside and play a bit. It would be shameful to waste the fresh air. Hannah, do you mind taking Jacob?"

Hannah picked up her youngest brother from Amanda's lap and led him out of the living room. The rest of the children all scrambled off the floor and headed outside, leaving Josiah and Amanda with Katharine.

"I'll have lunch ready in about an hour," Katharine called out after them.

"I'll prepare lunch, *Mamm*." Amanda rose from her seated position on the floor. "You'll stay here and rest."

Katharine nodded, leaning back against one of the small pillows that matched the pattern of the couch. "I'm not going to argue with you. I do feel tired." At Amanda's look of alarm, she added, "But I'm *fine*. I will admit, though, that this *boppli* is taking more out of me than the other *kinder* did." She let out a chuckle. "Guess that's what happens when you get old."

"You're not old, *Mamm*."

"You're sweet to say that. But I'm getting there, that's for sure."

Not wanting to eavesdrop on the conversation more than he

already had, Josiah turned to leave, grimacing when the floorboard squeaked beneath the heel of his shoe.

"Josiah?"

He turned at the sound of Katharine's voice. *"Ya?"*

"Danki for your help. You don't have to leave just yet. Please join us for lunch."

"I'm sorry, but I can't. I have a lot of work to do at the house. But I appreciate the offer."

"All right. Just know, Josiah, that you're always welcome here. Anytime. We're glad you've come back."

Josiah nodded as he met her gaze, then left the room.

"I know you're in a hurry to get back to work," Amanda said to him as they entered the kitchen. "But I want you to know how thankful I am that you were here to help me with *Mamm.* I don't know what I would have done . . . I couldn't have lifted her . . ." Her lower lip trembled.

Something broke inside of Josiah as he saw tears form in Amanda's eyes. Only now did she reveal how truly scared she had been for her mother. Then he remembered her encounter with Peter, and his heart went out to her. She'd had a rough morning. As one tear slid out of the corner of her eye, he couldn't resist wiping it from her cheek with the side of his thumb. At the sound of her soft sigh, he snatched his hand back, regaining his senses.

He cleared his throat, thrusting his hands into his pockets. "Glad I was here. I'll see you later." He paused, remembering he had to take care of something first. "I need to set things right with your brothers. Would it be okay if they helped me out for a few more days? If they get bored or tired of the work, I'll send them back home."

Happiness replaced the anxiety in her eyes. *"Nee,* they won't be bored. Hard work is *gut* for them, Josiah. They'll learn a lot from you."

Josiah wasn't sure about that after how he had treated them this morning, but he would feel better knowing he'd done something to make up for yelling at them. "Take care of your *mamm*," he couldn't resist adding as he opened the back door.

"I will."

He looked at her for one last moment, unable to pull his gaze from her pretty face. If only things were different. "*Ya*. I know you will. She couldn't be in better hands."

Chapter Ten

AMANDA STOOD AT THE BACK DOOR AND WATCHED AS Josiah made his way over to Andrew and Thomas, who were sliding down the plastic yellow slide attached to the swing set. Thomas listened at perfect attention, but Andrew hung back. After a few moments Josiah reached out and touched Andrew's shoulder. Her brother responded to the gesture by moving a little closer, then finally stood beside Josiah. Soon all three of them disappeared from view as they headed for Josiah's house.

She grinned, the tension draining from her. *Mamm* would be all right, as the Lord had watched over her today. Josiah had made amends with her brothers. Most important, he seemed to have opened up a little bit to her. She touched her cheek where his thumb had brushed away her tears. Such a kind gesture, and an unexpected one for so many reasons. Her skin still tingled from his gentle touch.

Turning away from the door, she went back and checked on her *mamm*. Her eyes were closed, and Amanda was glad to see her resting. She had been terrified when she'd seen her mother lying on the floor, unconscious.

Guilt pricked at her, and she realized she should have been here helping her *mamm* instead of over at Josiah's, who hadn't even wanted her there in the first place. If she had been here at the house, then her mother wouldn't have overdone it.

Amanda pressed her lips together. She wouldn't leave her mother alone again, not until the baby's birth. Even though Hannah and Rachel had been here to help, her mother clearly needed more rest.

"Amanda?"

"Did you need something, *Mamm?*"

Katharine shook her head. "Don't worry, *Dochder*. I'm still okay." She reached up and brushed back a strand of Amanda's hair that had escaped her *kapp*. "I just wanted to thank you for your help."

"I didn't do nearly enough." Amanda looked down at her hands. "I shouldn't have gone over to Josiah's."

"You think this is your fault?" Katharine tilted her head and gave her a gentle smile. "Amanda, these things sometimes happen. A person can pass out for any number of reasons. And I haven't been drinking water like I should. The doctor said to watch out for dehydration. So it's really my fault. Besides, you were right to go to Josiah's."

"He doesn't think so. He doesn't want my help anymore. Although he did tell Andrew and Thomas they could work with him for a few days."

"That's *gut*," Katharine said. "I'm sure he'll keep them busy."

"He plans to sell the house when he's finished."

Katharine appeared surprised. "He's selling it?"

Amanda nodded. "Then he's moving to Ohio."

"So that's where he's been."

"*Nee*. He lived in Indiana, but he's not going back there."

"Sounds like he has everything planned out."

"*Ya*," Amanda said, unable to hide the disappointment in her voice.

But if Katharine noticed her tone, she didn't mention it. "It's near lunchtime. Are you sure I can't help?"

"Positive. You rest."

"*Danki*, Amanda. You have been such a help to me."

"I'm happy to help."

"I know you are. You've been that way since you were a young child. And when we had Hannah, then the other *kinder*, I don't know what I would have done without you." She sobered. "But I worry I'm keeping you from your own life."

Amanda shook her head. "This is my life. Taking care of you and *Daed* and the children."

"But don't you ever think of having a family of your own?"

She paused. "Sometimes." More often than she wanted to admit. "But it seems God's plan is for me to stay right here, at least for now, until I meet the man He has set apart for me."

"Perhaps you've already met him."

"Oh, *nee*," she said, shaking her head vehemently. "Peter Yoder is not the man for me."

"I wasn't talking about Peter."

Amanda lifted her brow. "Then who?"

Katharine leaned back on the couch and closed her eyes. "You'll have to figure that out yourself."

A short while later Amanda had lunch prepared and served to the children. She took a tray of chicken soup and a cheese sandwich, along with a large glass of water, to her mother, but she was asleep. Setting the tray on the coffee table in front of the couch, Amanda tiptoed out of the living room.

As she made her way back to the kitchen, her mind began to whirl. What did her mother mean about her already having met the man God had set apart for her? Thank goodness she hadn't meant Peter. She thought about the other young men in her community. While there were some very nice ones, none of them had stirred any feelings inside her. Unlike Josiah.

Surely her mother hadn't meant him. That didn't make any sense, especially after Amanda had just told her that he wanted to sell his house and move to Ohio. Besides, Josiah had been back a total of three days, and they had barely rekindled their friendship.

But she couldn't deny that romantic feelings for him had started to grow.

How did everything get so complicated?

Josiah ran a brush through his hair, smoothing his bangs over his forehead. He needed a haircut, and maybe he would take the time to get one next week. But he couldn't worry about that now, not when he had to pick up Amanda in fifteen minutes.

Two weeks had quickly passed since Peter's visit. The more time passed, the more he regretted his snap decision to take Amanda to the singing. Everything had gotten too complicated too quickly. It wasn't that he didn't want to spend time with her—he did, more than he had a right to. But taking her to this singing meant facing even more of his past. He'd see people he grew up with, and they would undoubtedly ask him a lot of questions he didn't want to answer. At least with others he could be vague and not have to worry about them pressing the issue. Unlike Amanda.

He hadn't seen much of her the past two weeks except at a distance, when she and her sisters were working on their garden patch, pulling up dead weeds and spreading piles of compost on top of the garden to enrich the existing soil. To his chagrin he had spent more time watching her toil than he should have. But he couldn't help it. Her beauty stunned him, and she worked with such spirit and vigor. Any man would be proud to have her as his wife.

He would be especially proud. But he was also realistic.

Taking a deep breath, he slid his arms through his suspenders, then went downstairs to retrieve his hat. A worn-out brim, and a small stain near the hatband. He wished he had a new one to wear, but this would have to do.

A blast of brisk air greeted him as he stepped outside. It was near the end of October, when days were shorter and the air cooler. The temperature dropped a little bit as evening approached, cool enough to wear a jacket over his light blue long-sleeved shirt.

He glanced at the Grabers' house. Should he walk over and get Amanda, or hitch Tater to the buggy? Josiah didn't particularly care for the name Thomas had chosen, but the boy had a spark of pride in his voice every time he mentioned her by name.

Before he could make his decision, he heard the sound of a screen door shut and turned to see Amanda striding toward him. His mouth went dry as he gazed at her, taking in her dark green dress and white prayer *kapp*. She smiled as she neared, and it tugged at his heart.

He was in for a long night.

"Missed seeing you at church this morning," Amanda said as Josiah guided the buggy onto the road.

He shrugged, keeping his gaze straight ahead. He hadn't said more than two words to her since she'd met him at his house a few minutes ago. She glanced down at the plastic container filled with fresh-baked monster cookies—packed with oats, chocolate chips, and M&M's and rolled in powdered sugar. She had taken care with her appearance, knowing that the green dress brought out the green in her hazel eyes. But she shouldn't have bothered. She doubted Josiah even knew the color of her eyes, he so rarely looked directly at her.

Silence filled the space between them, and not for the first time she thought this was a bad idea. She hated feeling awkward around Josiah. After a few more minutes of only the sound of the passing cars and the clip-clop of Tater's hooves, she couldn't stand it anymore.

"You were right about Peter," she said.

He turned to her. "What?"

Finally, she had gotten his attention. "I expected at church this morning some of my friends would ask about our going to the singing together, but no one mentioned it."

"I'm not surprised. Like I said, Peter hates to lose."

"I'm not a prize, Josiah."

"Peter thinks so."

"Well, I don't care what he thinks." She settled against the seat. "I just hope he leaves me alone after this."

Josiah pulled on the reins, guiding the horse to make a right turn onto the road where Peter and his family lived. "You let me know if he doesn't."

She hid a smile at his protective tone. She'd never figure this man out. "I remember you spending a lot of time at your aunt and uncle's. I didn't realize you and Peter didn't get along."

"It's a long story."

"We've got time."

He glanced at her for a brief moment, then focused on the road ahead. "I suppose you'll keep asking until I tell you."

"You know me so well."

His lips quirked, but he didn't smile. "We were okay when we were younger. Then when I turned ten, I started helping my uncle in the shop. Peter wasn't old enough to do much more than clean up and be our gopher, which he hated. I think he resented the time my *Onkel* John and I spent together. And since Peter has five sisters, *Onkel* John appreciated the extra help."

"But then Peter worked in the shop too, right?"

Josiah nodded. "He wasn't quite as angry at that point, but we still didn't get along. Peter always had everything he wanted or needed, but he still never seemed happy. Then *Mamm* died." He swallowed. "My *onkel* was there for me more than my own *daed* was."

"I'm so sorry," she said, seeing the stricken look on his face. "I had no idea."

"I didn't want to talk about it. There's the house." He nodded toward a large white house several hundred yards away.

Amanda had only been to the Yoders' a few times before, for church services over the years and when Peter's oldest sister, Esther, had gotten married a couple of years ago. As the beautiful house came into view, she couldn't help but be impressed. Although there was nothing ostentatious about it, the size of the house, shop, and property bespoke of wealth. She had heard stories over the years of how generous John and Vera Yoder had been to families in the community that were struggling financially. She hoped Peter would keep up that family tradition.

Numerous gray buggies were parked in the large area near the shop. She spotted a volleyball net in the backyard behind the house, and several young women and men were already playing with a bright yellow ball. The scent of grilling meat greeted her as Josiah squeezed his buggy into the last space near the hitching post. Hamburgers, or maybe chicken, she couldn't tell. Her stomach growled.

They disembarked from the buggy, and Josiah tethered Tater. Amanda clutched her cookies while Josiah shoved his hands in his pockets. One look at his uncertain expression, and she knew they shouldn't have come here together.

"I'll take these cookies inside to your *aenti*," she said.

"I'll come with you." He fell in step beside her as they went to the house. "I want to say hello to her and *Onkel* John."

They entered through the side door and passed through a large mudroom before reaching the spacious kitchen, where plates and trays of desserts covered the oblong table. Giving the spread a cursory look, Amanda noticed at least four different kinds of cookies, a baking dish filled with date pudding, chocolate-frosted brownies, a huge hickory nut cake, and two double-crust apple pies.

"Looks *gut*," Josiah said, his hands still in his pockets. He nodded his approval, then glanced around the kitchen. "Wonder where *Aenti* Vera is."

Amanda looked out the large, multipaned window that exposed the Yoders' expansive backyard. Two more tables were set up near the gas grill manned by Josiah's uncle. Those tables were also filled with platters of food. "We won't starve here," she commented.

"*Nee. Aenti* Vera always makes sure everyone has plenty." Josiah walked over to the window and stared outside.

After shifting a few of the desserts around, Amanda made enough room for her container, then moved to stand by him.

"I don't know anyone here," he said, still looking outside. "Then again, I suppose most of our old friends are married by now."

"*Ya*, they are." She peered at a young woman and man standing off to the side, watching the volleyball game. From the way they stood close to each other, everyone could see they were a couple. "You remember Ben Weaver and Rebecca Miller, don't you?"

He hesitated, then nodded.

"Her twin sister drowned in a skating accident." Amanda shook her head. "Such a tragedy. Rebecca had a hard time dealing with it, not that anyone could blame her. She's found happiness with Ben, though."

"I can see that."

"They're getting married in a few weeks." She nodded toward another couple just arriving. "Leah and Aaron Lantz are here too. Leah Lantz was formerly Leah Petersheim. They married last year."

"I don't know them very well," he said.

"You'd like Aaron; he's a great guy."

Josiah didn't say anything for a moment. Then he looked at her. "I have to admit, I'm surprised you're not married yet."

"I could say the same thing for you."

He looked out the window again. "I don't plan on getting married."

Amanda did a double take. Choosing to remain single was almost unheard of among the Amish. She started to ask him why, when his aunt bustled into the kitchen.

"I know I put the extra napkins somewhere," she mumbled, tapping her chin with her index finger. Then she glanced in the direction of the window, and a wide grin appeared on her face. "Josiah!" She went to him, squeezing between the chairs around the table and the wall. "I had no idea you were here! When did you arrive?"

"Just a few minutes ago, *Aenti*. Amanda dropped off a dessert."

Vera looked at Amanda and smiled. "*Danki*. I hope you found room for it."

"I did. Everything looks wonderful."

"It's nothing," Vera said, batting away the compliment with her hand. "I just hope everyone has a *gut* time." She looked at Josiah and smiled. "Especially you."

Without replying, Josiah averted his gaze.

Apparently not noticing her nephew's reticence, Vera said, "Now, you two *geh* outside and have fun. They're starting up another volleyball game. You used to love to play, Josiah." She moved toward them and made shooing gestures with her hands. "Get out there before the game starts."

Amanda hid a smile as she and Josiah left the house and entered the backyard. Fragrant smoke drifted from the gas grill, scenting the air and making her mouth water. The Yoders had a large concrete patio, and several young people were sitting in plastic chairs, talking and watching their friends playing horseshoes and choosing teams for the volleyball game. She and Josiah stood on the perimeter, still unnoticed by everyone else. She turned to him. "Do you want to play?"

"*Nee*, not today."

"Oh, come on, Josiah," Amanda said. She enjoyed volleyball and remembered what a great player he'd been. Without thinking, she reached out and grabbed his hand. "It'll be fun."

Chapter Eleven

JOSIAH STARED AT HER SMALL HAND IN HIS LARGE ONE. Warmth traveled from his palm throughout his entire body as he reveled in Amanda's touch. The way she had grabbed his hand had been so smooth, so natural, he doubted she had thought twice about it, or that she had any idea how her touch affected him.

"I'm not taking no for an answer," she said, tugging on his hand. "Your *aenti* told you to have fun, and I'm going to make sure you do." She smiled at him, her cheeks rosy from the cool air, the ribbons from her prayer *kapp* fluttering around her shoulders.

Those ribbons weren't the only thing fluttering. Despite his efforts, he couldn't calm his heart rate.

Several girls and guys on the patio turned and looked at them, and he realized he either had to follow her to the volleyball net or risk making a scene. Taking off his coat, he took a few steps forward. "All right, you've convinced me. Or should I say you didn't give me much of a choice."

"Either one works for me." She grinned and released her grasp.

His hand had never felt so empty.

The underlying anxiety he'd felt since leaving his house threatened to surface as he approached the group of people near the volleyball net. He had spoken the truth to Amanda: he didn't know very many of them. Then his gaze landed on Ben Weaver, and he felt a little relief at seeing another friendly face.

"I see my cousin has decided to join us." Peter suddenly appeared and stood beside a pretty young *maedel* Josiah didn't recognize.

So much for relief.

"You all remember Josiah, don't you?"

A couple of people nodded, although Josiah wasn't sure who they were. Then he saw Ben tossing the volleyball up and down. Ben gave him a wide grin. "Hey, Josiah. Heard you were back in town. Glad you could make it."

Josiah nodded. He and Ben hadn't known each other all that well; Ben was a couple of years younger. But he'd always been friendly, and Josiah was glad to see that hadn't changed.

"We just finished picking teams," Peter said in an even tone, but Josiah could see a tiny spark of resentment in his cousin's eyes. "Since I'm one of the captains, I choose Amanda."

"We'll have Josiah," Ben said.

The teams assembled, and soon they started playing. Before long Josiah had shed any self-consciousness and immersed himself in the game. He hadn't played in a long time, but soon he fell into a comfortable rhythm and scored a couple of points.

At game point, it was his turn to serve. He tossed the ball in the air and executed a perfect serve—directly at Amanda.

"Mine!" she yelled, extending her arms and clasping her hands together in position to bump the ball either over the net or to one of the players on her team. Josiah watched her, hoping she would make a clean hit.

She missed the ball.

Josiah's team hollered and celebrated their victory, and a couple of the guys clapped him on the back. He accepted their congratulations and walked toward Amanda to tell her good game, but paused as he saw Peter moving to stand next to her.

"How could you have missed that?" His tone wasn't overly loud, but loud enough for Josiah to hear him.

Amanda, to her credit, didn't cower. "It was a *gut* serve. I misjudged it."

Josiah ducked under the net and went to Amanda. "Is there a problem here?"

"*Nee*," she said, looking straight at Peter, appearing a little upset.

"Food's ready!" *Onkel* John called out.

Peter walked away without another comment, but Josiah's anger continued to simmer. He wanted nothing more than to grab his cousin and knock some manners into him. But that wasn't the Amish way, and even if he were still living an *Englisch* life, he wouldn't have done anything to embarrass his aunt and uncle. He clenched his jaw, took a deep breath, then looked at Amanda, grateful everyone else had abandoned the volleyball court in favor of eating. "Sorry about that."

"You shouldn't apologize for your cousin's bad behavior." Glancing at Peter again, she added, "Maybe one day he'll grow up."

"We can hope."

Amanda turned and faced him, a smile on her face. "You haven't lost your touch at volleyball, I see."

"And you're still a graceful loser." He took a step closer to her, her gorgeous smile drawing him in. She had an adorable dimple in her left cheek. He had to fight the urge to bend down and kiss it.

"What?" She brought her hand to the dimple. "Is there something on my face?" She wiped at her cheek. "I wouldn't be surprised if it's grass or something."

He reached out and touched her hand, stilling her movements. "*Nee*," he said, bringing his hand up to touch her dimple with his thumb. "You're perfect."

❧

Amanda nibbled on her fingernail during the trip home in Josiah's buggy. The singing had ended fifteen minutes before, fortunately without any more confrontations from Peter. In fact, the rest of the evening couldn't have been better. Josiah sat next to her the entire time, even during the hymn sing. And although he had remained fairly distant since the end of the volleyball game, she couldn't get what he said out of her mind.

"You're perfect."

But it wasn't just the words that had made her emotions dance. His gentleness as he touched her hand and her face, the warmth in his eyes as he spoke—all those things made her dizzy with delight. Whether he meant to or not, Josiah had allowed her a glimpse into his heart.

She gazed straight ahead, taking in the beauty before her. Long narrow clouds streaked the pastel evening sky, as if God had skipped a paintbrush across the heavens. The sun had hidden behind the horizon a short while ago, leaving behind remnants of lavender, peach, and pink. The sharp clip-clop of Tater's shoes sounded against the pavement. There weren't many cars on the road to disturb the peaceful scene. The night was perfect.

"You're perfect."

She looked at Josiah's profile. His expression remained impassive, as usual. But she couldn't get the image of the way he looked at her out of her mind. Her body suddenly went hot, then cold as realization dawned. She shivered, hugging her arms around her body, despite the relative warmth of the evening.

It's Josiah, isn't it, Lord? He's the one You've set apart for me.

Perhaps she had always known, even when they were younger. That had to be the reason she'd been devastated by his leaving, and why his rejection upon his return had hurt so much. There had always been that hollow part inside her heart. Now she knew why she had never married, why no man had ever piqued her interest. Only one man held her heart, one man she loved completely, and one she suspected loved her in return.

Now if only she could figure out why he held those feelings back.

She waited for him to say something. Normally she would pepper him with questions and demand answers, but she had learned that method only pushed him further away. *Lord, what should I do?*

A short while later Josiah guided the buggy onto their dirt road.

Their houses came into view, and he still hadn't said anything to her. When he reached his driveway, he hesitated, clearly unsure whether to turn in or take her to her house.

"I can walk from your barn," she said, deciding for him.

He nodded and turned the buggy, making his way up the driveway.

Her frustration climbed as he yanked on the reins, signaling Tater to stop. "Josiah, you haven't said one word to me since we left. Is something wrong?"

"*Nee.*" He shrugged, then moved to get out of the buggy.

"I hate when you do that!" She knew she sounded as immature as Peter, but she couldn't help it. She was tired of Josiah being cold toward her one minute and hot the next.

"Do what?" He turned and looked at her.

At least she'd gotten his attention. "Shut me out. Don't you think we should at least talk about what happened tonight? And don't act like you don't know what I'm referring to."

He let out a long sigh. "I know what you mean. And I definitely don't want to talk about it."

She put her hand on his arm, her fingertips resting lightly on the bare skin of his forearm. The muscles twitched underneath her touch, spurring her courage. "Josiah, there's something going on between us. I feel it. I know you feel it."

"Amanda," he said, pain streaking his tone.

"Why are you running away?"

"Because that's how it has to be." His gaze bored into her, filled with intensity. "What I said to you tonight . . . it was a mistake."

He couldn't have hurt her more if he had tried. "A mistake?"

"*Ya.* I didn't mean it the way you thought I did."

"And how was that, exactly? Have you suddenly become a mind reader?"

"You've always been easy to read, Amanda. Look, I didn't mean to lead you on. I might have said . . . something . . . to make you think

I had feelings for you. But it was only out of friendship." He gave her a half smile. "We used to say goofy stuff to each other all the time, remember?"

She moved to withdraw her hand from his arm, her feelings stinging from his admission. But then she searched his face, met his eyes. "You're lying," she said softly, more confused than ever. "You've never lied to me before, Josiah Bontrager. Don't think you can start now."

He moved his arm from beneath her hand. "I've got to put Tater up." He turned his back to her and jumped out of the buggy.

Amanda clamped her lips together. He wasn't getting off this easily. "Josiah," she said as she got out of the passenger side. "You can't just walk away from this. From us."

He unhitched Tater from the buggy and started to lead her to the barn. "There is no us, Amanda."

She followed him. "There has always been an us, Josiah." She paused, waiting for him to lead Tater to her stall. When he latched the door shut, she continued. "We were inseparable as kids."

"We were friends," he said, his palm lying flat against the stall door.

"*Ya*, that we were. But when you left . . ." She took a deep breath, her body shaking with emotion. "You took a part of me with you."

He didn't say anything, only leaned his forehead on the stall door, his hat tilting back on his head.

The light continued to fade in the barn, and she had difficulty seeing his face. She moved closer, until only inches separated them. "You're still holding that part of me, Josiah. I don't know if you even realize it."

He drew in a sharp breath and stepped away from her. "Mandy," he whispered, his voice thick. "Don't . . . don't do this."

"Do what? Be honest with you? Tell you how I feel?" She had exposed her feelings this far, she might as well lay bare her soul. "Tell you I love you?"

Clamping both hands on his head, he exclaimed, "Don't say that!"

"I'm not like you, Josiah. I can't turn feelings off and on whenever it suits me."

He dropped his hands. "Is that what you think I'm doing?"

"That's exactly what you're doing. And I don't understand why."

"You want some understanding? You've got it. And when I'm finished, you'll wish you'd never known me."

⟳

Josiah gulped for air as Amanda looked at him, love brimming in her eyes. "Nothing you could say would drive me away, Josiah. I told you that before, and I meant it."

"That's because you don't know the facts." He took off his hat and tossed it on the stack of hay bales nearby. Then he ran his fingers through his hair, because if he didn't do something with his hands, he'd lose his mind. Why was she pushing so hard? She said she loved him, but he didn't deserve her love. He had to make her understand that.

He watched as she moved to the door of the barn. He thought she might leave, until she picked up one of the old lanterns hanging on a peg near the door. She retrieved a match from the match holder bolted to the wall and lit it.

She walked toward him, her beautiful face illuminated by the soft yellow glow. "I want to see your face when you tell me, Josiah," she said, moving closer to him. "And I want you to look at me. Because when you're finished telling me your secrets, I want you to see that I still love you."

His throat hitched. Unconditional love. That was what she was offering him, even before she knew what he had done. He did not think he could love her any more than he did at that moment. But it would only take a few words from him to destroy what she felt for him.

"Things were bad when *Mamm* got sick," he said, his memory sending him back to that terrible time when he had just turned twelve and he found out his mother had cancer. She had survived for almost a year before she succumbed. "*Daed* was angry all the time, especially when *Mamm* went into the hospital that last time. He'd always had a temper, but I never saw him raise a hand to her, ever. But . . ."

"He hit you?" She brought her hand to her mouth, her eyes widening. "Josiah, I had no idea."

"No one did. He'd always say he was sorry afterward. And he really didn't do it all that often . . . usually when I broke a rule or didn't do my chores."

"That's no reason to strike a child."

"I know that now. But when *Mamm* got sick, he started smacking me harder. More often. Sometimes he'd bring me out here." He glanced over his shoulder at the far corner of the barn, where the horse whip and stool remained. "He didn't always use his fists."

"Josiah, that's awful." Tears shimmered in her eyes.

"After *Mamm* passed, *Daed* just broke down. He stopped going to work, stopped caring about anything. He only spoke to me when I got in his way. After a while I avoided him as much as I could, and worked at my *onkel*'s shop every chance I got. Pretty soon the only income we had came from the money I made working there. I resented him for that, and it wasn't long before we were arguing all the time.

"Then one day I came home from the shop, and *Daed* told me to pack my clothes, that we were leaving. He didn't tell me where, or why, just that we had to *geh*. We drove into Paradise and met a man who had arranged to buy our buggy and horse, and then he hired someone to take us to Indiana. He planned it all out and didn't tell me anything." He paused and looked at her. "That's why I didn't tell you good-bye. I would have if I'd had the chance."

"I know, Josiah." She sniffed and wiped her cheek. "I never resented you for leaving. I just wished I had known what was going on."

"What could you have done about it? No one knew what *Daed* did to me. He made sure not to leave any visible marks. I don't know if my *aenti* and *onkel* had any idea either. Besides, at that point I figured I deserved what I got."

"How can you say that?"

"I was young; he was my dad. I believed him." Josiah started to pace the width of the barn. "I could never do anything right. I was in the way. Everything was my fault." He stopped and looked at Amanda. "You hear that enough, you begin to believe it's true."

Chapter Twelve

AMANDA COULDN'T BELIEVE WHAT JOSIAH HAD JUST TOLD her. How could she have lived next door to him all those years, been his best friend, and not known that his father abused him? But as more and more memories came to the front of her mind, she realized there were subtle signs. The fact that he never wanted to go near his barn. That the year after his mother died, he never invited her in his house. The underlying sadness she had attributed to grief over his mother's death.

"Did my parents know?" she asked, dread pooling in her belly. "Please tell me they didn't know."

"I'm not sure. It doesn't matter anyway. They couldn't have done anything."

"They could have confronted your *daed*! They could have gone to the bishop!" The lantern shook in her hand as she spoke.

"*Daed* would have just denied it. Besides, it would have made things worse for me."

"I don't see how they could get any worse."

"Trust me, Amanda. It did."

Her arms ached to hold him. She couldn't stand thinking about what he had suffered at the hands of his own father, and she could see by the tortured look in his eyes that he was reliving those memories.

"When we got to Indiana, we didn't know anyone. I think *Daed* thought the move would give us a fresh start. For a time things were okay. He got a job working in one of the RV factories there, and I did some odd jobs for some of the Amish and *Englisch* that lived near us.

He bought a small trailer, and we moved in. At least he stopped hitting me for a while. But that didn't last very long. A couple years later he started drinking. A lot, which made his temper worse."

"Oh no," Amanda whispered.

"I was almost seventeen and ready to move out anyway. I was sick of him yelling at me and smacking me around, and I had made some friends with a few *Englisch* guys. I moved in with them for a couple years. I tried living their fancy lifestyle—I even bought a car—but it wasn't for me. By this time my *daed* had drunk himself sick." Josiah went and sat on one of the hay bales, his shoulders drooping. "I ended up having to take care of him."

Amanda went to him and sat down, letting the handle of the lantern dangle from her fingers. "Josiah, why didn't you get in touch with me?"

He looked at her with a sad smile. "You couldn't fix this, Amanda. Although I have no doubt you would have tried."

"What happened to your father?"

"He died when I was twenty-two. He got drunk one night, and on his way to the bathroom he tripped and fell. Hit his head against the corner of his dresser. When I found him, he was dead."

"Josiah, I'm so sorry."

"I'm not." He stared straight ahead. "At least a part of me isn't. I didn't recognize him anymore. He wasn't my father by that point."

She reached for his hand, but he moved. "Josiah, don't pull away from me. Not now."

"I'm not finished. What I didn't tell you is that I not only didn't recognize my father anymore, I didn't recognize myself."

"What do you mean?"

He popped up from the bale. "I'm just like him, Amanda. Sometimes I get so angry I can feel it boiling inside my veins, running through my body. My temper is just as bad as his."

"But you're not him, Josiah. You would never hurt anyone."

"That's where you're wrong. I know how important it is for the Amish to be peaceful. To swallow their anger and turn the other cheek. Even though I didn't see that with my father, I understood that controlling those impulses is a basic tenet of the faith. And that's the problem. I can't control them." He looked at her, and she saw the shame in his eyes. "I hit my *daed*, Amanda. And not just once, either. We didn't just argue, we fought."

Amanda shut her eyes against what he had just revealed. She could barely fathom that gentle Josiah, the boy who wouldn't even step on a spider or squash a bug, would ever hit another person, much less his own father. Yet she couldn't doubt his words either.

"Now you see why I can't stay here. Why I keep pushing you away. Why I can't marry." He squatted down on the floor and held his head in his hands. "I can't risk hurting anyone else."

Heat emanated from the lantern, so she set it on the floor of the barn, well away from the hay bales and anything else that might catch fire. Tentatively she knelt down and put her arm around his shoulders, glad when he didn't pull away. "Josiah, listen to me. Everyone gets angry."

He looked up at her, his gaze narrowing. "Don't patronize me, Amanda. I know everyone gets angry. The difference is they can control it. I can't."

"With the Lord's help you can."

"The Lord's help?" He let out a bitter laugh, then sat on the ground, slipping out from beneath her embrace. "God abandoned me long ago."

"God is faithful, Josiah. He would never abandon us."

"Easy for you to say. Your *mamm* didn't die and your *daed* didn't beat you on a regular basis."

Amanda cringed, properly chastised. "I suppose it does sound like a platitude. I didn't live your life, and I can see where you might doubt God's presence." She said a silent prayer for the Lord to give her the right words before she continued. "But, Josiah, He was with you. You had to have amazing inner strength to survive what you did. That type of strength comes from God."

"I did what I had to do." He looked at her. "I'm still doing what I have to." He rose from the floor and retrieved his hat, then put it on. "I've told you everything, the whole sorry story."

She stood and faced him. "I know. And I'm still here."

He looked at her for a long moment, a myriad of emotions crossing his features. Shame. Anguish. And for a fleeting instance, hope. Then his expression hardened. "*Geh* home, Amanda. Forget we ever had this conversation."

"I can't just forget what you told me, Josiah."

"You have to. I'll be gone soon, once the house is sold."

"You think running away is going to fix everything? That didn't work out so well for your *daed*, did it? You can't keep running from the past, or from God. You'll never be free if you do."

"Maybe I don't deserve to be free. I hit my own *daed*, Amanda. What kind of *sohn* does that?"

"A *sohn* who was abandoned by his *vatter*, and who thought everyone else had abandoned him too."

He didn't look convinced. "I know you want to fix this, Amanda. To fix me. But you can't."

"Oh, I know I can't. Only God can do that." She reached for his hand, squeezing tightly when she sensed him pulling away. "I want to pray for you, Josiah. Will you let me do that much?"

Pain like he'd never experienced welled up inside him. He had thought, or at least sincerely hoped, that when he had confessed everything to Amanda, she would leave him alone. But he should have known better. Amanda Graber never knew an underdog she couldn't champion or a lost cause she wouldn't support. She just couldn't understand he wasn't worth saving.

That thought had hit home when she had admitted she loved him. The words lifted up his heart while crushing his soul. Other than his mother, and for a short while his uncle, Amanda had been the only good thing in his life. Then when he moved, when she had been taken away from him, he knew God had written him off. Somehow he'd managed to go through the motions of life since then, not feeling much of anything except rage at his father, a rage he had expressed with his fists, just like his *daed*. He'd only punched his *daed* twice, but the look of shock and betrayal on Levi Bontrager's face was permanently stamped on Josiah's memory.

Why couldn't she see how dangerous he was? Even if he could afford to entertain the thought of a future with her, she could never trust that he wouldn't lose his temper with her or their children. Yet she stood strong, wanting to pray for him. "It won't do any *gut*," he muttered, knowing if he refused she would persist until he gave in.

"I think you'll be surprised at how much *gut* it will do." She gripped his hand and bowed her head. The words of her prayer skimmed over him, having little effect on his emotions or his opinion of himself. When she finished, she looked up at him, her eyes consumed with anticipation.

Her hand felt so soft and warm in his, he never wanted to let go. But he did. "It's late, Amanda. You need to get home."

She'd obviously expected some kind of miracle from her little prayer. He knew from experience that prayer didn't work. He'd said enough prayers after his mother became ill to last a lifetime.

"All right, I'll *geh*." She started for the door, only to turn around and rush toward him.

She threw her arms around him, drawing him against her. "This isn't the end, Josiah," she whispered in his ear. Her embrace tightened. "I still love you. God loves you too. One day you'll believe both of us." She released him, then turned and fled.

He stood in the center of the dusty barn, his arms slightly lifted. He realized he had been about to return her embrace. Although her hug had been brief, her warmth had flowed straight through him, and he ached to hold her again.

Tater whinnied, pulling him out of his stupor. The horse had been amazingly quiet during his conversation with Amanda. Weariness suddenly overcame him, both emotional and physical. He wanted to fall into bed and try to get this entire evening out of his mind.

But as he headed for the house, he realized that wouldn't happen. He couldn't put Amanda's reaction out of his mind. She truly believed in God's faithfulness, and a part of him wished he had her conviction.

◦◦◦

Sleep didn't come easily to Amanda that night. She tossed and turned, her emotions somersaulting as she tried to process everything Josiah had told her. She felt so clueless, so sheltered. Were there others in their community suffering the same fate as Josiah? Would she be able to tell if they were?

Unable to rest, she left her bed, walked to the window, and opened it. From here she had a clear view of Josiah's house, although a large oak tree that stood between the two properties partially obscured the barn. The lights were out in his house, and she wondered if he was already asleep.

Despite her confusion about everything else, her love for Josiah hadn't wavered. She had no idea how to convince him of that, or how to convince him of God's love. After spending a few minutes breathing in the fresh air, she returned to bed. As her eyelids closed, she prayed not only for Josiah, but for herself.

◦◦◦

The smell of smoke pulled her out of her fitful sleep. *Fire!* Panic shot through her as she jumped out of the bed. She ran to her brothers' room and woke them up. "Outside, now!"

"What's wrong, Mandy?" Thomas said sleepily.

"Don't ask questions, just *geh!*"

She woke up the rest of her siblings and chased them down the stairs. Where was the fire? Where were her parents? Her terror increased as she realized the fire might be downstairs where she had sent the children. But if that was the case, why didn't she see smoke?

"Amanda, what are you doing?" Her father met her at the foot of the stairs, his hair standing up in disheveled tufts all over his head. "Why are the *kinder* down here?"

"Can't you smell the smoke, *Daed?*" But even as she spoke the words, she realized the scent wasn't as strong down here. Maybe the fire was upstairs after all.

Daed inhaled deeply. "*Ya*, I smell something. But I don't think it's in our house." He dashed to the front door, Amanda dogging his heels. He threw open the door and both of them stepped out on the front porch. The thick scent of smoke filled the air.

"Josiah!" Amanda exclaimed, realizing the smoke was coming from his property. She ran toward his house, ignoring her father's calls. When she reached Josiah's driveway, she saw huge flames coming out of the slats of the old barn. Her head jerked back and forth as she searched for Josiah, or a sign that Tater had escaped the fire. When she saw a dark figure dash inside the barn, she rushed toward the burning structure.

"Amanda! *Halt!*" Her father came up behind her and put his hands on her shoulders, holding her back. "You can't go in there."

She spun around. "Josiah's inside!"

"I called the fire department from our call box. They'll be here in a few minutes. There's nothing else we can do."

"If Josiah's in there, he doesn't have a few minutes." Her nerves were stretched to their limits. "I can't lose him, *Daed*. Not again."

"You can't save him, either, Amanda."

Tears and smoke clogged her throat. She saw no sign of either

Josiah or Tater. She grasped at a thin thread of hope that she'd been seeing things. He might be in his house, safely away from the fire. But seeing the fierceness of the blaze in front of her, she knew Josiah couldn't possibly be in the house. He would be in the barn, trying to save his horse.

She folded her hands and tucked them under her chin, praying harder than she had ever prayed in her life. She squinted, willing him and Tater to come out. *Please, Lord. Save them!*

Then, in a direct answer to her plea, she saw them exit the barn, Josiah clinging to Tater's bridle as he hunched over and coughed. As soon as he was clear, he let the horse go and fell to the ground.

"Josiah!" She ran and knelt next to him. Even though they were well clear of the blaze, she could feel the heat searing her back through her thin nightgown. The shrill sound of fire sirens pierced the air.

"Josiah," she said again, cradling his head in her hands. Soot colored his face, and he remained very still. She leaned down and kissed his cheek, her unbound hair falling in a curtain around them both. "Say something. Please."

He opened his eyes slightly, then coughed, his chest heaving from the effort. "Tater?" he asked in a hoarse voice.

She glanced up to see her father guiding the horse farther away from the burning barn. "*Daed*'s got her. She looks all right."

Two fire trucks pulled alongside the driveway, engulfing Amanda and Josiah in their swirling light. Suddenly two men in paramedic uniforms hovered over her.

"Let us take a look at him," one of them said. "Step back and give us room."

She acquiesced, silently praising and thanking God for bringing Josiah out alive. His cough sounded horrible, and his T-shirt and pants were black. The paramedics helped him to a sitting position and gave him an oxygen mask. After he settled, one of the men came over to her.

"Looks like he'll be all right. We wanted to take him to the hospital to get checked out, but he refused. Your husband is a very lucky man to have gotten out of there alive."

Amanda started to correct him, then stopped. "*Ya*, he is. He's a very lucky man."

Chapter Thirteen

JOSIAH STOOD A FEW FEET FROM THE BARN, STARING AT its charred remains, watching thin tendrils of smoke snake up in the air as they greeted the rising sun. The firefighters had extinguished the blaze over an hour ago, but there were still a few hot spots in the rubble. They had assured him the fire had been completely put out. Not that it mattered anyway. The entire structure had burned to the ground.

He took a deep breath and felt a catch in his lungs. He coughed, the burn in his throat and chest mixing with his despair. The barn was a total loss. And while he supposed he should be grateful the fire hadn't spread to the house or the Graber property, and that his horse had been spared, he couldn't summon a speck of gratitude. He couldn't afford to replace the barn. Even if he could, it would take him months to do it himself. He could sell the house and property without it, but without the barn he would take a significant loss.

His gaze landed on his buggy, which had caught fire after the fire department arrived. It also sustained damage, although it hadn't been completely destroyed. Scorch marks streaked the gray enclosure and oak frame. He could probably do the repairs himself, but he would have to purchase the materials. Another expense he couldn't afford.

"Josiah?"

He didn't respond. When Amanda stood beside him, he couldn't bring himself to look at her. He vividly remembered hearing her voice when he collapsed after leading Tater out of the barn. How she knelt beside him and kissed his cheek, her soft brown hair brushing against his face, keeping him from slipping into unconsciousness. If he allowed himself a single glimpse of her, he might fall apart right there.

"We just finished breakfast. I saved some for you." She stepped closer to him, apparently waiting for him to answer.

"Not hungry."

She hesitated a moment longer before saying, "*Daed* said Tater can stay in our barn as long as you need her to."

"Tell him *danki* for me." His voice sounded flat and emotionless to his own ears, reflecting how he felt inside. Empty. Hopeless.

"Did they tell you how the fire started?"

"The lantern exploded. I forgot and left it lit in the barn last night."

"Josiah, I'm so sorry."

He shrugged. "No need for you to feel sorry. It was my own *dumm* fault."

"But if I hadn't lit the lantern—"

"It was *my* fault," he snapped.

Amanda moved to stand in front of him. "I know you're upset—"

"*Upset?* Why would I have any reason to be upset?"

"You can replace the barn, Josiah."

"*Nee,* I can't. I don't have the money, Amanda." He looked over her shoulder at the pile of black remains. "Or the will." His gaze found hers again. "I guess God let me know how much He cares about me."

"Surely you don't believe this is God's fault."

"He didn't stop it, did He?"

"*Nee.* But, Josiah, you're alive. Your horse is alive." She gestured to the burned barn behind her. "This pile of burnt wood and ash can be replaced. You can't." Her hand went to her mouth for a moment, and she swallowed. "I don't know what I would have done if I lost you last night, Josiah." She wrapped her arms around his waist and leaned her cheek against his chest.

He stood motionless for a second before succumbing to her embrace. Closing his eyes, he rested his chin on the top of her head, touching the stiff fabric of her *kapp*. Fatigue seeped into his bones. He was tired of the struggle, of fighting against everything—his feelings for Amanda, his past, his uncertain future. Only now, as he felt her tighten her arms around him, as he breathed in the sweet scent of her freshly shampooed hair, did he feel a semblance of peace. He longed to hold her forever, to tell her how much he loved her. But he didn't dare. She'd said he had amazing inner strength, but compared to her, he had none.

"Amanda! Mr. Josiah!"

They broke apart as Andrew and Thomas neared. His first instinct was to send them away. They didn't need to bear the brunt of his foul mood again. Yet he couldn't bring himself to do it. Instead he walked toward them, meeting the boys at the edge of his driveway and the grassy yard.

"Wow," Andrew said, gaping at what little remained of the barn. "That was some fire."

"*Mamm* made us stay in the house." Thomas rubbed his nose with the palm of his hand. "I wanted to come over, but she said *nee*."

"I wanted to come over too!" Andrew stepped in front of his brother. "But we had to watch from the window." His eyes grew wide with amazement. "Never seen a fire that big before."

"Or so many fire trucks." Thomas moved to Andrew's side, not content to remain in his brother's shadow for very long. He took in a deep breath. "It sure does stink! What are you going to do about the barn?"

"Not much I can do. It would cost me too much to fix it."

The young boy's face fell. "I'm sorry, Mr. Josiah." Then he leaned over and whispered something in Andrew's ear. Andrew nodded, and both boys took off running toward the house.

"Wonder what that's about," Amanda said.

"With those two, there's no telling."

"They think the world of you." She moved closer to him. "So do I."

He looked at her, incredulous. "Even after everything I told you?"

She nodded.

"Amanda, I can't be trusted to hold my temper in check. I'm afraid . . . I'm afraid I might hurt you."

"I'm not. I could never be afraid of you, Josiah." She reached up and brushed back a lock of his hair from his forehead. "If I have to, I'll spend the rest of my life convincing you of that."

"Mr. Josiah!"

He turned at the sound of Thomas's voice. The boys bounded toward him, each of them holding something in his hand. As they neared, he saw that each held a small, clear plastic baggie halfway filled with coins. The change jingled as they ran.

"Here." Andrew held out his baggie to Josiah, and Thomas followed suit. "It's all we got, but you can use it to rebuild your barn."

Josiah crouched down in front of the boys, unshed tears burning his eyes. The bags were filled mostly with pennies, and he doubted they had more than six dollars between them. He could only imagine how long it had taken for them to save such a meager amount. Yet they were ready to part with it willingly, expecting nothing in return.

"*Danki, buwe*," he said, then cleared his throat. He closed his hands over each of theirs, gently pushing the money back toward them. "I appreciate the offer, but keep your money. Spend it on something special."

"But we are," Thomas said.

"You have to have a barn, Mr. Josiah," Andrew piped up. "Tater needs a place of her own." He shoved the money back at Josiah.

"Take it," Amanda said quietly as she crouched beside him. "I'm not the only persistent one in my family."

"I can see that." He accepted the small bags.

Andrew grinned. "I can help you clean up the mess, Mr. Josiah."

"Me too!" Thomas added.

Josiah's spirits suddenly lifted, and he nodded, smiling back. "You know I can use the help. I've got a broom in the house, but the shovel was in the barn."

"I'll get the broom," Thomas volunteered and dashed to the house.

Not to be outdone, Andrew said, "And I'll fetch *Daed*'s shovel. He won't care if we borrow it for a little while."

When the boys disappeared, Josiah turned and looked at Amanda. The scent of smoke still hung heavy in the air, but things didn't seem as bleak as they had moments before.

She gave him a small smile. "The *buwe* will be back soon, eager to get started."

"*Ya.*" He couldn't move away from her, not yet.

"I have to get back home and help *Mamm*. Today is supposed to be washday, but I think we'll wait until the smoke clears completely."

"*Gut* idea. You don't want to smell like a barbecue."

"*Nee*, we don't." She reached up on tiptoe and kissed his cheek. "I love you," she whispered. "Just wanted to remind you of that."

He turned and watched her walk away, wondering what he had done to deserve her love. Then he realized he had done nothing, because he didn't deserve it.

"I found the broom, Mr. Josiah."

"*Gut*," Josiah said, still watching Amanda, waiting until she disappeared inside. He didn't know how he would be able to walk away from her, from everything here.

But somehow he had to.

❧

Josiah woke up the next morning to the sound of hammers pounding nails. He popped out of bed and ran to the window, rubbing his eyes as he tried to fathom what he saw. Amish men, at least twenty of them, were in his backyard, working in perfect sync. They had already nailed several beams of wood together where the south side of his barn had been, creating a partial wall.

They were raising a new barn.

He threw on his clothes, dashed downstairs and out the door. A few of the men looked at him. He recognized Ben Weaver and Aaron Lantz, who both waved at him, then continued their work, with Ben holding up one of the six-by-six square poles while Aaron nailed a two-by-four to the base of the pole at an angle for support. Several of the other men were doing the same. To his shock he even saw Peter pitching in, although he didn't look too happy about it.

"You look surprised, Josiah." Uncle John came up beside him.

"I am." He pushed his hat back on his head, surveying the scene in front of him. "I truly am."

"You shouldn't be." John clapped a hand on his shoulder. "You know our ways. When a person loses something in our community, the rest of us help out."

"But I'm not part of your community."

"That could change, you know. It's up to you. You're family, a part of ours, and a part of the Lord's." He dropped his hand from Josiah's back. "Better get to work. Here," he said, handing Josiah a hammer. "*Geh* and help Ben and Aaron. I don't think that beam is straight."

The beam looked straight enough, but he eagerly joined the others, still incredulous that so many had turned out to help him. As the day progressed, even more men showed up. By the noon hour the women had arrived and were setting up tables of food on the Grabers' lawn. It seemed the entire community had put their own lives on hold for a day to help him build his barn. And while he knew this was the Amish way, their generosity humbled him, a generosity he doubted he could ever return.

"Beautiful day for a barn raising, *ya?*" Leah Lantz stood to Amanda's left and unwrapped a huge bowl of chicken salad. The faint scent of chicken, celery, and salad dressing wafted through the air.

"*Ya,*" said Rebecca Miller, on Amanda's other side. She placed a tray of thinly sliced ham, turkey, and roast beef on the table. "That chicken salad smells delicious, Leah. Did you make it?"

"That's the only thing she knows how to make," Leah's sister Kathleen said from the other side of the table.

Leah smirked at her. "I'll have you know Aaron loves my chicken salad."

"He'd better. He'll be eating it every day for the rest of his life."

Leah just responded to the dig with a soft smile.

Kathleen left to help some of the other women inside, clearing Amanda's view of the men working on the barn. Her gaze zeroed in on Josiah, who was working near Ben and Aaron. Still holding the hammer, he pushed his hat back and wiped his forehead with the back of his hand. He had rolled his shirtsleeves up, exposing his tanned forearms.

"The barn is coming along quickly, isn't it?" Rebecca asked.

"It always does when everyone helps out," Amanda replied. She tucked the ribbons of her white *kapp* into the front of her dress and waved her hand in front of her heated face. The day had turned sultry, but the heat didn't impede the men's progress.

"Don't get me wrong," Leah said, moving closer to the other two women. "I'm not glad Josiah's barn burned down, but I love a *gut* barn raising."

"Me too," Rebecca echoed. "It's *wunderbaar* to see everyone come together to help someone in need."

Amanda nodded, glad Josiah had accepted the community's help without an argument. Maybe this outpouring would help him see God's hand in his life. She had prayed almost continually for that to happen after leaving him yesterday morning. She knew she couldn't convince him herself, that her words about God's faithfulness had passed right through him with no effect. She had to let Josiah go and let God take over. It hadn't been easy, but when she woke up this morning, she felt the Lord lift that burden from her.

She surveyed her yard and Josiah's, taking in everyone who had shown up for the barn raising. The turnout was nothing short of amazing, considering it was a last-minute event. Yet so many men and women had taken part of or even the whole day off to come and help. Many children were there, too, running around the Grabers' backyard and playing on the swing set. She saw Sarah Fisher chasing after her toddler. She called out for her father, who was busy sawing a long section of wood into pieces. She also saw Miriam Fisher talking to her sister, Lydia King. Their husbands, Seth and Daniel, had spent the morning working alongside Josiah, Aaron, and Ben.

"Here come the men," Rebecca said a few moments later. "They look *hungerich* too!"

"Aaron's always *hungerich*." Leah stuck a spoon in the chicken salad.

They lined up at the end of the table, and the women served them buffet style. When Ben reached them, Amanda noticed the tender look he gave Rebecca, and how she blushed in response. Aaron stood right behind him, and he lingered longer than he should have in front of Leah and her chicken salad.

"Hurry up, Aaron," Peter called from farther down the line. "The rest of us need to eat too."

Aaron winked at Leah and moved on.

In between dishing out spoonfuls of colorful carrot salad, Amanda glanced around for Josiah but didn't see him in line. Then she caught a glimpse of him still working on the frame of the barn. Her father walked over to him, carrying a plate of food and a drink. The men spoke for a few minutes, then Josiah dropped his hammer and headed for the food line.

Since he was the last in line, some of the other women had already stopped serving and gone inside to help with the cleanup. Only Rebecca and Leah had stayed, and when Josiah approached them, they quietly disappeared.

Josiah thrust out his plate, which held two fresh yeast rolls and a large pat of butter. Amanda scooped some of Leah's chicken salad onto the plate, then a generous helping of carrot salad.

"*Danki*," he said, picking up a plastic fork and piling on slices of ham. He glanced at her, his face red and streaked with dirt from working. "Are you to thank for all of this?"

"*Nee*," she said. "Your *Onkel* John organized everything. I happened to mention it to him yesterday."

"Because you just *happened* to be over there."

She merely smiled.

"Is there enough for seconds?" Seth Fisher approached the table, flashing a charming grin.

"For you, always." Amanda served Seth, who had a reputation for being a bottomless pit when it came to food. She then turned to talk to Josiah again, only to find he had disappeared.

Chapter Fourteen

JOSIAH WALKED THROUGH THE FRAMED-IN POLE BARN, breathing in the scent of fresh oak. Everyone had left a little over an hour ago, making sure they got home before dark so they could do their own chores and take care of their families. Plenty of work lay ahead, but the men had managed to frame the barn and put up the supports for the roof. He could do the rest of the job himself.

As he examined their handiwork, he marveled at the gift they'd given him. Before his uncle left, Josiah tried to find out how much the materials had cost so he could pay everyone back. His uncle refused to say, reminding him that the materials and labor were donated. He didn't owe anyone a dime.

He paced off the length of the barn, stopping at the back corner. The frame of the barn extended at least four feet on all sides beyond its original size. Another gift.

As he sank to his knees, it took a moment for him to realize he'd knelt down in the exact same spot where his father had beaten him with the horse whip shortly after his mother had died. He ran his hand on the dirt ground in front of him, then looked at his palm. Brown dirt mixed with black ash and sawdust. Not a trace of the short stool his *daed* made him sit on before applying the punishment. Not a sign of the horse whip anywhere. Both had burned up in the fire.

Josiah closed his eyes, tears streaming down his cheeks. The heaviness that had weighed on his heart and soul for so many years slowly drained away. He could sense God's presence now, in the midst of the ashes of his past. Now he knew why he had returned to Paradise. Not to fix up an old house and sell it so he could keep running away from the relentless memories. God had brought him back here to face those memories—and let them go.

I'm ready, Lord. Please take this pain from me . . .

He didn't know how long he prayed, but when he opened his eyes, it was nearly dark. His father's image formed in his mind, the man's face contorted with anger as it usually had been during the last years of his life. But instead of the usual resentment and guilt, Josiah experienced peace. "I forgive you, *Daed,*" he whispered into the darkness. He not only said the words, he felt them. "I forgive you."

❧

Although she was tired from helping with the barn raising the day before, Amanda had difficulty sleeping that night. Right before sundown she had gone outside to check on Lucy, who had given birth to four kittens earlier that morning in the barn. On the way she had spotted Josiah kneeling inside the barn, and she had fought the urge to check on him. But a niggling inside her soul held her back. She couldn't keep rushing to his side all the time, attempting to fix something she wasn't equipped to fix. She had to let him go, and if that meant his leaving her for Ohio, then she'd have to deal with it.

Yet as she tossed and turned, fighting the tears and praying to the Lord, she knew letting Josiah go would be the hardest thing she'd ever have to do.

She rose even earlier than usual, well before sunup. Quickly she donned a long-sleeved light gray dress, brushed her hair and pinned it up, then secured her *kapp* to her head. Picking up her flashlight off the nightstand, she quietly slipped out of the house to the backyard. While she wanted to check on Lucy and her adorable kittens again, she didn't dare go in the barn and disturb the animals. Instead, she walked to the swing set and sat down on a swing.

Amanda closed her eyes. A few birds were twittering in the surrounding trees, getting ready to start their day. The scent of smoke that had been in the air yesterday had disappeared completely, and she breathed in the sweet scent of grass. The chilly morning didn't bother her. She started to hum a hymn as she gently swung back and forth. When she finished the song, she opened her eyes, startled to see Josiah there. She hadn't heard him approach.

"Don't stop on my account," he said.

Dawn had started to break, but she couldn't make out his features clearly. He wore a coat over his white T-shirt and gray pants, but he'd left his hat at home. How long had he been standing there listening to her?

"I was finished anyway." She dug the toe of her shoe into the dirt and pushed the swing back. "You're up early."

"Had trouble sleeping."

"Me too."

Josiah stood next to her. "You mind?" he asked, pointing to the empty swing.

"*Nee.*" What was he up to? She'd become used to him fleeing from her or outright avoiding her, not seeking her out.

He sat down on the swing, which hung lower than the other two so the smaller children could reach it. His knees came halfway to his chin, but he didn't seem to care.

Neither of them spoke for a moment, but instead of the silence feeling awkward between them, it felt natural. Like it had been when they were kids. From their vantage in Amanda's yard, they had a perfect view of the sunrise. Amanda sighed.

"Something wrong?"

"*Nee,*" she said, twisting in the swing so she could see him. "God's gifted us with another *brechdich* morning."

Josiah looked at her and smiled. Beams of new sunlight lit up his face.

Amanda stared at him for a moment, content to take him in.

Then she realized it wasn't just the sun that made him shine. Tears sprang to her eyes. "Josiah?"

His grin widened. "I get it now, Mandy. You were right. All that time I thought God had left me. Turns out I ran away from Him. I lived in fear of becoming like my father, and I tried to steer clear of everyone because of that. But it didn't matter. Running away, blaming God, being afraid . . . I had already *become* my father. Maybe I wasn't as openly cruel, but I had turned bitter inside. But God and *mei* . . . we had a long talk yesterday. I know I don't have to live like that anymore. I finally forgave my father and let the past *geh*."

Happiness surged through her. "Oh, Josiah! I'm so happy for you!"

"I don't think I would have figured it out on my own. Not without your help." He took her hand. "I'm sorry, Mandy," he said softly. "I'm sorry for everything."

She glanced down at their hands as they hung suspended between the two swings. Their fingers entwined together, the intimate clasp sending a pleasant wave of emotion through her body. "It's all right, Josiah. I understand why."

"*Nee*, it's not all right. You've never been anything but honest with me, and I should have told you the truth a long time ago. Maybe if I had said something, everything would have been different."

"And maybe it would have stayed the same. You can't spend your life second-guessing the past."

"I know. I'd rather talk about the future."

"What about the future?"

"There's a Realtor coming here later on today. I talked to him a few days ago. He seemed really excited I was fixing up the place, but he thought it would go for a *gut* price even without the renovations. Of course, I'll have to finish the barn, but I only have to do minor repairs on the house."

"I see." She removed her hand from his grasp and stared at her lap, fighting the lump forming in her throat.

KATHLEEN FULLER

"He even quoted me a number. It's a lot of money, plenty enough for me to get started in Ohio."

"That's . . . great." So she'd been wrong about his feelings for her after all. So very, very wrong. Pain seared her heart as she comprehended what he'd just said. He really was leaving. It wouldn't take long to complete the barn and address the minor problems in the house. A week, maybe two at the most, then he'd be gone.

Wrapping her arms around her body, she wished she could disappear. She thought she had prepared herself for this, but she could barely contain her heartache. She never should have told him she loved him—she never should have let herself fall in love with him. And she'd been wrong about God, too, at least about His setting Josiah apart for her. Somehow she'd find the strength to mend her heart, but right now she couldn't even look at him. If she did, she'd burst into tears.

She rose from the swing, her arms still crossed over her chest. "I've got to get inside. *Daed*'s probably up already, and I'll have to make breakfast. I'll send the boys over when we're done." Unable to stop herself, she faced him. "Just do me one favor, before you leave."

He jumped up from the swing. "Amanda—"

"Make sure you say good-bye." Whirling around, she started for the house, only to stop in her tracks when he gently grabbed her arm. He tugged her toward him, and before she could say a word, he kissed her.

A few seconds later, they parted. "Just for the record, that was *not* a good-bye kiss." His gaze lingered over her face. "I'm not going anywhere."

Her lips still tingling, she said, "But the Realtor—"

"Is making a trip out here for nothing."

Joy surged through her. "You're not leaving?"

"*Nee*. I love you, Mandy. That's something else I haven't been honest about. I've loved you for a long time, I think even before I left Paradise. You've always been the only woman for me."

Her eyes widened. "I had no idea."

"I never let on. I didn't want to ruin our friendship, for one thing. Also . . . I thought you'd laugh in my face if I told you."

"I would never do that."

"I know that now. I've made a lot of mistakes, Mandy. I'm not a perfect man. I still have a temper, but I'm hoping with God's help I can control it. I also don't have much to offer. I only have this house and part of a barn to my name. I'll never have money like Peter does."

"You know I don't care about that."

He grinned. "It's one of the reasons I love you. One of many." He ran his thumb over her cheek. "I love your enthusiasm, your spontaneity, your spirit, your unconditional belief and love." Then his expression grew somber. "I've spent the last ten years longing for something I never thought I'd have. A wife. Family. A place of my own."

"You can have all of those things, Josiah." Her voice trembled as she put her arms around him.

"I can?"

"*Ya*," she said, resting her cheek against his chest. "All you have to do is ask."

WHAT THE
HEART SEES

To my daughter Sydney.
I love you!

Chapter One

ELLIE CHUPP SAT STRAIGHT UP IN BED, HER NIGHTGOWN soaked with sweat and sticking against her clammy skin. Her chest heaved as she fought for breath. After a year's reprieve, the nightmare had returned with a vengeance. Her fingers curled around her quilt as the vivid memory finally faded—the sound of metal scraping against metal, the car flipping over, the scent of burning rubber, Caroline's scream—

She gripped both sides of her head, willing her heart to slow and the images to slide away. She fell back against the bed. Darkness surrounded her. Why had the dream returned now? Five years should be long enough to heal. Long enough to forget.

But the nightmare proved she would never forget.

She tried to fall back asleep, but remnants of emotion kept her awake. Pain. Fear. Anger. Regret. All of them mixed in her mind and soul as she tossed and turned.

Finally she reached for the watch on her nightstand and read the time. Four thirty. Might as well get up. She slipped on her dress, then she put her white apron over it and quickly pinned up her hair before fastening her white prayer *kapp*. She made her way downstairs to the kitchen and put on a pot of coffee, knowing her father would want a cup when he got up.

With the coffee percolating, Ellie sat at the table, bowed her head, and began her morning prayer time with the Lord. But the dream still haunted her.

Please, Lord, take these memories away. Help me face life with the courage only You can give. Guide my heart, my thoughts . . . and my dreams.

As she finished praying, she heard the heavy tread of her father's footsteps down the hallway. Ellie rose and poured him a cup of coffee as he entered the kitchen. A moment later the hiss of the gas lamp filled the room.

"*Danki*, Ellie." He took the cup from her hands and slurped. "*Sehr gut.* Just what I needed this morning. Your *mamm* was up half the night making lists about what she needed to do to help your *aenti* with Isaiah's wedding."

Ellie smiled, found the chair next to him, and sat down. In a couple of weeks her cousin Isaiah would marry one of her dearest friends, Sarah Lynne Miller. Her mother was consumed with the preparations. "That sounds like her."

The cup hit the table with a soft thump. "You'd think we were marrying off one of our own the way she's carrying on."

Ellie's smile faded a tiny bit.

Her father suddenly cleared his throat. "Ah, what's for breakfast, *dochder*?"

"Eggs, bacon, and toast."

"Sounds *gut*." He rose from the chair, the legs scraping against the wood floor. "I'll be back after I tend to the animals."

Ellie's smile slid completely from her face. *Daed* had meant no harm, yet his unspoken message hurt. Still, she accepted the reality of her situation. An Amish man needed a healthy wife. A whole wife, one who could take care of the home and the children without impediment. Ellie couldn't be that wife to anyone. Because the accident that still haunted her hadn't just taken the life of her best friend, Caroline. It had also taken Ellie's sight.

⚬~⚬

Christopher Miller looked at the packed duffel bag on his bed and ground his teeth. He could still change his mind about going to Paradise. He'd done it before, many times. But he couldn't keep running away from the past. He'd spent the last five years ignoring God's prodding. Like Jonah avoiding Ninevah. But Chris couldn't keep ignoring God's will, no matter how much he tried.

He sat on the bed and withdrew his mother's latest letter from his pocket. He'd been in the *bann* for five years, since Caroline's death, and she had written him almost every month during those years, telling him that life wasn't the same since he left. But it was the last paragraph that had stirred him the most.

> *If you could just come home*, mei sohn, *we would all be grateful. We all miss you, Christopher, including your* daed. *I pray for you every single day . . .*

Chris shot up from the bed and shoved the letter back into his pocket. Her words echoed in his brain, and he could almost hear her soft voice, as if she stood right there in his one-bedroom apartment in Apple Creek, Ohio, looking at him, pleading not only with her words but with her light gray eyes. But she wasn't. She, along with everything he loved, was back in Paradise.

Pacing the length of the room, he fought with himself. More than once he had packed up his few belongings, jumped in his used car, and headed for Pennsylvania. But every time the memories stopped him. The pain of losing Caroline had sent him in a downward spiral that ended with his being shunned and leaving his family. One act could reinstate him in the church and reunite him with his parents, his brothers, and his sister, Sarah Lynne. But he couldn't do it. Not when they were wrong and he was right.

A knock sounded on the door, yanking him from his thoughts. He opened it, and his landlord, Mr. Russell, walked in. The stout man's red-and-black-plaid shirt stretched over his rotund belly, barely covering it.

"I was just about to turn in the keys," Chris said, stepping to the side.

"Thought I'd save you the trip." Russell strolled around the apartment, his eyes narrowing beneath overgrown graying eyebrows. "Didn't do much with the place while you were here, did ya?"

Chris shook his head. Even living as one of the *Englisch*, he'd maintained a sparse existence the past five years. His furniture was minimal: a lumpy couch, an old recliner, a small kitchen table, and his bed, all secondhand. Living alone, he hadn't needed much. What he had was enough. Or so he thought.

Russell faced Chris and gestured to the furniture. "Sure you don't want to take any of this with you?"

"Like I said, get whatever you can for the stuff. I don't need it anymore."

Russell glanced around the room. "I'll probably just dump it. Won't get more than a few bucks anyway. Hardly worth the effort."

Chris shrugged. "Whatever you want to do."

"Sorry to see you go. You're a good tenant. Paid your rent on time and never caused me no trouble. Can't say the same for all the renters I got here. Sure wish you were sticking around." He held out his hand.

Chris put the two apartment keys in Russell's beefy palm. It would be easy for him to stay. But lately he'd been thinking more and more about home, about the Amish faith he'd turned his back on but was still entwined with every fiber of his soul. He'd lived an *Englisch* life since the day he'd been shunned, cutting his hair, buying *Englisch* clothes, even getting his driver's license and purchasing a beat-up car. Shortly after arriving in Apple Creek, he found a job with a construction company, building houses all over Knox and Holmes counties. Before long he was making more than enough money to afford an apartment and a better car. He even joined a Mennonite church. On the outside, he'd made a successful transition from Amish life.

On the inside, it was anything but.

He snatched up a faded brown baseball cap and plopped it on his head, then he slung his duffel bag over his shoulder. "Thanks for that, but I've got to get going."

Russell nodded. "Good luck."

Chris left the apartment and went to his car. He felt freer than he had in a long time, but doubts plagued him. He stopped in front of his car and looked up at the cloudless sky, questions and doubts battering him. Had he made the right decision? Could he reconcile with his family and the church? Could he forgive the person who'd ruined his life? Could he ask the community to forgive his transgressions?

He wasn't sure if he could. But he had to try.

⌘

Sarah Lynne carefully aligned the simple label on the jar of strawberry jelly, then smoothed it against the glass. *Ellie's Jellies* it said in black print, with a small picture of a cluster of grapes above the name. She breathed in the sweet scent of cooking fruit and sugar wafting throughout Ellie's kitchen as the next batch of jelly simmered on the gas stove. Her lips curved into a smile. "Did I tell you it smells *gut* in here?"

"About a dozen times," Ellie said.

Ellie's light blue eyes were directed just beyond Sarah's shoulder. They held no expression, but from the twitch of Ellie's lips, Sarah Lynne could see the compliment pleased her friend. "Here's another jar." She placed it in Ellie's outstretched hands.

Ellie gripped the jar with her left hand, then guided it into one of the six square openings inside the box. "It's nice of you to take the time to give me a hand. I know how busy you are with wedding preparations."

"I'm happy to do it. Especially since I know I can get all the free samples I want."

Ellie chuckled. "Does Isaiah know what a sweet tooth you have?"

"*Ya*. He quickly learned the way to my heart and has been keeping me supplied with treats ever since."

"He's a *gut mann*, your Isaiah." Ellie rose from her chair, turned, and made her way to the gas stove a few steps from the round kitchen table. She picked up a wooden spoon from beside the stove and stirred the pot of strawberries and sugar.

"He is, *ya*." Sarah Lynne watched her friend move about the kitchen with ease. Ellie never ceased to amaze her. Completely blind from a car accident five years before, she didn't let her disability stop her from creating her own line of jams and jellies, which she sold at Yoder's Pantry. Before losing her sight she had been a cook at the restaurant, a job she had loved.

Last year she had announced her new venture to her former employers. Sarah Lynne worked as a waitress at the Pantry, and she clearly remembered the scrumptious samples Ellie had brought with her that day. One taste and everyone was sold.

Sarah Lynne put her elbow on the table and leaned her chin on her hand. So much had happened over the past year, not the least of which was her falling in love with Ellie's cousin Isaiah. She'd known him forever and had never had a romantic thought toward him for most of her life. But then she'd been without a ride home from a Sunday singing, and he offered to take her. She was drawn to his shy manner and strong faith, and soon they were dating. Now she couldn't imagine spending the rest of her life with anyone else.

"You've gotten quiet over there." Ellie tapped the handle against the lip of the pot, letting the residual ruby-colored jelly slide off the spoon. She placed the spoon on the rest by the stove and sat down again. "Anything you want to talk about?"

Sarah Lynne looked at her friend's eyes. They were so beautiful, like tiny ovals of blue glass, with round black pupils that never changed size. The accident hadn't damaged her eyes, nor had it left any physical scars. Her blindness was due to blunt force trauma, damaging her optic nerve. From a glance one would think Ellie Chupp absolutely perfect, with her pale blonde hair, slender figure, and those gorgeous eyes. Sarah Lynne looked away, feeling guilty even though she knew Ellie had no idea she was staring at her.

"Are you worried about the wedding?" Ellie folded her hands on her lap. Her posture, as always, was perfect.

"*Nee*. Well, maybe a little." She dropped her hand from her chin and leaned forward. "*Mamm*'s been writing to Chris. I don't think *Daed* knows. If he did, he might be upset. He's very strict about the *bann*."

"Do you agree with him?"

"*Nee*. But we're not going to argue with him about it."

Ellie leaned forward. "I don't understand that. How can we possibly bring our loved ones back to the faith if we send them away? If we don't let them know how fervently we pray for them?"

"I wouldn't let Bishop Ebersol hear you say that."

"Don't worry, I won't." Ellie sighed. "It's not like I'll ever have to worry about that."

"Being in the *bann*?" Sarah Lynne smiled at the thought of her friend doing something worthy of shunning.

"*Nee.*" Ellie lowered her voice to an almost inaudible level. "Having a *kinn* to worry about."

Sarah Lynne's eyebrows lifted. She'd rarely heard a self-pitying word cross Ellie's lips. "Ellie, you can't say that."

"*Ya*, I can. I've accepted that I may not ever have a husband. God has helped me to see that I can find fulfillment in other ways."

"Like your business. We can't keep your jelly in stock at the Pantry."

"That's *gut* to hear. I'm glad the customers are enjoying it."

"Enjoying?" Sarah chuckled. "They're devouring it."

Ellie smiled. "Then I'll have to keep making more." She leaned forward and searched for Sarah Lynne's hand. When she found it, she gripped it. "But we're not talking about me. We're talking about you. And about Chris. Did your *mutter* mention the wedding in any of her letters?"

"I don't know. We don't talk about what she writes. But I would be surprised if she did." Having Chris here for the wedding would be a complete disaster. Yet Sarah Lynne wished her brother would come home. She missed him.

"I can understand why she wouldn't say anything." Ellie paused. "But your family has wholeheartedly accepted Isaiah into their fold. Perhaps Chris can find it in his heart to do the same."

"Someday, perhaps." Knowing the history between the two men, Sarah Lynne doubted it. In fact, her brother's complicated relationship with Isaiah had kept her from accepting Isaiah's first marriage proposal. But when he asked her a second time, she knew she couldn't put her happiness on hold waiting for her brother to come around. "I'm not counting on it. And it doesn't matter, really. If *Mamm* told him about the wedding and he decides to come, then we'll deal with it. And if he doesn't, we'll still have a *gut* time." This was her wedding, her time to celebrate. She wouldn't let Chris ruin that.

Ellie squeezed her hand and let it go. "How is Chris faring in Ohio?"

"I guess he's doing fine. *Mamm*'s the only one who has contact with him, and like I said, she doesn't tell me anything." She sighed. "It would be wonderful if Chris would realize how wrong he's been. *Mamm* hasn't been the same since he left."

"I'm sure it's been hard. On all of you. I'll pray he comes back and reconciles with your family and the church."

"*Danki*, Ellie. We've all been praying for that as well. Especially Isaiah." A lump formed in her throat. "He's still carrying around so much guilt."

Ellie gripped the table, her light brows furrowing. "He shouldn't."

Her forceful reply surprised Sarah Lynne. "That's what I keep telling him—"

"Because we've all put the past behind us, *ya?*"

"*Ya.* Ellie, is something wrong?"

Ellie released the edge of the table, the lines of strain fading from her face. "*Nee,*" she said, putting her hands in her lap. "Isaiah shouldn't punish himself after all this time. What's done is done, and it can't be changed."

"I know that. He knows that. But . . ." She couldn't bring herself to say the words out loud. Her future husband would never be at peace as long as Chris stayed away. She looked at Ellie. "It seems to me the only person who should be angry with Isaiah is you."

"Me?" Her mouth tugged down in a frown. "Sarah Lynne, I could never be angry with Isaiah. Look at what a wonderful *mann* he's become. He's so strong in our faith—everyone knows that. And whenever there's a need in our community, he's there, not only providing help with his hands, but with his time and his money. There isn't a more generous *mann.*"

Hearing about her fiancé's qualities made Sarah Lynne's heart swell with love. His image came to mind. The smoky gray eyes that were always filled with kindness, the soft, low tone of his voice, the mop of curly, sandy blond hair that could never be fully tamed into the bowl-shaped Amish haircut.

Ellie was right. Isaiah shouldn't carry so much guilt. It wasn't fair, not when the one person who should really resent him had forgiven him long ago. Sarah Lynne couldn't wait to be his wife, and if her brother couldn't give him the peace he needed, she'd spend the rest of their lives making up for it.

Chapter Two

AFTER SARAH LYNNE LEFT, ELLIE WIPED OFF THE COUNTER-tops in case any jelly had spilled. Then she rinsed the rag and hung it on the divider between the double sink. The window above the sink was cracked open a bit to let out some of the heat that had built up in the kitchen. But now that she had finished canning the jelly, the late October air brought a chill into the room. She groped for the sash, then closed the window.

She lifted the plastic lid on her Braille watch—something Bishop Ebersol had given her special permission to wear—and checked the time. Nearly five o'clock. Her parents would be home soon, her father from his construction job and her mother from visiting her older brother Wally's children, who lived a few miles down the road. Ellie usually accompanied her mother on her visits—she adored her nieces and nephews—but she had to finish up the jelly. God had seen fit to bless her small venture, keeping her plenty busy. She needed to be busy. She needed to be *needed*. And this new business met that need.

For now.

She shoved the thought away. Ellie didn't like thinking of the future, not anymore. Before the accident thoughts of the future consumed her—a future with John Beachy. When would they marry? How many children would they have? Would they have all boys, all girls, or a mix of both? She'd even wondered how many grandchildren she might have.

But in an instant all those hopes had been dashed, forcing her to live in the present, taking each day as the blessing it was. She'd spent years adapting to a life without sight, relearning the simplest tasks, things she used to do automatically. To pin up her hair, she needed to place the hairpins in the same spot every day. If she put them somewhere else, or if someone moved them, she might never find them, and then she would have to depend on someone else to locate them. The day John left, she decided she would never depend on anyone. She didn't want people's pity. She spent enough time pitying herself.

Ellie turned from the window. That was all behind her now. Her future was in God's hands. Her sole focus was today, and at the moment, on what she would make for supper.

Twenty minutes later she had a fragrant beef stew bubbling on the stove, filled with potatoes and carrots from the root cellar and canned meat from the cow her parents had butchered last month. She pulled a loaf of bread she'd baked that morning from the breadbox on the counter and was slicing it when her mother walked into the kitchen.

"That smells great, *dochder*." *Mami's* soft footsteps sounded against the wooden floor in the kitchen as she moved to stand next to Ellie. "Did you use homemade broth?"

"Of course."

"And are those barley pearls I see?"

"Absolutely." Ellie smiled as she placed the palm of her left hand on the loaf of bread, using the tip of her finger to find the edge. She moved her fingertip back about an inch, then she placed the knife close to it before slicing off a big piece of soft bread. Laying that on the plate nearby, she repeated the process again as she tilted her head in the direction of her mother's voice. "I'm using the restaurant's recipe tonight."

"Your specialty? Mmm, I can't wait to taste it. You have a gift for cooking, Ellie. You always have."

Ellie was grateful she hadn't lost her ability to work in the kitchen. It had taken months and months to acquire the new skills and techniques until she had mastered again what she had once taken for granted. More than once she had felt the slip of the knife blade into her finger as she learned how to slice bread, and the splash of hot water from the kettle as she practiced pouring. Yet she'd never had a major accident and had almost regained her former confidence in the kitchen. But the satisfaction of cooking at home would never replace what she had permanently lost.

She would never have her job back at Yoder's Pantry, a job she loved. She'd never know the pleasure of cooking for the customers again, both Amish and *Englisch*, and seeing them enjoy the food she prepared. The compliments hadn't stoked her pride; they only spurred her on to become a better cook. She loved inventing tiny twists on common Amish meals, such as adding a touch more thyme to the chicken and noodles or a bit of orange zest to the cherry pie filling. She loved it when customers asked what was in the recipes, trying to identify that one flavor they just couldn't pinpoint.

Now she had to be content with pleasing her parents and occasionally families in the church when she brought a meal to potluck.

Her father arrived, and after he cleaned up from work they all sat down at the table. After saying a silent prayer, they started to eat.

"I see you got your jelly jars finished today." Her mother's voice broke the silence that had settled over them once they dug into the meal.

"*Ya*, Sarah Lynne came over and helped me." Ellie found the lip of the bowl with her left hand and guided her spoon into the stew. From the temperature of the bowl she knew the stew was still pretty hot. She gently blew on the spoon before putting it in her mouth. The flavors exploded on her tongue, and the beef chunks were so tender they almost melted before she could chew them.

"That reminds me, I need to visit her *mamm* and find out how the wedding preparations are going. Did she mention anything to you?"

Ellie turned her head in the direction of her mother's voice. She'd learned in rehabilitation the importance of looking at the person speaking. She'd been amazed how quickly she had stopped doing that after the accident. Now it had become natural again. "They're going well. Sarah Lynne asked if I'd make a couple of desserts."

"Brownies."

She directed her sightless gaze to her father's deep voice at her left. "Brownies?"

"You should take your brownies, the cream cheese ones. Best dessert I ever had."

She warmed at the compliment, which she knew her father didn't give lightly. "*Danki, Daed.* I'll do that. And I'll make an extra pan just for you."

"That'll do."

Ellie could imagine the small smile twitching on her father's face, the crinkles forming in the corners of his eyes. As she usually did, she tried to imagine what he looked like now, at age fifty-five. Was his beard close to full gray? Did he still wear his hat at a slight left angle? Did he have more wrinkles? She'd never know, as she would never ask him such strange questions, nor would she ask her mother. What were looks anyway? She'd never thought about them too much when she had her sight, knowing that God saw the inside of a person, not the outer shell. Character was the important thing. But she had to remind herself of that, instead of being curious about what her family and friends looked like.

"I wonder if Chris knows about the wedding," her father said before taking another slurp of his stew. "If he does, maybe he'll come back."

"I certainly hope not," her mother responded. "At least not before he repents of his sin."

Ellie could sense her mother shaking her head, as she always did when she became indignant.

"He's in the *bann*. He must be willing to make things right with God and the church."

"I don't think you should judge him so harshly, *Mami*," Ellie said. "He lost someone very important to him."

"And you losing your sight wasn't important?" Her tone held an edge. "He would do well to follow your example, *dochder*. You were able to do as God calls. You were able to forgive. That *bu* has done nothing but cause pain for his family. His poor *mutter*." She clucked her tongue. "At least he should think of her. It breaks my heart to see the sadness in her eyes, even after all this time."

Ellie reached for her bread, which was on a small plate to the left of her bowl. She tried to set her place as consistently as possible, using a mental clock face as a guide. Her plate was the center, her water glass at one o'clock, her bread plate at eleven, and her fork and knife situated close to the plate on the right and the left.

Her mother had always been strict about her faith, even more than her father. She'd never been shy about expressing her support of *meiding*, even when others, including herself, in the community were less sure about the fairness of the practice. Her mother had balked about her father having a cell phone in the small appliance repair shop that he used to run before he started to work in construction, but even Bishop Ebersol approved of having the phone for business purposes.

"Maybe he is thinking of her," Ellie said, putting her bread back down on her plate.

"What?" her mother asked.

"Maybe Chris is thinking about his mother. If he's not ready to repent, then staying away is the right thing to do. Being close by would be even more painful for her, *ya*? Besides, who's to say what's in his heart? People forgive in their own time. Or rather, in the Lord's time, I like to think."

"Humph. It's been five years, Ellie." She felt her mother's hand on her arm. "You have such a gentle heart, *dochder*. You see the *gut* in everyone. But sometimes people aren't *gut*, even Amish people."

Ellie pulled her arm away. She hated when her mother spoke to her like she wasn't smart enough to figure things out. She was blind, not stupid, and it was on the tip of her tongue to say so, but she held the words in. "I just like to give everyone the benefit of the doubt. That's all."

"And that's very admirable." Her mother took another quiet bite of the stew.

As usual, her father remained silent. She heard him slide his chair from the table.

"*Sehr gut*, Ellie. As always." His knees creaked as he rose and walked out of the room.

Ellie had expected to hear the heavy thud of his work shoes on the wooden floor, but he must have removed them before supper because she barely sensed his soft footsteps as he left.

She and her mother ate the rest of the meal in silence. She finished off the stew, dipping the last few bites of her bread into the rich broth.

After praying at the end of the meal, her mother spoke. "I'll get the dishes." The clink of silverware against the plates filled the kitchen as her mother started to clear the table. "Oh, and I brought another book from the library. I think you'll like it."

"Is it about the Amish?"

"*Ya.*" She leaned close to Ellie, her voice lowered to a whisper. "And it's a *romance*."

Ellie tamped down a giggle. Her mother sounded like she was smuggling something illegal into the house. Before the accident she had expressed disdain over Ellie's choice of reading material. Her mother had always preferred Bible reading, or a few nonfiction books. She claimed to never have time for "that nonsense."

But Ellie was glad that her mother had softened and brought home books she knew Ellie would enjoy.

"*Danki*," Ellie said. "I can't wait to read it. Are you sure you don't need any help?"

"*Nee*. You just go on, I'll take care of this. It's the least I can do in return for such an *appeditlich* meal."

Ellie nodded, then stood from the table and made her way to the living room, which was through a small hallway just off the kitchen. She didn't use her white cane at home. Her parents had kept everything the same for years, even before the accident. That made navigating through the house a lot easier.

As she walked into the room, she breathed in deeply and smiled. Her father had started a fire in the woodstove in the corner. She loved the rich smell of smoke and went to sit in the chair near the newly crackling fire.

Her father tossed another log in the fire, then eased himself into the chair on the opposite side of the fireplace. The soothing warmth covered her body, seeping through the thin fabric of her pale green dress. She leaned back in the comfortable chair and closed eyes, enjoying the peace. She heard the soft rustle of her father opening the daily newspaper.

"Any news worth mentioning?" she asked.

"Not too much." He turned a page. "Sure are a lot of jelly jars on the counter in the kitchen. Looks like your business is doing well."

"It is, *Daed*. Even I'm surprised." She angled her body toward his voice, the heat from the fire warming her legs through her dark blue knee socks. "I thought a few people might want to buy a jar of jelly every once in a while, but I can barely keep up. Every day I have to *geh* to the grocer's to get more fruit."

"You using frozen?"

"I have to. Fresh is so expensive right now and will be until next summer. I can tell a difference in the quality of the jelly, but

Sarah Lynne says the customers can't. A few have asked if they can buy it by the case."

Her father lowered his voice. "Now that your *mutter*'s out of sight, I can say this. I know I'm not supposed to have a speck of pride in my bones, but I can't help it when it comes to you. You've done real well for yourself, Ellie. You let that *Englisch* woman come here. The one that taught you Braille and how to use your cane and stuff. What was her name?" He snapped his finger.

"Mrs. Neeley." Ellie smiled at the thought of her rehabilitation teacher. They hadn't always gotten along, especially in the beginning. She'd been a stubborn student at first, still struggling to accept her blindness and John's increasing retreat from her life. But the woman never lost patience with her. Ellie owed her much more than she could ever repay.

"*Ya*, that's her. And you stuck with it. And never once did I see you feel sorry for yourself."

Ellie tilted her chin down. He may not have seen her piteous moments, but she'd had plenty over the years.

His voice started to quaver. "Now you've got your thriving business. And you've done it on your own."

"Not exactly on my own, *Daed*." She'd been raised to deflect any praise, but hearing the emotion in her father's voice brought tears to her eyes. She fought to keep them from sliding down her cheeks. "The printer in town gives me a *gut* discount on the labels. Sarah Lynne helps me with the packaging. *Mami* drives me to the store when I can't get a taxi and takes me to the Pantry when she can. I've had lots of help."

"I reckon you're gonna need more if things keep going like this." He cleared his throat. "You've done *gut*, *dochder*. You've done *gut*."

Ellie took a deep breath. If her mother came in and saw her crying, even happy tears, she'd pepper her with endless questions. And Ellie didn't want to reveal what her father had told her. She loved her mother, but Ellie's personality meshed more with her father's, and she'd always felt closest to him. Knowing that he thought well of her meant everything.

"Dishes are all done." Her mother entered the room and huffed. "Goodness, Ephraim, you're going to roast us in here. Turn down the damper!"

A moment later the damper squeaked closed.

"There. That's much better. Here you are, Ellie." Her mother handed her the portable CD player. "The librarian said if you enjoy this one she can order the other two in the series."

"*Danki*. I'm sure I'll enjoy it." She was glad Bishop Ebersol had given her special permission to listen to books on her battery-operated CD player. If not, she would have to depend on her mother or father to read to her, and they would never read a romance out loud, even a Christian one. Her father would probably die of embarrassment if she even hinted at it.

Her mother had slipped the CD in the player for her already. But as the story floated through the speakers of her headphones, she could barely focus on the words. She had made her father proud. She would carry his praise with her for a long time.

Chapter Three

"Two weeks is a long time."

Sarah Lynne peered around Isaiah's shoulder as they sat on the swing on the front porch of her parents' house. Satisfied that no one was peeking through the window, she threaded her fingers through Isaiah's, her palm pressing against his large, calloused hand. The air had a bit of a chill in it, but she didn't care. Not only did her jacket keep her warm, but so did the man sitting next to her. "It's a long time to me too."

"I wish we had scheduled the wedding for the first of November." He leaned back in the swing, pushing against the wooden porch with the toe of his work boot.

"Patience is a virtue."

"*Ya*, but it's hard to be patient when I'm about to marry the best *maedel* in Paradise." He turned to her. "Make that the world."

The sun had dipped past the horizon, but there was enough daylight to see the redness of his cheeks and his slightly crooked teeth as he smiled. He was handsome and kind. He was also so shy that they hadn't even shared a kiss on the cheek since they'd started courting. She squeezed his hand. Isaiah wasn't the only impatient one.

She tore her gaze away before her thoughts got her in trouble. "We should focus on the wedding preparations. And who we'll be visiting afterward."

"Your parents, of course. Then mine."

"There's also my cousin. Although she has seven *kinner* and is expecting another one, so she may not notice we're even there."

They continued to talk about visiting various friends and relatives after their wedding. They both had large extended families, so there would be plenty of visiting going on before they were settled in their own house, which Isaiah had just purchased a few weeks ago. Located down the street from his family, it was a modest house, but with plenty of room for a growing family.

"I thought maybe next week we could go shopping for furniture." He started the swing moving again. "We'll need a couch, a table for the kitchen, a bed . . ." His voice trailed off and he averted his gaze.

Laughing, she lightly tapped his arm with her hand. "You're the shyest *mann* I know." She sighed. "I wouldn't have you any other way."

Out of the corner of her eye, she saw the headlights of a car coming down the long, winding dirt driveway. Her parents' house was at least a half mile from the road, and rarely did cars venture here, except the occasional taxi when necessary. She released Isaiah's hand and stood up. "Wonder who that is."

"Are you expecting anyone?"

She shook her head. "Not tonight."

"Maybe your parents are?"

As the car neared she said, "They didn't say anything to me about it."

The dark blue two-door car pulled up near the house. When the door opened, a tall, slender man with short black hair stepped out, then reached back inside the car to pull out a big duffel bag. Finally he turned around.

Sarah Lynne gasped. Was the dim light playing tricks on her? "Christopher?"

Then the man grinned, and her heart tripped. Even with his short hair and *Englisch* jeans and leather jacket, she knew him. "Christopher!" She ran toward him, her arms outstretched, then stopped short. She couldn't hug him, not while he was still shunned.

She hadn't seen him since she was fifteen years old. Suddenly she didn't care that he was in the *bann*. Her brother was here, and that was all that mattered. She reached out to him, and he held her tight.

They finally separated and she looked up at him. He tweaked her nose. "Can't hardly call you my little *schwester* anymore, can I? You're all grown up."

"And you've become *Englisch*, I see."

He immediately sobered. "Not completely, Sarah Lynne. In my heart, I'm still Amish."

Her breath caught in her throat. "Does that mean you're coming back to the church?"

He didn't say anything, just looked past her shoulder to Isaiah, who was standing several feet away. She glanced over to see that he had put on his hat, pulling it low over his forehead.

Just at that moment she saw Chris lock eyes with him, and her stomach twisted like a metal spring. Her pulse thrummed as the two men stared at each other.

"What's he doing here?" Chris sounded like he'd just chewed a mouthful of glass.

"We should go inside. *Mami* and *Daed* will want to see you—"

"I want him to answer me first." Chris directed the question to Sarah Lynne but kept his eyes on Isaiah.

Sarah Lynne stepped to the side, her gaze shifting from one man to the other. Isaiah kept his eyes on the ground. His broad shoulders slumped, like the confidence had whooshed out of him. Even as Chris strode toward him, he didn't look up. Then she realized why. He wouldn't engage her brother. He couldn't and still adhere to the Amish tenant of nonviolence. And with the anger coiling off Christopher right now, Isaiah had clearly made the right decision.

"Christopher!" Sarah Lynne grabbed the crook of his elbow and pulled him to the side. She lowered her voice, not wanting Isaiah to hear. "Why are you here?"

Chris pulled his gaze from Isaiah. "I came back to . . . to . . ."

He shot another look at Isaiah. "Why won't anyone tell me why he's here?"

Sarah Lynne put her hand on her brother's shoulder, steeling herself for his reaction. "Things have changed since you left." The knot in her stomach suddenly unwound as a sudden peace fell over her. She loved her brother, and always would, but her place was beside Isaiah. "A lot of things."

Chris looked at her, then back at Isaiah, who lifted his head to gaze at Chris directly but without confrontation. Chris focused on her again. "What are you talking about?"

She took a deep breath. "Chris, Isaiah and I are engaged."

Chris froze for a moment, then he turned around and walked a few steps to his car. He kicked the tire, then whirled to face them. "You're marrying him? After what he did to our family?"

The front door opened, and Chris saw his father, closely followed by his mother, come out to the porch.

"What's going on here?" His father, still nimble for a man in his midfifties, hurried down the steps. "Christopher?"

Mamm came down the stairs, the white strands of her *kapp* flying behind her shoulders. She passed by her husband, Isaiah, and Sarah Lynne, and rushed straight to Chris. *"Sohn?"* Her voice was thick with tears. "Is it really you?"

Chris's posture softened as he looked down at his mother. *"Ya, Mami."*

She reached up to embrace him, only to freeze at her husband's approach.

"Melvin——," his mother said, moving to stand in front of him. But when he waved her to the side, she stepped back.

"Are you here to ask forgiveness? Are you ready to come back to us?"

Chris's gaze darted from his father to his mother and finally to Sarah Lynne. He had thought he was ready to let go of the past and repent, but how could he do that now? "I'm not sure."

A muscle in his *daed's* cheek twitched. "Then why are you here?"

"I . . . I don't know."

His father turned to their mother. "*Geh* in the *haus*."

"But, Melvin—"

"I said . . . *geh* in the *haus*." He didn't raise his voice or even change the tone. Just spoke the words slowly as he moved closer to her.

Without another protest, his mother turned around. But Chris saw her wipe at her nose with the back of her hand before disappearing inside.

His father turned toward Sarah Lynne and Isaiah. "Isaiah, it's time you head home. Sarah Lynne, *geh* inside with your *mamm*."

Chris's stomach turned as he saw Isaiah and Sarah Lynne gaze at each other for a long moment. Even in the dim light of approaching night he could see the emotion in their eyes.

Isaiah turned and headed behind the house. He must have parked his buggy near the barn, probably in the same spot Chris used to keep his buggy . . . the one he'd bought to surprise Caroline on their wedding day. The twist in his gut tightened.

Sarah Lynne took one more look at Chris before running into the house. He hoped she could comfort their mother. It didn't seem he'd have the chance.

Why hadn't his mother told him Sarah Lynne was marrying Isaiah? How could his parents approve of this? Why would they allow their daughter to marry a criminal? They had all betrayed him. Every last one.

Isaiah's buggy appeared from the opposite side of the house. Long ago Chris's father had formed a crude but effective circular dirt driveway that made parking the buggy easy. It also made for a quick getaway for Isaiah. He didn't have to directly pass by either of them to get to the road.

Chris's *daed* kept his back to him, watching Isaiah. When Isaiah turned his buggy on to the main road, his *daed* faced Chris again. "You may stay here tonight. But we will follow the rules of *meiding*. Understand?"

Chris shook his head. He couldn't stay here, not after what he had learned. "*Danki*, but I made other arrangements." He hadn't, but his father didn't need to know that.

His *daed's* nod was almost imperceptible. Then he turned around and went back in the house.

The wind suddenly picked up, and Chris drew his black leather jacket closer to his body as he leaned against his car. His gaze drifted to the large picture window, focusing on the soft, yellowish glow cast by a gas lamp. A few seconds later the light was extinguished, leaving him in darkness.

He grabbed his duffel and tossed it inside the car, then he hurled himself into the driver's seat and yanked the door shut. But instead of turning on the engine, he leaned his forehead against the steering wheel, trying to make sense of his feelings. He should head back to Apple Creek. He had a good life there. No lies. No betrayal.

No family. No faith. No real connection to God.

A heavy sigh escaped him. He had no idea what to do, but he knew he couldn't stay in his parents' driveway. He lifted his head and reached for his keys in the pocket of his coat. A knock sounded on the window, making him jump. He turned and saw Sarah Lynne tapping on the glass.

He turned on the ignition and pressed the button for the automatic window. Even though he was furious with her, he couldn't turn her away. "What?"

She leaned forward, hugging her shoulders with her hands. "*Mamm*'s upset, Christopher. And so am I."

"*You're* angry?"

"*Ya*, I am. For starters, I don't appreciate the way you treated Isaiah."

He gaped. "I treated him the way he deserves."

"*Nee*. You didn't. You're acting like a little *kinn*, Christopher. Just like you did when you left Paradise."

"I didn't have a choice. I'm in the *bann*, remember."

"That's your own doing."

"Look, I don't know how this became about me, but—"

"It's always about you, Christopher. You saw *Mami* tonight." She paused. He couldn't see her expression clearly, but he heard resentment creeping into her voice. "And now *Daed*'s all upset. Do you have any idea how hard this has been on him? You're his only *sohn*."

Her words pierced his heart, but he wouldn't let her see it. Instead he focused on the real offense. "How can you marry him, Sarah? After what he did to Caroline?"

"Because I love him," she said without hesitation. "And he loves me. There's no finer man in Paradise."

"I find that hard to believe."

"Believe it."

He slumped against the seat. The exhaust from the engine reached his nostrils, and Sarah Lynne had started to shiver. "I don't want to argue with you," he said. "Not now."

"I don't either."

"Then you should *geh* back inside."

"I will. I just came out here to find out where you're staying."

"Staying?"

"*Ya. Daed* said you were staying somewhere else. Don't be thick, Christopher."

"I'm not being thick, and I'm not staying." If he had waffled before about leaving for Ohio, he had just made up his mind. His family had chosen sides. There was no point in hanging around here any longer.

"But you can't leave." Distress colored her tone. "You saw how excited *Mami* was to see you. She couldn't take it if you left now."

Alarm shot through him. "Is there something wrong? Is she sick?"

"Sick? *Nee*, she's not sick. Unless you count heartsick. *Daed* is too. I know he won't talk to you, but I'm sure *Mamm* will. So where are you staying? She can meet you there tomorrow. I'll call the taxi myself."

Chris paused. He wanted to see his mother one last time before he went back to Apple Creek. "I'm not sure."

"Let me know in the morning. I'll be at the Pantry starting at seven. My shift ends at three, so don't wait too long to come by."

She stepped away from the car. "There's a bed-and-breakfast near the restaurant that has a vacancy. They're rarely busy during the week."

He nodded, then rolled up his window and watched her shadowy form run back to the house. So much for leaving Paradise tonight.

Chapter Four

ELLIE SLID INTO A BOOTH NEAR THE FRONT WINDOW OF THE
Pantry. She folded up her cane and laid it beside her on the bench
seat. She really didn't need it. She had worked there for over four
years, from the time she was sixteen, and she knew the restaurant
inside and out. But she carried the cane anyway, more as a way to
alert others that she was blind.

She checked her watch. Two o'clock. She couldn't believe a
couple of hours had passed since the taxi had brought her here
to drop off the jelly jars. She'd gotten sidetracked visiting. Her
stomach rumbled. Definitely time for some lunch.

She ran her hand across the smooth tabletop. It was white,
and she could see the entire layout of the restaurant in her mind.
Yoder's Pantry hadn't changed its décor in years.

Ellie heard footsteps approach. Probably the waitress to take
her order. She always got the same thing—a grilled chicken salad
with a wedge of Swiss cheese on the side and a cup of chicken
noodle soup. Sometimes she would splurge on vanilla ice cream
for dessert, but not often, and not today.

"I hope you don't mind me bothering you."

Her eyebrows lifted. It wasn't the waitress she'd been expecting, but Levina Lapp, one of her mother's friends. "*Nee, Frau*
Lapp. You're not bothering me at all."

"I'll only be a minute. I just wanted to tell you that your jellies
are the best I've ever tasted. I've bought too many jars to count
lately."

Ellie smiled. "*Danki*. I appreciate that."

"I wondered if you ever took special orders."

"I can. Is there a particular flavor you want?"

"I was actually thinking more of amounts. I'd like to purchase a couple cases of all the different flavors, if that's all right."

Ellie's jaw dropped. "Cases?"

"At least four. I think they'll make lovely Christmas presents for my family in Indiana. I've been raving to them about your jellies."

Ellie was still trying to wrap her head around such a large order. "When would you need them?"

"Mid-November should be fine."

"Then you shall have them mid-November."

Levina touched Ellie's shoulder. "*Danki*, Ellie. You have a fine day, now. And we'll be in touch."

As Levina walked away, Ellie tried to calculate how much fruit she would need to prepare four cases of jelly. She still couldn't believe she'd made such a large sale. Levina's order alone would ensure she could stay in business for the next several months, even if she didn't sell another jar.

Footsteps approached. This time it had to be her waitress. But she was wrong again when she heard someone slide into the seat across from her, then let out a big sigh, one she immediately recognized.

"Doesn't sound like you're having a *gut* day, Sarah Lynne."

"I'm not." Another sigh.

Ellie put thoughts about Levina's order out of her mind and focused on her friend. "What's wrong? Please tell me you and Isaiah aren't fighting."

"I'm fighting with someone, but not him."

Ellie waited for Sarah Lynne to elaborate, but her friend remained silent. Not wanting to pry, she changed the subject. "I thought Brandy might be coming over here to take my order."

Sarah Lynne gasped. "Oh, I'm sorry. You must be starving. It's well past lunchtime."

"I'm not starving, exactly—"

"I don't know where Brandy is, but I'll make sure you get some bread right away, fresh from the oven. I'll be right back."

When Sarah Lynne left, Ellie smiled and turned her face toward the window. The sun warmed her skin as it streamed through the glass. The sounds of the restaurant filled her ears—the low hum of conversations, the clinking of silverware against dishes, the faint ding of the cash register bell up front. From what she could tell, there weren't too many customers at the moment. Then again, it was after two on a Wednesday afternoon.

Ellie waited awhile longer, letting the sun shine in her face and warm her through. As the minutes ticked by she wondered where Sarah Lynne had gone. It wasn't like her to forget.

Her stomach growled again, spurring her into action. Scooting herself out of the booth, she started toward the front of the restaurant. She walked along the narrow aisle that separated the booths from the tables, which were situated in the center of the large room.

Suddenly something hit her in the face. Hard. She sank to the ground.

Chris didn't need any more reasons to leave Paradise. However, he'd just found another one. He knelt beside the young woman he'd knocked to the floor as he'd entered the restaurant. The door had hit her square in the face.

"Are you okay?" He looked down at the woman. Her arms were propping her up, but her eyes were still closed. Then they opened.

His sister rushed up to them, kneeling down on the opposite side of the woman. "Chris, what did you do?"

"It was an accident, okay?"

The woman still seemed dazed, her eyes unfocused. A small bump had already formed on her forehead. What if he'd given her a concussion?

Sarah Lynne shot him an irritated look as she tried to help the woman to her feet. Chris ignored it and assisted on the other side, putting his arm around her slim waist. When she got to a standing position, he let go, marveling at how petite she was. The top of her head, covered in a white prayer *kapp*, barely reached his shoulder.

But the weird thing was how she didn't look at him. In fact, there was no expression in her eyes at all.

"I'm really sorry." He moved closer to her, wondering why she didn't glance in his direction. Was she that angry? Not that he would blame her.

"Nothing to be sorry about," she said. Finally she turned toward him, but stared at his chest instead of his face. "I forgot my cane."

Cane? Why would a young woman like her need a cane?

"You should sit down." Sarah Lynne put her arm around the woman's shoulders and guided her to one of the booths near the back of the restaurant. Chris followed, trying to ignore the stares of the other patrons. The woman was doing a good job of that herself, keeping her attention focused directly in front of her.

Sarah Lynne guided her into the booth. "Do you need some water? Ice?"

She shook her head. "I could use some bread. I'm starving." She smiled, looking, yet not looking, directly at Sarah.

But Chris had stopped paying attention to her gaze. Instead he was transfixed by her smile. Wow. It was wide and genuine. Then he paid attention to the rest of her face—the light dusting of freckles that gave her fair complexion a darker hue, the roundness of her cheeks, the upturn of her nose. She about snatched the breath right from his lungs.

"Oh, I meant to bring the bread to you."

Sarah Lynne touched the woman's shoulder, as she often did when she spoke to people she knew. His sister had never been stingy with affection.

"When I went back to get the bread, a party of eight walked through the door and into my section. But I found Brandy, and she said she'd bring it over. I don't know what happened to her . . . You're late, by the way."

"I'm what?"

"Not you, Ellie. I was talking to Chris."

Ellie's face registered her surprise. "Your brother?"

"*Ya.* He was supposed to meet me this morning." Sarah Lynne's gaze shot through him like an arrow. "Remember?"

He nodded but kept his focus on the woman in front of him, wondering how she knew him. Then he suddenly realized who she was . . . and why she wasn't looking at his face. "Ellie Chupp?"

"*Ya.*" She tilted her head up, but not enough to look him square in the eye.

He couldn't help but stare at her eyes. They were a bright crystal blue that nearly matched the color of her long-sleeved dress. She had long, almost transparent lashes that brushed the tops of her cheeks when she blinked. How could he not have recognized Caroline's best friend? They had hung around together for years, ever since they were in school. But for some reason she looked so different to him. Except for those eyes. He'd noticed how striking they were, even back then.

"Ellie, I'm really sorry." Now he felt like a double heel. Not only had he hurt a woman, but a blind one at that. "I should have been paying attention."

"And I should have been using my cane. I left it here in the booth. I wasn't even thinking." Her slender fingertips touched the bruise on her forehead. "Does it look bad?"

He shook his head. Then, realizing she couldn't see the motion, he added, "*Nee*. Just a little black and blue."

She smiled again. "I've been through worse."

Her words were like a knife twisting inside. In his grief over losing Caroline, he'd paid little attention to what happened to Ellie. He'd heard she'd been in the hospital for a long time.

Sarah Lynne interrupted his thoughts. "I'll be getting off soon. Is your car outside?"

"*Ya*." Without thinking he stole another glance at Ellie. Her gaze was focused straight ahead.

"*Gut*. I'll meet you there. I'm off in half an hour." Sarah Lynne laid her hand on Ellie's arm again. "I'll have someone bring you that bread. And take your order, which will be on the house for all your trouble."

"You don't have to do that."

"I know, but you deserve it after waiting all this time, then getting hit in the head." She fired another glare at Chris, who gave her a cool glance in response. "I'm sure the boss will okay it," she continued, looking back to Ellie. "He loves your jelly, too, you know."

As his sister sped away to take care of her customers, Chris turned his attention back to Ellie. He tried to pinpoint why she looked so different. Or maybe she hadn't changed as much as he thought? He hadn't noticed her too much when they were growing up, not when his attention was always on Caroline.

He sure was noticing her now.

⁓◦

Ellie's forehead ached, but the pain didn't compare with the ache of embarrassment she felt. She kept her hands underneath the table and fiddled with the hem of her white apron. She felt like an idiot, allowing herself to get smacked like that. She knew better than to walk so close to the door. Chris probably thought she was completely helpless, not to mention stupid.

He didn't speak, but he didn't move away either. Why didn't he leave? Questions swirled in her mind, but she couldn't ask him a single one.

Finally he spoke. "I'm really sorry about hitting you with the door, Ellie."

His deep voice flowed over her. Had his voice always been so rich and appealing? She didn't know—maybe it had. But since she lost her sight, she noticed the quality of voices much more than before.

"It's all right," she said. "It was more my fault, really."

"*Nee*, it wasn't. I'm the one who messed up."

He paused for a moment, and she wondered what he was doing. Not being able to see facial expressions or body movements was one of the hardest things for her to deal with, especially when no one said anything. She only had her imagination to fill in the blanks.

He finally spoke. "I'll leave you alone now." She heard him move, and his voice sounded closer. "There are a couple of older *fraus* looking at us. They've already started whispering to each other."

"Maybe they're discussing the weather. Or the Pantry's apple pie recipe."

"I don't think so. Not by the dark looks they're giving me. And here . . ."

His hand suddenly touched hers, and she jumped.

"I'm sorry."

She knew why he was apologizing. According to the *bann*, they were forbidden to touch.

"I just wanted to let you know, lunch is on me. The restaurant shouldn't have to pay for my mistake."

She swiveled toward him, forgetting everyone else in the

restaurant. "You don't have to do that. I should have been paying better attention."

"How could you? You can't even see." He drew in a sharp breath. "There I *geh* again, putting *mei* foot into *mei* mouth."

She chuckled. "Now that's something I wish I could see!"

To her surprise he let out a quiet laugh. "I'm putting the money on the table. Please take it. It would make me feel a lot better."

"All right, if you insist." Ellie folded the open bills and placed them on the table near the window. She expected to hear him walk away, but he remained in place. "Chris? Did you need something else?"

He paused before answering. "Um . . . just wondering if the pretzels are still *gut*."

"*Ya*, they're delicious."

"Then I guess I'll get one of those before I leave. Haven't had one since . . ." He cleared his throat. "*Gut* seeing you, Ellie."

She angled her face toward him. "*Gut* seeing you, too, Chris." Then he left.

Her heart pinched at the sadness she'd heard in his voice. Clearly he still wasn't over Caroline's death. She also had moments when she missed Caroline terribly. Her infectious laugh and her excitement about the future were just two aspects of Caroline's bright personality that had touched everyone.

She heard the jangle of Brandy's trademark thin, silver bangles as the *Englisch* waitress approached. "Here you go." Brandy sounded rushed as she placed a basket of bread on the table. "I'm sorry, Ellie, I meant to get this to you earlier. We had a bit of a catastrophe back in the kitchen."

Ellie tilted her head up. "Is everything okay?"

"It is now." Her tinkling laugh sounded above the restaurant's din. "Thought we might have to call the fire department."

"That doesn't sound *gut*."

"Hey, it's all good. So . . ." Brandy slid into the seat across from Ellie. "Who was your *friend*? Haven't seen him around here before."

Brandy's not-so-subtle connotation made Ellie look away for a moment. "He's Sarah Lynne's brother, Chris. And he's not my *friend*. Not like that anyway."

"Well, that's too bad, because he's really cute."

"He is?" The words were out of her mouth before she could stop them.

Chris had been nice looking, if a little gangly, when they were younger. She wondered how much he'd changed over the years. She wished she could find out for herself.

"Yup. Although I didn't know Sarah Lynne had a brother who wasn't Amish."

"What do you mean?"

Brandy's bracelets chimed together again. "His hair's cut short in the back and on the sides."

"Is it still black?" Why couldn't she keep her questions to herself? Her curiosity had taken control of her common sense.

"Yes, it's still black." Brandy's voice had a sly sound to it. "Black and straight. He has it parted to the side."

Ellie tried to picture Chris with an *Englisch* haircut, but she couldn't.

"He looks a lot like Sarah Lynne. They both have the black hair and greenish eyes. He's also got the most incredible mouth, with these full lips that are so cute—"

"Brandy!" Ellie blushed.

"What? You asked me to describe him."

"*Nee*, I didn't!"

"I can tell you're curious. I would be, too, if I were you. He's got a dreamy voice, but you probably already know that."

She did, but she wasn't about to admit it.

"Maybe *curious* isn't the right word. How about *interested*?"

"I'm not interested in Christopher Miller." Ellie lowered her voice.

"Why not?"

Ellie touched her teeth to her bottom lip. She couldn't reveal the reason. Talking about something this sensitive and private constituted gossip, and she wasn't about to spread it around to anyone. "I'm just not."

"Okay, I won't ask. But let me get back to describing that gorgeous guy to you."

"Brandy, you don't have to—"

"Oh yes, I do—this is the most fun I've had all day. Oh nuts, he's leaving. I didn't even get a chance to talk to him. Why isn't he dressed Amish, again?"

Striving for patience, Ellie said, "He's not Amish anymore." Just admitting that out loud saddened her.

"Oh. Hmm."

"What are you *hmm*-ing about?" Sarah Lynne suddenly appeared and touched Ellie's shoulder.

"Your brother." Brandy slid from the booth. "Where have you been hiding that hottie all this time? Is he available?"

"Nee." Sarah Lynne's tone was firm. "Absolutely not."

"Now that's a shame." Brandy's voice dripped with disappointment.

"Brandy, why don't you *geh* check on Abby and Joseph Lambert?" Sarah Lynne said.

"I just gave them a refill on coffee."

"Well, maybe they want dessert or something." Impatience edged Sarah Lynne's tone.

"Humph," Brandy said. "I can take a hint, Sarah Lynne. Why don't you just say you need to talk to Ellie?"

"I need to talk to Ellie."

"Fine. Nice seeing you again, Ellie. Thanks for bringing the jelly. I've already put three jars in the back for myself."

KATHLEEN FULLER

"I can't believe she's interested in Chris," said Sarah Lynne after Brandy went back to work. She sat across from Ellie. "The nerve! She's not even Amish!"

"Neither is he," Ellie said softly. But she had felt a tiny twinge in her chest when Brandy had asked Sarah Lynne about Chris. Which was ridiculous. He'd been engaged to her best friend. And she had no business thinking about any man, for that matter. She'd learned her lesson with John. To stray from that reality would only mean heartache, and she didn't need any more of that.

"Right now he isn't Amish. But why would he come back if he wasn't ready to forgive Isaiah? Although that might never happen now."

"Why? What happened?"

"He came to the house last night. While Isaiah was there."

Ellie said a quick silent prayer, then reached for a slice of bread. "That had to be a shock."

"Not as much as when I told him we were getting married. He was so angry, Ellie—like he was when Caroline died. He threatened to leave last night, but I persuaded him to stay and see *Mami* one more time before he left. But then what happens after that? How can someone hang on to all that anger for five years?"

So that's why Sarah Lynne had been out of sorts this morning. Ellie found the small bowl of peanut butter spread and put some on her bread. As she spread it with a knife she said, "How is your *mami* going to talk to him?"

"I said she'd meet him at the bed-and-breakfast. She and *Daed* are really upset. When *Daed* asked Chris if he was ready to ask forgiveness, Chris said *nee*."

Ellie took a bite of the bread, but it wasn't as tasty as she'd anticipated. Hearing about Sarah Lynne's and Chris's problems had curbed her appetite. "I'm so sorry, Sarah Lynne. Not just for you and your parents, but for Chris too."

"I appreciate that, Ellie." She paused for a moment. "I've got to *geh*. Can you say a little prayer for me—actually for all of us? Isaiah feels really bad about all of this. I thought he might come by today and we could talk about it, but he never showed up."

"I will." Ellie nodded. "If there's anything I can do to help, let me know." It was an empty promise. This was Sarah Lynne and her family's problem, not hers. But she wanted to give Sarah Lynne her support.

"Actually, there might be something."

"What?"

"I don't know yet, but I may need your help." Sarah Lynne slid out of the booth. "*Ya*, you might be able to fix this after all."

"Wait a minute—"

"I'll let you know!" Sarah Lynne called out.

Chapter Five

"I DON'T THINK THERE'S ANYTHING ELSE TO SAY."

Sarah Lynne touched her fingertips to her forehead. Her brother was more stubborn than a thousand mules. And since Isaiah owned a couple, she knew what she was talking about. Why wouldn't Chris listen to reason? "All you have to do is say you forgive him. Why can't you do that?"

"Because it would be a lie, Sarah Lynne. And I can't get up in front of God and the church and lie."

"Then make it the truth. Forgive Isaiah, really forgive him. Then you can repent with a clear heart."

They were in the parking lot in the back of the Pantry, near the Dumpster. He had been pacing back and forth while they were talking, and she could tell he was battling something inside himself.

Finally he halted and faced her. "You're asking me to do the impossible."

"Then why did you come back here, if you weren't ready to forgive him?"

"I thought I was. But it's different now. You're marrying him. He's going to be my *bruder*." He spat out the last word. "That changes everything."

"It should change nothing." She clenched her fists at her sides, catching a slight rancid whiff of the garbage from the Dumpster.

A muscle twitched in his jaw. "Every time he's around I'll be reminded of what happened to Caroline."

"Haven't you spent every day of your life thinking about that?" He didn't answer.

"Christopher, you have to let this *geh*. You have to let her *geh*."

He remained silent, his back toward her. She saw his shoulders slump, and for the moment she pitied him. But he had the power to change the situation, and it made her almost *ab im kopp* that he refused.

A horse and buggy clip-clopped past the restaurant, followed by three cars. They couldn't stand here all day at an impasse.

"Christopher?"

After a long moment he turned around, his expression haunted with grief. "What?"

Her heart went out to him. "Come home. Come back to the house and talk to *Mami*."

"I can't. You know how *Daed* feels."

"I don't mean right now. Come back tomorrow while *Daed*'s at work."

He rubbed his chin, but his expression was no less tortured. "I should just *geh*. It would be easier on everyone."

"Oh *ya*, you running off will make us all feel a lot better." She crossed her arms over her chest, bunching the front of her navy blue jacket. "Please, Chris. Can't you see how selfish you're being?"

Chris stared at his sister, her sharp words slicing through him. He shouldn't expect her to understand. But deep down he knew he was being selfish, at least where his mother was concerned. "All right. I'll come over tomorrow. But just for a little while. I can't promise more than that."

Sarah Lynne let out a long breath and hurled herself into his arms. "*Danki*, Chris. This will mean so much to *Mami*. And to me." She stepped back and looked at him, her smile dimming.

"I'm not trying to make light of your pain over losing Caroline. If anything happened to Isaiah, I don't know what I'd do."

He ground his teeth at Isaiah's name. He'd spent the last five years trying to erase the memory of what that man had done to him and Caroline. And now he could see he had failed. Just seeing Isaiah again brought back all the resentment and anger he'd held inside for so long. And soon Isaiah would be his brother-in-law, and the father to his nieces and nephews, should God choose to bless them with children. Isaiah had taken Caroline's life, and now he would have what Chris had been denied—a wife and family. *How is that fair, God?*

He turned away. He couldn't be around Sarah Lynne anymore, not with the emotions wrenching inside him. "Tell *Mami* I'll see her tomorrow." He walked away.

"Christopher?"

He looked back at his sister, five years his junior. He had been her tormentor when they were little, her protector as they had gotten older. But he had failed at that too. Maybe if he hadn't left, he could have stopped Isaiah from insinuating himself into her life. "What?"

"I have to ask you one more thing." She went to him, her eyes wide and hopeful, the way she used to look when they were little and their parents promised them a special treat if they behaved in church. "I'm begging you. Give Isaiah a chance."

Chris felt the muscles tense in his cheek.

"He's not the same *mann* he was five years ago. The accident changed him, Christopher. And it still haunts him."

"*Gut.* He deserves to be haunted."

"How long should he have to pay for one mistake?" Her voice cracked.

"He *never* paid. Not the way he should have."

"That was your judgment. Not the community's. Not even the police agreed with you."

Chris knew that firsthand. After Caroline had died from her injuries, he went to the police to have charges filed against Isaiah. That started his downward spiral, resulting in his shunning.

"Everyone else has forgiven him, Christopher, including Caroline's family. Why can't you?" She whirled around and headed back into the restaurant.

He stood there for a moment, letting her question sink in. Why couldn't he forgive Isaiah? All it would take was a confession in front of the church. In front of God. But God knew his heart, saw the black spot of anger etched on it. He couldn't lie, not even to make his mother and his sister happy. God would know his confession wasn't sincere.

"Would you mind dropping me off at the cemetery?" Ellie held her folded white cane across her lap. "It's not far from my *haus*. I can walk home from there."

Trish Moore, the young woman Ellie paid for rides to and from Paradise, sucked in her breath. "I don't think that's a good idea, Ellie," she said from the front seat. "There are no sidewalks on your road. It's not safe."

"I don't walk on the side of the road. I cut across the fields between the cemetery and my *haus*."

"Aren't you afraid of tripping over something?"

"I've got my cane." Ellie held it up and smiled, leaning forward a little in the backseat. She set it down in her lap and said, "I promise, I'll be fine. I've done this before."

"I don't mind waiting for you," Trish said. "I've got a magazine to keep me occupied."

Ellie shook her head. "I don't want to keep you from your family, Trish. Your children will be getting home from school soon, *ya*?"

"They'll be all right by themselves for a little while. Trevor's thirteen—he can watch the other two."

Ellie could feel her patience slipping away. "I appreciate it, but I'd prefer if you dropped me off."

"Oh."

Ellie heard the small hint of hurt in Trish's voice. She wanted to apologize, but Trish might take that as agreement. A few minutes later she felt the car come to a stop. *"Danki,"* she said, opening the car door.

"Ellie, if something happens to you—"

"Don't worry, I won't hold you responsible. Please don't worry about me."

Trish sighed. "All right. As long as you're sure."

Ellie opened the door and stepped out of the car. She was perfectly capable of making her way home on her own. It wasn't that far, and she knew those fields as well as she knew the layouts of her house and the Pantry. When would everyone realize she could take care of herself?

Turning around, she opened her cane, which was three parts that telescoped into one long piece. The cemetery had been here since before Ellie's birth, and from memory she knew it had a narrow asphalt driveway that led to the entrance of the burial ground. She glided the tip of the cane in front of her, arcing it smoothly to detect any debris that might be in the way and to keep herself walking straight on the path. Before long she reached the short chain-link fence that surrounded the cemetery and swung open the unlocked gate.

After the accident she'd often come to visit Caroline's grave. At first it was out of grief over what she'd lost. Over the years, coming here had brought her comfort and peace. But since she started her jelly business, she had neglected her visits. Talking to Chris today had impelled her to come back.

She made her way around the perimeter of the graveyard,

stopping at the upper west corner. Leaning down, she searched for the small, plain stone slab that marked her friend's grave. When she found it, she knelt down, placing her cane beside her.

"Christopher came back, Caroline." She ran her finger along the grassy edge of the site. "I pray it's for *gut.*"

❧

Christopher turned into the narrow gravel drive that led to the cemetery where Caroline was buried. He turned off the car engine and leaned his head back against the seat. He'd driven past the burial ground three times before finally summoning the courage to pull in. Closing his eyes, he searched for the will to step out of the car. He hadn't been here since the day Caroline was buried.

Taking a deep breath, he opened the door and stepped out, breathing in the crisp fall air. Orange, yellow, and brown leaves skittered across the drive and the fields of grass surrounding the cemetery. He looked up at the clear sky, the sun still shining bright, its heat seeping through his leather jacket. Growing up, he'd spent such autumn days outside as much as he could, helping his father with the chores or playing baseball and volleyball with his friends. When he and Caroline started courting, he took her for open-air buggy rides, something she had always loved.

Before him he saw the small cement markers identifying each grave, a stark contrast to the large headstones and statues in an *Englisch* cemetery. The chain-link fence reached his waist, and he opened the short gate. He scanned the small cemetery, which was less than an acre in size.

"Hello?"

The female voice came from the back corner of the burial ground. A woman suddenly rose to her feet, not looking in his direction. Ellie Chupp.

He should turn around and leave. He didn't want to intrude.

Besides, he wasn't sure coming here was a great idea. He hadn't made too many smart decisions lately.

"Hello? Is someone here?"

He could simply walk away without speaking. She would never know. But he couldn't sneak off. That wouldn't be fair. "It's me. Christopher Miller."

"Oh, hello, Chris." She bent down to pick up something. When she stood, he could see it was her cane. "I was just leaving."

"You don't have to leave on my account. I'll *geh*."

She shook her head and walked toward him, moving the white cane in front of her at an angle. "Please. Stay. Caroline would be glad you were here."

Her words held him in place. "It's been a long time since I was here."

"I know." Ellie reached him, stopping a few feet in front of him. She tilted her chin up, gazing at him with those stunning blue eyes. "It's been awhile since I visited her too. I used to come here all the time after the accident. But lately I haven't had the chance."

"Is John picking you up?"

She frowned. "Why would he do that?"

"I thought . . . Didn't you two get married?"

Her frown turned into a bitter smile. "*Nee*. We decided we weren't . . . suited for each other."

Chris wanted to kick himself. That was the second time he'd said something insensitive to her. But from what he remembered of Ellie and John, they were very much in love. Caroline had been certain they would soon get married. His gaze strayed to the corner of the cemetery, to Caroline's grave site.

"I'll get out of your way," Ellie said, moving her cane in front of her. It tapped his foot, and he stepped aside.

Suddenly he didn't want her to go. She was his last tangible link to Caroline. But he couldn't ask her to stay. "You're not in my way, Ellie."

"And you're still as polite as you used to be." She smiled. "I'm glad you came back. I know Sarah Lynne is."

"She's not too happy with me now."

"Maybe not, but I'm sure that will change."

"I don't know about that." He glanced down at her, taking in her cane, the way her gaze was off center. "How did you do it?"

"Do what?"

"Forgive Isaiah." The question had flown out of his mouth. But now that it was out there, he wanted an answer. "After what he did to you?"

Her lips pinched together. "Isaiah didn't make me blind. The accident did that."

"But it was his fault." Chris shoved a hand through his close-cropped hair and leaned against the fence. He rammed his hands into the pockets of his jeans. "He was driving the car."

"Which he wasn't supposed to be doing." Ellie's expression grew soft. "Chris, he was sixteen and trying the *Englisch* ways. We were all guilty of that before we joined the church."

"I never drove a car."

"You do now."

"That's different. Never mind." He started to move past her, but she held out her hand to stop him. When it landed on his waist, she jerked it back.

"Sorry." Her cheeks turned the color of a strawberry. "I didn't mean to upset you."

Without thinking he touched her on the shoulder. "It's all right."

Chapter Six

ELLIE FELT THE WARMTH OF CHRIS'S HAND THROUGH HER lightweight coat, and for a moment she was frozen in place. A shiver coursed through her body.

He let go of her shoulder. "You're cold."

She wasn't cold at all. From the tingling in her belly at his touch to the heat on her face, cold was the last thing she was feeling.

"I should let you get home," he said. "Some people might get the wrong idea if they see us together."

The cemetery was fairly secluded, situated in the middle of two fields, the houses far enough away that visitors could have privacy as they visited their loved ones. And it didn't matter if they were in an empty cemetery or in a crowded room, she couldn't ignore the pain in Chris's voice when he asked her about forgiving Isaiah. "I'm not worried about anyone seeing us."

"You should be. I'm in the *bann* for a *gut* reason. At least the church thinks it is."

"What do you think?" Ellie asked.

He didn't say anything for a moment. Neither did he move away. She wasn't quite sure how close they were to each other, but she detected the scent of his leather jacket, a smell she found appealing.

"I think they're right," he said.

"You do?"

"I went against the church. That I'll admit. But it doesn't mean I wasn't right about going to the police." His low voice cracked with emotion. "When they refused to press charges, I knew there wasn't any hope for justice."

"It's not our job to dispense justice. Only God can do that."

"You sound like Sarah Lynne."

Ellie heard the sound of his shoes against the pebbles littering the grass. When he spoke again he sounded farther away. "I can't believe she's marrying him."

"She loves him, and he loves her. My cousin is a *gut mann*, Chris. You can ask anyone in the community. He's changed—"

"I know, I know. I've heard it from Sarah Lynne. That doesn't change what he did to Caroline. What he did to you. How can you forget about that?"

"I haven't." She was surprised at the tremor in her voice. Since the accident she had said little about what happened. She had to be strong, not only for Isaiah's sake. The accident had plunged him into a deep depression, and her entire family had worried about him. She had never wanted to pile on more guilt. She also had to be strong for her parents. And for John, although in the end that didn't matter. Her blindness had doomed their relationship.

But there was another reason she rarely spoke of that day. One she couldn't tell a single soul.

"Ellie, I shouldn't have said that." He moved closer, enough that she could smell the spicy-sweet scent of the cinnamon gum he chewed. "Please don't be upset."

"I'm not upset." She fought for the inner strength she had relied on for so many years. The last thing she wanted was Chris's pity. "I can't forget about the accident. I'm reminded of it every day."

⁂

Chris looked down at Ellie, seeing the sorrow in her face. She was only inches from him, the ribbons of her prayer *kapp* trailing down the back of her short navy blue jacket.

Then she lifted her chin, her expression composed. "But I was able to put what happened in the past, where it should stay."

She did what he found impossible. "You're a better person than I am."

"That's not true." She turned her head away from him. "I'm not a saint, Chris. Don't make me out to be one." She moved her cane in front of her, angling it to the side. "I have to get back home."

"How are you getting there?"

"Walking." Ellie turned to the right and pointed. "I live across the field over there."

He looked where she was pointing. "The white house?"

She chuckled. "Aren't they all white?"

"*Ya.* I suppose they are." He grinned, his first smile since he'd arrived in Paradise. "You're going to walk that far by yourself?"

"I've done it before."

"I could give you a ride." He bit his lip, forgetting that he wasn't allowed to drive her anywhere.

"I'll be fine." She brushed past him, her steps faster than they had been moments before. "I can manage."

"All right." He watched as she hurried out the cemetery and made a sharp right turn. The brown grass reached her knees, but it didn't seem to bother her as she used her cane to guide her steps. He admired her determination and fearlessness. She really was different than he remembered. Back then she was more cautious and unsure of herself. No one could deny she had confidence now. But while she seemed capable of making her way home, it didn't seem right to let her go alone. He rushed after her, reaching her quickly and adjusting his long strides to match her shorter ones.

She kept her gaze straight ahead. "What are you doing?"

"Walking you home."

She sighed. "I told you I don't need any help."

"I didn't say I was *helping* you home, did I?"

She didn't answer right away. "I guess you didn't. But it's what you intend to do, right?"

"So you have a sixth sense or something?"

"What?"

"You know, like mind reading. Because that's the only way you could know my intentions. You're amazing, but not supernatural."

He nearly tripped over his feet as the words slipped out. But it was true, she was amazing. The way she had forgiven Isaiah, how well she managed despite being blind, the fact that she had taken the time to talk to him even though he was in the *bann*. He just hadn't intended to say it out loud.

But his compliment seemed to irritate her further. "Don't patronize me, Chris."

"I didn't realize that's what I was doing."

"You are." She stared straight ahead again, her mouth set in a thin line. "You don't have to feel sorry for me either."

Now that remark hit home. He *did* feel sorry for her, at least he had a little while ago. But that feeling had gone away during their conversation. "I don't."

She didn't respond. Her cane hit a large stone, and she side-stepped it with ease.

"You don't believe me, do you?"

"*Nee.*" She quickened her pace, the sound of the grass brushing against her legs filling the air.

"Okay, I'll prove it to you." He stopped and watched as she walked away. She had gone a few feet before she stopped too. "Chris?"

"I'm back here."

She turned around, moving her cane in front of her. "Why?"

"I told you I don't feel sorry for you, so *geh* ahead and walk home by yourself."

Her mouth opened, then shut. For the second time that afternoon, he smiled.

"Okay," she said, suddenly sounding unsure. "Well, then I guess this is good-bye."

"I guess it is." He put his hands in the pockets of his jacket.

Then her expression softened. "I hope it's not forever, Chris. I mean it."

His smile faded as she turned and walked away. "I hope not either," he whispered.

Ellie didn't know what to think. In many ways Chris was exactly the same as he'd been five years ago—polite, caring, and a little self-deprecating. Yet she could hear the bitterness in his tone, hanging on the edges even when he was being nice. His grief over Caroline had thoroughly permeated him.

She was glad he had gone back to the cemetery. He had come there to visit Caroline, and if he had walked her home she would have taken up more of his time, which wasn't fair.

"You're amazing . . ."

Ellie's stomach fluttered. His words hadn't registered when he said them, because she'd been aggravated by his accompanying her. But now they hit her full force. He thought she was amazing? Her mouth tilted up in a smile.

And her foot landed in a shallow hole. Her ankle twisted, and she'd have gone down if it weren't for the support of her cane. She grimaced, regaining her balance. That's what she got for losing her concentration. But when she stepped forward, pain shot through her ankle and foot, making her bend over and nearly lose her balance again.

"Ellie!" Seeing her trip, Chris sprang into action. He sprinted toward her. "Ellie!"

She righted herself, hanging on to the white cane as she regained her balance. Thank goodness for that thing. He had just reached her side when he saw her step forward, then almost fall again.

"Are you all right?" he asked.

She stood up, nodding. "I'm fine. Just twisted my ankle."

He looked down at the ground. Although it was partially hidden by the tall grass, he saw the shallow hole she'd stepped into. His gaze went back to her face. "You're not fine."

"*Ya*, I am." She put her cane in front of her and hobbled forward two steps. "See," she said through gritted teeth.

"I bet you sprained your ankle." He went to her, putting his hand on her arm to make her stop. He didn't care that she couldn't accept a ride from him. There was no way she'd be able to walk home now. "Let me take you home."

"It's not that far to walk."

"Ellie, you're nowhere near your *haus*."

"I can make it." She tried to walk again and winced.

"And Sarah Lynne says *I'm* stubborn." He moved to block her path. "I'm taking you home."

She tilted her head up. Those eyes again. For a second he was lost in their beauty. It didn't matter that she wasn't looking exactly at him. He barely even noticed.

"If I can walk back to your car, I can make it home," she said.

"Who said anything about you walking?" He scooped her up in his arms and started toward his car.

"Chris, put me down!"

"I will when we get to my car."

Her face was inches from his, and something stirred inside him, emotions he hadn't come close to experiencing since Caroline's death. He nearly stumbled himself as he looked at her face, his gaze lingering on her lips, then traveling to her gorgeous eyes again.

"What if someone sees us?"

Her voice sounded small, and he felt her grip tighten around his neck, her cane lightly bouncing against the back of his shoulder as he walked. He wasn't supposed to touch her, much less carry her.

"I'll take full responsibility." And he would too. He wouldn't do anything to get her in trouble with the bishop or the church.

She relaxed in his arms, and he held her a little closer, partially out of not wanting to drop her, but mostly because he wanted to. He had no idea what had gotten into him this afternoon. He was saying and doing things that surprised him. But he was here for Ellie when she needed him, and that was all that mattered right now.

When they reached his car, he stopped. "I'm putting you right next to the car. You can lean against it while I open the door." Gently he lowered her to the ground, not letting go until he was sure she had her balance. When she did, he opened the car door and moved to pick her up again.

"I can get in the car," she snapped, her expression stormy.

He took a step back and watched her hop on one foot as she got in the car. She collapsed her cane with jerky movements.

He braced his hands on either side of the door opening and leaned close. "Just so you know, I would have helped you whether you were blind or not." He shut the door and walked around to the other side.

Chapter Seven

ELLIE FLINCHED AS THE CAR DOOR SLAMMED. SHE FELT LIKE a fool. He had helped her, and she treated him badly for it. "I'm sorry," she said when he got in on his side.

"It's okay."

She heard him let out a long breath.

"I just wanted you to know I didn't help you because I feel sorry for you. I helped you because you needed it."

She nodded, breathing in the scent of the car's interior. It smelled like him—cinnamon gum and leather. She closed her eyes for a moment, savoring the scents. Then she heard him start the car.

Her eyes flew open, and she gripped the door handle.

"Ellie? Are you okay?"

"*Ya.*"

His concerned voice did little to soothe her. Irrational fear took hold, and for a moment she thought about getting out of the car. But her ankle throbbed, and he would chase her down again. Should she ask him if she could move to the backseat? But that was ridiculous. She was less than a mile from her house. She could sit in the front seat for five minutes.

"You don't sound okay." She heard him shift in his seat. When he spoke he sounded closer, as if he were leaning toward her. "You're pale."

Her breathing grew shallow as she tried to calm herself. The accident was five years ago. She shouldn't be acting like this now.

Images of the crash exploded in her mind. The car speeding

toward her. Caroline's blood-chilling scream piercing the air. Her own body pitching forward, then jerking back as the car slammed into the side of Isaiah's vehicle, making them spin into the center of the intersection—

"Ellie, you're worrying me." Chris shut off the car. "Is it your ankle?"

"*Nee.*" She leaned forward. Darkness surrounded her as it always did. But this darkness was different. Suffocating. The memories continued to flash through her mind, accelerating her heartbeat. A panic attack. She'd had them before, especially soon after the accident. But time had diminished them. Until now.

She felt his hand cover hers. "It's okay, Ellie. Take a deep breath."

"I'm . . . trying." And she was, but her lungs wouldn't let the air in.

Then his fingers entwined with hers. "Lean back. That's it." His arm went around her shoulders, his free hand gripping her and gently guiding her back against the seat. "There you *geh.*"

His voice and touch were her anchors. Her heart slammed against her rib cage, but she was able to draw breath.

"It's all right, Ellie. You're okay." He kept talking, his low, rich voice providing a comforting cocoon, forcing the panic from her body. The images retreated. Her pulse slowed. Her breath evened out. But even then he held on to her hand and kept his arm around her.

"Ellie?" He squeezed her hand.

"I'm okay." She still sounded breathless, but the strangling sensation was gone. "I'm . . . okay."

"Thank God." He moved his arm from her shoulders but kept holding her hand. "Scared me for a minute. What happened?"

She dipped her head, embarrassed. It wasn't enough that she'd walked into a door and fallen into a hole, now she had to have a complete meltdown in front of him. How could she explain?

But she didn't have to.

"Is it the car? I didn't even think how that might affect you."

She shook her head. "It's not the car. Well, it is . . ." She shut her eyes against the humiliation. "I haven't been in the front seat in five years."

He squeezed her hand again. "That makes sense."

She opened her eyes. "It does?"

"*Ya*. You were in a horrible accident."

"Five years ago." She finally relaxed against the seat. "Long enough to get over it."

He didn't say anything for a moment, and she wanted to take back the words. He hadn't gotten over Caroline in five years. Anyone could see that.

"Ellie, don't be hard on yourself. We were talking about the accident. It probably triggered a memory." He lowered his voice. "I'm sorry you had to *geh* through that."

His words moved her, touching her heart in a place she had shut away from the rest of the world. The light pressure of his palm against hers warmed her through.

"I could carry you to your *haus*," he added, a bit of humor entering his voice. "You don't weigh much."

She shook her head and removed her hand from his. She still felt the strength of his arms around her when he picked her up. Her hand had brushed against the back of his head, where she felt his short, soft hair. She had been shocked, then upset, when he picked her up. But those emotions had changed into something else by the time he set her down on the ground. She didn't think she could handle him holding her any more.

"You can drive me. I'm all right now."

"Would it be better if you sat in the back?"

"*Nee.*" She took a deep breath. "I can do this. I *need* to do this. I learned a long time ago to face my fears. That's the only way I can overcome them." She fumbled for the seat belt, tamping down her frustration as she tried to locate it.

"Let me." Chris leaned over, his body close to hers as he reached for the seat belt.

Normally she'd insist on doing it herself, but she was too weary to argue. His leather jacket brushed against her shoulder, and she tried not to be obvious as she breathed him in. He brought the seat belt across her and snapped it in place.

"*Danki.*"

"No problem. I'm turning the car on now. You sure you're gonna be all right?"

"*Ya.*" And she would, even if she had to cling to the edge of her seat all the way home.

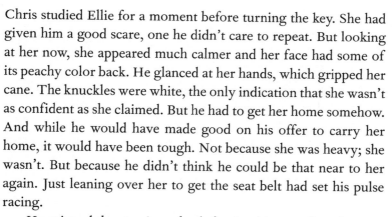

Chris studied Ellie for a moment before turning the key. She had given him a good scare, one he didn't care to repeat. But looking at her now, she appeared much calmer and her face had some of its peachy color back. He glanced at her hands, which gripped her cane. The knuckles were white, the only indication that she wasn't as confident as she claimed. But he had to get her home somehow. And while he would have made good on his offer to carry her home, it would have been tough. Not because she was heavy; she wasn't. But because he didn't think he could be that near to her again. Just leaning over her to get the seat belt had set his pulse racing.

He gripped the steering wheel, forcing his gaze from her. He turned the key and the engine roared to life. A quick glance told him she was still okay. Slowly he backed his car down the long driveway, turning it around at the wider portion at the end. "Talk to me, Ellie."

"I'm *gut.*" Her voice sounded as if it were being pushed through wire mesh.

"Tell me about your jelly."

"What?"

"Sarah Lynne said something about her boss loving your jelly." He had to get her mind off the drive. Jelly was the only thing he could come up with.

"You heard that?"

"*Ya.* Do you make it yourself? Or is it just your recipe?"

"Both." She sounded a little more relaxed. "I've had my own business for the past year. Ellie's Jellies."

He smiled. "Perfect." He looked to his left, making sure no cars were coming. "I'm going on the street now."

"*Danki* for telling me."

"What kind of jelly do you sell, Ellie?" He meant to make the rhyme, and he was glad to hear her tiny chuckle.

"All kinds. Name a fruit, and I make jelly out of it."

He turned onto the road, driving well below the speed limit. "Gooseberry."

"When they're in season, *ya.*"

"Orange?"

"I make a great orange marmalade. Or so I've been told."

He smiled at her humility. "What about kumquat?"

"Kum-what?"

A horn blared behind him, making them both jump. Chris glared at the car as it whizzed by, the driver making a rude gesture. He looked at Ellie. She had the death grip on her cane again.

"What happened?" she asked, sounding nervous again.

"*Nix.* Just some bozo in a hurry. So you were telling me about kumquats."

"I don't even know what a kumquat is." She angled her head toward him. "Do you?"

"*Nee.* Just wanted to see if I could trip you up. Which one is your *haus*?"

"It's the one set back farthest from the road. There's an old swing set in the side yard. My *mamm* has been trying to get *Daed* to take it down, but he won't. Says the *grosskinner* still have fun with it."

Chris spotted the house several yards ahead. He glanced at the speedometer. Five miles per hour. A horse could go faster, but he didn't care. He'd never driven his car this slow in his life. "How many grandkids do they have?"

"Four. My sister has two and my brother has two with one on the way. Do you see *mei haus*?"

"Just about to turn in the driveway." He sneaked a look at Ellie. She appeared to be back to normal. He let out a breath as he maneuvered his car onto the drive. For the first time he noticed how low the sun was in the sky. It had almost dipped below the horizon. He had no idea so much time had passed.

He pulled his car to a stop near the house. It was a typical Amish home, painted white with no shutters or decoration of any kind. Two steps led up to the porch, which spanned the length of the front. Chris could see part of a white barn in the back.

"*Danki*, Chris." She opened the door and started to get out.

"Wait a sec." He jumped out of the car and met her on the other side. He put his hand under her elbow to help her up.

"I'm okay. It feels better actually."

But from the pained look on her face, he could tell it didn't. He looked down at her feet. "Your ankle is pretty swollen."

"I'll put some ice on it when I get inside." She had already opened up her cane and was leaning against it. For a second he wished she'd lean against him.

"Ellie?"

Chris looked up to see an older woman come out of the house. She had a white apron over her gray dress, and her graying hair peeked from beneath her white *kapp*. Her gaze narrowed as it landed on Chris. "Who are you?"

He didn't answer right away. He shouldn't be surprised that Ellie's mother didn't recognize him. He looked *Englisch*, drove a car, and had just brought her daughter home. He'd be suspicious too. It would be better for Ellie if he kept his identity hidden from her. But before he could come up with a fake name, Ellie spoke.

"It's Christopher Miller, *Mamm*." She hobbled around the car door, forcing him to take a few steps back. "I hurt my ankle and he brought me home."

"You did what?" Ellie's mother practically shoved Chris out of the way. She looked down at Ellie's ankle and scowled. "How did you do that?" She whirled around and glared at Chris. "Did you have something to do with this?"

Chris held his hands up. Since his *meiding* he was used to being ignored, not turned against.

"*Nee, Mamm*. He was only helping me home. I twisted my ankle all on my own."

Frau Chupp turned her back on him. Now that's what he'd expected.

"I thought Trish was bringing you home."

"She did, but I asked her to leave me at the cemetery."

Frau Chupp put her hands on her hips. "Why didn't she wait for you?"

Ellie's face was pinched. Chris could see she was in pain, and standing there leaning on a thin cane while her mother fired questions at her wasn't helping. "Ellie should *geh* inside. She needs to get her ankle up."

Frau Chupp didn't acknowledge Chris's statement. "Answer me, Ellie."

"I didn't want her to have to wait around. She has a family to take care of." Ellie gripped the cane and leaned against the car. "Besides, I've made that walk home several times."

"That was when you could see! What kind of person lets a blind *maedel* fend for herself?"

Ellie's bottom lip shook for a moment. Then she lifted her chin. "Can I *geh* inside now?"

"*Ya.*" Her mother took a step backward, giving her daughter room to walk. Ellie positioned her cane and started limping toward the house. She stopped in front of Chris and turned her face toward him. "*Danki,*" she said, her voice whisper-soft.

"Ellie Chupp! Inside, now." Her mother shot another glare at Chris.

Ellie's face contorted into a mix of pain and irritation. But she didn't say anything else. He watched as both women walked into the house, her mother finally lending a hand to Ellie when they reached the steps.

When the door closed behind them, Chris shut the passenger door, then got in on the other side. He started the car and reached for the gearshift on the steering column. He glanced at the empty seat next to him, remembering how tightly Ellie had held on to his hand when he offered it to her. He was glad he'd driven her home, despite her mother's treatment. Ellie was nothing like *Frau* Chupp. He was glad about that too.

He drove down the road toward the bed-and-breakfast, making sure he drove the speed limit this time. Only when he passed by the cemetery did he realize he hadn't visited Caroline's grave.

Chapter Eight

SARAH LYNNE PACED THE LENGTH OF HER FRONT PORCH, her fists opening and closing. Where was Isaiah? Since they had gotten officially engaged, he had stopped by after work every day except Sunday. Now it was nearly seven o'clock and almost dark.

She plopped down on the swing, letting the force of the movement push her back and forth. She wondered if Chris would keep his word about meeting with *Mamm* tomorrow. She was off work and would make sure her mother didn't go anywhere until Chris arrived. But what if he'd left Paradise already?

She couldn't believe her brother hadn't forgiven Isaiah after all this time. He could at least do it for *Mamm's* sake, if not his own. She had never thought Chris could be this selfish. He was clinging to his bitterness like it was his life raft.

At the sound of a horse's hooves, she looked out at the street and saw Isaiah's buggy coming down the driveway. She should have known he wouldn't let her down. She jumped out of the swing and rushed down the porch steps to meet him.

But when Isaiah got out of the vehicle, her relief disappeared. "Isaiah, what is it?"

He'd never looked so forlorn.

He stood next to the buggy, not moving toward her, his gaze fixed on the house behind her instead of her face. Finally he spoke. "I'm not sure we should do this."

"Do what?" She went to him and grabbed his hand, not caring if her parents saw. "Do what, Isaiah? Get married?"

His Adam's apple bobbed up and down as he looked at the

ground. Then he met her eyes, tears shining in his. "*Ya*. Maybe we shouldn't get married. Not after what happened last night."

She gripped his hand. "I will not let my brother's selfishness stand in the way of our happiness. I love you, Isaiah. And I'll love you no matter what Chris does."

Isaiah ran the back of his hand over her cheek. She closed her eyes against his touch.

"I love you, too, Sarah Lynne. More than I thought possible. The thought of living without you . . ." His voice cracked. "But I can't stand to see you so upset, and you've been that way since your *bruder* came back. He's angry because of me."

"*Nee*, not because of you. And Chris will come around." But she couldn't be completely sure.

Isaiah gazed down at her, doubt alive in his eyes. "I want to marry you more than anything. But is our marriage worth tearing your *familye* apart?"

"Chris is doing that, not you!" She wished she could take away the pain she saw in his eyes. "Don't let him break us apart, Isaiah. I love my family, but I love you more. And if I have to choose between them . . . I will always choose you."

Without warning Isaiah pulled Sarah Lynne into his embrace. She leaned her cheek against his chest, her arms going around his waist. His heart thrummed against her temple, and she felt his hand splay across her back.

"You can't get rid of me, Isaiah Stolzfus," she said, her voice muffled against his chest. "So you might as well stop trying."

He held her from him, his blue eyes still filled with sorrow. "That's the last thing I want to do, Sarah Lynne. But—"

She reached up and touched the cleft in his chin, stopping his words. "Then don't."

"But what about Chris? Maybe if I talked to him about how much I love you and about how sorry I am about the accident, he could forgive me."

She considered his words, then shook her head. She doubted Chris would listen to him. Instead he'd probably be even more resentful. She didn't want Isaiah to deal with that. "I love you for offering, but we have to give this to God, Isaiah. There's nothing we can do to make him change his mind. Only the Lord can do that."

"I know. And I've tried to let this *geh.*" He took a step back and rubbed the back of his neck, staring at the ground. "But I can't. I don't want to cause any more problems for you or your *familye.*"

Sarah Lynne pressed her palm against his cheek, causing him to look at her. "What about me, Isaiah?" Her voice trembled. "You're breaking my heart."

He closed his eyes and pulled her against him. "I'm sorry," he said, his arms tightening around her. "I just thought—"

"You thought wrong." She looked up at him, willing him to understand that they couldn't sacrifice their happiness for Christopher. "I want my brother to find peace too. But only God knows if it's possible."

"Ellie Chupp, I can't believe you would disobey the church and allow that *mann* to drive you home." Ellie's mother balanced a kitchen towel filled with ice cubes on Ellie's ankle. "I don't know what's gotten into you."

Ellie winced as her mother adjusted the ice. She was sitting on the couch near the fireplace with her leg propped up on a pillow.

"I hurt my ankle, *Mamm.* He was nice enough to help me." She didn't mention that he had first carried her across the field.

"You shouldn't have been alone." Ellie heard her mother step back from the couch. "How many times have I told you that?"

More than I can count.

She understood her mother's worry. At first she had even appreciated it. But over the past year her *mamm's* admonishments had grated on Ellie's nerves, undermining her confidence. She didn't want to go back to the days when her mother hovered over her every move. "I can't have someone watching me every minute of the day," she blurted.

"You're blind. You need—"

"I know I'm blind!" She turned her head in the direction of her mother's voice. "I don't need you to tell me that. I live with it every day."

"There's no need to be snippy, *dochder*."

"I'm sorry." Ellie leaned back against the armrest of the couch and gave up. To argue with her mother further would be disrespectful, and it would earn not only her ire but Ellie's father's reprimand. Besides, her mother would never understand how much Ellie craved her independence.

Despair filled her at the thought of always living with her parents, of spending the rest of her life under her mother's thumb. But what other choice did she have?

"Christopher Miller has become *Englisch*," her mother said. "I see that he's fully embraced their ways now. He's turned his back on his family and on God. You are not to have any dealings with him, not until he has reconciled himself with God and the church. If he ever does."

Ellie clamped down on her lip to keep from arguing. She couldn't keep that promise. Chris deserved more than a whispered thank-you for what he'd done. She had no idea how to thank him, but she would figure out a way, hopefully before he left Paradise.

"I wonder if his *mutter* knows he's here. I can only imagine her heartbreak if she sees him, his hair cut off and driving a car. Clearly he's not here to ask forgiveness."

As her mother continued to speculate about Chris, Ellie tuned her out. She didn't want to hear any more negative comments about him. She tried to ignore the pain in her ankle, too, but it throbbed. Her skin had felt tight and warm before she applied the ice.

"Is the ice helping?"

Her mother's sudden question intruded on Ellie's thoughts. "What?"

"The ice? Does your ankle feel any better?"

"It's fine. I'm sure I'll be able to walk on it soon."

"*Gut.* But I don't want you working in the kitchen or going anywhere for a couple of days." When Ellie started to protest, she cut her off. "I'm serious, *dochder.* You must let the ankle heal."

With a sigh Ellie nodded. She couldn't be independent, but at least she was needed. And since she had delivered a large supply of jellies and jams to Yoder's Pantry today, she wouldn't have to make any more for a few days. That would give her time to rest her ankle and catch up on her reading. She still had plenty of the audio book left to listen to.

"Will you be all right for a few minutes? I need to make supper."

"*Ya.*" Ellie paused. "I'm sorry about this, *Mamm.* I just wanted to spend some time alone with Caroline. I still miss her."

"I know you do." Her mother's voice softened. "I only ask that you use common sense next time."

"I will."

Her mother left the room, and Ellie exhaled. Suddenly weary, she closed her eyes and tried to rest, but images crowded her mind. The panic she'd felt in Chris's car sent quick warmth to her face. She recalled the way Chris's hand felt on hers. The way his low, mellow voice soothed her overwrought fears. John would never have acted that way. He would have grown angry, told her to snap out of it. But Chris seemed to have infinite patience, enough to drive slower than a buggy to keep her panic at bay. Ellie's mouth formed a half smile. Caroline had been a lucky woman to love and be loved by a man like Christopher Miller.

Sarah Lynne lifted up the curtain in the living room and peeked out the window. It was past noon and Chris still hadn't shown up. She shouldn't be surprised. All these years she'd tried to understand why he had turned against the church and left the community and his family behind. Especially since falling in love with Isaiah, she could empathize with how Caroline's death had devastated him so deeply. She didn't know what she'd do if she lost Isaiah. But she had never thought Chris a coward. Until now.

"Are you expecting someone?"

Sarah Lynne turned at the sound of her mother's voice and joined her on the opposite end of the cushioned couch. She picked up the scarf she had been knitting and started working the needles again, avoiding the curious lift of her mother's graying eyebrow. "*Nee*. Just thinking about taking a walk outside. It's a nice afternoon."

"Oh. I thought . . ." Her mother's gaze dropped to her husband's torn work shirt perched on her lap. She twisted the silver thimble protecting the tip of her middle finger. "You haven't heard from Christopher, have you?"

Sarah Lynne paused. She didn't want to lie to her mother, but getting her hopes up about Chris coming over wouldn't be fair to her either. She saw the sorrow in her mother's eyes, sorrow that had never completely disappeared since Chris's *meiding*.

Sarah Lynne shook her head. "*Nee*," she said, silently asking for forgiveness.

"Then I guess he went back to Apple Creek." Her mother's lower lip trembled, but her eyes remained dry. She picked up the shirt again and drew the white thread through one of the ripped buttonholes. She cleared her throat but didn't look up. "I'm going out myself, after I finish your *daed's* shirt."

Sarah Lynne hid her surprise, which was quickly turning to

panic. Until her father came home in a couple of hours there was still a chance Chris might show up. She didn't want her mother to be gone if he did. "Where are you going?"

"Bertha Chupp's. She's been a great help to me with the wedding plans. Ellie too. I hear she's making some of her famous brownies." Her mother shook her head, revealing a slight smile. "The things Ellie can do amazes me. She's a marvel, *ya?*"

"That she is."

"I just hope she can find happiness in her circumstances."

Sarah Lynne set down her knitting. "What do you mean?"

Her mother put the shirt down in her lap. "I always thought Ellie would marry John, you know? And then the accident happened and everything changed. So much loss." Her mother looked away again. "At least Ellie's mother still has her daughter."

"What time are you planning to leave?"

"Probably in an hour. I shouldn't be gone too long."

She nodded, giving up on Chris. She wouldn't try to stop her mother from leaving. "Don't worry about supper," Sarah Lynne said, fighting to keep an even tone. "I'll take care of it. Stay at *Frau* Chupp's as long as you like."

"*Danki.*" Her mother smiled, but as always since Chris left, her expression held a tinge of sadness.

A knock sounded at the door, and Sarah Lynn jumped up from the couch and ran to answer it. But when she opened it, Chris wasn't standing on the front porch.

"Ellie."

"I hope it is all right that I stopped by," Ellie said. "I won't stay too long." She frowned a little. "I can come back if this is a bad time."

Sarah Lynne tamped down her disappointment and smiled. Even though Ellie couldn't see the expression, Sarah Lynne knew her friend would hear it in her voice. "*Nee,* this is a great time. Come on in."

Ellie stepped inside, holding her cane. In her other hand she held a small basket. As she took a step forward, Sarah Lynne saw she was limping. She offered Ellie the back of her arm, as she usually did to help guide her. "Did something happen to your foot?"

Ellie gripped Sarah Lynne's arm right above the elbow and followed her lead. "I twisted it yesterday. I thought I might have sprained it, but it's better today."

"I'm glad to hear that."

As they walked into the living room, Sarah's mother looked up from her sewing. "Hello, Ellie. What brings you by today?"

"I came to talk to Sarah Lynne for a few minutes."

"*Gut*. I think she was getting restless this afternoon." Her mother tied off the thread and snipped it with a tiny pair of sewing scissors, then started folding the shirt. "I was just telling her I'm paying your *mutter* a visit in a short while."

Ellie turned her face toward *Frau* Miller. "She mentioned that to me. I wondered if I could catch a ride home with you when you leave? My *daed* just dropped me off. He's on his way to Paradise to run an errand for work."

"Of course." She lifted the folded shirt and stood. "I have a couple more things to do upstairs, then I'll be ready."

"All right. I'm not in a hurry."

When her mother left, Sarah Lynne led Ellie to the chair across from the couch, putting Chris out of her mind. "What did you want to talk about, Ellie?"

Ellie sat, setting her cane on the floor beside her. She touched the sides of the small basket in her lap. It was Amish made, with tightly woven straw-colored thin strips of wood, while the handle was one solid, curved piece. "Have you seen Chris today?"

"*Nee.*" She sat down, unable to keep from frowning. Then she glanced toward the staircase near the living room, making sure her mother wasn't close by. Still, she lowered her voice. "He was supposed to come by today to see *Mamm* before he went back to Apple Creek, but he hasn't shown up. I doubt he's coming."

Ellie's expression turned troubled. "So he's definitely not coming back to the community?"

"That's what it looks like." Sarah Lynne's heart ached. "I'm trying not to be angry with him, but I can't help it. I don't understand why he can't let this go."

Ellie sighed. "I'm not sure either. I saw him yesterday—"

"You did? Where?"

"At the cemetery. He came to see Caroline, and I was there visiting her." Ellie touched the handle of her basket. "That's why I stopped by here. He helped me with something yesterday, and I wanted to thank him. I didn't know where he was staying, so I thought you could give him this, if you see him again." She picked up the basket. "It's just a couple jars of jelly and some homemade bread. I don't have much else to offer him."

Sarah Lynne took the basket from her. "I'm sure he'll appreciate it. What did he help you with?"

Ellie's fair cheeks turned red. "He gave me a ride home when I twisted my ankle, that's all."

Sarah Lynne didn't know why Ellie was blushing. Maybe she was embarrassed about twisting her ankle. She knew how important it was to her that she be independent and capable.

"Well, it's *gut* to know that deep down he's got some redeeming value. Lately he hasn't shown it to us." She set the basket on the floor. "I'll keep this, but honestly, I don't know if I'll be able to give it to him. I'd go into town and look for him, but *Mamm*'s taking the buggy over to your *haus*." She sighed. "Maybe I should just forget about him. He's forgotten about us."

"I'm sure that's not true."

"Did he say anything about coming by here?"

Ellie shook her head. "I'm sorry, he didn't. But he's still struggling with what happened to Caroline, and finding out about you and Isaiah. Learning that you two are marrying shocked him."

"Well, if he'd been here all along, he wouldn't be shocked."

Sarah Lynne grimaced at the look on Ellie's face. "Sorry. I'm frustrated. Chris isn't the only one upset about this. Can you believe Isaiah tried to call off the wedding last night?"

Ellie's brows went up. "Oh *nee!*"

"*Ya.* I think I convinced him not to, though."

"You think?"

"I don't know." Sarah Lynne curled her bottom lip. "I told him he's stuck with me, no matter what."

"And he's lucky he is."

Sarah Lynne tried to smile but couldn't. This was supposed to be an exciting, happy time for her and Isaiah. Instead they were both miserable. "He's not feeling lucky, and neither am I. He's filled with guilt." Sarah Lynne rubbed one of the ribbons of her prayer *kapp* between her thumb and forefinger. "I'm sorry to say this, but I wish Chris hadn't come back. He's upsetting everyone. *Mamm*'s sadder than usual. She just asked me about him, and I had to lie." She rubbed the ribbon harder. "I didn't want to get her hopes up that she would see him again."

Ellie nodded but didn't say anything.

"And *Daed* has been so quiet lately. It was hard on him to turn his back on Chris." She released the ribbon, her shoulders drooping. "I'm supposed to be focusing on my wedding. Instead I'm worried there might not be one."

Ellie reached in the air for Sarah Lynne's hand. Sarah Lynne grabbed it, comforted by her friend's touch. "I'm sorry. I'm so sorry about this."

Sarah Lynne squeezed Ellie's hand. "It's not your fault. Christopher's to blame for all of this."

Ellie suddenly released her hand. "*Nee*, he's not, not completely—"

At the knock on the door, she and Ellie looked up. Sarah Lynne walked to the door and opened it, her breath catching in her throat.

Chapter Nine

CHRIS SHOVED HIS HANDS INTO THE POCKETS OF HIS JEANS and looked down at his little sister as she stood in the doorway, her mouth agape. He shouldn't blame her for being surprised; he had almost decided not to come. He still wasn't sure why he was here, other than he had to see his mother one last time before he went back to Apple Creek. He wished he could see his father, too, but judging from the way his *daed* had reacted the last time they were together, he knew that was impossible.

Sarah Lynne finally spoke. "You came."

He nodded, glancing away for a moment. He'd spent the first twenty years of his life here, playing on this front porch, learning how to break and ride a horse, helping his father and mother raise a garden and take care of the house and land. Yet never had he felt more like an outsider than he did at this moment.

He looked back at Sarah Lynne. "Can I come inside?"

She nodded and stepped away so he could walk in. As he strode into the living room, a mix of bittersweet memories flooded him. Everything was the same, including the way the old, plain furniture was arranged.

Then he saw Ellie Chupp sitting on the couch, reaching for her cane as she moved to stand. He started toward her. "How's that ankle?"

"Better, *danki*. I only twisted it." She lifted her face in his direction.

He stood there for a moment, an unfamiliar warm sensation

spreading through his stomach as he looked at her. She was the last person he'd expected to see here, but for some reason her presence comforted him. "I didn't see another buggy outside. I hope you didn't walk here."

She shook her head. "My *daed* dropped me off."

At the sound of his sister clearing her throat, he turned around. She had an odd look on her face, a blend of surprise and bewilderment.

"What?"

"Ellie brought something for you." Sarah Lynne went to the easy chair near the couch and picked up a small basket. But instead of handing it to him, she put it in Ellie's hand. "I'll *geh get Mamm*," she said, hurrying out of the room.

Chris scratched his head. "What's wrong with her?"

Ellie shrugged, but the way she tilted her head away from him he knew something was up. "Ellie, what happened? Why is my sister acting strangely?"

Ellie hesitated. "She's upset, Chris. I probably shouldn't tell you this, but yesterday Isaiah tried to call off the wedding."

Chris's brows lifted. "He did? Why would he do that?"

"I don't know. Maybe because he doesn't want Sarah Lynne to be unhappy?"

"That's a weird way to show it. Anyone can see she's crazy about him. Unless he's just stringing her along. I wouldn't put it past him."

"Stop."

He snapped his mouth shut at Ellie's exclamation. Her light blonde brows pinched together, strain showing around her mouth. Even the color of her eyes had darkened with anger.

"Isaiah would never ruin Sarah Lynne's life. He loves her so much he was willing to give up his own happiness because he thought it might bring you back into the family." She moved toward him, stopping just short of stepping on his toes. "You don't know *mei* cousin. What he's sacrificed over the years. How he's had to live with . . . how the accident changed him."

"He doesn't seem to have suffered too much." Chris couldn't stop the bitter words from escaping.

"You have no idea."

Her voice trembled, touching Chris deep inside. She wobbled for a moment, and he remembered her ankle. "You should sit down." He put his arm around her shoulder, but she shrugged him off and walked past him.

"Your *schwester* is right. You are selfish. You would rather blame Isaiah for your bitterness than face the real reason for it." The tone of her voice suddenly grew thick, as if something clogged her throat. "It's not my cousin's fault you're unhappy. You've managed that all on your own." She turned and walked out the door.

Chris stood frozen, her words stinging him. What did she know about his unhappiness? If it hadn't been for Isaiah, he would be married right now, and probably a *vatter* too. He'd have his own house and wouldn't be at odds with the community. Isaiah had stripped him of all that and more. Most of all, he'd robbed him of his peace.

"Christopher."

He turned to see his mother standing in the living room, her lips pale. Had she heard what Ellie said?

Sarah Lynne appeared, standing behind their mother. The same deep green eyes and dark eyebrows. So alike, and yet his mother had aged over the years, more than he had expected her to. Frown lines rimmed her mouth, and her gaze didn't hold the same spark as Sarah Lynne's. Guilt dug at him, accusing him.

"Where's Ellie?" Sarah Lynne stepped around their mother.

"She left." He caught his mother's gaze, and he knew she had heard their conversation.

"And you let her *geh?*" Sarah Lynne exclaimed. "She's hurt and doesn't have a ride."

He'd been so distracted he hadn't thought about that. "I didn't have a choice. She walked out the door."

Sarah Lynne stormed over to him, her bare feet pounding on the wood floor. "There's always a choice, Christopher. Someday you'll learn to make the right one." She rushed outside, the screen door slamming behind her.

Without a word Chris's mother went and shut the inner door. Then she turned around and faced him. "Why are you here?"

Chris turned around, trying to get control of his emotions. He couldn't even answer her simple question. Everything had been so clear a few days ago, and he thought he was following God's lead to return to Paradise. Now he didn't know what to do.

He felt his mother's hand on his arm. He turned and faced her, swallowing the lump that had appeared in his throat.

"It's all right, *sohn*." Tears welled in her eyes. "It's all right." She lifted her arms to him.

Overwhelmed with emotions he couldn't understand or define, he embraced his mother, holding her close for the first time in five long years.

⌒⌒⌒

"Ellie! Ellie!"

Ellie heard Sarah Lynne's footsteps hurrying down the few steps leading from the front porch to the yard. When her friend called her name again, she sounded farther away, as if she had headed toward the street.

"Over here." Ellie lifted her hand from where she sat. After leaving Chris, she had made her way to the end of the porch and sat down on one of the Millers' wicker chairs. Her ankle had started to throb shortly after she arrived at their home. Knowing she had no choice but to wait on *Frau* Miller to give her a ride home, she waited on their porch. For the first time in years her blindness angered her. If she had her sight, she would have driven a buggy over here. She wouldn't be stuck waiting for someone to give her a ride.

"Thank goodness." Sarah Lynne stood in front of her, sounding breathless. "I thought you were trying to walk home."

Ellie shook her head. "Too far." She heard the edge in her own voice, but she couldn't help it. Chris had infuriated her with his stubbornness. She didn't blame Sarah Lynne for being upset with him. He didn't deserve her understanding.

Ellie heard Sarah Lynne plop into the other wicker chair next to her. "You didn't have to leave, you know. We're almost *familye*, and besides, you know everything about the situation with Chris."

"They needed their privacy." Which was true, even though it wasn't the reason she'd left. She couldn't bear to listen to him complain about Isaiah any longer.

"They have it now." Sarah Lynne sighed. "I hope *Mamm* can talk sense into him."

Ellie doubted it, but she remained quiet. Ellie didn't know what it would take for Chris to let go of the grudge he held against Isaiah. "Caroline wouldn't want him to do this," she said, thinking aloud.

"What?"

She turned to Sarah Lynne. "If Caroline were here right now, she'd be able to convince him to let *geh*. The last thing she'd want would be for him to live like this, separated from everyone, unable to move on with his life."

"Then maybe you should tell him that." Sarah Lynne's voice rose as she spoke.

"Me?" Ellie shook her head. "He's not going to listen to me."

"I think he will. Ellie, I hope this doesn't offend you, but you didn't see the way my brother looked at you a few minutes ago."

"*Nee*, I'm not offended. But I am confused."

"Me, too, but I know what I saw. When he was talking to you

about your ankle, it was like I wasn't even in the room. And when he offered you a ride and you refused, he got this hangdog look on his face that I haven't seen since . . ."

"Since when?"

"Since Caroline." Sarah Lynne's voice softened. "*Mei bruder* looks at you like he used to look at Caroline."

Chris downed the iced tea his mother gave him, then set the glass on the kitchen table. He looked at her sitting directly across from him, her hands tightly clasped in front of her. The hug they exchanged gave him relief, as if she had somehow taken part of his burden as her own. Then again, she probably had carried his pain with her for the past five years. Once more he was reminded of what his choices had cost everyone else.

"I'm glad you came by," she said in her usual soft voice. "I prayed you would."

"I couldn't leave without seeing you."

Her eyes filled with sadness. "Then you're going back to Apple Creek for certain?"

He started to nod but stopped. Since he arrived in Paradise and learned about the wedding, all he could think about was going back to Ohio. But now he wasn't so sure. "I don't know."

"What is your life like there?" She leaned forward, her gaze seeking his.

"It's . . . all right. Fine, actually. I have a *gut* job, a nice apartment." He'd had those things but had given them up to come here. Still, he didn't think it would be too hard to get either back . . . if he needed to. Right now he didn't know what he needed.

"*Freinds?*" Worry creased her brow.

"*Ya.* I have *freinds.*" They were more like acquaintances, but he wouldn't admit that.

"What about an *aldi*?"

He shook his head, frowning. Her questions were starting to irritate, but he couldn't blame her for wanting to know about his life. "*Nee*. I don't have a girlfriend."

She unclasped her hands and reached for his. "Are you happy, Christopher? Because if you're happy, then I can be happy for you too. It would set my mind at ease knowing you have made a new life for yourself, one that is pleasing and satisfying."

He gave her fingers a light squeeze and released her hand. Was his life in Apple Creek pleasing and satisfying? Far from it. "*Nee, Mamm*. I'm not happy."

She nodded. "I didn't think so."

"Am I that easy to read?"

She smiled, though it didn't reach her eyes. "You are my *sohn*, Christopher. How could I not know these things? But I thought . . . I hoped . . . when you came back it was because you had finally made peace with the past." She looked beyond him, her gaze unutterably sad, making Chris's gut clench. "I see now that's not true."

He didn't answer right away, embarrassed to admit the truth. "If Sarah Lynne was marrying anyone else . . . Why does it have to be Isaiah?" He gripped the empty tea glass. "How can I find peace in that?"

She took his other hand. "By forgiving, Christopher." She squeezed his fingers. "By following the Lord's example. He sent His Son to forgive our sins. What makes us better than God?"

"I don't think I'm better than God. I don't think I'm even worth His mercy."

Her thin lips smiled. "None of us is. Yet He gives it to us freely if we but ask. Forgiveness leads to peace in our hearts. But peace and strife can't live together. That's the battle you're waging, and it's one you can't win, not unless you let your bitterness *geh*."

Chris shoved his hands through his hair. He looked around

the kitchen. Like the living room, it hadn't changed since his childhood. The table and chairs were the same, the walls painted the same white color he remembered. And just as the house had remained the same, his mother was as wise as ever. He was pulled in different directions, his head pounding with indecision.

"When are you heading back?"

He looked at her. "Tonight. I was going to head out after I said good-bye to you and Sarah Lynne."

"Please. Stay one more *daag*." She took his hand again, this time holding it tightly in both of hers.

"What difference will a *daag* make?"

For the first time since she sat down, his mother looked unsure. "I don't know. I just know God wants me to say this to you. Don't leave until tomorrow night."

He took a deep breath, then blew it out. "All right. I'll stay." He squeezed her hand again. "For you."

Chapter Ten

ELLIE GRIPPED HER CANE, STILL UNABLE TO BELIEVE SARAH Lynne's words. "You're seeing things that aren't there."

"*Nee*, I'm seeing what is there. At first I couldn't believe it—"

"Then don't. Because it's not true."

Christopher Miller couldn't possibly have feelings for her. And not just because they'd only been around each other a short while. No, the reason Chris couldn't feel anything for her was the same reason John had left her, and why no other man had shown any interest in her. Her blindness robbed her of her independence, made her helpless. He had witnessed that firsthand.

"I'm sure he just feels sorry for me."

"*Nee. Nee!*" Sarah Lynne touched her shoulder, the pressure of her hand firm. "That's not what I meant at all. The only person my brother feels sorry for is himself. The reason I'm surprised is because he's been so wrapped up in his own issues he can't look beyond them. But leave it to you to reach through all that."

Ellie shook her head, even as the thought of Chris showing interest in her sent a tiny thrill through her. She had spent most of a sleepless night trying to erase the sound of his rich voice, his woodsy scent, the way he touched her. He didn't make her feel foolish or weak for having a panic attack. If she hadn't twisted her ankle, she knew he would have let her walk home alone from the cemetery. He was one of the few people who seemed to understand how she wanted to be treated. Warmth and an attraction she could not deny tugged at her, but she tried to ignore it. Was she so starved for male attention? How pitiful she must seem.

"You have to talk to him, Ellie. You're right about Caroline, and as her best friend you're the only who can remind him that Caroline wouldn't want him to wallow in self-pity and give up his family."

"You can say the same thing." She didn't want to get involved with this. But even as the thought popped into her mind, she knew she was already involved.

"It's not the same. He's angry with me for marrying Isaiah. You're the only one who can reach him. Please, Ellie. Just talk to him. It could be his last chance."

She sighed. How could she stay mad at Chris, knowing his deep pain fed his stubbornness? Still, she didn't know how she could convince him of anything.

She heard the rusty squeak of the door hinge. Chris's heavy footsteps sounded on the porch floor, followed by the softer steps of his mother. Ellie stood and gripped her cane, conscious not to put too much weight on her sore ankle.

Sarah Lynne walked over to her mother and brother, and Ellie tried not to listen to what they were saying. Even though she turned away and they lowered their voices, she could hear parts of their conversation.

"I'm glad you decided to stay a little longer," Sarah Lynne said, sounding relieved.

"*Ya.* I better get going."

He sounded agitated, and Ellie surmised his discussion with his mother hadn't gone well.

"It's too late for me to *geh* to the Chupps'," *Frau* Miller said. "Sarah Lynne, could you take Ellie home?"

"I can take her."

Ellie's brows lifted at the swiftness of Chris's offer—and that he'd offered at all.

"I think that's a great idea." Sarah Lynne's enthusiasm sounded a little too obvious. "Don't you, Ellie?"

And though she knew her friend had Chris's best interests in mind, she couldn't help but feel manipulated.

"Nee," *Frau* Miller said. "You should be the one to take her, Sarah Lynne."

Frau Miller didn't have to explain any further. Ellie knew she was thinking of how her mother would react if Chris dropped her off.

"But by the time I get the buggy hitched up, Chris could have her home."

Sarah Lynne was starting to sound desperate, and Ellie second-guessed her resolve to stay neutral. She needed to try to reach Chris one more time for Sarah Lynne's sake, and riding in the car with him would be the perfect opportunity. She'd explain it to her mother later.

"Sarah Lynne's right. If Chris doesn't mind, I'll *geh* with him."

"I don't mind at all."

The emotion in his tone sent a shiver through her. Could Sarah Lynne be right? Was Chris feeling more for her than friendship? Was that even possible?

Frau Miller didn't respond for a long moment. Then she sighed. "I can't stop you."

Ellie moved to the porch steps, trying not to limp too much on her sore ankle. The last thing she needed was for Chris to carry her to the car in front of his mother and sister. That would send Sarah Lynne's imagination running rampant.

Chris said his good-byes to them. She heard his heavy foot-steps as he descended the stairs, and she was surprised he didn't offer to help her down them, as so many other people would have.

"The car's to your right," he said.

She lifted a brow, turning her head toward his voice. He'd

known she'd need a verbal cue without her saying anything. She walked toward the direction of his voice. *"Danki."*

"You can sit in the back if you want. I'll still *geh* slow."

"Nee, I need to sit up front. I can't let fear rule my life."

He didn't say anything to that, but she heard the car door open. Using her cane to find the passenger side door, she got inside and sat down, this time doing the seat belt herself.

"Wait!" Sarah Lynne came rushing toward them. "Ellie, you forgot this." She put the basket in Ellie's grasp then leaned forward. "Don't forget what we talked about. I will owe you forever if you persuade him to forgive Isaiah."

She might as well have asked Ellie to pluck the moon out of the sky and hand it over on a silver platter. But Ellie nodded anyway. "I'll see what I can do," she said, lowering her voice to match Sarah Lynne's.

Chris got into the car, and from the scent filling the interior, she realized he had his leather jacket on. She heard the vehicle roar to life.

"I'm surprised you agreed to this."

"Sarah Lynne was right. It's easier if you take me home."

The car jerked into reverse.

"Ready, Ellie?"

She gripped the basket, but her nerves were steady. "Ready."

"Like I said, I'll drive slow. I'm not in any hurry."

"You can drive normally." She didn't want him to be overly cautious on her account. "I think I'm over my anxiety."

"I think you are too. You haven't lost the color in your cheeks yet, and we're already on the road."

Ellie let her grip on the basket relax. Then, remembering why she had it in the first place, she said, "Oh. This is for you."

"What? The basket?"

"Ya. It's not much, but I wanted to thank you for taking me home the other day."

"You don't have to thank me," Chris said. "I'm glad I could be there. What's in it?"

"A loaf of homemade bread and some jelly."

"Ellie's jelly?"

His tone held a touch of humor, which put her at ease a bit. "*Ya*. My very own jelly. I'm afraid it's not kumquat, though."

"Well, that's disappointing. What's a *mann* got to do to get some kumquat jelly around here?"

"I don't know, but I hope you like strawberry."

"I do." His voice lowered. "It's my favorite. *Danki*, Ellie. That's the first gift I've gotten in a long time."

She felt sad for him. She didn't know what his life was like in Apple Creek, but she suspected he wasn't happy there. "Why are you leaving?"

"What?"

"Why are you leaving Paradise? Is there something, or someone, waiting for you there?"

He hesitated a long moment before replying. "*Nee*. There's not much for me back there."

"Then you should stay here."

The heaviness of his sigh filled the car. "You know it's not that simple, Ellie."

She heard the sound of him flipping on the turn signal and sensed the car moving to the right. "I never said it was simple. Often the most worthwhile things are hard." She curved her hand around the base of the basket. "Caroline wouldn't want this for you, Chris. You know that."

A low squeak sounded, like he was rubbing his palm back and forth on the steering wheel. "If she were here, I wouldn't be going through this."

"But she's not here. That's a fact, just like I'm never going to see again and your sister is going to marry Isaiah."

"Ellie, I don't want to talk about this anymore." His

good-humored tone turned curt. "I know how you and my mom and Sarah Lynne feel. And I'm sorry I'm hurting my *familye*. But why does everyone expect me to forgive Isaiah just like that?"

"It's not 'just like that.'" She couldn't keep the frustration out of her tone. "It's been five years. You've spent five years of your life hanging on to Caroline." She leaned back in her seat, her eyes growing wide. "That's it."

"What?"

She angled her face toward him, wishing she could see his expression. She was missing so much by only hearing his voice. "This isn't about Isaiah at all."

"*Ya*, it is. It's all about Isaiah."

She shook her head. "It's not, Christopher. You can't forgive Isaiah because you can't let *geh* of Caroline. And until you do . . . you'll never move on."

Chris gripped the steering wheel so hard his knuckles started to ache. Was Ellie right? Did his refusal to forgive Isaiah stem from his not wanting to let Caroline go? Maybe it was part of it. "But not all," he whispered.

"Not all what?"

He glanced at Ellie, not realizing he'd even spoken aloud. He pulled his gaze away, something he found difficult to do. She looked so pretty today. She was dressed the same as yesterday, except her dress was dark purple instead of blue and her blonde hair was pulled tightly from her face. He liked that nothing obscured the view of her amazing eyes that were so beautiful, yet unseeing. But he was learning fast that Ellie saw much more of him than anyone else. She saw his heart.

"Chris?"

Turning his gaze back to the road, he spoke. "I can't remember what she looked like. At least not completely. I can still see her smile sometimes, and every once in a while I hear her laugh." His jaw jerked. "At one time I thought I'd never forget her."

"And you haven't. Just because the physical memory has faded doesn't mean you don't carry her in your heart. A part of you always will."

"Like you with John?"

Her head dipped. "That's different. John is still here. He's married and has a family." Then she lifted her chin. "Which was for the best. His wife is a very nice *frau*. From all accounts he's happy."

Chris wished he hadn't brought John up. He could tell she was trying to put his marriage in a positive light, but there was a tinge of sadness to her voice. "I'm sorry. I shouldn't have mentioned him."

"*Nee*, it's fine. God has a way of working things out for the best."

"I'm not so sure about that. I can't see how Caroline's death was *gut* for anything."

"Sometimes we can't see God's plan while we're in the midst of it."

He looked at her again. "You really believe that, don't you?"

She turned to him again, a smile forming on her lips. "*Ya*. I really do. I pray that someday you will too."

They neared Ellie's house. He slowed down the car, not wanting his conversation with Ellie to end. He continued to be amazed by her capacity to forgive, to completely trust God and accept what happened to her.

"Are we at my *haus*?" she asked.

"*Ya*. We're nearly there."

"Could you do me one last favor? You know how *Mamm* is. I don't want her to see you dropping me off."

He nodded. He didn't want her getting into trouble with her mother on his account. "Where do you want me to drop you off?"

"Near the end of the drive will be fine. I can make my way to the *haus* from there."

He didn't like the idea of her walking the long length of the driveway on her sore ankle, but he didn't have a choice. He also didn't like the idea of parting company with her so soon. He pulled his car to the side of the road, then brought it to a stop. But before she could open the door, he blurted, "Can I see you again?"

She froze, and he wished he could take back the words, or at least say them in a less abrupt manner.

"I . . . don't know." Ellie turned to him, her delicate brows forming a V shape above her jewel-like eyes.

"Please?" He was practically begging her, but he couldn't help it. He had to see her once more before he left Paradise. She was the only one who came close to understanding him. He needed her to listen, needed the advice and wisdom she so easily offered. When she didn't reply, he couldn't help himself from reaching out and taking her hand. It was so soft, warm, and small in his palm. He clung to it like a lifeline. "I need to talk to you again."

"Chris, I . . ." Her head bent down as if she were looking at their hands clasped together. Then she pulled hers out of his grasp. She opened the door, and he sat back in the seat.

He should have known he was pushing it. Besides, she didn't owe him anything. Certainly not her time, especially at the risk of her mother's anger. That didn't stop the rush of regret flooding him as she left.

Her foot landed on the gravel, crunching beneath her black lace-up shoes. "Meet me at the cemetery tomorrow morning. Before eight." Then she handed him the basket, took her cane, and quickly exited the car.

His regret turned to surprise as he watched her unfold her cane and limp toward her *haus*. He stayed there until she walked inside. As he drove away, he glanced at the basket in the passenger seat before easing his car onto the road. He smiled. Eight o'clock couldn't come quickly enough.

⟋⟍⟍

"Something on your mind, Ellie?"

Ellie turned her head toward her father's voice. They were sitting in the living room again, the crackling fire warming the room. Her mother was in the kitchen cleaning up the supper dishes. On the surface, tonight seemed to be like every other night. But not for Ellie. She couldn't stop thinking about Chris and wondering if she'd made a mistake in agreeing to meet him. Yet she thought she had kept her inner strife to herself.

"How did you know?"

"I think I know you pretty well. Plus that player has been lying in your lap for the last half hour. Usually you're eager to listen to your book."

Ellie set the player to the side on the couch. She couldn't focus on her reading, especially a romance. Not when her thoughts were consumed with Chris. She let out a sigh, then heard the soft flutter of a newspaper page being turned.

"Anything you want to talk about?"

She started to shake her head but stopped. Maybe her father would have some insight into Chris. She certainly couldn't talk to her mother about him. Her *daed* was less stringent about the rules of *meiding* and might be more sympathetic to Chris and his plight. Then again—

"It's all right if you don't," her father said. "Never been too *gut* understanding women stuff anyway. Ask your mother."

Ellie chuckled. "You're not that bad, *Daed*. Besides, I think I need a *mann's* opinion about this anyway."

Her father shifted in his chair. "What about?"

She told him about her decision to meet Chris in the cemetery, explaining everything that had happened since Chris's return. When she finished, her father didn't say anything, and she wondered if she had made a mistake confiding in him.

"I see why you didn't want to talk to your *mamm* about this," he finally said. "She would be very upset if she found out you were meeting with him."

"Are you saying I shouldn't?"

"*Nee*, Ellie." He lowered his voice. "I think you should. Just be careful about it, that's all."

"I will." She appreciated her father's support. "But I don't know what else I can say to him. If his *mutter* and Sarah Lynne can't convince him to forgive Isaiah, how can I be expected to?"

He paused again, and she imagined him tugging on his beard, something he always did when he was deep in thought. "Maybe he doesn't need any more convincing. He might just need a *freind*."

Ellie nodded. Her father's words put things into perspective. Chris did need a friend. That had to be what Sarah Lynne was interpreting as romantic interest on his part. And she would be that friend to him when they talked tomorrow.

But she couldn't help but feel disappointed that there wasn't something more between them.

Chapter Eleven

THE NEXT MORNING DAWNED COOL AND CRISP. AN ABUN-
dant array of leaves fluttered across the grassy field surrounding
the cemetery. Chris got out of his car and shut the door, then he
shoved his hands into his pockets and walked over to the small
burial ground. The gate squeaked open as he stepped through.
A strong breeze kicked up, making the colored leaves swirl and
chilling the tops of his ears. He wished he had his wide-brimmed
hat, but he'd given that up along with the other articles of Amish
clothing he used to wear—the broadfall pants, homemade shirts,
and suspenders—after being shunned. But since he'd returned to
Paradise he longed for those simpler clothes.

He slowed his pace as he headed toward the corner of the graveyard where Caroline lay. He glanced around, looking for Ellie. He
was a good fifteen minutes early, but still . . . it was in the back of his
mind that she might not show up. He stood in front of his fiancée's
grave and looked down at the small, plain concrete marker, the same
shape and size as the rest of the headstones. He knelt down beside
the faded green grass that covered the grave and closed his eyes.

Memories of the funeral and burial flooded his mind. How
he had balled up his grief that day, trying to keep himself from
breaking down in front of family and friends as they viewed her
casket in her parents' basement per Amish tradition. The hours
before taking her casket to the graveyard had been excruciating, and the only way he had gotten through it was by plotting
his revenge against Isaiah. He clearly remembered standing by

Caroline's graveside and vowing that Isaiah would pay for her death, and pay dearly.

He opened his eyes and ran his palm along the grass. "I failed, Caroline." His voice was thick with the emotion he had allowed to fester for all these years. But even now he couldn't let the grief flow, not when faced with how he had let Caroline down. Isaiah had gotten off free from blame and consequences while the woman he had loved lay in the cold ground. How was he ever supposed to let that go?

"Christopher?"

He turned and stood at the sound of Ellie's voice. He hadn't heard her approach. She was standing just outside the gate, as if waiting for his permission to come in. He strode over to her and opened the gate for her. Her limp was less noticeable than it had been yesterday. "How did you get here?"

"*Daed* dropped me off on his way to work."

Chris was surprised; he hadn't even heard the buggy approach. "Didn't he see my car?"

She nodded.

"And he didn't care?"

"He's not as strict as *Mamm* is." She turned toward the sun and closed her eyes, allowing the warm beams to shine on her face.

He tried not to stare at her, but he couldn't help it. "I'm glad you came."

She turned toward him. "You thought I wasn't going to show up?"

"The thought did cross my mind."

Ellie shook her head. "I wouldn't do that to you, Chris."

And he believed her. Ellie kept her word. That was the type of woman she was. Strong. Filled with faith and forgiveness. She was perfect, while he was so flawed. He turned away, trying to fight his emotions, even though he knew she couldn't see his expression. Then he felt her touch his arm.

"Chris?"

He faced her again and, without thinking, moved closer. "I failed her, Ellie. I didn't realize it until this moment. I promised her that day that I would make Isaiah pay for the accident. He never did."

"You didn't fail her, Chris. That promise was given out of pain and grief. Believe me, Isaiah has paid dearly for what happened."

He let out a sigh. "I think we all have."

She nodded. "Why did you ask to see me again?"

Her blunt question caught him off guard. How could he admit he just wanted to be with her, to hear her voice, to listen to her say things that spoke to his heart? He couldn't tell her, not without scaring her off. He was scared enough by the abruptness and intensity of his feelings. The thought of leaving her tomorrow was almost unbearable.

But she wasn't the only thing keeping him here. If he had really wanted to leave, he would have done it as soon as he heard about Sarah Lynne's engagement. Yet he didn't. Something else kept him from going back to Ohio. God had brought him back to Paradise, and He was telling Chris to stay.

"I think I'm ready," he said, taking her hand from his arm and holding it in his. Her touch warmed his soul much like the sun warmed him through the leather of his jacket.

Her brows shot up. "Ready to do what?"

"Ask for forgiveness and rejoin the church."

Ellie pulled her hand out of his grasp and stepped away, almost losing her balance. She used her cane for support, not only because she had almost tripped, but to contain her surprise. "You're ready to repent?"

"*Ya.*"

She heard him approach her again, and she moved away until she felt the fence against the small of her back.

"You're right," he said. "*Mamm*'s right. Even Sarah Lynne's right, although she'll never let me live it down." His chuckle held more mirth than she'd heard from him since his arrival in Paradise. "Just talking about letting this *geh* is freeing."

Ellie was speechless. It was what she and so many others were praying for. Yet it seemed so sudden. Yesterday he had still been filled with bitterness. Now he was ready to let go. Perhaps God had done the work in his heart that they had all longed for. And who was she to question God?

"Ellie?" His tone changed from happiness to trepidation. "Why aren't you saying anything? I thought you'd be happy."

"I am. It's just so . . . sudden."

"I don't call five years sudden."

"*Nee*, that's not what I mean." What did she mean? Doubt niggled at her head and heart. "I am glad, very glad that you've decided to ask for forgiveness."

"But?"

"There are no buts." She bit her tongue.

"*Gut.*" He stepped away from her. "Now that I've made the decision, I don't know why I didn't make it before. I think it was because I was trying to hold on to Caroline, like you said. Her memory slipped away from me, and at least by being angry I felt *something*, instead of being dead inside. But you've shown me that I can't live my life like that anymore."

"I have?"

"*Ya.* You're the example of what I should have done all along. I should have left the past in the past. I shouldn't have put my family through all this."

He was saying all the right words, but she still wasn't sure. "What about Isaiah? Have you stopped blaming him for Caroline's death?" She held her breath while waiting to hear his answer.

"If that's what I need to do to get back with the church, then I will."

Her heart sank. It was what she feared. His forgiveness wasn't coming from his heart. It was a means to an end.

"Ellie, what's wrong?"

She felt him move closer. She was backed up against the fence and there was no place for her to go. Despite her disappointment that his repentance was less than genuine, she suddenly realized she didn't mind being this close to him. An attraction stronger than anything she'd ever felt before bloomed inside her.

"Ellie, I want this. I don't want to *geh* back to Apple Creek, to an empty apartment, to no *familye*, and to people I barely know being the only *freinds* I have. This is where I belong, I know that now." His voice lowered. "You showed it to me. I don't know how I can ever repay you for that."

"You don't owe me anything, Chris." She willed her pulse to slow, but it wouldn't. His rich voice, a tone she could listen to all day, flowed over her. He had on his leather jacket again, and his breath smelled sweet, as if he'd had flavored coffee for breakfast.

"Ellie, I . . ."

She heard him gulp, giving her the first indication that he might be nervous. But why? He cleared his throat but didn't step away.

"I'm going to see Bishop Ebersol today and ask him to take me out of the *bann*. When is the next church service?"

"This Sunday." Which was only two days away.

"*Gut*. I don't want to wait longer than that. And, Ellie, once I'm back in the church, I don't want us to stop seeing each other."

Ellie's belly swirled. "We won't," she said, fighting for an even tone. "We're *freinds*, Christopher. We were before the accident, and we always will be."

"That's not what I mean."

She drew in a sharp breath when she felt his palm cup her

cheek, then release it quickly. The touch was light, nearly imperceptible, but enough to make her heart almost leap out of her chest. Sarah Lynne was right—Christopher did like her. Or at least he thought he did. One thing was for sure, he was a very mixed-up *mann*.

✩

Ellie had Chris drop her off at the Pantry on his way to visit Bishop Ebersol. She hadn't answered him directly about what would happen between them after he was accepted back in the church, and he didn't press.

"Say good-bye to the car," he said as she was getting out. "I'm selling it after I see the bishop."

She paused. "You're serious about this."

"I'm serious about everything I said, Ellie. It's time for me to move on with my life. For the first time since Caroline died, I'm looking forward to it."

Ellie recalled his last words as she slipped into a booth in the back of the restaurant. She had told her mother she would be gone to Paradise for most of the day and asked to be picked up this afternoon at Stitches and Things in downtown Paradise. At least she didn't have to worry about dealing with her *mamm* for the rest of the day. She had enough things on her mind as it was.

"Hello, Ellie. How are you today?"

Ellie turned, recognizing the cheerful voice. Tillie always seemed to be in a good mood. "Hi, Tillie." She was grateful her tone sounded friendly and even. "How are you?"

"Doing great. We've got some delicious specials today. I've already snuck a few bites." She lowered her voice, giggling. "But don't tell anyone."

Ellie managed a smile. "I won't."

"Would you like a menu?"

"*Nee.* I'll just have a cup of coffee." She didn't even want that, but she couldn't sit in the booth taking up space without paying for something. "Is Sarah Lynne here?" She prayed she would be.

"*Ya.* She just came in an hour ago. I'll send her over with the coffee."

Ellie checked her watch as Tillie walked away, then she drummed her fingers against the hard plastic tabletop, her nerves strung taut.

"I'm so glad you're here!" Sarah Lynne set the coffee cup on the table and slid into the seat in front of her. "We're in between breakfast and lunch rush, so I have some time to talk. How did your ride home with Chris *geh* yesterday?"

"*Gut.* We talked—"

"Did you tell him about Caroline? Did you convince him to stay? Did he say anything about coming back to the community?"

Ellie held up her hand. "*Ya.* Sorta. *Ya.*"

"Wait a minute. So he's staying?"

"I don't know—"

"And he's going to forgive Isaiah?" Sarah Lynne grabbed her hand. "Ellie, you're amazing. Well, I've always thought you were amazing, but now you're double amazing. How did you do it?"

Ellie swallowed. This conversation wasn't going the way she planned—much like her last conversation with Chris. Events were spinning out of control, and she couldn't reel them back in.

"Sarah Lynne, I think your *bruder* is really confused right now. He says he wants to come back to the church. In fact, he went to see Bishop Ebersol after he dropped me off."

"He did? That's great. How is that confused? Sounds like he's finally making sense."

"He's doing the right thing, but I'm not sure it's for the right reason. I asked him if he forgave Isaiah. He said if that's what it took to get back to the church, then he would. Then he said something else."

"What?" Sarah Lynne gripped Ellie's hand tighter.

"I think he wants to court me after he's been accepted into the church."

"I knew it!" Sarah Lynne released Ellie's hand. "I told you he likes you. I love it when I'm right."

Ellie shook her head. Sarah Lynne was missing the point. "That's what I mean by him being confused. For one thing, he can't possibly like me."

"Why not?"

"You know why. Everyone knows why." Surely she didn't have to say it out loud.

"Because you're blind? Ellie, obviously that doesn't matter to him."

"It mattered to John."

"Because John was an idiot. I'm sorry, but he was. And Chris isn't like that. He's stubborn, but he isn't shallow."

Ellie shook her head. "It's not just that. His repentance doesn't come from the heart, Sarah Lynne."

"Did he say that to you?"

"*Nee*, but—"

"When Chris first came here and I asked him to forgive Isaiah, he said he could never get up in front of the church and say something that wasn't true. He wouldn't be doing this if he didn't really feel it deep in his heart." Ellie heard Sarah Lynne slide out of the seat. "I've got to run, but this is the best news! I can't wait to tell Isaiah. We'll all finally be happy."

As Sarah Lynne walked away, Ellie wondered if it would ever be possible. Especially when everyone learned the truth.

Chapter Twelve

ELLIE KNOCKED ON THE DOOR OF HER COUSIN'S HOUSE, praying he would be home. She heard the taxi she'd hired drive away. After talking with Sarah Lynne, she knew she had to speak to Isaiah. He often worked from home, but sometimes he would go out into the community to work on various construction projects.

Her aunt Roberta opened the door. "Why, hello there, Ellie. What a lovely surprise. Did your mother come with you?"

"*Nee*. I came alone. I need to talk to Isaiah for a minute. Is he home?"

"*Ya*, he's out in the workshop. You want me to take you there?"

She shook her head. "I remember where it is."

"All right. I'll be out in a minute with some fresh iced tea."

What she had to say was for Isaiah's hearing alone. "That's all right, *Aenti*."

"Okay, but if you change your mind, let me know. I have a fresh pitcher, just made it a little while ago."

"*Danki*, I'll keep that in mind."

Ellie turned away from the house as her aunt shut the door. Although she and her mother were sisters, they weren't anything alike. Aunt Roberta hadn't changed the way she treated Ellie since the accident, and occasionally Ellie heard her aunt admonish *Mamm* for hovering so much, especially after the accident.

As Ellie made her way to the workshop behind the house, she

could hear the sounds of the cows and pigs her cousin's family raised. She could smell them, too, and the scent helped her find her way to the workshop instead of the barn, which were right next to each other. The sound of the hydraulic-powered saw reached her ears. She waited a few moments for the whirring to stop, then with a firm fist she rapped on the door, hoping Isaiah heard her. She didn't dare walk into the shop, not knowing the layout of the building or where Isaiah kept his tools.

Soon she heard the muffled thud of footsteps coming toward the door. When it opened, she felt a slight breeze and inhaled the scent of fresh sawdust.

"Ellie." He sounded surprised to see her. "What are you doing here?"

"I need to talk to you. Now, and alone."

"All right. Let me tell *Daed*, and I'll be right out." Isaiah walked away, and she could hear him speaking with her uncle. Then Isaiah walked back to her. "Let's go behind the barn. That's a *gut* place to talk."

Ellie reached for Isaiah's arm, grasping it just above the elbow, letting him lead her to the back of the barn. A few moments later they stopped.

"There's a wood fence right in front of us," he said.

She reached out and touched the rough, splintered wood, holding her cane.

"I think I know why you're here," Isaiah said. "I also hope I'm wrong."

She leaned against the fence, as if its support would give her the strength to say what she should have said a long time ago. Over the years she had accepted what Isaiah had done. And up until Chris's return, she had seen no need to have this conversation with her cousin. But after hearing what Chris told her today, she knew she couldn't keep silent anymore. "We have to tell them, Isaiah. We have to tell everyone what really happened."

"And are you willing to fully repent of your sins? Of going against the church and trying to have your brother in Christ prosecuted?"

Chris looked at the bishop, who was peering at him over the rims of his spectacles. He fidgeted in his chair, gripping the mug of coffee the bishop's wife had offered him. The older man's steel-colored eyes made him feel like a child again, and perhaps that was the point. He had been acting childishly. He knew that now. Unfortunately, it had taken him far too long to realize it.

"*Ya,*" he said, sitting up a little straighter in his chair. "I ask that you forgive my sin against Isaiah Stolzfus."

"It isn't I who needs to forgive you, Christopher. Forgiveness must come from the congregation, and ultimately from God."

Chris nodded, understanding. All the way over here he'd prayed, harder than he ever had before, asking God to heal his heart for good this time, to give him the strength he needed not only to stand up in front of the church on Sunday and admit his guilt, but also to face Isaiah, which would be much harder. At the forefront of everything was Ellie. He could almost hear her prodding him on, and he wished he had thought to ask her to come with him. But she would have refused, and rightly so. This was his battle, and he had to face his past on his own before he could let it go.

Bishop Ebersol stroked his long, graying beard. The man had been bishop of their district for as long as Chris could remember.

"I'll have to speak with the other ministers about it, but I don't think they would have any disagreement about you making your plea on Sunday. I believe they will think, as I do, that this has been long overdue. Your absence has been missed, Christopher, not only by your *familye*, but by all of us."

Chris hadn't expected the surge of emotion that ran through him. He blinked back the tears, swallowed the lump in his throat.

"Danki," he said, his voice cracking.

The bishop nodded, his expression still stern. He looked Chris up and down. "You'll have to give up your fancy clothes and car. You realize that, *ya?*"

Chris set the cup down on the coffee table in front of him. "They mean nothing to me." His car was a convenience, nothing more, and he had no attachment to the clothes. Everything of worth he had in his duffel bag, which he could easily give up. He would be coming back to the community with nothing, ready to fully embrace the Amish life again.

Bishop Ebersol steepled his fingers beneath his fuzzy beard and stared at Chris for a long moment, enough to make Chris squirm again. Finally the man spoke. "What made you come to this decision, Christopher? It's been five years. Your sister is marrying the man you tried to have sent to jail, the *mann* who was at fault for your fiancée's accident."

Chris rubbed his palms over his jean-clad thighs. Was the bishop trying to rile him up? He gripped the tops of his kneecaps. "I realize that."

"Then how have you found it in your heart, after all these years, to forgive Isaiah?"

He leaned back in the chair, suddenly serene. "Someone has changed my heart," he said, smiling. "Someone very special."

"So you are doing this because of a *maedel?*" The bishop's gaze narrowed, and he looked more stone-faced than ever. "Does your change of heart come from God . . . or from her?"

"I don't want to talk about this," Isaiah said. "What's done is done."

She could hear Isaiah's voice drifting away, indicating he was walking away from her. She took a tentative step toward him, using the fence as a guide. "Things have changed, Isaiah. We both know that. I should have said something before now—"

"Ellie, I said I don't want to talk about it. The past is past. Remember? It's what we say to each other when we forgive, *ya?*"

"Isaiah, please don't be angry."

"I'm . . . not." He sounded closer now, and she could tell he was facing her. "I'm not angry with you, Ellie. I'm still mad at myself. I should have never driven that car."

"Caroline and I got in there with you. We trusted you."

"And look what happened." Isaiah touched her shoulder. "You've suffered enough, Ellie."

She moved her head up. "As have you."

"Not as much as I deserve." He sighed, dropping his hand from her shoulder. The wood fence creaked as he leaned against it. "Why are you bringing this up now? Is it because of the wedding? Because of Chris?"

"Both. And because of my conscience."

"Your conscience should be clear."

"But it's not. I've been talking to Chris, Isaiah. He said he's ready to forgive you and come back to the church."

She heard him move.

"He did? That's great! Sarah Lynne will be so happy."

"She is. I just told her about it."

He let out a deep breath. "I prayed so hard for this, Ellie. Sarah Lynne has been so sad since Chris came back. I think it was worse with him being here than when he was in Apple Creek. I offered to call off the wedding, to spare Sarah Lynne's *familye* any more pain. I thought stepping aside might make Chris change his mind about me."

"Not one of your smarter decisions."

"I realize that now. But, Ellie, listen to me." He gripped both of her shoulders, almost hard enough to make her wince. "The decision we made five years ago was a *gut* one."

"You didn't give me much of a choice at the time. I was in the hospital, still hurt and confused."

"I did what needed to be done. At the time I didn't know what would happen. Caroline was dead, you were blind . . . I had no idea what would happen to either of us. That's why I did what I did. And I'd do it all over again." He released her, but he didn't step away. "Just drop it, Ellie. Chris is forgiving me. He's coming back to the church."

"But I don't think he's doing it for the right reason. I don't think he's forgiving you with his heart."

"Who are you to make that judgment? Ellie, please. Just leave it alone. After all this time, everything is finally getting back to normal. I have to get back to work." He brushed past her, then added, "Can you make your way back to the *haus?*"

She nodded, not wanting to press the matter further. Her cousin had made up his mind, and she wasn't about to change it. "I'm fine. You *geh* on."

Once Isaiah left she turned, feeling the fence pressing against her waist. She couldn't mistake the pleading in her cousin's voice, nor his admonishment about her judging Chris's heart. He was right about that; she had no right to assume what Chris was feeling. After five years he was practically a stranger to her. And she knew judging others was frowned upon, not only by other Amish, but by God. Why did she have a hard time letting this *geh?*

But she knew the answer to that. And even though her cousin wanted her to keep their secret, she wasn't sure she could do it anymore.

⌒⌒⌒

After his visit to Bishop Ebersol's, Chris drove his car back to the bed-and-breakfast in Paradise and checked out. He loaded his duffel bag into the back and put the basket Ellie had given him in the passenger seat. As he turned the key in the ignition, he realized this might be last time he would drive this car. He didn't have a single regret. Smiling, he headed to his parents' house, his nerves steady until he got a few feet from their driveway. He glanced at the clock on the dashboard. It read four thirty. His father usually arrived home before five.

He turned in the driveway, excited to see his mother's face. She had been right about staying one more day. Talking with Ellie had put things into perspective. She was a special woman, and once he rejoined the church, he hoped she would be willing to let him court her.

He pulled his car to a stop and hopped out, went to the front porch, and knocked on the door. A few moments later he knocked again. After a third time, he frowned. No one was home? His sister and father were probably still working, and his mother sometimes visited friends in the afternoon. But he didn't mind waiting for them to return.

Chris left the porch and went around to the backyard. He saw a couple of cows grazing in the pasture next to the barn. He strode toward the white wood fencing, then leaned against it, watching the cows nibble on the tender blades of grass. Peace filled him like he hadn't experienced in so long. Why had he fought so hard all this time? He could barely remember his reasons.

He wasn't sure how long he stood there, soaking in the afternoon sun and watching the cows in front of him. But when he heard the sound of a car in front of the house, he dashed around to find out who it was. He didn't recognize the car, but he knew the woman stepping out of it. Ellie. He went to her just as she was taking out her cane.

"Here, let me get that." He dug into his back pocket for his wallet so he could pay her taxi fare.

"Get what? Oh." Then she nodded. "*Nee*, I've already paid." She turned to the driver. "*Danki*, Mrs. Jones."

"You're welcome, Ellie."

Chris ducked to see an elderly woman behind the wheel of a car that seemed to swallow her whole.

"What time do you want me to pick you up?" Mrs. Jones asked.

"Half an hour will be fine," Ellie replied.

"You don't have to pick her up." Chris stepped beside her and leaned over, poking his head through the passenger doorway. "I can take her home."

"Are you sure?"

He heard Ellie say something behind him, but he didn't let her finish. "I'm positive. Thanks anyway."

"Okay."

Chris stood up and shut the car door. After Mrs. Jones started pulling away, he turned to Ellie. He opened his mouth to speak but shut it when he saw her stormy expression.

"I wanted Mrs. Jones to pick me up."

"I'm sorry. I thought I'd save her a trip and take you home. I should have asked."

"*Ya*, you should have. Just because I'm blind doesn't mean I can't take care of myself."

The strength of her irritation surprised him. "I never said that you couldn't. I didn't think you'd mind. It's not like I haven't driven you home twice before."

"You shouldn't assume anything about me, Chris. You don't know . . . You don't know the real me. And once you do . . ."

The break in Ellie's voice made Chris go to her. But when he touched her shoulder, she shrugged him off. "What's going on here, Ellie? I don't understand why you're upset with me."

"I'm not." She took in a deep breath. "But I need to talk to you. Privately."

"No one's home, so you have me all to yourself." That didn't come out exactly right, but at that moment he didn't care. He bit the inside of his cheek. Remembering her sore ankle, he said, "Let's sit on the front porch."

She nodded, and he followed her as she made her way to the porch. Even though she obviously knew the way, her steps were slow. A few moments later they were both seated in the wicker chairs. But she didn't speak. "What did you want to talk to me about, Ellie?"

"Did you see the bishop today?"

He nodded. "*Ya.* Everything is ready for Sunday. But I thought I'd go over to Isaiah's on Saturday and talk to him. I think a conversation is long overdue."

Her hands clutched the ends of the wicker chair. "Whatever he tells you about the accident, don't believe him."

He looked at Ellie and frowned. What was she talking about?

"Maybe Isaiah was right," she murmured. "Maybe I should leave this alone."

"Leave what alone?"

"But I have to tell the truth. I should have told the truth a long time ago."

Her words unnerved him. He leaned forward in the chair and reached for her hand, not caring if his mother and father showed up and saw them together. Soon everyone would know how much he cared for Ellie. But just as before, she shirked from his touch.

"Ellie, please, talk to me."

Her body started to shake before she turned toward him. "Chris, Isaiah isn't to blame for Caroline's death. I am."

Chapter Thirteen

ELLIE COULDN'T STOP SHAKING. EVERY BONE IN HER BODY quaked. She pulled her light jacket closer to her body. She'd said the words aloud, the secret she had kept inside for five long years.

"What are you talking about?"

An edge had crept into his voice, which she had expected. Once he knew the full truth, he wouldn't want to see her again. She heard him get up and start to pace the front porch. Then he suddenly stopped.

"What happened? And start from the beginning."

"Caroline spent the night at my house the night before the accident. We both had to work the afternoon shift at the Pantry, and I was going to call a taxi when Isaiah showed up. He had borrowed one of his *Englisch* friends' fancy cars." She sighed. "I lost patience with him right away. We were trying to arrange a ride to work, and he kept bugging us to *geh* for a ride with him. Finally Caroline pointed out that we could make Isaiah happy and get to work on time if we would ride with him. 'It'll be fun, Ellie,' she said. With both of them trying to convince me, I gave in. She got in the back, and I got in the front.

"As he drove us, Isaiah told us it was the first time he'd ever driven a car. I panicked and held my breath. Neither he nor Caroline noticed how nervous I was; Caroline was enjoying the ride, telling him to go faster. The car had one of those sunroof things, and he opened it up and put one hand through it, leaving only one hand on the wheel. When we got to the intersection right before Paradise I saw a car coming at us. I grabbed his arm and squeezed, screaming for him to look out." She tilted her head downward. "He already had one hand off the wheel. When I grabbed him, he let go and lost control of the car. That's when he spun out of control and rammed into a tree. Caroline was thrown out and . . . you know the rest."

Chris didn't say anything for a long time. She hadn't expected him to. She thought by telling him about the accident, a burden would have lifted, but it didn't. Instead she felt worse. She had never admitted any of this to anyone else. Saying the words out loud made her feel ashamed.

"Why didn't Isaiah say anything?" he finally asked.

"That was the way he wanted it. He came to see me in the hospital the day after the accident." She could still remember the sound of his crutches hitting the floor. He had broken his left leg and had just been released by the doctors. "They had given me some kind of drug for the pain, and I wasn't sure exactly what he was telling me, but it was something about not mentioning my part in the accident. At the time I didn't care—all I thought about was Caroline and my injuries. Later on I heard he had taken complete blame for the accident. I tried to talk to him about it after I came home from the hospital, but he wouldn't listen. He said no matter what, the accident was his fault. He was the one driving. He also said I had suffered enough."

She paused, waiting for him to speak. His silence drove her to distraction. She wished she could see his face, because then she could gauge his reaction. Now she could do nothing except sit there, waiting for him to tell her what she already knew. She was a coward and a liar.

But he didn't say either of those things. "Is that all?"

She angled her head toward his voice, which sounded like it was coming from the far end of the porch. She nodded, shame robbing her of her voice.

"Why are you telling me this now?" He approached her, his footsteps harsh against the wooden porch floor. "Why tell me at all?"

"I should have told you a long time ago. I should have admitted it to everyone, instead of letting Isaiah shoulder the blame on his own. I even talked to him about it today, but he still insisted on keeping the secret."

"Does Sarah Lynne know?"

"*Nee*. Only Isaiah and me. And now you." She took a deep breath. "You should have been angry at me as well all these years, Chris. I'm sorry about that. I'm sorry I was too weak to speak the truth. It was easier to let Isaiah carry it all. But if you're going to forgive him . . . you'll have to forgive me too."

In the distance she heard the clip-clop of the horse's hooves. She also heard Chris walking away, stepping down from the porch. She wanted to call out to him, but she couldn't. She wouldn't blame him if he never talked to her again. The sound of a buggy and horse traveling over gravel reached her ears, and she knew Sarah Lynne or her parents were home. Standing up, she reached for her cane and made her way down the porch steps. The buggy pulled to a stop, and she heard someone get out.

"Chris!" Sarah Lynne said, her tone exuberant.

Sarah Lynne rushed over to her brother. It had to be a good sign that he was at the house, knowing their father usually came home at this time. But instead of looking happy, he seemed miserable. Then she spied Ellie standing a couple feet away, her shoulders drooping and her head dipped.

Her mother came up behind her. "Chris?" she asked, moving toward him. "Christopher, is something wrong?"

He glanced at Ellie, his dark eyes narrowing, then shifted his gaze to his family.

"I came to see if I can stay here tonight. I checked out of the bed-and-breakfast earlier today."

Sarah Lynne heard her mother suck in a breath. "Just for tonight?"

He looked at Ellie again. "Maybe."

Their father nodded, and Sarah Lynne's heart swelled. "Does this mean you're coming back for *gut*?"

He didn't answer right away, just glanced at the ground, his hands going deeper into his pockets.

Ellie spoke. "Sarah Lynne, could you give me a ride home?"

Sarah Lynne was about to suggest that Chris do it, but then he looked at her and shook his head.

"*Ya*. I can take you home."

"*Danki*."

Chris turned around and walked into the house, not saying good-bye to Ellie. Bewildered, Sarah Lynne looked to her mother, who shrugged and followed Chris inside. Her father went behind the house, presumably to check on the cows. The tension in the air was almost suffocating. She went to Ellie and put her hand on her shoulder. "Ready to *geh*?"

Ellie nodded, straightening her shoulders and her posture. "Where's the buggy?"

Sarah Lynne told her, and she walked to the driveway and climbed inside. Sarah Lynne joined her, and soon they were on the way to Ellie's house. She was determined to find out what was going on with her friend and her brother.

❧

Ellie was miserable. She knew Chris wasn't going to give her a ride home once he heard her news. She doubted he'd ever want to see her again. The thought filled her with sadness.

"Ellie, what happened with you and Chris?" Sarah Lynne

asked, sounding as perplexed as Ellie felt. "I thought everything was settled already. Now it looks like he's not sure he's going to stay."

Ellie wasn't sure how to answer. Maybe she should just tell her the truth, as she had told Chris. But she saw what Chris's reaction was. Who knew how Sarah Lynne would react, knowing her fiancé had been less than truthful to everyone? She brought her fingertip to her temple. How did this all get so complicated?

"Are you all right?" Sarah Lynne asked. "You've gone pale, Ellie. Is it your ankle?"

"Nee." She tried to keep her voice steady, but she failed. "I'm . . . fine."

"You don't look or sound fine." The buggy slowed. "Ellie, you have to tell me what happened. Did Chris do something?"

She let out a bitter chuckle. "He didn't do anything wrong. He's done everything right." If only she could say the same thing for herself.

"Then why are you both upset? Chris looked like someone kicked him, and you're on the verge of tears." Sarah Lynne took her hand. "I care about you both so much. I can't stand to see you unhappy like this."

"I'll be okay, and so will Chris." She remembered telling Chris how God worked out everything for good. She held on to those words, now more than ever before.

◦───

Chris stumbled into the dark bedroom, not bothering to turn on the small lamp on the nightstand. Instead he walked into the hallway and made his way to the kitchen, turning on the gas lamp in there. He glanced at the battery-operated clock on the wall. Two thirty in the morning. He had hoped it would be at least closer to dawn. He hadn't slept a minute the entire night. How could he, when all he could think about was Ellie?

He sat down at the kitchen table, slumping in the chair. Stark silence enveloped him. It had been so long since he'd spent the night in an Amish home, and the quiet unnerved him. But he'd get used to it again.

Hard to believe more than a few hours ago everything had been so simple, and coming back to the church had seemed so clear, so God-ordained, that he had felt better about himself than he had in years. But Ellie's news had been like a punch in the mouth. The accident had been her fault as much as Isaiah's? Her fault that Caroline was dead? And the man he had resented for the past five years, whom he had tried to put in jail, had been protecting Ellie all this time. How was he supposed to make sense of that?

Isaiah had been behind the wheel . . . but if Ellie hadn't panicked and distracted him, the wreck might not have happened at all. And she had lived with this secret for five years. Even when he returned, she had said nothing to him about it. What had made her change her mind? A part of him wished she had stayed quiet. It was easier to resent Isaiah than her.

And what of his feelings for her? He cared about her, had wanted to court her after he set things right with God and the church. Had those feelings changed? He couldn't tell, not when they were competing with the confusion in his heart and soul.

"Christopher?"

He looked over his shoulder to see his father walking into the room, wearing his broadfall pants and a white T-shirt. Chris looked down at his own T-shirt and boxer shorts. He'd been so preoccupied that he hadn't thought not to wear shorts in the house. That would have to change too.

"Everything okay?" His father sat down next to him.

It was the most his *daed* had said to him since he'd come back to Paradise. Even during supper he had been quiet, excusing himself right after he finished eating to go outside and check on the animals. Chris had thought to go with him, but he didn't want to push it. He was lucky his father was allowing him to stay here, because technically he was still in the *bann*.

But his father had come to him on his own volition, concern shining in his dark brown eyes. Chris looked at him for a moment. Like his mother, his father had more gray in his hair and beard, more creases at the corners of his eyes and mouth. But the man was still built like a small bull, his thick chest and muscular arms a testament to his profession as a blacksmith and farrier. His hair was mussed from sleep, and his eyes looked tired.

"Sorry I woke you up," Chris said.

"It's all right. I saw the light come on from the bedroom and thought you might be up. How about some coffee?"

Chris nodded, marveling at how his father's demeanor had changed in such a short time. It was as if the past five years had never happened. He rose from the chair. "I'll make it."

His father gestured for him to sit down. "I got it. Still like it strong enough to paint the side of the barn?"

With a chuckle Chris said, "*Ya.* I do."

His father filled the percolator with water from the sink, put a couple of scoops of coffee in the basket, then set it on the gas stove, putting the lid on top of the pot. He turned the stove on, and the hiss of gas filled the room. Then he came back and sat down.

"Your *mamm* says you're coming back to the church."

Chris frowned. He hadn't said anything for sure about it to anyone other than Ellie and Bishop Ebersol. "What makes her say that?"

He shrugged. "She said she just knew. Knew the day you showed up here that God had brought you home. You've been fighting Him the whole time, apparently."

"*Ya.* Been doing a lot of that lately."

"So is she right? Are you rejoining the church?"

Chris ran his thumb along the edge of the oak table. "It looks that way."

"Well, that doesn't sound exactly definite." His *daed* scooted his chair back and rose. As he got two mugs down from the cupboard, the percolator started bubbling. He poured them each a cup and carried them to the table.

Wrapping his hands around the warm mug, Chris sighed. "I'm pretty confused right now."

"I can tell. That's what happens when you've been away from the Lord. The devil takes hold and mixes everything up." *Daed* took a sip of his coffee and made a face. "*Ya.* You should like this."

But Chris pushed the mug away. "But that's just it, *Daed.* I haven't been straying from the Lord. Even when I was in Apple Creek I went to church. I prayed. Read my Bible. And when I came back here, I knew it was God's leading, so *Mamm* was right about that. Then I found out about Sarah Lynne and Isaiah—"

"And there went your best-laid plans."

"*Ya.* Still, I had come to a place where I could finally let the past lie." *Thanks to Ellie.* "And I was ready to come back. I even talked to Bishop Ebersol and stopped by the used-car dealership in Paradise to talk to them about selling my car."

"That's *gut* to hear, Chris. Sounds like you are where God wants you to be. So what's the problem?"

"I found out something today. Something I didn't know." He toyed with the idea of confiding in his father, but he couldn't bring himself to spill Ellie's secret.

"And it's affecting your decision to come back to the community?"

"*Nee,* not that." He looked at his father.

"Does this have something to do with Ellie Chupp? I saw her here earlier."

"You could say that."

"You have feelings for her, don't you?"

Was he that transparent? "*Ya.* I do. After Caroline died, I never even looked at another woman. I wasn't interested in dating. Then I spend a couple days with Ellie and everything's changed."

"That's the way it was for me and your mother. We grew up together, but one day when I was seventeen I saw her at a singing, and it was like I'd seen her for the first time. I was gone after that. But she wasn't as easy to convince."

"Ellie isn't either. And then she told me something today . . ." He looked at his *daed*. "I can't betray her confidence."

"I wouldn't want you to." He took another drink of coffee and set down the mug. "But let me tell you this—you can't come back to the church because of Ellie or anyone else. There has to be a change in your heart and a willingness to forget the past, as God calls us to do."

Now he sounded like Bishop Ebersol.

"Believe me, I know."

His father stood up and yawned. "Can't believe I'm still sleepy after drinking that stuff, but I'm heading back to bed. Pray about your confusion, Chris. And know that God is not the author of it. Follow His leading. Not anyone else's."

"*Danki, Daed.*"

After his father left for bed, Chris thought about his advice. He had been praying all along, but had he been praying for the right thing? He'd asked God to help him forgive, but not to change his heart. Would that be the answer? He didn't know, but there was one way to find out. He got out of his chair and knelt on the hardwood floor, praying harder than he'd ever prayed before.

Chapter Fourteen

ON SUNDAY MORNING ELLIE ARRIVED THIRTY MINUTES early at the home of the Keims, who were hosting church. She hadn't had a choice about the early arrival, as her mother always liked to be punctual. She greeted everyone, then took her seat on the outside bench and folded her cane.

The Keims didn't have enough room in their house to hold church inside, so they held it in their barn, the benches lined up in neat rows in the center. Ellie listened to the commotion around her, the low sounds of murmuring as people said hello and found their seats. She breathed in the scent of fresh hay and horses, knowing the Keim family would have spent hours making sure the barn was in pristine condition to hold church.

Normally Ellie was serene at the beginning of services, but this morning she was far from it. She couldn't stop twisting the hem of her apron. She hadn't spoken to Chris or Sarah Lynne since Friday. Which wasn't a surprise, since she'd kept to herself all day yesterday, not leaving the house under the ruse that her ankle still ached.

Her mother was pleased. "It's about time you listened to me about that ankle."

But Ellie didn't reveal the real reason she didn't want to leave the comfort of home, or why she was so quiet her father asked her what was wrong at least three times. Each time Ellie had told him everything was fine. How she wished that was so.

She fiddled with her hem some more, then stopped before her

mother sat next to her and admonished her. Instead she clasped her hands tightly together, wondering if Chris would come to church today. She had thought about him all day yesterday, when her guilt over keeping her secret kept her mind in turmoil. She prayed that revealing her secret hadn't made him change his mind about the church. But then again, if he had, he wasn't coming back for the right reasons. Regardless of her feelings for him, she wanted him to reconcile with God and find peace on his own terms, not because of anything she said or did.

Her mother came and sat down beside her. It was her habit right before the service to spend the last few minutes in prayer, preparing her heart and mind. Ellie would do well to follow her example. She closed her eyes.

Heavenly Father, whatever happens today, please be with Chris. Show him the only true way to peace is to follow You, to surrender to You completely.

Before long the service began, and Ellie tried not to think about Chris, keeping her mind focused on Christ. After the congregation spent twenty minutes singing hymns, one of the ministers gave a short sermon on forgiveness, mentioning James 5:16. *"Confess your faults to one another, and pray one for another, that ye may be healed."* God's words spoke to Ellie's heart, causing a tiny spark to light within.

When the sermon ended, the congregation remained quiet, save a few murmurs from young children who were fidgeting in their seats. Ellie felt more relaxed than she had in days. She waited for the next part of the service to start. She recognized the familiar sound of Bishop Ebersol clearing his throat.

"Christopher Miller. Are you ready to confess your sin to God and the church?"

Ellie sucked in a breath as she heard Chris answer from the opposite side of the room.

"Ya."

He sounded penitent yet confident. The bishop asked him a few more questions, with Chris answering them all, including apologizing to Isaiah for trying to have him thrown in jail.

"Christopher, the past is in the past. It is forgotten, never to be brought up again."

Tears welled up in Ellie's eyes. He had come back to church. It had taken a great deal of courage to do what he had done. More courage than she had. Because while Chris had opened up his heart to forgiveness, she still kept her secret. Yet she wasn't sure if she could keep it any longer.

The first hour after the service was a whirlwind for Chris. He had gone from being ignored by almost everyone to being welcomed back to the community with open arms, literally. Friends he hadn't seen or talked to for five years told him how glad they were to see him and how they'd have to get together soon. His uncle even offered him a job at his blacksmith shop, and he'd been invited to two singings during the next couple of weeks. It amazed him how the words Bishop Ebersol had said after Chris's confession were so true. They would never bring up the past again.

But he had some unfinished business to take care of before he could settle the matter completely. Once he had a break from talking with everyone, he left the barn and headed for the Keim house, where he expected to find Ellie helping the women get lunch prepared. He searched for her in almost every room. He even approached her mother, who was suddenly as friendly as a golden retriever.

"She was in the living room last time I saw her." *Frau* Chupp put a plate of sandwiches out on the kitchen table. "She wanted to help in here, but I had to tell her *nee*." She lowered her voice.

"Look how tiny this kitchen is. I didn't want her to trip or fall over anything. One injury a week is enough." She suddenly rubbed her hands together. "Let me know when you find her. I don't approve when she takes off on her own like this."

Chris held in his irritation. Ellie could take care of herself, and hopefully one day her mother would realize it. He smiled politely, leaving *Frau* Chupp to bustle around the "tiny kitchen," which to him seemed a good size. He went outside to the backyard but didn't see her right away. Where could she be? Had she left? He hoped not, but she had seemed so unnerved when he saw her during the service, maybe she had decided to go home.

A crisp breeze kicked up, slicing through his white dress shirt and pressing against the brim of his black hat. He glanced down at the black pants and vest he wore. His Sunday best. He'd found the clothes hanging in his closet, just as he'd left them five years ago. The trousers were a little loose at the waist, but between his mother's cooking and plenty of Ellie's homemade jelly, they would soon fit right.

He continued to look for her and had just about given up when he saw her walking along the pasture fence on the other side of the Keims' barn. He jogged to her, stopping short a few steps behind so as not to startle her. But she must have heard him anyway, because she halted her steps and turned around.

"Congratulations," she said, facing him but not looking directly at him. For some reason he thought that was on purpose. A smile formed on her face, but it was halfhearted. Even he could tell that.

"Can we talk, Ellie?"

She paused for a moment, then nodded.

He glanced around. They were pretty secluded behind the barn, although he could hear the sound of some of the kids playing a game of tag in the backyard. "I wanted to thank you again. If it weren't for you, Ellie, I wouldn't be standing here, welcomed back by my *familye* and friends."

She shook her head, her smile disappearing. "Please," she said, her voice sounding thick. "Don't say that."

❦

Ellie gripped her white cane, trying to keep a tight rein on her emotions, but failing. Her fingers went numb and she relaxed them, but only a little. She couldn't believe he was standing here thanking her. He should be angry with her for holding back the truth. Just as she was angry with herself.

"Ellie, it's true." She heard him move closer to her, as he tended to do when he talked to her. "You showed me how I could move on—"

"I lied to you." She couldn't keep the words inside any longer. "I lied to you and everyone else. I let Isaiah suffer for what I did."

"*Nee*, listen to me—"

"Don't try to make me feel better. It won't work." She released the cane and wiped her finger under her eye. "I still have nightmares sometimes. They're so vivid and clear, it's like I'm reliving the accident. Over and over." She hung her head. "I suppose that's what I deserve."

His hands suddenly covered her shoulders, and she jerked. "Are you done?"

She sniffed, nodding.

"*Gut*, because I see I need to set you straight on a few things. For one, you didn't lie to me."

"I did—"

His fingertip covered her mouth, sending a shiver through her spine. She froze. "If I have to," he said, his voice husky, "I'll make you stay quiet."

She didn't say anything else. How could she? He had taken not only her voice away but also her breath and heartbeat with just one simple gesture.

He removed his finger. "Ellie, I understand why Isaiah did what he did. I probably would have done the same thing to protect you. You admitting your secret finally showed me that I'd been unfair to him all along. But I should have realized that when I came back. My *schwester* wouldn't have picked a lesser *mann* to marry. She tried to tell me that. You did too. I was too thickheaded to accept it, not to mention I needed him to take the brunt of my anger. Because I couldn't blame the person I was really angry with."

"Who?"

"Caroline." He took a step back. "I'll admit, I was shocked when you told me the real story of what happened. I'd been told Isaiah had begged you all to ride with him, and that you and Caroline hadn't actually wanted to. But when I learned that Caroline was the one to suggest it . . . I didn't want to believe it at first. Then I had to, because she would do something like that. She was free-spirited, always willing to walk on the edge of danger."

Ellie nodded, remembering her friend's penchant for excitement. "Like the time she tried to get me to skate with her on the thin ice in the middle of her cousin's pond."

"Or when we were *kinner* and she dared me to jump off the roof of her *haus* onto the trampoline underneath it."

"I hope you had the *gut* sense to tell her *nee*!"

"Um, not exactly. What self-respecting ten-year-old would refuse a dare from a *maedel*?"

Ellie laughed, the tension draining out of her. She hadn't reminisced about Caroline this way for a long time. "Since you put it that way, you're right."

He chuckled, but it quickly faded. "When you told me about the accident, everything changed. I couldn't go on being angry at Isaiah. And I couldn't be angry at you." His fingertips skimmed across her cheek. "God showed me that."

She flinched at his unexpected gesture. His touch had been fleeting, and blissful. "I deserve your anger, Chris."

"*Nee*. The last thing you deserve is that. But even knowing the truth, I still had this pain inside me—there was something I couldn't let *geh*. I realized I was angry with Caroline."

"And now?"

"Did you hear what Bishop Ebersol said? The past is in the past. And for me, finally, it truly is."

Ellie smiled, her heart swelling with joy. There was a peace in Chris's tone, one she had never heard before. Yet despite her happiness for him, there was a sliver of guilt still burrowing its way through her.

"I know what you're thinking," he suddenly said.

"So now *you* have a sixth sense?"

"When it comes to you, *ya*, I do. You want to confess your part in the accident."

She nodded. "Isn't that the right thing to do?"

He took her hand and squeezed it. "It is. But you don't have to do it alone."

Ellie couldn't keep the tears from falling. She always thought she'd be alone. She had accepted it. Even fought for it at times. But now she didn't have to be.

❧

"Are you ready to *geh* home?"

Sarah Lynne looked at Isaiah and smiled. Church had ended awhile ago, and she was still happy from seeing her brother reconciled with the community. Once the service was over, a burden had seemed to lift from Isaiah too. He was grinning as he led her to the buggy, and all she could think about was how happy she was that things finally were the way they should be. Their wedding was in less than two weeks, and her brother would be there. Her family was finally intact. *Thank You, Lord*.

But as she started to get into the buggy, she heard Ellie call out her name. She turned around to see Ellie and Chris approaching from behind the barn. She couldn't help but smile as she saw how her brother led her friend to the buggy. He'd not only come back to the church but possibly found love again. She couldn't think of anyone better for Chris than Ellie.

Yet as they neared, she could see something was wrong. Redness rimmed Ellie's eyes, and Chris's mouth was set in a grim, straight line. She stepped away from the buggy and walked toward them. "Ellie? Is something wrong?"

Isaiah appeared at Sarah Lynne's side. The two couples stood across from each other. She glanced at Isaiah, whose happy expression had melted into wariness. But instead of directing his gaze to Chris, he was looking at Ellie.

"I need to talk to you, Sarah Lynne," Ellie said. She moved a little closer to Chris. "There's something you need to know."

"Ellie, don't." Isaiah stepped toward her.

Ellie's brows lifted as she turned to Isaiah, as if she were surprised he was here. "*Nee*, Isaiah. We can't keep this a secret anymore. Chris already knows."

Isaiah looked at Chris, who nodded.

"What secret?" Sarah Lynne's gaze darted from Isaiah to her brother.

"Ellie, you don't have to do this."

She stepped toward him. "Isaiah, I do. I should have told everyone a long time ago. You know that."

"But you don't have to tell everyone."

"Tell everyone what?" Frustration bubbled to the surface. "Will someone tell me what's going on?"

Ellie turned to Sarah Lynne. "The accident wasn't just Isaiah's fault. I'm to blame too."

Sarah Lynne listened as Ellie revealed how she caused the car crash. When Ellie finished, Sarah Lynne looked at Isaiah. He cast his gaze downward, and she knew Ellie was telling the truth.

"Why didn't you say anything about this before?" she asked him.

"Don't be angry with Isaiah." Ellie groped for Sarah Lynne's arm. When she found it, she squeezed. "He was only protecting me."

"I'm not . . . angry." Hurt welled in her chest. "I don't understand. Why didn't you tell me?" She looked at Isaiah. "Why didn't either of you trust me enough to tell me the truth?"

"We didn't tell anyone."

"But I'm going to be your wife!" She faced Christopher. "When did you find out?"

"The other day. When I came to the *haus* to stay." He moved closer to Ellie. "You and Isaiah need to talk."

"I'm sorry," Ellie said, her eyes shining with tears. "I really am."

When Chris and Ellie left, Sarah Lynne turned her back on Isaiah. He had lied to her, to everyone. And so had Ellie. She felt Isaiah touch her shoulder, but she stepped away. "Take me home, Isaiah."

They climbed into the buggy and didn't say anything for a long while as he drove to her house. Finally Isaiah spoke. "Don't blame Ellie for this. She was just doing what I asked her to."

She glanced at him. "So the accident wasn't her fault?"

He gripped the reins with both hands. "I was driving the car."

"But she distracted you."

"Not on purpose." He let out a long breath. "I did what I thought was right at the time. But now . . ." His shoulders slumped. "I don't know anymore."

Sarah Lynne moved closer to Isaiah and touched his arm. "I understand."

He looked at her. "You do?"

She nodded. "But I'm glad Ellie said something. I don't want any secrets between us, Isaiah."

He grinned. "There won't be. That was the only one."

KATHLEEN FULLER

Returning his smile, she leaned back in the seat. Now everything was truly right.

Two weeks later Ellie sat in the swing on Christopher's porch, breathing out a sigh of contentment. Isaiah and Sarah Lynne were married, and the gathering afterward was winding down. Her desserts had been a success, especially the cream cheese brownies. Her father had been right about bringing them.

"Mind if I join you?"

She smiled at the sound of Chris's voice and nodded. He sat down, making the swing propel forward.

"Great wedding," Chris said.

The swing continued to move back and forth.

"*Ya*."

"You know what I'm going to ask you next."

Her shoulders tensed. "I do."

"And you know I'll keep asking until you say yes."

She turned toward him. He had been asking her to go out with him since that Sunday he had made his confession, and she had put him off. They were close friends, there was no denying that, just as there was no denying she wanted more. But she couldn't let it happen.

"Chris, there are plenty of other *maed* that are more—"

"Suitable, I know." He scooted a little closer to her. "What I don't understand is why you refuse to realize that you're the one suited for me."

She shook her head. "It's complicated."

"*Nee*, it's not. Ellie, I get it. You're worried I'm going to leave you like John did. I'm not like him."

And he wasn't. He had proved that over and over.

"But what if you find out you can't handle my being blind?"

"If you can handle it, which you do, then I can handle it too."
He touched her chin, turning it toward him. "I care for you, Ellie
Chupp. More than I ever cared for anyone in my life. I want us to
go together, and not just on one or two dates. I'm talking about a
lot of dates. But I don't want you to feel you have to compete with
Caroline's memory."

"I don't feel that way."

"And I don't want to compete with John's. You once told me
I'd have to let *geh* of Caroline to move on." He dropped his hand.
"Can you let *geh* of John and move on with me?"

His question made her pause. She had gotten over John a long
time ago. That wasn't what she had to release.

"I'm afraid," she said in a small voice.

"It's okay, Ellie." He kissed her cheek. "Whatever you're
afraid of, I promise, we'll face it together. As long as you promise
me one thing."

"What?"

"That someday, maybe even when we're old and gray, you'll
make me some kumquat jelly."

She laughed and leaned against him, suddenly knowing that
Chris meant everything he said. God had changed his heart . . .
and through him, God was healing hers.

KATHLEEN FULLER

Bonus excerpt from *Treasuring Emma,*
the first in the new Middlefield Family series.
Available August 2011 from Kathleen Fuller.

"I WON!" EMMA SHETLER HELD UP HER HANDS IN VICTORY
as she looked across the table at Adam Otto.

Adam glanced up from his cards and grinned. He leaned backward in her father's old hickory rocker, the back of it touching the white siding on the house. She and Adam usually played cards on Saturday afternoons after he got off work. Today they decided to play outside on her front porch. "You won because I let you."

"You say that every time I win."

"I have to defend my bad playing somehow." He winked, making her heart melt. Emma sat in her mother's matching rocker and ran her fingers along the smooth edge of the round wooden table, trying to collect herself. Lately all it took was his innocent smile or trademark wink to set her stomach fluttering.

She tried not to stare at Adam's hands as he gathered the Dutch Blitz cards. The light blue sleeves of his shirt were rolled up to mid-forearm. His fingers were long, with short, well-shaped nails. Even though he worked at Fisher Lumber processing hardwoods, his skin wasn't overly rough. He'd told her after he first started at the mill a little over three years ago that it didn't take long for him to get his fill of splinters. Now he wore gloves whenever he could. She glanced at his hands again, wondering for the thousandth time what his fingers would feel like wrapped around hers. *Stop it.*

"Did you say something?"

"Me? *Nee*, I didn't say anything." She bit the inside of her lip, hoping he believed her.

"Sounded like you did." Adam shuffled the cards.

She couldn't let her gaze linger on his hands again. Instead she concentrated on his face. Big mistake. She could stare at the adorable freckles scattered across the tops of his cheeks and bridge of his nose all day. Not to mention his honey-colored eyes, his perfect mouth . . . Emma gripped the edge of the table. What was wrong with her? Adam wasn't just her next door neighbor he was also her best friend. But she couldn't even look at him without her heart turning inside out, and it had been this way for months.

Suppressing a sigh, she pulled her navy blue sweater closer around her body. It was early October and the late afternoon air had turned cool. She thought to button it, then remembered the bottom button didn't quite fasten around her hips. That was the last thing she wanted Adam to notice. It wasn't as if she could ever ignore it herself.

"Are you up for another game?" His eyes twinkled. "This time I won't be so easy on you."

She was nothing if not competitive, at least when it came to Dutch Blitz. "You're on."

Adam dealt the cards and then grinned at her. Her heart fluttered. Why did he have to be so cute? So nice? So . . . Adam?

"Emma?" He reached across the table and tapped her hand. "Hello, Emma? You there?"

Emma blinked, startled. "What?"

"I said *geh* and you just sat there." His grin had faded and his dark brown eyebrows formed a V. "Do you want to play or not?"

"I do. Sorry." Her cheeks grew hot and she focused on the cards on the table. She picked up her pile. "Ready?"

When Adam said go, they both started to play. He got a jump start on her and suddenly she was behind. Dutch Blitz involved skill and speed, and she scrambled to catch up with him. But he zipped through his stack of cards, slamming the last one on top of the pile. He gave her a victorious smile.

Emma smiled. "Congratulations. You played a *gut* game." She set her last three cards to the side and started to pick up the others.

"That's one thing I like about you, Emma. You're not a sore loser."

She froze, her fingers grasping a green card. *He likes me.* But she knew exactly what he meant when he said those words. For the past fifteen years he'd told her how much he liked her. As a *friend*. Nothing more. It wasn't his fault her feelings for him had changed. He'd never been anything but honest with her, from the day he and his parents moved in next door from Kentucky. Even back then he was cute, with shaggy brown hair and a stick-thin body that didn't fill out until he turned eighteen. She put her fingertip to her temple. Why couldn't she keep her thoughts straight when she was around him?

"Got a headache?"

More like heartache. She moved her hand and shook her head. "*Nee.* I'm fine."

He nodded and pushed the rocker back a few inches, then stood. He picked up his yellow straw hat from the opposite side of the table and put it on. "I better get going. Christine won't be happy if I'm late again."

Emma felt a twinge in her heart at the sound of Adam's girlfriend's name. "She's not one for patience, is she?" The last sentence slipped out, and it sounded catty, even though it was true. She frowned, wishing she could take the words back.

Adam shrugged. "I suppose she's not."

She quickly snatched up the cards and slid them into the box. Standing, she decided to drop the subject of Christine before she said something she might regret. "*Danki* for coming over yesterday and mowing the lawn." She gestured to the expansive front yard, which was now nicely trimmed. He'd even edged around the flowerbeds and the stone path that led to the porch. "I meant to do it but—"

"Don't mention it. It doesn't take that long to mow."

"It took you over two hours." Emma's house sat back nearly a quarter mile from the road. She remembered how he'd come straight home from work and started mowing, sawdust still covering his clothes. "Plus the time it took to use the edger. So it was a big deal to me, and I appreciate it."

"I thought it would be one less chore for you to do."

"I don't mind doing chores."

"I know you don't. Just like I don't mind helping you out." He smiled again, his bottom lip dipping a little to the right as it always did. Her breath hitched

"That's what friends are for, Emma."

His words brought her back to reality. Friends. It's all they ever had been, all they ever would be. She had to keep telling herself that. Her mind knew it, but her heart didn't want to listen.

Reading Group Guide

"A MIRACLE FOR MIRIAM"

1. Miriam allowed Seth's youthful rejection to affect her self-confidence, even as an adult. Instead of seeing herself as a beautiful woman of God, she continued to see herself as unattractive and undesirable. What can we do to protect our hearts against the thoughtless and cruel words of others?
2. Proverbs 29:23 states, "A man's pride shall bring him low; but honor shall uphold the humble in spirit." How did Seth's accident "bring him low"? How did he vow to change?
3. List some reasons why Miriam didn't trust Seth. Think back to a time where you had difficulty trusting someone else. What allowed you to trust again?
4. The Amish value *demut* (humility) over *hochmut* (pride), and strive to be as humble as possible in all situations. Is humility difficult to achieve? How can we practice humility in our daily lives?

"A PLACE OF HIS OWN"

1. When Josiah arrives in Paradise, he's determined not to depend on anyone else. Has there ever been a time in your life when people let you down? How did you learn to trust again?
2. Amanda is a "fixer"—she's eager to solve everyone's problems. What lesson did she learn in the story?
3. Although it's not stated in the story, do you think Josiah asked for and accepted God's forgiveness? Why or why not?

4. Sometimes it seems easier to blame God for our troubles than to ask Him to help us during times of hardship. Why do you think we tend to do this? What should we do instead?

"What the Heart Sees"

1. After the accident, Ellie wants to be as independent as possible. Eventually she learns that she has to accept help from others and from God. Think about a time in your life when you wanted to do things on your own. What made you realize you needed God? How did his help change the situation?
2. Christopher's refusal to forgive kept him apart from his family and separate from God. How could Christopher have handled things differently after the accident?
3. Ellie's mother is overprotective, while her father respects her need for independence. Was one parent's reaction to Ellie's blindness better than the other's? Why or why not?
4. Christopher and Ellie both found healing by accepting God's forgiveness. Has there been an event in your life where you had trouble accepting God's forgiveness? What helped you to ultimately accept it?

CREAM CHEESE BROWNIES

1 pkg. German chocolate cake mix
¾ cup flour
½ cup sugar
1 egg
1 T vegetable oil
⅓ c water
1 t. baking powder

8 oz. cream cheese, softened
1 egg
½ cup sugar
½ cup milk chocolate chips

1. Preheat oven to 350 degrees F.
2. Prepare cake mix as directed on the box, plus add the flour, sugar, egg, vegetable oil, water, and baking powder.
2. Pour batter into a jelly roll pan.
3. Mix remaining ingredients—cream cheese, egg, sugar, and chocolate chips—and drop by tablespoon onto batter.
4. Cut through batter with knife several times for marbled effect.
5. Sprinkle with additional chocolate chips and nuts (optional).
6. Bake for 25 to 30 minutes. Cut when cool.

Amanda Graber's Monster Cookies

1 ½ sticks butter
1 cup white sugar
1 cup brown sugar
4 eggs
1 pound crunchy peanut butter

2 ½ t. baking soda
¼ cup flour
4 ½ cups quick oats
½ pound M&Ms
12 ounces chocolate chips

1. Preheat oven to 350 degrees F.
2. Cream together butter, white sugar, and brown sugar.
2. Add eggs and peanut butter. Mix until blended
3. Mix in baking soda, flour, and oats.
4. Mix in M&Ms and chocolate chips
5. Dough will be stiff. Form teaspoon sized balls and roll in powdered sugar.
6. Bake for 10 minutes. Do not overbake.

Shoestring Apple Pie

4 cups peeled, finely chopped apples
1 cup white sugar
2 T flour
¼ cup water
2 eggs, beaten
½ t. cinnamon
4 T butter, divided

1. Preheat oven to 450 degrees F.
2. Grease two 9-inch glass pie plates with cooking spray.
3 Combine the first six ingredients until sugar is dissolved and apples are moist. Divide mixture between the two pie plates.
4. Dot each pie with two tablespoons of butter.
5. Bake for 15 minutes, then turn down the temperature to 350 degrees F and bake for 20 more minutes or until apples are soft

Acknowledgments

A MIRACLE FOR MIRIAM

This book wouldn't have been possible without the help of several spectacular people. Thank you to my terrific editor, Natalie Hanemann, for putting this project together, and for her amazing editing skills and encouragement. It's a privilege to work with her. I also express my gratitude to LB Norton, who told me to trust my writing. Those words really clicked with me. Another big thank-you to the team at Thomas Nelson, who are all fantastic. And a special thank-you to Barbie Beiler, who graciously read the manuscript for accuracy.

A PLACE OF HIS OWN

My deepest thanks to Natalie Hanemann and LB Norton for helping me bring this story to life. Their experience and insights were invaluable. As always, thanks to my family for their patience and understanding, especially during deadline time!

WHAT THE HEART SEES

There are so many people to thank for helping me tell Ellie and Christopher's story. Thank you to my wonderful and insightful editors, Natalie Hanemann and LB Norton, for their advice, encouragement, and direction. To my agent, Tamela, who is always just a phone call away. To Cecelia Dowdy for reviewing the story and for answering my questions about living with someone who is visually impaired. To my former student, Hannah Bowser, who for four years allowed me a glimpse of the world through her eyes. A big thank-you to Beth Wiseman and especially Barbie Beiler for reading over the manuscript and helping me with the details. And to my wonderful friend and critique partner, Jill Eileen Smith. Thank you for making sure I kept the story on track and for your invaluable feedback.

Kathleen Fuller is the author of the bestselling novels *A Man of His Word* and *An Honest Love*. When she's not writing, she enjoys traveling and spending time with her family and farm pets.